# UNDER WESTERN EYES

broadview editions
series editor: L.W. Conolly

# UNDER WESTERN EYES

## Joseph Conrad

*edited by John G. Peters*

broadview editions

**Library and Archives Canada Cataloguing in Publication**

Conrad, Joseph, 1857-1924
  Under western eyes / Joseph Conrad ; edited by John G. Peters.

(Broadview editions)
Includes bibliographical references.
ISBN 978-1-55111-721-8

  1. Russia—History—1904-1914—Fiction.  I. Peters, John G. (John Gerard)  II. Title.  III. Series: Broadview editions

PR6005.O4U5 2009      823'.912      C2009-905641-0

**Broadview Editions**

The Broadview Editions series represents the ever-changing canon of literature in English by bringing together texts long regarded as classics with valuable lesser-known works.

Advisory editor for this volume: Denis Johnston

Broadview Press is an independent, international publishing house, incorporated in 1985. Broadview believes in shared ownership, both with its employees and with the general public; since the year 2000 Broadview shares have traded publicly on the Toronto Venture Exchange under the symbol BDP.

We welcome comments and suggestions regarding any aspect of our publications—please feel free to contact us at the addresses below or at broadview@broadviewpress.com.

*North America*
Post Office Box 1243, Peterborough, Ontario, Canada K9J 7H5
2215 Kenmore Avenue, Buffalo, NY, USA 14207
Tel: (705) 743-8990; Fax: (705) 743-8353
email: customerservice@broadviewpress.com

*UK, Europe, Central Asia, Middle East, Africa, India, and Southeast Asia*
Eurospan Group, 3 Henrietta St., London WC2E 8LU, United Kingdom
Tel: 44 (0) 1767 604972; Fax: 44 (0) 1767 601640
Email: eurospan@turpin-distribution.com

*Australia and New Zealand*
NewSouth Books
c/o TL Distribution, 15-23 Helles Ave., Moorebank, NSW, Australia 2170
Tel: (02) 8778 9999; Fax: (02) 8778 9944
email: orders@tldistribution.com.au

www.broadviewpress.com

This book is printed on paper containing 100% post-consumer fibre.

Typesetting and assembly: True to Type Inc., Claremont, Canada.

PRINTED IN CANADA

# Contents

# Acknowledgements

I would like to thank Francis King for permission to reprint (in Appendix E) his translation of "To the Whole Russian Peasantry," which can be found in the original Russian in N.D. Erofeev's compilation *Partiia sotsialistov-revoliutsionerov: dokumenty I materialy 1900-1907* (Moscow: Rosspen, 1996), 153-55. I would also like to thank Laurence Davies and Cambridge University Press for permission to reprint material from Conrad's letters (Appendix A); Edward Judge for pointing me to sources I might not have discovered on my own; Robert Trogden and those associated with The Center for Conrad Studies at Kent State University for materials and advice they offered; the librarians and student workers at the Inter-library Loan Office of the Willis Library at the University of North Texas, especially Pamela Johnston and Lynne Wright, for their diligent work in helping me to find various materials necessary for completing this volume; and the Office of the Vice President of Research at the University of North Texas for financial support. I would like to thank George L. Snider for help on classical references, Sheila Gunter for running down some of the biographical information on Russian figures and for otherwise helping on the project, and Robyn Jackson, Elizabeth Dwelle, and Noah Geisert for proofreading. Also, I would like to thank Keith Carabine, Nic Panagopoulos, Laurence Davies, Leonard Conolly, Mark Larabee, Marina Tetereva, Henry Eaton, Werner Senn, Jeremy Hawthorn, Olga Velikanova, Dreanna Beldan, Nicole Smith, Natalia Zazovskaya, Olga Grieco, J.H. Stape, Michael Gibson, Richard Spence, Philippe Rigaud, and Edward Hoyinski for their advice and suggestions and for their help on some difficult references and other such matters. Finally, I would like to thank my wife Deanna and daughter Kaitlynne for their support.

# Introduction

## Biography

Joseph Conrad was born Józef Teodor Konrad Korzeniowski on 3 December 1857 in Berdyczów in a predominantly Polish part of Ukraine. His parents, Apollo Korzeniowski (1820-69) and Ewelina Bobrowska (1833-65), were members of the Polish gentry or *szlachta*. At the time of Conrad's birth, Poland did not exist. Some sixty years earlier, it had been partitioned among Russia, Prussia, and Austria-Hungary. Conrad's father was heavily involved in the more radical elements of the Polish population working for independence, and in 1862 he was convicted of seditious activities by the Russian authorities and sent into exile in Russia. His wife and young son accompanied him. Both parents developed tuberculosis as a result of their experience in exile, Conrad's mother dying in 1865 and his father in 1869, shortly after he was allowed to return to Poland. Thereafter, Conrad was raised primarily by his maternal uncle Tadeusz Bobrowski (1829-94).

At seventeen years of age, Bobrowski allowed Conrad to move to France to study for his chosen profession: a life at sea. After four years of study, Conrad joined the British Merchant Marine service, despite speaking no English at the time. He spent roughly the next fifteen years pursuing that profession, eventually rising to the rank of captain in 1888, when he served as the captain of the *Otago*. During his maritime career, Conrad traveled extensively throughout the East (and elsewhere), experiences that would serve as the basis for much of his future writing. A particularly important episode in Conrad's maritime career occurred in 1890 when he worked in the Congo. His time there appears to have significantly affected his perception of Western civilization and the nature of human existence and provided the basis for such works as "An Outpost of Progress" (1897) and *Heart of Darkness* (1899). In 1893, while serving as first mate aboard the *Torrens*, Conrad met John Galsworthy (1867-1933), who would later become a famous novelist, playwright, and a lifelong friend. Galsworthy's was the first of a number of literary friendships that Conrad would develop over the years, as he became friends with such authors as Stephen Crane (1871-1900), H.G. Wells (1866-1946), Arnold Bennett (1867-1931), Henry James (1843-1916), R.B. Cunninghame Graham (1852-1936), and Ford Madox

Ford (1873-1939). Conrad's friendship with Ford would be particularly important as they seem to have helped one another develop their literary skills. They actually collaborated on two novels, *The Inheritors* (1901) and *Romance* (1903), and a story, "The Nature of a Crime" (1909).

In 1894, Conrad's life changed drastically as a result of two events. When his tour of service on the steamer *Adowa* ended, he had difficulty finding work. His employment situation, coupled with the completion of his first novel, *Almayer's Folly* (upon which he had been working intermittently for some five years), forever altered the course of his life, and he thereafter embarked on a career as a full-time writer. That same year, Conrad's uncle Tadeusz Bobrowski died. Bobrowski had been a second father figure to Conrad, who felt the loss keenly. While it appears that Conrad initially had not thought beyond the writing of his first novel, apparently Edward Garnett (1868-1937) suggested that he try to write another and thus Conrad's writing profession was born.

Shortly after the publication of his second novel, *An Outcast of the Islands*, in 1896, Conrad married Jesse George (1873-1936). The couple seems to have had little in common, but despite Conrad's sometimes difficult personality and fiery temper, the relationship appears to have been quite successful: their first son, Borys, was born in 1898. From 1897 to 1911, Conrad produced a remarkable number of important works: *The Nigger of the "Narcissus"* (1897), "Youth" (1898), *Heart of Darkness* (1899), *Lord Jim* (1900), "Typhoon" (1902), *Nostromo* (1904), *The Secret Agent* (1907), "The Secret Sharer" (1910), and *Under Western Eyes* (1911). This body of work firmly established his reputation as a major figure in British literature, but despite his literary success, Conrad often found writing excruciating, and, to make matters worse, his works, although typically well received by the critics, were not particularly popular with the reading public. As a result, Conrad often suffered from physical, emotional, and especially financial difficulties. Not until the publication of his novel *Chance* in 1914 did he achieve a popularity that would relieve him of financial worries.

After the success of *Chance*, Conrad continued to write, although at a slower pace than previously. Besides achieving some financial independence, he received increasingly greater critical acclaim. Conrad came to be regarded as one of the foremost figures in British letters, so much so that many of his later works, such as *The Arrow of Gold* (1919), *The Rescue* (1920), and *The*

*Rover* (1923), were more appreciated when they first appeared than they often are now. On 3 August 1924, Conrad suffered a heart attack and died, leaving behind his unfinished novel *Suspense* (1925). After his death, a number of Conrad's friends wrote reminiscences of him. The common themes among them are the warmth of Conrad's friendship and his concern for the well-being of his friends.

## Historical and Political Contexts for the Novel

Having lived in Poland, France, Russia, and the Orient, Conrad was much more cosmopolitan than most of his fellow writers in England. As a result, important historical events on the European continent, as well as those in England, affected Conrad and influenced his writings, even more than they did many of his contemporaries in British literature.

In the case of *Under Western Eyes*, political turbulence in both Poland and Russia underlie the events of the novel, and the intertwining of their histories during the nineteenth century irrevocably altered Conrad's life. After the third partition of Poland in 1795 (the first two occurring in 1772 and 1793), it ceased to exist as an independent nation for over a century, and its lands were divided among Prussia, Austria-Hungary, and Russia. Conrad's family lived in the Russian-controlled part of Polish territories. The Poles had a rich cultural tradition and were strongly nationalistic. They chafed against Russian rule and periodically revolted, the two most widespread revolts occurring in 1830 and 1863. The first of these began in Warsaw in November 1830, but it soon spread across Polish territories in general and was not finally suppressed until September 1831. As a result of the revolt, the Poles suffered severe reprisals, and Russian control became even more oppressive. One prominent member of the 1830-31 revolt was Prince Roman Sanguszko (1800-81), whom Conrad is said to have met as a boy. Conrad would later memorialize him in "Prince Roman" (1910), a story completed shortly after *Under Western Eyes*.

Beginning around 1861, Polish opposition to Russian rule began to increase. In Warsaw, for example, demonstrators battled with Russian troops. Hoping to reduce the unrest, the Russians authorities chose Aleksander Wielopolski (1803-77) to govern Poland, but he was hated by both the Whites (the more moderate opposition) and the Reds (the more radical opposition), and both groups began underground resistance movements. Conrad's father, a member of the Reds, participated in the resistance and was exiled as a consequence. These underground activities eventually erupted into a full-scale revolt in January 1863. It took until the fall of 1864, but the Russians finally put down the uprising and executed Romuald Traugutt (1826-64), the leader of the Reds. In addition to his father's sentence, some of Conrad's other relatives were either killed or imprisoned during the uprising and in its aftermath. In the years following the revolt, Poles again experienced strong reprisals and repressive measures. Undoubtedly as a result of these experiences, Conrad was ever suspicious of political activity of any kind, and his youth in Poland and Russia certainly played a large role in the dark, skeptical outlook on the world that became a hallmark of his fiction and that appears so prominently in *Under Western Eyes*.

As important an influence as the relationship between Poland and Russia was on Conrad's fiction in general, the history and politics in Russia during the nineteenth century was even more important to *Under Western Eyes* (see Appendix F). With Napoleon's defeat in 1815, Russia became the pre-eminent European land power for nearly forty years, first under Tsar Aleksandr I (1777-1825) and then under Tsar Nikolai I (1796-1855). Nikolai I was a tireless defender of monarchal autocracy amid widespread democratic upheaval across Europe, but his absolute rule, together with a corrupt bureaucracy that seemed to permeate all facets of Russian society, became increasingly out of step with the political reform occurring in Europe and with the desires of the Russian people.

Russia's defeat in the Crimean War of 1853-56 illuminated its weaknesses, and Aleksandr II (1818-81), who became Tsar shortly before the end of the war, began to institute changes meant to modernize Russia and return it to its position of European pre-eminence. Aleksandr proceeded to reform the judicial system and abolish serfdom, as well as implementing other changes. Nevertheless, the Russian people remained dissatisfied, wanting greater political and social reforms. Aleksandr resisted greater change and a reduction of autocratic power, and in 1876 the Land and Freedom Party was organized in response. Some of the party's members favored terrorist tactics, which eventually led to the forming of the People's Will Party, a more radical wing of the Land and Freedom Party, whose members actively pursued violent revolutionary activities—including the assassination of Aleksandr II in 1881. Resistance to Russian authority increased steadily and violently after the famine of 1891 until the Russian Revolution of 1917. During this period, the People's Will became a part of the Socialist-Revolutionary Party, who carried out a number of assassinations of Russian officials, most notably Viacheslav Konstantinovich de Pleve (1846-1904), Minister of the Interior in 1904 (see Appendices C, D, and E). Although Conrad took some of the details of the assassination of Mr. de P—— from accounts of Aleksandr II's assassination, de Pleve's name and many of the details and circumstances surrounding his assassination served as the primary basis for the political events in the novel (see Appendix C).

Along with the historical context of Russia and Poland, significant influences from nineteenth-century revolutionary politics in Europe, particularly the Socialist and Anarchist movements, can be found in *Under Western Eyes*. In *What is Property?* (1840) and other works, Pierre-Joseph Proudhon (1809-65), generally viewed as the founder of nineteenth-century Anarchism, outlines what he considers the basic problems of society—private property and political power. Anarchist thought centers on these two problems, especially on the structure of political power. Despite the differences in the various strains of Anarchist thought, one idea they have in common is that the ills of society can be greatly lessened by moving from a centralized state to smaller regional governments. Not surprisingly, the Anarchists particularly targeted the extremely centralized Russian autocracy as a prime example of the problems associated with a powerful, centralized government.

Proudhon's ideas influenced many important political thinkers, including Mikhail Bakunin (1814-76), a Russian exile. Despite this influence, however, Bakunin's political ideas also differ significantly from those of Proudhon, particularly regarding methodology. Where Proudhon proposed a peaceful and gradual transition to a stateless and propertyless society, Bakunin advocated any method through which political change could be realized, particularly favoring revolutionary violence. Ultimately, Bakunin was the more influential on later Anarchists, and evidence of his methods can be seen in the violent revolutionary activities of so many of those Anarchist organizations that arose in the latter part of the nineteenth century.

Closely related to the Anarchist movement of this time was the Socialist movement. Recognized founders of Socialism in the nineteenth century include Henri de Saint-Simon (1760-1825),

François-Marie-Charles Fourier (1772-1837), Étienne Cabet (1788-1856), Louis Blanc (1811-82), Louis-Auguste Blanqui (1805-81), Karl Marx (1818-83), and Friedrich Engels (1820-95), as well as Proudhon. The very appearance of Proudon on this list emphasizes the common origins and resemblance of the Anarchist and Socialist movements, as do the notorious revolutionary activities of Blanqui, so similar to those of the Anarchists. Among the many figures linked to the beginnings of Socialism, Karl Marx and Friedrich Engels are the most important. Their *Communist Manifesto* (1848) appeared at the same time that democratic movements swept across the European continent. Marx and Engels saw capitalist economics and social class as the root of social ills and advocated instead a classless society with a redistribution of wealth such that the workers rather than the industrialists would reap the rewards of their labor. In Russia, following in the footsteps of Marx, Engels, and other thinkers, Aleksandr Ivanovich Herzen (1812-70) considered the peasant communities to be a model for a Socialist society and hoped to bring about a widespread peasant revolt that would result in social change.

Although the Socialists and Anarchists agreed upon the evils of capitalist economics and private property (the consequences of which had become magnified with the rise of industrialism), the two groups also had important differences, and they split during the 1870s. The main cause for the division was related to the roles of private property and government. While Anarchists rejected the ideas of a strong, centralized government and of private property, some Socialist groups accepted this kind of government and some limited private property. Nevertheless, distinguishing between nineteenth-century Anarchism and Socialism is often difficult, since some Socialist groups advocated a less centralized form of government, much like that favored by the Anarchists; the situation becomes yet further complicated by the fact that despite the split between the two political camps, revolutionary wings of the Socialist movement arose, whose methods and aims closely resembled those of the Anarchists. For instance, although Herzen and many of his followers argued—as Proudhon had—for a peaceful, evolutionary approach to social change by disseminating political propaganda and educating the peasant population, some of his followers became impatient and broke away, forming more radical political groups. The lines between these more radical Socialist groups and the radical Anarchist groups blur significantly, and to many it was difficult to distinguish clearly between them. In fact, it is not entirely clear that Conrad himself fully recognizes the differences between the radical Anarchists and radical Socialists in *Under Western Eyes* since it was the Socialist-Revolutionary Party (responsible for most of the terrorist activities and assassinations in Russia) that carried out the assassination of de Pleve, while in the novel blame for the deed seems to be assigned to the Anarchists. Regardless of whether Conrad fully understood the nuances between the Anarchists and such Socialist groups as the Socialist-Revolutionary Party, however, he clearly drew upon the more violent activities of both Socialists and Anarchists in constructing the events in the novel and the attitudes of the various revolutionary figures who appear in it.[1]

## Composition of the Novel

*Under Western Eyes* was serialized in 1910 and published in book form in 1911 at roughly the mid-point of Conrad's writing career. It not only marked the end of the middle period of his literary career but was also one of Conrad's more difficult writing projects (see Appendices A5 to A9). Initially conceived as a short story entitled "Razumov," the work gradually grew into the lengthy novel we know today. Conrad began writing *Under Western Eyes* in late 1907 and completed the manuscript in early 1910. During the course of the writing, he struggled as he did with no other novel. In a March 1908 letter to Ford Madox Ford, Conrad writes, "I am stuck dead with R[*Razumov*]. Inventions [*sic*] dead. And yet the imagination works dans le vide.[2] Its [*sic*] a

---

1  For more information on the historical and political background to the novel, see, for example, Edward H. Judge, *Plehve: Repression and Reform in Imperial Russia 1902-1904* (Syracuse, NY: Syracuse UP, 1983); Peter Marshall, *Demanding the Impossible: A History of Anarchism* (New York: HarperCollins, 1992); Paul Avrich, *The Russian Anarchists* (Princeton, NJ: Princeton UP, 1967); G.D.H. Cole, *A History of Socialist Thought*, 7 vols. (London: Macmillan, 1953-60); Hugh Seton-Watson, *The Russian Empire, 1801-1917* (Oxford: Clarendon, 1967); and Piotr S. Wandycz, *The Lands of Partitioned Poland, 1795-1918* (Seattle: U of Washington P, 1974).

2  *dans le vide*: in a vacuum (French).

most cruel torture."[1] In another letter, written in April 1908 to Henry Mills Alden (1836-1919), Conrad remarks, "I am now struggling with the end of a long novel of Russian life and daren't turn my eyes another way. I find it a tougher job than I expected" (4: 74). Later, in a September 1909 letter to John Galsworthy, Conrad again comes back to the difficulty of writing the novel: "If I could only write at night when everybody is asleep I would not care. I've tried all last week. It's no go" (4: 271-72). To make matters worse, near the end of 1909, J.B. Pinker (1863-1922), Conrad's agent, became impatient with the delay in completing *Under Western Eyes* and apparently threatened to withhold his regular payments if he did not receive the novel shortly. Conrad fumed over this ultimatum, threatening to throw the manuscript into the fire and remarking in a letter to Perceval Gibbon (1879-1926), "You imagine how charming it is to be following the psychology of M<sup>r</sup> Razumov under these conditions. It's like working in hell" (4: 302). Shortly thereafter, he remarked in a letter to Norman Douglas (1868-1952), "There's neither inspiration nor hope in my work. It's mere hard labour for life" (4: 309), and around the same time he wrote to Pinker, "I havent [sic] done anything for nearly a week. I simply could not think and absolutely felt too listless to hold the pen" (4: 317). Conrad appears to have struggled not only with financial straits, illness (mental and physical), and writer's block, but also with personal emotions: spending so much time on a novel dealing with Russia and revolutionary politics could only force him to reflect upon his own early-life experiences resulting from his father's conviction for revolutionary activities. Although Conrad often suffered emotional trauma after finishing a lengthy writing project, the aftermath of completing *Under Western Eyes* was unusually severe, as he suffered a complete mental and physical breakdown. In a letter to David S. Meldrum (1864-1940) dated 6 February 1910, Conrad's wife, Jesse, wrote:

The novel is finished, but the penalaty [sic] has to be paid. Months of nervous strain have ended in a complete nervous breakdown. Poor Conrad is very ill and D<sup>r</sup> Hackney says it will be a long time before he is fit for anything requiring mental

---

1 Frederick R. Karl and Laurence Davies, eds., *The Collected Letters of Joseph Conrad*, vol. 4 (Cambridge: Cambridge UP, 1990), 69. Hereafter, citations from Conrad's letters will appear parenthetically.

exertion.... There is the M.S. complete but uncorrected and his fierce refusal to let even I touch it. It lays on a table at the foot of his bed and he lives mixed up in the scenes and holds converse with the characters.[1]

After having recovered to some extent, Conrad wrote to John Galsworthy in March 1910, "I have stood up today for several minutes, the first time in six weeks" (4: 321). Shortly thereafter, he wrote again to Galsworthy remarking, "I am still extremely limp both mentally and physically; but I shall to morrow try to go on with the revision of MS and discover how far I am capable of sustained mental effort. I am afraid it will not be a very brilliant result. I am growing desperate with the pain and weariness and the worry of this fatal stoppage of work" (4: 322). Even in June 1910, Conrad was little better; in a letter dated 8 June 1910, Conrad remarks to T. Fisher Unwin (1848-1935), "I don't think that [Hugh] Clifford[2] exaggerated; I've been very ill for four months and even now I am not myself yet."[3]

The completion of *Under Western Eyes* marked the end of Conrad's most productive period and may have resulted in more than merely the breakdown he suffered. For many commentators, the novel is the last of Conrad's great works, and it may be that in writing this novel the strain exhausted not only his physical and psychological health but also his creative genius.

## Reception of the Novel and Critical Trends

From the time that *Under Western Eyes* was first published, the critical response has been almost universally favorable. As Clement King Shorter (1857-1926) observed, "Mr. Conrad's novel, *Under Western Eyes*, has been hailed everywhere as his greatest achievement."[4] Further evidence of Shorter's assessment appears throughout the early reviews of the novel. The anonymous reviewer for *The Standard*, for example, remarks, "It may be considered, for its inevitable tragedy, Mr. Conrad's finest work,"

---

1   Joseph Conrad, *Letters to William Blackwood and David S. Meldrum*, ed. William Blackburn (Durham, NC: Duke UP, 1958), 192.

2   Sir Hugh Clifford (1866-1941) was governor of a number of British colonies and author of various books of fiction and nonfiction.

3   See John G. Peters, "Conrad to T. Fisher Unwin: An Uncollected Letter of June 1910," *The Conradian* 34.2 (autumn 2009): 125-26.

4   C[lement] K[ing] S[horter], "A Literary Letter: The Most Popular Novels of the Hour," *The Sphere* 47 (11 November 1911): xvi.

while the anonymous reviewer for *Evening Standard and St. James's Gazette* comments that the novel is Conrad's "finest—except 'Lord Jim.'" Similarly, Richard Curle (1883-1968) concludes that the novel "is a literary event of the first importance," and William Morton Payne (1858-1919) refers to *Under Western Eyes* as "Mr. Conrad's masterpiece." James Douglas (1867-1940) absolutely gushes over the novel: "Mr. Joseph Conrad has written a very great novel, 'Under Western Eyes' (Methuen[1]). It is incomparably finer and bigger than anything he has ever done. It places him among the giants of prose fiction."[2] Frequently, early reviewers noted two aspects of the novel: its psychological drama surrounding Razumov's betrayal of Haldin and its similarity to Russian novels of the nineteenth century. All of the reviews appearing in Appendix B comment on one or both of these aspects. Similarly, these issues arise in the reviews that appeared in *The Scotsman, The Morning Post, The Times, The Sun,* and *The Daily Telegraph.*[3] For instance, the reviewers typically comment on the psychological investigations in the novel, more specifically Razumov's character and his moral wrestling with his betrayal of Haldin and his struggles to recognize and finally come to terms with his remorse. Of the Russian novelists, Conrad is most often compared to Dostoevskii, and Conrad's ability to reveal the inscrutable Russian character to Western readers is particularly noted.

Two other issues also appear with some degree of frequency: the novel's narrative methodology and its bleak atmosphere. As with many of Conrad's works, reviewers and readers often noted Conrad's narrative experimentation. Of *Under Western Eyes,* the anonymous reviewer for *T.P.'s Weekly* concludes that "it is a masterpiece of contributory circumlocution rather than of direct power," while the anonymous reviewer for *The New York Tribune*

---

1 Methuen & Co. (London) first published the novel on 5 October 1911.

2 See "Novels of the Week," *The Standard* (20 October 1911): 5; "Mr. Conrad Ashore," *Evening Standard and St. James's Gazette* (12 October 1911): 5; Richard Curle, "Mr. Conrad's New Novel," *Manchester Guardian* (11 October 1911): 5; William Morton Payne, "Recent Fiction," *The Dial* (16 February 1912): 134; James Douglas, "Books and Bookmen: 'Under Western Eyes,'" *The Star* (16 October 1911): 7.

3 "*Under Western Eyes,*" *The Scotsman* (16 October 1911): 2; "The Middle of Russia," *The Morning Post* (12 October 1911): 3; "The World of Books," *The Sunday Times and Sunday Special* (15 October 1911): 7; "Some Russian Souls," *The Sun* 79 (4 November 1911): 9; [W.L. Courtney], "*Under Western Eyes,*" *Daily Telegraph* (25 October 1911): 4.

remarks that Conrad "is read not only for his substance but for his form, for his method. Indeed, half the pleasure of reading him is ordinarily derived from contemplation of his technical adroitness, an adroitness curiously spiritualized and very original. His method counts for much in this new novel." Other reviewers are less unequivocal in their praise of Conrad's narrative technique. The anonymous reviewer for *The Times Literary Supplement*, for example, comments, "Possibly Mr. Conrad's arrangement of his material is open to objection. The course of the story is twisted in order to keep up the pretence that the reader has not guessed what the English narrator had not guessed; but one can only admire the way in which Mr. Conrad has made use of his self-imposed difficulty," and the anonymous reviewer for *Punch* remarks that the novel "is as remarkable as any work by Mr. Joseph Conrad must needs be; but at the same time my impression of it, after turning the final page, is that as a story it is not without some unnecessary and irritating tricks of style, which may wear the patience of a reader who is less than a disciple."[1] Finally, some commentators noted what they saw as the novel's bleakness. For instance, despite their appreciation of the novel, the anonymous reviewers for *The North American Review* and *The Outlook* particularly note the novel's bleak atmosphere, commenting that the novel "is too unrelieved"[2] and "One finishes the book with a feeling of profound relief that Providence in its mercy has seen fit to save us from being a Russian subject."[3]

Despite the preponderance of positive reviews, the occasional negative notice also appeared. For example, the anonymous reviewer for *The Book Monthly News* complained that the novel was "so prosy in style that one is tired of it long before the end is reached" and that the author should not apologize about his not possessing the gift of imagination (the reviewer evidently confuses Conrad with the narrator in this complaint).[4] A surprisingly cool review of the novel came from H.L. Mencken (1880-1956). Usually a tireless supporter and promoter of Conrad's work,

---

1  "A Russian Book," *T.P.'s Weekly* (3 November 1911): 566; "A Brilliant Analytical Study by Joseph Conrad: The True Russian," *The New York Tribune* (28 October 1911): 8; "*Under Western Eyes*," *Times Literary Supplement* (12 October 1911): 385; "Our Booking-Office," *Punch* (1 November 1911): 326.

2  "*Under Western Eyes*," *North American Review* 194 (December 1911): 935-36.

3  "*Under Western Eyes*," *The Outlook* (21 October 1911): 546.

4  "*Under Western Eyes*," *The Book Monthly News* 30.5 (January 1912): 346.

Mencken did not particularly appreciate *Under Western Eyes*, remarking that "its central situation comes perilously near to banality,"[1] and of Razumov's falling in love Mencken comments "but let us stay our snickers!" At the same time, though, Mencken does conclude that although the novel "is not, to be sure, Conrad at his greatest ... it is certainly Conrad at a level of achievement which not many other men of the day ever reach."[2] Probably the most negative review of the novel appeared in *The New Age*: the anonymous reviewer writes, "Nothing redeems it" and "It is a preposterous invention, and by no means serves its purpose of excusing a story that after Turgeniev's 'Fathers and Children,'[3] ought never to be have been written."[4] These few negative reviews, along with a few other lukewarm ones, represent by far a minority view.

Unlike some of Conrad's later novels, which were well received during his lifetime but whose reputation later declined, *Under Western Eyes* has consistently been admired as one of his best works; and as noted by early reviewers of the novel, issues of betrayal and psychological struggle, as well as the relationship between *Under Western Eyes* and Russian novelists (particularly Dostoevskii), have also attracted a good deal of attention from later commentary. Indeed, such commentary has considered the novel's treatment of betrayal and its associated psychological struggle as a particularly complex problem. For instance, Anne Luyat sees betrayal in the novel as the source of tragedy, while Robert Hampson investigates Razumov obtaining his identity through betrayal and moving from a state of isolation ultimately to one of community as a result. George A. Panichas views the novel as a movement of moral ascent and discovery in which Razumov eventually finds his soul by repudiating his betrayal of Haldin. Similarly, R.A. Gekoski sees Razumov's confession as a moral victory, and John E. Saveson considers the novel to be one of moral discovery. In contrast, John Hagan argues that it is not

---

1　H.L. Mencken, "Conrad, Bennett, James et al," *The Smart Set* 36.1 (January 1912): 154.

2　Mencken, 156.

3　Ivan Sergeevich Turgenev (1819-83), Russian fiction writer, poet, and playwright. He is best known for his short story collection *A Sportsman's Sketches* (1852), his novel *Fathers and Sons* (1862), and his short story "A Lear of the Steppes" (1870). Methuen promoted *Under Western Eyes* as being similar to the work of Turgenev, an assertion with which the reviewer clearly does not agree.

4　"*Under Western Eyes*," *The New Age*, n.s. 9.26 (26 October 1911): 615.

the guilt of betrayal but rather the need for self-respect that impels Razumov to confess. In this way, commentators have seen the issue of betrayal as one of the crucial aspects of the novel and one that radiates in various directions.[1]

One of the most popular topics among commentators has been the relationship between *Under Western Eyes* and Russia, particularly in regard to Dostoevskii. David R. Smith, for example, argues that despite his protestations Conrad actually admired Dostoevskii in some ways, and that although *Under Western Eyes* may begin as a parody of *Crime and Punishment* it ends as a novel that Dostoevskii himself might have written. Similarly, Barbara Block Adams notes that the women in the lives of Raskolnikov and Razumov are primary influences in bringing these men out of their lives of loneliness. Unlike some commentators, Keith Carabine addresses the significant differences between Dostoevskii's *Crime and Punishment* and Conrad's *Under Western Eyes*, arguing that Conrad wholly rejected Dostoevskii's idea of Christian salvation and that in the end the similarities between the two novels are really more superficial than they may initially appear to be. Other commentators have focused more broadly on Conrad's relationship with Russia and Dostoevskii in order to understand better the relationship between *Under Western Eyes* and Russia. For instance, L.R. Lewitter compares Conrad's view of Russia and Dostoevskii's view of Poland. The historical context Lewitter provides makes Conrad's antipathy toward Dostoevskii much more understandable and clarifies why *Under Western Eyes* would necessarily diverge from Dostoevskii's novel. More broadly, Marcus Wheeler focuses on the background surrounding Conrad's relationship with Russia, arguing that although he clearly hated the Russian government he did not necessarily hate Russians themselves (hence the sympathetic portraits of such characters as Razumov, Tekla, and Sophia Antonovna). Bernard C. Meyer, on the other

---

1   See Anne Luyat, "Betrayal and Revelation: The Double Source of Tragedy in *Under Western Eyes*," *L'Époque Conradienne* 18 (1992): 153-62; Robert Hampson, *Joseph Conrad: Betrayal and Identity* (London: Macmillan, 1992), 167-95; George A. Panichas, *Joseph Conrad: His Moral Vision* (Mercer, GA: Mercer UP, 2005), 79-98; R.A. Gekoski, *Conrad: The Moral World of the Novelist* (New York: Barnes & Noble, 1978), 152-71; John E. Saveson, *Conrad, the Later Moralist* (Amsterdam: Rodopi, 1974), 71-91; John Hagan, "Conrad's *Under Western Eyes*: The Question of Razumov's 'Guilt' and 'Remorse,'" *Studies in the Novel* 1.3 (fall 1969): 310-22.

hand, emphasizes the psychological effect of Russia on Conrad as an influence on how he wrote the novel.[1]

Unlike in the early reviews, the politics of *Under Western Eyes* has been a major point of interest for later commentators. Irving Howe was the first to present an extended discussion of Conrad's politics,[2] identifying Conrad as a political conservative who supports the established government because of his relationship to Polish nationalism and who could not believe in the values that formed the basis for radical and liberal politics. In the end, Howe sees *Under Western Eyes* as flawed because of its negative portrayal of revolutionaries. Although Howe's book opened the door to more extended treatments of Conrad's politics, the two most important commentaries on this topic are those by Eloise Knapp Hay (*The Political Novels of Joseph Conrad*) and Avrom Fleishman (*Conrad's Politics*).[3] Published in the 1960s, both books remain almost definitive in their contributions to understanding the politics in *Under Western Eyes*. Like Howe, Hay views Conrad as rather conservative politically (though not to the degree that Howe does). Hay sees Conrad as rejecting revolutionary ideas and siding (perhaps somewhat reluctantly) with established governments. In contrast to Howe and Hay, Fleishman places Conrad in the context of a much more democratic Polish, English, and European political tradition. In Fleishman's reading of Conrad's politics, Conrad is not as conservative as other commentators had concluded.

Except for the novel's political aspects, perhaps no topic in

---

1   See David R. Smith, "Dostoevsky and Conrad," *The Conradian* 15.2 (January 1991): 1-11; Barbara Block Adams, "Sisters under Their Skins: The Women in the Lives of Raskolnikov and Razumov," *Conradiana* 6.2 (May 1974): 113-24; Keith Carabine, "'Where to?': A Comparison of Dostoevsky's *Crime and Punishment* and Conrad's *Under Western Eyes*," in *Inter-Relations: Conrad, James, Ford and Others*, ed. Keith Carabine and Max Saunders (Boulder, CO: Social Science Monographs, 2003), 211-60; L.R. Lewitter, "Conrad, Dostoevsky, and the Russo-Polish Antagonism," *Modern Language Review* 7.3 (July 1984): 653-63; Marcus Wheeler, "Russia and Russians in the Works of Conrad," *Conradiana* 12.1 (spring 1980): 23-36; Bernard C. Meyer, "Conrad and the Russians," *Conradiana* 12.1 (1980): 13-21.

2   Irving Howe, *Politics and the Novel* (New York: Horizon Press, 1957), 76-113.

3   See Eloise Knapp Hay, *The Political Novels of Joseph Conrad: A Critical Study* (Chicago: U of Chicago P, 1963) and Avrom Fleishman, *Conrad's Politics: Community and Anarchy in the Fiction of Joseph Conrad* (Baltimore: Johns Hopkins UP, 1967).

*Under Western Eyes* has been more discussed than Conrad's narrative methodology, in both earlier and later commentary. In contrast to the early reviews, however, later commentary has tended to focus more heavily on the novel's narrator than on its fractured chronology. These discussions have revolved around such issues as what the narrator knows, his reliability, and whether the views expressed at various points in the novel are his own or Razumov's or the narrator's other sources.[1]

## Narrative Methodology

An important aspect of the novel is its narrative methodology. Unlike most traditional novels, *Under Western Eyes* employs neither an omniscient narrator nor a strictly first-person narrator. Instead, the unnamed British teacher of languages narrates his personal experience, but he also records the information set forth in Razumov's journal. In so doing, though, he does not simply record Razumov's writings word for word but rather takes that recorded information and narrates the events and information much as an omniscient narrator would; at times it is difficult to separate Razumov's views from those of the narrator, particularly when he employs free indirect discourse. The benefit of the choice to use the teacher of languages to relate Razumov's experience instead of using Razumov's own words (except in a few isolated instances) is that Conrad is able to present Razumov's

---

1  See, for example, Keith Carabine, *The Life and the Art: A Study of Conrad's "Under Western Eyes"* (Amsterdam: Rodopi, 1996), 209-51; Ronald Schleifer, "Public and Private Narrative in *Under Western Eyes*," *Conradiana* 9.3 (autumn 1977): 237-54; Robert Secor, "The Function of the Narrator in *Under Western Eyes*," *Conradiana* 3.1 (autumn 1970-1971): 27-38; Tony Tanner, "Nightmare and Complacency: Razumov and the Western Eye," *Critical Quarterly* 4.3 (autumn 1962): 199-200; Gail Fincham, "'To make you see': Narration and Focalization in *Under Western Eyes*," in *Joseph Conrad: Voice, Sequence, History, Genre*, ed. Jakob Lothe, Jeremy Hawthorn, and James Phelan (Columbus: Ohio State UP, 2008), 60-80; Kenneth Graham, "'Like a Traveller in a Strange Country': Narrative Dynamics in *Under Western Eyes*," in *Studies in English and American Literature: In Honour of Witold Ostrowski*, ed. Irena Janicka-Świderska (Warsaw: Państwowe Wydawnictwo Naukowe, 1984), 63-70; Robert E. Kelley, "'This Chance Glimpse': The Narrator in *Under Western Eyes*," *University Review* 37.4 (June 1971): 285-90; Frank Kermode, "Secrets and Narrative Sequence," *Critical Inquiry* 7.1 (autumn 1979): 83-101; and Gene M. Moore, "Chronotopes and Voices in *Under Western Eyes*," *Conradiana* 18.1 (spring 1986): 9-25.

experience filtered through the consciousness of the narrator, thus giving readers the perspective of both Razumov and the teacher of languages. Furthermore, the title *Under Western Eyes* also emphasizes that everything filters through the narrator: his are the Western eyes of the title, and he represents the Western view of the world. In a March 1909 letter to Henry-Durand Davray (1873-1944), Conrad stressed the novel's perspective: "It is written from the English point of view" (4: 203). Of course, the narrator attempts to render Razumov's thinking when narrating the events contained in his journal, but otherwise the reader sees the world through the eyes of the narrator.

Conrad chooses such a narrative strategy for several reasons. First, he wishes to render experience as it actually occurs. In other words, the reader's experience in accessing information resembles the way human beings typically access information, piecing it together from various sources and discovering it at different points in time. Because the reader can access information only as it is filtered through the narrator's perception, which information has already been filtered through Razumov's perception or that of other characters such as Natalia Haldin and Sophia Antonovna, Conrad demonstrates that nothing can be known with absolute certainty since nothing can be accessed except through human consciousness. Perspective and point of view alter the nature of phenomena, and thus the choices the characters make, particularly those of Razumov, become that much more difficult to judge because of the relativity of all knowledge to the context in which it appears.[1]

Furthermore, Conrad wishes to show that the West can see things only from its own perspective. For example, the British teacher of languages consistently demonstrates his inability to understand Russia. Early in the novel, he remarks, "Yet I confess that I have no comprehension of the Russian character. The illogicality of their attitude, the arbitrariness of their conclusions, the frequency of the exceptional, should present no difficulty to a student of many grammars; but there must be something else in the way, some special human trait—one of those subtle differences that are beyond the ken of mere professors" (49-50). Furthermore, in his various discussions with Natalia, the narrator shows a similar lack of understanding, and later remarks, "But this is not a story of the West" (257). Lest the reader assume,

---

1 For more on this concept in general, see John G. Peters, *Conrad and Impressionism* (Cambridge: Cambridge UP, 2001), 16-34.

however, that this difference in perception is simply an idiosyncrasy of the narrator himself, Conrad juxtaposes the views of the populations in general. Of the expatriate Russians, the narrator comments:

> The shadow of autocracy all unperceived by me had already fallen upon the Boulevard des Philosophes, in the free, independent and democratic city of Geneva, where there is a quarter called "La Petite Russie." Whenever two Russians come together, the shadow of autocracy is with them, tinging their thoughts, their views, their most intimate feelings, their private life, their public utterances—haunting the secret of their silences. (125)

For the Russians, their homeland experience colors how they see every other place. In contrast, elsewhere the narrator remarks, "I observed a solitary Swiss couple, whose fate was made secure from the cradle to the grave by the perfected mechanism of democratic institutions in a republic that could almost be held in the palm of one's hand" (175). Unlike the Russians, the Swiss see this same setting (Geneva) wholly differently because their experience differs from that of the Russians. This difference between Western and Eastern perceptions of the world further emphasizes the relativity of all knowledge that becomes apparent through Conrad's choice of narrative methodology, but even more so it represents the idea that in Conrad's view the West simply does not and cannot understand the East—although typically those of the West do not even recognize this blind spot (the teacher of languages being an exception because of his Russian background and his extensive interaction with Russians). Implicit in this contrast is not just that the West does not realize that others view the world differently, but also an inherent criticism of a Western ethnocentricism.

Finally, the title *Under Western Eyes* emphasizes that the events in the novel all occur under the eyes of the West. In other words, Conrad clearly delineates the implications of Russian autocracy and revolutionary activity for those living in the East and caught between these two forces. In the midst of this tragedy, the West merely looks on. In the back of Conrad's mind is perhaps a similar issue: the fate of Poland. With their country having been partitioned, Poles had been consistently fighting for their freedom from foreign rule. Appeals to the West fell on deaf ears, as those nations, particularly the powers of France and England, viewed the Polish problem as the internal affairs of Russia, Prussia, and Austria-Hungary. In emphasizing the Western eyes of the novel, Conrad appears to be criticizing the West once again and showing it, by its tacit consent, to be complicit with Russia in the oppression of so many under its rule.

## Politics of the Novel

*Under Western Eyes* is best known as the third and last of Conrad's overtly political novels, following *Nostromo* (1904) and *The Secret Agent* (1907). It has both similarities to and differences from these earlier novels and in some ways most clearly solidifies Conrad's political views. As noted earlier, the novel is based upon the 1904 assassination of Russia's Minister of the Interior, Viacheslav Konstantinovich de Pleve, by members of the Socialist-Revolutionary Party. Conrad uses this event as the jumping-off point to consider the actions and philosophy of Russian revolutionaries and the Russian autocracy.

After the assassination of de P——, Conrad's fictional perpetrator, Victor Haldin, seeks refuge in the rooms of a fellow student, Kirylo Sidorovitch Razumov, assuming that Razumov is a sympathizer with the revolutionary cause. In fact, Razumov is only mildly sympathetic to the cause and is extremely troubled by Haldin's presence under such circumstances, feeling the "sentiment of his life being utterly ruined by this contact with such a crime" (59). Given the political climate of the time, Haldin's mere presence would be enough to implicate Razumov and ruin his future. The narrator comments, "It is unthinkable that any young Englishman should find himself in Razumov's situation.... He would not have an hereditary and personal knowledge of the means by which a historical autocracy represses ideas, guards its power, and defends its existence" (65). As a result of this dilemma, after offering to help Haldin escape (just to get rid of him) but finding the sleigh driver drunk and incapable of spiriting Haldin away, Razumov decides to turn Haldin over to the authorities. By so doing, he hopes to serve his country and to save himself from suspicion. Despite Razumov's service to the government, though, he remains a suspect in the minds of the authorities. General T—— remarks, "And you say he came in to make you this confidence like this—for nothing—*à propos des bottes*," to which the narrator notes, "Razumov felt danger in the air. The merciless suspicion of despotism had spoken openly at last" (82).

Shortly thereafter, the police search Razumov's rooms. Later, Councillor Mikulin, looking to make further use of Razumov, eventually recruits him to be a double agent. In this atmosphere of extreme suspicion, however, even a high-ranking official such as Mikulin is not safe. Later, the narrator notes, "[D]uring one of those State trials which astonish and puzzle the average plain man who reads the newspapers, by a glimpse of unsuspected intrigues. And in the stir of vaguely seen monstrosities, in that momentary, mysterious disturbance of muddy waters, Councillor Mikulin went under, dignified, with only a calm, emphatic protest of his innocence—nothing more" (270), and concludes, "It seems that the savage autocracy, no more than the divine democracy, does not limit its diet exclusively to the bodies of its enemies. It devours its friends and servants as well" (271). Conrad's indictment of the Russian autocratic government and its jealous protection of power at the expense of everything else is unrelenting throughout the novel.

Despite his criticism of Russian autocracy, however, Conrad does not endorse the revolutionary cause that opposes it. As in his other political fiction, Conrad is critical of both sides of the political divide. Although there is some sympathy in his portrayal of Sophia Antonovna, Ziemianitch, and Victor Haldin, Conrad is otherwise scathingly critical of the revolutionaries. In the revolutionary camp in Geneva, Madame de S—— appears to have little political fervor and supports the revolutionaries as a means to address her own personal agenda. Her priorities later become particularly apparent when we learn, after her death, that she bequeathed none of her money to the revolutionary cause. In addition, Conrad paints her as a ghoulish figure with a precarious grip on sanity. Of Peter Ivanovitch, Conrad shows him to be more interested in personal power than in the revolutionary ideas he espouses. Conrad ridicules his "feminism" and represents it as hypocritical, merely a means to obtain power over women. Julius Laspara is described as a tiny man, a "violent pamphleteer clamouring for revolutionary justice" (255), who does nothing of significance. Worst of all is the brutal Nikita, who turns out to be a double agent and who clearly takes more pleasure in the havoc he wreaks than in any political ideology. Despite some sympathy in Conrad's treatment of Sophia Antonovna, she is singularly deceived as to Razumov's politics, and her unequivocal support of Peter Ivanovitch in the closing line of the novel ("Peter Ivanovitch is an inspired man" [325]), in the face of his overwhelming shortcomings, tips the balance against her in the end.

Conrad's treatment of the revolutionaries in St. Petersburg is no more sympathetic. Kostia is represented as a fool. The unnamed red-nosed student appears as an ineffectual, idealistic dreamer. Similarly, despite some sympathy for Ziemianitch, he is otherwise depicted as a drunken sentimentalist, who is unavailable when most needed. Even Victor Haldin is described as having "the dream-intoxication of the idealist incapable of perceiving the reason of things" (70); particularly telling is his disregard for Razumov's safety by coming to his rooms after assassinating de P———. Haldin tells Razumov, "For some weeks now, ever since I resigned myself to do what had to be done, I tried to isolate myself. I gave up my rooms. What was the good of exposing a decent widow woman to the risk of being worried out of her mind by the police? I gave up seeing any of our comrades"; to which Razumov reasonably thinks, "Upon my word, he seems to have thought of everybody's safety but mine" (89). Even more telling, Conrad carefully notes the great number of innocent bystanders who are killed or injured during the assassination of de P———, thus ultimately condemning Haldin's actions and suggesting that one must consider the cost of so many innocent lives against the gain of removing even a much-despised figure.

More telling examples of Conrad's scorn of both sides of the political fight appear in the character of Nikita and in various statements in Conrad's "Author's Note" to Under Western Eyes. As noted earlier, we discover late in the novel that Nikita is a double agent, spreading death and destruction for and against both sides of the struggle. Nikita thus becomes a symbol of the devastation wrought by both sides, and his role highlights their amorality in courting the services of ruthless characters like him in order to further their own political ends, regardless of the consequences. Conrad's most significant political statement regarding his rejection of both sides, however, appears in his "Author's Note" to the novel (written some ten years after the book's completion) when he prophetically remarks:

> The ferocity and imbecility of an autocratic rule rejecting all legality and in fact basing itself upon complete moral anarchism provokes the no less imbecile and atrocious answer of a purely Utopian revolutionism encompassing destruction by the first means to hand, in the strange conviction that a fundamental change of hearts must follow the downfall of any given human institutions. These people are unable to see that all they can effect is merely a change of names. The oppressors

and the oppressed are all Russians together; and the world is brought once more face to face with the truth of the saying that the tiger cannot change his stripes nor the leopard his spots. (46)

At a time when most writers of political fiction chose one side of a political debate, Conrad wrote a most unusual political novel in its consistent condemnation of both sides.

## The Individual and Society

Conrad's indictment of politics arises not so much from philosophical pessimism (of which he is often accused) but rather from what he saw as the all-too-costly price of politics in human terms. For Conrad, so often the individual (particularly the innocent bystander) was the greatest victim on the battlefield of political warfare. Examples of those crushed between the two opposing political forces go much further than those passers-by killed during de P——'s assassination, as both sides see individuals merely as political means rather than political ends.

Typically, in Conrad's political fiction, there are two general storylines—the larger life of political struggle and the smaller life of the individual—that are intertwined and reflect upon one another. *Under Western Eyes* is no different; in fact, the novel may be the best example of Conrad's investigations into the relationship between the individual citizen and political society. Three characters in particular are at the center of such scrutiny: Natalia Haldin, Mrs. Haldin, and Razumov. In the cases of Natalia and Mrs. Haldin in particular, Conrad clearly condemns the devastating effects of Victor Haldin's politics. Because of his revolutionary activities, Victor casts suspicion upon his sister and mother while they are living in Russia, then uproots them, forcing them to flee to Geneva and live in a foreign and unfamiliar environment. In the end, he loses his life as a result of his role in the assassination of de P——, and his family is left adrift. Conrad closely delineates the near-worship Victor's sister and mother have for him, and their subsequent desolation at his death. Natalia is eventually better able to cope with this loss, but her mother never can. In effect, at the moment she learns of Victor's death, Mrs. Haldin dies as well. Natalia tries to console her mother, but to little avail. As Natalia laments, "Then, when I was left alone with poor mother, all this seemed so wrong in spirit, something not worth the price she is paying for it" (297-98).

Conrad implies that the idealistic revolutionary views of Victor Haldin are a poor price to pay for the individual tragedies left in their wake. One wonders whether in chronicling the plight of Natalia and her mother Conrad did not have in the back of his mind his parents' premature death and his own life as an orphan as a consequence of his father's revolutionary activities.

Most tragic perhaps is Razumov's fate. He simply wants to be left to his studies and his efforts to write an essay worthy of the silver medal so that he can secure a future academic career. Neither political camp, however, will allow him this freedom, despite the fact that Razumov has little sympathy for either the revolutionaries or the government authorities. His main reason for first trying to help Haldin escape and his main reason for later turning him in are in essence the same: to protect himself and maintain a life divorced from politics. The great tragedy in the novel is the impossibility of such a desire in the political climate of the time. When Razumov's rooms are searched, the revolutionaries welcome him as a fellow traveler. On the other hand, the authorities search his rooms because they suspect that he was involved with Haldin. Why else would Haldin have sought out Razumov after de P——'s assassination? Later, the authorities place Razumov in a position where he has little option but to accept their offer to become a double agent and infiltrate the revolutionary circles abroad. Councillor Mikulin's chillingly prophetic query that closes Part I of the novel underscores Razumov's plight. When Razumov gets up to leave, saying that he wishes "to retire," Mikulin quietly asks him, "Where to?" (119). The implication is clear: Razumov no longer has anywhere to go. Ironically Razumov, the most politically neutral character at the beginning of the tale, later becomes its most politically involved character.

Once Haldin arrives in Razumov's rooms, Razumov's life forever changes. Beset by guilt and embraced by both the revolutionaries and the authorities (while still feeling he is also under suspicion from the authorities), he cannot return to his studies; and because his whole existence had been focused on the future and predicated upon a successful academic career, Razumov feels his life is over once that possibility disappears. As a result, when Councillor Mikulin recruits him as a double agent, Razumov accepts the offer. He quickly discovers, however, that this new life will not provide meaning for his existence either and instead destroys what little remains of it.

Further emphasizing Razumov's plight, and despite its great emphasis on politics, the most powerful aspect of *Under Western*

*Eyes* is the moral and psychological dilemmas with which Razumov struggles. Conrad remarked of the novel in a March 1908 letter to Henry-Durand Davray, "It will be called *Razumov* and will be Russian, very Russian in fact. Absolutism and Revolution—and the moral pangs of the above-mentioned Razumov—quiet student—who dies of them" (4: 59). Conrad places Razumov in an untenable position, focusing on the moral and psychological struggle he must endure in which he has no good options. Knowing the danger that Haldin's presence poses, Razumov feels that he must choose between his own safety and Haldin's. He wrestles with this dilemma and finally turns Haldin over to the authorities, hoping thereby to return to his previous existence. Not until much later does he recognize that his inescapable feelings of guilt as well as his moral sensibility (rather than the political demands of the revolutionaries and authorities upon him) prevent him from returning to his previous life. In the end, Razumov concludes, "In giving Victor Haldin up, it was myself, after all, whom I have betrayed most basely" (310); and once he realizes the moral implications of his actions, he concludes: "therefore perdition is my lot" (310). For Conrad, people like Natalia Haldin, her mother, Razumov, and all other innocent bystanders matter much more than any political ideas.

Conrad further privileges individuals over ideas—political or otherwise—in the consistent value he places on human relationships in *Under Western Eyes*. Ziemianitch, Tekla, and Razumov best exemplify this aspect of the novel. In the experience of Ziemianitch, Conrad first demonstrates the importance of the individual in the political world. The keeper of the eating house says of Ziemianitch, "A proper Russian driver that. Saint or devil, night or day is all one to Ziemianitch when his heart is free from sorrow" (68). Since Ziemianitch's sorrow always results from the loss of a woman, his priorities are clear: human relationships are more important than politics. "Ziemianitch's passionate surrender to sorrow and consolation had baffled" (70) Razumov because such priorities are foreign to him, as he later confesses: "I've never known any kind of love" (310). Nor does Sophia Antonovna understand Ziemianitch's priorities. After learning of his suicide, she assumes that he has hanged himself out of remorse for having betrayed Haldin. She does not imagine that he killed himself over his failure to win back the woman he loved. Razumov, however, knows that "[t]his was a drama of love, not of conscience" (253). Unlike Haldin and many of the other revolutionaries, whom Razumov accuses of "the dream-intoxication of the idealist" (70), Ziemianitch's intoxication results from the sorrow of lost love. Not until much later does Razumov begin to understand Ziemianitch's priorities.

Tekla even more so demonstrates Conrad's emphasis on the importance of human ties over abstract ideas. She leaves a comfortable existence with her family because she recognizes that her family's comforts result from the privations of others. Her father has a favorable appointment in the Russian bureaucracy, but Tekla turns her back on that life in order to join the ranks of the revolutionaries. Unlike the other revolutionaries in *Under Western Eyes*, though, Tekla's revolutionary ideas are always closely linked to individual human beings. She finds far greater value in helping her "poor Andrei" by trying to nurse him back to health after the police release him than in direct revolutionary discussions and activity. For her, helping people is the most important thing she—and particularly the revolution—can do. For this reason, she becomes wholly disillusioned with the revolutionaries in the Geneva circle, as they seem to have forgotten (or never known) the value of the individual human being. Peter Ivanovitch best represents this failing while dictating to Tekla his revolutionary writings meant for the betterment of humanity. Tekla relates her experience to Natalia:

> First of all, you have to sit perfectly motionless. The slightest movement you make puts to flight the ideas of Peter Ivanovitch. You hardly dare to breathe. And as to coughing— God forbid! Peter Ivanovitch changed the position of the table to the wall because at first I could not help raising my eyes to look out of the window, while waiting for him to go on with his dictation. That was not allowed. He said I stared so stupidly. I was likewise not permitted to look at him over my shoulder. Instantly Peter Ivanovitch stamped his foot, and would roar, "Look down on the paper!" It seems my expression, my face, put him off. Well, I know that I am not beautiful, and that my expression is not hopeful either. He said that my air of unintelligent expectation irritated him. (155)

Peter Ivanovitch, it seems, can theorize about improving humanity, but he cannot put his theory into practice, and in his disregard for Tekla's humanity he destroys her faith in the ideas he is dictating: she remarks, "I am quite willing to be the blind instrument of higher ends. To give one's life for the cause is nothing. But to have one's illusions destroyed—that is really almost more than one can bear" (156). As a result of her experience at the hands of the Geneva revolutionaries, Tekla no longer has any faith in their ideals, and so when she meets Razumov she latches onto him, remarking, "It was your humane manner. I have been starving for, I won't say kindness, but just for a little civility, for I don't know how long" (217). As was the case with her devotion to her "poor Andrei," she offers a similar devotion to Razumov: "'Yes, if you were to get ill,' she interrupted eagerly, 'or meet some bitter trouble, you would find I am not a useless fool. You have only to let me know. I will come to you. I will indeed. And I will stick to you. Misery and I are old acquaintances—but this life here is worse than starving'" (217). Tekla's revolutionary ideology consists simply in valuing humanity, and she is as good as her word. After Razumov is run over by the tramcar, she follows him to the hospital and cares for him, and when he is released from the hospital, she takes him into her care and stays with him. For Tekla, the concrete human being matters more than the abstract idea, and ideas divorced from humanity have no value.

Razumov's case is similar. As noted earlier, at the opening of the novel he is detached from the politics of both sides. After Haldin draws Razumov into the conflict and he cannot facilitate Haldin's escape, Razumov then convinces himself (or rather believes that he convinces himself) that Haldin is a menace to Russia and determines to turn him over to the authorities. Later, when Razumov finds that he can no longer focus on his studies and realizes that his imagined future has been destroyed, he accepts Mikulin's offer to become a double agent, in part because of what he believes to be patriotic reasons but even more so because he wishes to exact revenge upon the revolutionaries, whom he holds responsible for ruining his life. Consequently, the ideas of hate, revenge, and patriotism rule him. In the end, though, Razumov finds such ideas to be hollow, leading to an empty existence because he ignores humanity in their pursuit. Razumov reveals this emptiness in the journal entry he directs toward Natalia. After first meeting her, he had decided to revenge himself upon Haldin through his sister: "And do you know what I said to myself? I shall steal his sister's soul from her.... I was thinking, 'Yes, he [Haldin] himself by talking of her trustful eyes has delivered her into my hands!'" (309). Soon, however, Razumov finds that he cannot carry out his plan when confronted with Natalia's purity:

> For days you have talked with me—opening your heart. I
> remembered the shadow of your eyelashes over your grey

trustful eyes. And your pure forehead! It is low like the forehead of statues—calm, unstained. It was as if your pure brow
bore a light which fell on me, searched my heart and saved me
from ignominy, from ultimate undoing.... Your light! your
truth! I felt that I must tell you that I had ended by loving
you." (310)

Razumov discovers that his feelings of patriotism and particularly
of hatred and revenge crumble in the face of Natalia's virtue. Like
Ziemianitch and Tekla, Razumov too comes to realize that
human connections matter most of all.

As a result of Razumov's discovery, he confesses his betrayal to
Natalia and to the revolutionary circle in Geneva. This decision
results in not only Razumov losing a chance to further his relationship with Natalia, but also his being attacked by Nikita and
consequently run over by a tramcar. At the end of the novel,
although Razumov is crippled, deaf, and likely to die young from
his injuries, Conrad reveals that Razumov is better off than he
was earlier—not only when he was full of health (and also full of
hate) but even at the opening of the novel when he actively culti-
vated his isolation from humanity. As Sophia Antonovna concludes, "It was just when he believed himself safe and more—infinitely more—when the possibility of being loved by that
admirable girl first dawned upon him, that he discovered that his
bitterest railings, the worst wickedness, the devil work of his hate
and pride, could never cover up the ignominy of the existence
before him. There's character in such a discovery" (323). In the
end, Razumov best reflects Conrad's emphasis on the necessity of
choosing the reality of human ties over the illusion of mere ideas.

## Conrad's Universe

The universe that Conrad portrays is one in which individuals are
subject to the whims of chance and have little control over their
existence. At the outset of *Under Western Eyes*, Razumov believes
that he can shape his destiny: by working hard and writing an
essay worthy of the silver medal, he believes that he can secure an
academic position for his desired future. Once Victor Haldin
appears, however, Razumov loses all control over his existence.
Certainly Razumov *chooses* to betray Haldin, but he does so out
of the very real belief that to do otherwise would implicate him
and leave his future in ruins. What he does not realize is that his
future was already ruined the moment Haldin appeared and that

turning Haldin over to the authorities has not enabled Razumov to reclaim his future. Once he recognizes the gravity of Haldin's presence in his rooms, Razumov tries to regain control of his existence by agreeing to facilitate Haldin's escape, but he despairs when he discovers Ziemianitch in a drunken stupor. Later, Razumov once again appears to have an opportunity to resume his life as it was prior to Haldin's arrival. Despite the search of his rooms and the suspicion he remains under and despite his interview with Councillor Mikulin over the Haldin affair, it turns out that Mikulin "would have simply dropped him [Razumov] for ever" (271) except for the chance occurrence of Mikulin's promotion to another position, at which point he "saw great possibilities of special usefulness in that uncommon young man [Razumov] on whom he had a hold already" (271). At that point, Mikulin actively recruits Razumov as a double agent.

Still later, fate again comes into play in Razumov's life. Arriving in Geneva, he seeks once more to master his fate and avenge himself on the revolutionaries, but by chance Natalia Haldin and her mother happen to be in Geneva and also by chance it turns out that, contrary to his usual practice, Victor Haldin had mentioned a fellow student (Razumov) and spoke highly of him. This combination of circumstances brings Razumov and Natalia together and ultimately leads to Razumov's confession. Again, the fact that Nikita was in Geneva at that time and was present when Razumov confesses and, perhaps most tragically and most ironically, the fact that the tramcar happened to be passing at the very moment that Razumov was crossing the tracks demonstrate Razumov's precarious position in the world and how little say he has in the workings of his life. Furthermore, in telling this tale, Conrad seeks to represent the plight of people in general as they confront an absurd universe in which they are subject to the whims of chance, can make no sense of the world in which they find themselves, and can exert no ultimate control over their existence. Only in confronting such a universe in the full knowledge of its nature and yet choosing those moral values that affirm humanity despite the absence of any transcendent foundation for such values, as Razumov chooses, does human existence become meaningful for Conrad.

*Under Western Eyes* is perhaps Joseph Conrad's most unusual novel. It is the fictional work closest to some of his most painful memories; it is his most human novel; and it is generally considered to be the final work of his most productive (and for many his greatest) period of writing. In many ways, the novel embodies

Conrad's most important ideas. Issues of solidarity, betrayal, politics, the individual in society, and the nature of human existence all find their way into this tale. After *Under Western Eyes*, Conrad's writing (with only rare exceptions) was never the same. It would seem perhaps that everything Conrad had to say in his previous works and later works comes together in *Under Western Eyes*: thus the novel may be seen as a culmination of Conrad's unique and remarkable literary career.

# *Joseph Conrad: A Brief Chronology*

1762    Catherine II (Ekaterina II) or Catherine the Great becomes Empress of Russia.

1772    Part of Poland is partitioned between Russia, Prussia, and Austria.

1793    More of Poland is partitioned between Russia, Prussia, and Austria.

1795    The remainder of Poland is partitioned between Russia, Prussia, and Austria.

1796    Paul I (Pavel I) becomes Tsar of Russia.

1801    Aleksandr I becomes Tsar of Russia.

1812    Russia is invaded by France, but ultimately weathers the invasion and emerges victorious as the premier power on land in Europe.

1825    Nikolai I becomes Tsar of Russia.

1830    Polish insurgents revolt against Russian rule. The insurrection is not put down until almost a year later. Severe reprisals follow.

1853    Russia enters the Crimean War of 1853-56 and is ultimately defeated.

1855    Aleksandr II becomes Tsar of Russia.

1857    Józef Teodor Konrad Korzeniowski (Joseph Conrad) is born in Berdyczów, Ukraine on 3 December.

1862    Conrad's father, Apollo Korzeniowski, is sentenced to exile in Vologda, Russia.

1863    Polish insurgents again revolt against Russian rule. The insurrection is not put down until nearly two years later. Again, severe reprisals follow.

1865    Conrad's mother, Ewelina Bobrowska Korzeniowska, dies of tuberculosis.

1868    Apollo Korzeniowski is allowed to return to Poland.

1869    Apollo Korzeniowski dies of tuberculosis contracted during exile.

1874    Conrad goes to Marseilles, France, to study to become a sailor.

1876    The Land and Freedom Party is formed in Russia, to seek social reforms.

1878    Conrad joins the British Merchant Marine service.

1879    The People's Will wing of the Land and Freedom Party is formed with the express intent of carrying out terrorist activities against the Russian government.

1880 Conrad passes his officer's examination.

1881 Aleksandr II is assassinated by members of the People's Will. Aleksandr III becomes Tsar of Russia.

1886 Conrad passes his master's examination for a captaincy, and becomes a British citizen.

1888 Conrad becomes captain of the *Otago*.

1889 Conrad begins writing *Almayer's Folly*.

1890 Conrad signs on with a Belgian trading company to command a steamboat on the Congo River.

1891 Conrad becomes first mate of the *Torrens*.

1891 In Russia, a famine across the land re-invigorates revolutionary activity against the Russian government.

1893 Conrad meets and becomes friends with Edward Lancelot Sanderson and John Galsworthy on a return voyage from Australia aboard the *Torrens*.

1894 Conrad finishes his tour of duty aboard the *Adowa*, never to return to his profession at sea. Later that year, he completes *Almayer's Folly*, and he meets and becomes friends with Edward Garnett.

1894 Nikolai II becomes Tsar of Russia.

1895 *Almayer's Folly* is published.

1896 *An Outcast of the Islands* is published. Conrad meets and becomes friends with H.G. Wells. He marries Jessie George.

1897 *The Nigger of the "Narcissus"* is published, and Conrad meets and becomes friends with Henry James, R.B. Cunninghame Graham, and Stephen Crane.

1898 *Tales of Unrest* is published. Conrad meets and becomes friends with Ford Madox Ford. His first son, Borys, is born.

1899 *Heart of Darkness* is published.

1900 *Lord Jim* is published and James B. Pinker becomes Conrad's literary agent.

1901 *The Inheritors*, written in collaboration with Ford, is published.

1902 *Youth and Two Other Stories* is published.

1903 *Typhoon and Other Stories* is published. *Romance*, written in collaboration with Ford, is published.

1904 *Nostromo* is published.

1904 Vyacheslav Konstantinovich de Pleve, Russian Minister of the Interior, is assassinated by members of the Socialist-Revolutionary Party.

1905 "Autocracy and War" is published.

1905 The Bloody Sunday massacre occurs in St. Petersburg, setting off a year-long revolution in Russia.

1906 *The Mirror of the Sea* is published. Conrad writes "The Nature of a Crime" in collaboration with Ford. Conrad's second son, John, is born.

1907 *The Secret Agent* is published.

1908 *A Set of Six* is published.

1909 Conrad writes "The Secret Sharer."

1910 Conrad completes *Under Western Eyes* and suffers a complete physical and emotional breakdown.

1911 *Under Western Eyes* is published.

1912 *Some Reminiscences* (*A Personal Record*) and *'Twixt Land and Sea* are published.

1913 Conrad meets and becomes friends with Bertrand Russell.

1914 With the publication of *Chance*, Conrad achieves public fame and financial security. He travels to Poland with his family and is caught behind Austrian lines at the outbreak of World War I in August; narrowly missing being detained for the duration of the war, the Conrads arrive back in England in November.

1915 *Within the Tides* and *Victory* are published.

1917 *The Shadow-Line* is published.

1917 The Russian Revolution occurs, overthrowing the monarchy once and for all.

1919 *The Arrow of Gold* is published.

1920 *The Rescue* is published.

1921 *Notes on Life and Letters* is published. Conrad translates Bruno Winawer's play *The Book of Job* from Polish into English.

1923 *The Rover* is published and Conrad travels to America on a promotion tour.

1924 Conrad dies of a heart attack, leaving his novel *Suspense* unfinished.

1925 *Tales of Hearsay* and *Suspense* are published.

1926 *Last Essays* is published.

# A Note on the Text

The textual history of *Under Western Eyes* is a difficult one. Until late in his career (when he began dictating some of his works), Conrad wrote his manuscripts by hand. As he did typically, Conrad had the manuscript of *Under Western Eyes* typed as he completed sections, first as a "rough type," which was then heavily corrected, and then later as a "clean copy," which would have fewer corrections. The extant typescript, which appears to consist of more than one actual typescript, is held at the Philadelphia Free Library, while the manuscript is held at Yale University. It is also possible that there were yet other typescripts that have not survived.

After the manuscript was completed in January 1910, Conrad revised it in preparation for serial publication. He made extensive cuts for the serial versions of the novel that he initially intended to re-insert into the book versions, but later he seems to have either changed his mind or did not want to go to the trouble of restoring the deleted material, since he was already working on other projects by that time. In December 1910, serial publication began in England in *The English Review* and in America in *The North American Review*. Conrad also seemed to go back and forth regarding yet further corrections, writing to Austin Harrison (1873-1928), the editor of *The English Review*, to send him "early proofs, in duplicate" (4: 371) for correction, while later writing in October 1910 to John Galsworthy, "I didn't care whether he [Harrison] printed the novel forwards or backwards with a title or without" (4: 381-2). Later still, in August 1911, in preparation for the first American edition, Conrad wrote to his agent J.B. Pinker asking that Harper and Brothers "send me over galley slips" for correction (4: 467). The novel was published in book form in October 1911 by Methuen in England and by Harper and Brothers in America.

The entire process of revision appears to have been both rushed and also perhaps somewhat confused, and as a result there are differences not only between the manuscript and typescript versions of the novel but also among the published serial and book versions as well. Unfortunately, no proofs for any of the published versions are known to exist; hence differences among the various versions cannot be ascribed solely to authorial intention with any strong degree of confidence, nor can any clear genealogy be constructed regarding which changes are authoritative and which are either errors of some sort or examples of editorial intervention. Nor are artistic criteria more helpful, since all of the early published versions of the novel contain some unique differences that seem artistically superior to the other versions.

With numerous early drafts of the novel (whether manuscript or typescript), as well as serial and book versions in both England and America, all with substantial differences among them, it would be difficult enough to determine authorial intention; but given that Conrad was making revisions while still ill from his nervous breakdown after finishing the manuscript, and later wondered himself whether some of the deleted material should have been deleted, determining a definitive text is all but impossible. In letter to John Galsworthy in October 1911, Conrad remarked of the manuscript: "You know there are about 30000 words more than the printed text. Revising while ill in bed I am afraid I have struck out whole pages recklessly.... There are passages which should have remained. I wasn't in a fit state to judge them" (4: 486; See Appendix A10).[1]

This Broadview text is based upon a full collation of the manuscript, typescript, and English and American serial and first editions, as well as the other editions of the novel published during Conrad's lifetime. I have used the first English edition (1911) as my copy text, since it is known that Conrad made revisions in preparation for this edition that were not made in preparation for some of the other editions. Nevertheless, I have silently corrected obvious errors and regularized obvious inconsistencies such as the spelling of "judgement" and "judgment" and "Victor Haldin" and "Viktor Haldin," and the capitalization of "Silver Medal" and "silver medal" and "Western" and "western," all of which appear in the first English edition. In each case, I have chosen the spelling or capitalization that appeared most often. I also changed the heading "Part Four" to "Part Fourth" to be consistent with the other section headings ("Part First," "Part Second," and "Part Third"). Hesitant to assume too much regarding Conrad's intentions, particularly given the uncertain genealogy of the various versions of the novel, I have only emended the text of the first English edition in a few places where there was a precedent from another version that Conrad clearly had a hand in produc-

---

1  For more on the cuts Conrad made to the manuscript, see David Leon Higdon and Robert F. Sheard, "Conrad's 'Unkindest Cut': The Canceled Scenes in *Under Western Eyes*," *Conradiana* 19.3 (autumn 1987): 167-81.

ing and that also seemed obviously more correct. Precedents for these changes to the first English edition (E1) come from the manuscript (M), typescript (T), American serial (AS), English serial (ES), and first American edition (A1), and are noted in footnotes throughout the text with the precedents following in parentheses. Finally, throughout this Broadview edition, my ellipsis points appear with no space between the points, while all others appear with a space between the points.

# UNDER WESTERN EYES

# AUTHOR'S NOTE

It must be admitted that by the mere force of circumstances *Under Western Eyes* has become already a sort of historical novel dealing with the past.

This reflection bears entirely upon the events of the tale; but being as a whole an attempt to render not so much the political state as the psychology of Russia itself, I venture to hope that it has not lost all its interest. I am encouraged in this flattering belief by noticing that in many articles on Russian affairs of the present day reference is made to certain sayings and opinions uttered in the pages that follow, in a manner testifying to the clearness of my vision and the correctness of my judgment. I need not say that in writing this novel I had no other object in view than to express imaginatively the general truth which underlies its action, together with my honest convictions as to the moral complexion of certain facts more or less known to the whole world.

As to the actual creation, I may say that when I began to write I had a distinct conception of the first part only, with the three figures of Haldin, Razumov, and Councillor Mikulin, defined exactly in my mind. It was only after I had finished writing the first part that the whole story revealed itself to me in its tragic character and in the march of its events as unavoidable and sufficiently ample in its outline to give free play to my creative instinct and to the dramatic possibilities of the subject.

The course of action need not be explained. It has suggested itself more as a matter of feeling than a matter of thinking. It is the result not of a special experience but of general knowledge, fortified by earnest meditation. My greatest anxiety was in being able to strike and sustain the note of scrupulous impartiality. The obligation of absolute fairness was imposed on me historically and hereditarily, by the peculiar experience of race and family, in addition to my primary conviction that truth alone is the justification of any fiction which makes the least claim to the quality of art or may hope to take its place in the culture of men and women of its time. I had never been called before to a greater effort of detachment—detachment from all passions, prejudices, and even from personal memories. *Under Western Eyes* on its first appearance in England was a failure with the public, perhaps because of that very detachment. I obtained my reward some six years later when I first heard that the book had found universal recognition in Russia and had been re-published there in many editions.

The various figures playing their part in the story also owe their existence to no special experience, but to the general knowledge of the condition of Russia and of the moral and emotional reactions of the Russian temperament to the pressure of tyrannical lawlessness, which, in general human terms, could be reduced to the formula of senseless desperation provoked by senseless tyranny. What I was concerned with mainly was the aspect, the character, and the fate of the individuals as they appeared to the Western Eyes of the old teacher of languages. He himself has been much criticised; but I will not at this late hour undertake to justify his existence. He was useful to me, and therefore I think that he must be useful to the reader both in the way of comment and by the part he plays in the development of the story. In my desire to produce the effect of actuality it seemed to me indispensable to have an eye-witness of the transactions in Geneva. I needed also a sympathetic friend for Miss Haldin, who otherwise would have been too much alone and unsupported to be perfectly credible. She would have had no one to whom she could give a glimpse of her idealistic faith, of her great heart, and of her simple emotions.

Razumov is treated sympathetically. Why should he not be? He is an ordinary young man, with a healthy capacity for work and sane ambitions. He has an average conscience. If he is slightly abnormal it is only in his sensitiveness to his position. Being nobody's child he feels rather more keenly than another would that he is a Russian—or he is nothing. He is perfectly right in looking on all Russia as his heritage. The sanguinary futility of the crimes and the sacrifices seething in that amorphous mass envelops and crushes him. But I don't think that in his distraction he is ever monstrous. Nobody is exhibited as a monster here—neither the simpleminded Tekla, nor the wrongheaded Sophia Antonovna. Peter Ivanovitch and Madame de S—— are fair game. They are the apes of a sinister jungle and are treated as their grimaces deserve. As to Nikita—nicknamed Necator—he is the perfect flower of the terroristic wilderness. What troubled me most in dealing with him was not his monstrosity but his banality. He has been exhibited to the public eye for years in so-called "disclosures" in newspaper articles, in secret histories, in sensational novels.[1]

---

1 Conrad was particularly aware of David Soskice's article "The Russian Spy System: The Azeff Scandals in Russia," *English Review* 1.4 (March 1909): 816-32, which served as one of Conrad's chief sources for Nikita and which he undoubtedly has in mind in this passage.

The most terrifying reflection (I am speaking now for myself) is that all these people are not the product of the exceptional but of the general—of the normality of their place, and time, and race. The ferocity and imbecility of an autocratic rule[1] rejecting all legality and, in fact, basing itself upon complete moral anarchism provokes the no less imbecile and atrocious answer of a purely Utopian revolutionism[2] encompassing destruction by the first means to hand, in the strange conviction that a fundamental change of hearts must follow the downfall of any given human institutions. These people are unable to see that all they can effect is merely a change of names. The oppressors and the oppressed are all Russians together; and the world is brought once more face to face with the truth of the saying that the tiger cannot change his stripes nor the leopard his spots.

J.C.
1920

---

1　A government in which a single person or small group possesses absolute power, often used in conjunction with tsarist Russia of the nineteenth and early twentieth centuries.
2　A reference to the Russian Revolution of 1917, as well as to revolutions in general.

To
Agnes Tobin[1]
who brought to our door
her genius for friendship
from the uttermost shore
of the west

---

1  Agnes Tobin (1864-1939), of San Francisco, California, was a friend
   of Conrad, the Irish poet William Butler Yeats (1865-1939), and other
   literary figures.

*"I would take liberty from any hand*
*as a hungry man would snatch a piece of bread."*
MISS HALDIN

# PART FIRST

To begin with I wish to disclaim the possession of those high gifts of imagination and expression which would have enabled my pen to create for the reader the personality of the man who called himself, after the Russian custom, Cyril son of Isidor—Kirylo Sidorovitch—Razumov.[1]

If I have ever had these gifts in any sort of living form they have been smothered out of existence a long time ago under a wilderness of words. Words, as is well known, are the great foes of reality. I have been for many years a teacher of languages. It is an occupation which at length becomes fatal to whatever share of imagination, observation, and insight an ordinary person may be heir to. To a teacher of languages there comes a time when the world is but a place of many words and man appears a mere talking animal not much more wonderful than a parrot.

This being so, I could not have observed Mr. Razumov or guessed at his reality by the force of insight, much less have imagined him as he was. Even to invent the mere bald facts of his life would have been utterly beyond my powers. But I think that without this declaration the readers of these pages will be able to detect in the story the marks of documentary evidence. And that is perfectly correct. It is based on a document; all I have brought to it is my knowledge of the Russian language, which is sufficient for what is attempted here. The document, of course, is something in the nature of a journal, a diary, yet not exactly that in its actual form. For instance, most of it was not written up from day to day, though all the entries are dated. Some of these entries cover months of time and extend over dozens of pages. All the earlier part is a retrospect, in a narrative form, relating to an event which took place about a year before.

I must mention that I have lived for a long time in Geneva.[2] A whole quarter of that town, on account of many Russians residing there, is called La Petite Russie—Little Russia. I had a rather extensive connexion in Little Russia at that time. Yet I confess that I have no comprehension of the Russian character. The illogicality of their attitude, the arbitrariness of their conclusions, the frequency of the exceptional, should present no difficulty to a

---

1 A number of commentators have noted that the name Razumov comes from the Russian word "razum" which means "reason," thus associating Razumov with reason.

2 A city in western Switzerland.

student of many grammars; but there must be something else in the way, some special human trait—one of those subtle differences that are beyond the ken of mere professors. What must remain striking to a teacher of languages is the Russians' extraordinary love of words. They gather them up; they cherish them, but they don't hoard them in their breasts; on the contrary, they are always ready to pour them out by the hour or by the night with an enthusiasm, a sweeping abundance, with such an aptness of application sometimes that, as in the case of very accomplished parrots, one can't defend oneself from the suspicion that they really understand what they say. There is a generosity in their ardour of speech which removes it as far as possible from common loquacity; and it is ever too disconnected to be classed as eloquence. . . . But I must apologize for this digression.

It would be idle to inquire why Mr. Razumov has left this record behind him. It is inconceivable that he should have wished any human eye to see it. A mysterious impulse of human nature comes into play here. Putting aside Samuel Pepys,[1] who has forced in this way the door of immortality, innumerable people, criminals, saints, philosophers, young girls, statesmen, and simple imbeciles, have kept self-revealing records from vanity no doubt, but also from other more inscrutable motives. There must be a wonderful soothing power in mere words since so many men have used them for self-communion. Being myself a quiet individual I take it that what all men are really after is some form or perhaps only some formula of peace. Certainly they are crying loud enough for it at the present day. What sort of peace Kirylo Sidorovitch Razumov expected to find in the writing up of his record it passeth my understanding to guess.

The fact remains that he has written it.

Mr. Razumov was a tall, well-proportioned young man, quite unusually dark for a Russian from the Central Provinces. His good looks would have been unquestionable if it had not been for a peculiar lack of fineness in the features. It was as if a face modelled vigorously in wax (with some approach even to a classical correctness of type) had been held close to a fire till all sharpness of line had been lost in the softening of the material. But even thus he was sufficiently good-looking. His manner, too, was

---

1    A member of the British Parliament and civil servant, Pepys (1633-1703) is best known for the extensive diary he kept from 1660 to 1669, which contains much valuable information regarding that period in English history.

good. In discussion he was easily swayed by argument and authority. With his younger compatriots he took the attitude of an inscrutable listener, a listener of the kind that hears you out intelligently and then—just changes the subject.

This sort of trick, which may arise either from intellectual insufficiency or from an imperfect trust in one's own convictions, procured for Mr. Razumov a reputation of profundity. Amongst a lot of exuberant talkers, in the habit of exhausting themselves daily by ardent discussion, a comparatively taciturn personality is naturally credited with reserve power. By his comrades at the St. Petersburg University,[1] Kirylo Sidorovitch Razumov, third year's student in philosophy, was looked upon as a strong nature—an altogether trustworthy man. This, in a country where an opinion may be a legal crime visited by death or sometimes by a fate worse than mere death, meant that he was worthy of being trusted with forbidden opinions. He was liked also for his amiability and for his quiet readiness to oblige his comrades even at the cost of personal inconvenience.

Mr. Razumov was supposed to be the son of an Archpriest[2] and to be protected by a distinguished nobleman—perhaps of his own distant province. But his outward appearance accorded badly with such humble origin. Such a descent was not credible. It was, indeed, suggested that Mr. Razumov was the son of an Archpriest's pretty daughter—which, of course, would put a different complexion on the matter. This theory also rendered intelligible the protection of the distinguished nobleman. All this, however, had never been investigated maliciously or otherwise. No one knew or cared who the nobleman in question was. Razumov received a modest but very sufficient allowance from the hands of an obscure attorney, who seemed to act as his guardian in some measure. Now and then he appeared at some professor's informal reception. Apart from that Razumov was not known to have any social relations in the town. He attended the obligatory lectures regularly and was considered by the authorities as a very promising student. He worked at home in the

---

1　A university established by Tsar Peter I or Peter the Great (Pëtr Alekseevich) (1672-1725) in 1724, and still one of the premier universities in Russia today. The city of St. Petersburg, capital of Russia at the time of the novel, is located in northwestern Russia on the Baltic Sea at the Gulf of Finland.

2　A priest in the Russian Orthodox Church who supervises a number of parishes. Unlike in the Roman Catholic Church, Russian Orthodox priests are permitted to marry.

manner of a man who means to get on, but did not shut himself up severely for that purpose. He was always accessible, and there was nothing secret or reserved in his life.

## I

The origin of Mr. Razumov's record is connected with an event characteristic of modern Russia in the actual fact: the assassination of a prominent statesman—and still more characteristic of the moral corruption of an oppressed society where the noblest aspirations of humanity, the desire of freedom, an ardent patriotism, the love of justice, the sense of pity, and even the fidelity of simple minds are prostituted to the lusts of hate and fear, the inseparable companions of an uneasy despotism.

The fact alluded to above is the successful attempt on the life of Mr. de P——,[1] the President of the notorious Repressive Commission of some years ago, the Minister of State invested with extraordinary powers. The newspapers made noise enough about that fanatical, narrow-chested figure in gold-laced uniform, with a face of crumpled parchment, insipid, bespectacled eyes, and the cross of the Order of St. Procopius[2] hung under the skinny throat. For a time, it may be remembered, not a month passed without his portrait appearing in some one of the illustrated papers of Europe. He served the monarchy by imprisoning, exiling, or sending to the gallows men and women, young and old, with an equable, unwearied industry. In his mystic acceptance of the principle of autocracy he was bent on extirpating from the land every vestige of anything that resembled freedom in public institutions; and in his ruthless persecution of the rising generation he seemed to aim at the destruction of the very hope of liberty itself.

---

1  Based upon the 1904 assassination of Viacheslav Konstantinovich de Pleve (1846-1904), Minister of the Interior, although the actual details of the assassination as they appear in *Under Western Eyes* resemble more those surrounding the assassination of Tsar Aleksandr II (Aleksandr Nikolaevich) (1818-81) in 1881. The Russian novelist Andrei Belyi (1880-1934) also wrote an important novel, *Petersburg* (1913), based on this assassination.

2  A fictitious order and fictitious saint. Conrad may have taken the name from Procopius of Cæsarea (c. 500-c. 565), a Byzantine scholar, best known for his book *Secret History* (1623), an exposé of corruption at the court of Byzantine emperor Justinian I (483-565).

It is said that this execrated personality had not enough imagination to be aware of the hate he inspired. It is hardly credible; but it is a fact that he took very few precautions for his safety. In the preamble of a certain famous State paper he had declared once that "the thought of liberty has never existed in the Act of the Creator. From the multitude of men's counsel nothing could come but revolt and disorder; and revolt and disorder in a world created for obedience and stability is sin. It was not Reason but Authority which expressed the Divine Intention. God was the Autocrat of the Universe. . . ." It may be that the man who made this declaration believed that heaven itself was bound to protect him in his remorseless defence of Autocracy on this earth.

No doubt the vigilance of the police saved him many times; but, as a matter of fact, when his appointed fate overtook him, the competent authorities could not have given him any warning. They had no knowledge of any conspiracy against the Minister's life, had no hint of any plot through their usual channels of information, had seen no signs, were aware of no suspicious movements or dangerous persons.

Mr. de P—— was being driven towards the railway station in a two-horse uncovered sleigh with footman and coachman on the box. Snow had been falling all night, making the roadway, uncleared as yet at this early hour, very heavy for the horses. It was still falling thickly. But the sleigh must have been observed and marked down. As it drew over to the left before taking a turn, the footman noticed a peasant walking slowly on the edge of the pavement with his hands in the pockets of his sheepskin coat and his shoulders hunched up to his ears under the falling snow. On being overtaken this peasant suddenly faced about and swung his arm. In an instant there was a terrible shock, a detonation muffled in the multitude of snowflakes; both horses lay dead and mangled on the ground and the coachman, with a shrill cry, had fallen off the box mortally wounded. The footman (who survived) had no time to see the face of the man in the sheepskin coat. After throwing the bomb this last got away, but it is supposed that, seeing a lot of people surging up on all sides of him in the falling snow, and all running towards the scene of the explosion, he thought it safer to turn back with them.

In an incredibly short time an excited crowd assembled round the sledge. The Minister-President, getting out unhurt into the deep snow, stood near the groaning coachman and addressed the people repeatedly in his weak, colourless voice: "I beg of you to keep off. For the love of God, I beg of you good people to keep off."

It was then that a tall young man who had remained standing perfectly still within a carriage gateway, two houses lower down, stepped out into the street and walking up rapidly flung another bomb over the heads of the crowd. It actually struck the Minister-President on the shoulder as he stooped over his dying servant, then falling between his feet exploded with a terrific concentrated violence, striking him dead to the ground, finishing the wounded man and practically annihilating the empty sledge in the twinkling of an eye. With a yell of horror the crowd broke up and fled in all directions, except for those who fell dead or dying where they stood nearest to the Minister-President, and one or two others who did not fall till they had run a little way.[1]

The first explosion had brought together a crowd as if by enchantment, the second made as swiftly a solitude in the street for hundreds of yards in each direction. Through the falling snow people looked from afar at the small heap of dead bodies lying upon each other near the carcases of the two horses. Nobody dared to approach till some Cossacks[2] of a street-patrol galloped up and, dismounting, began to turn over the dead. Amongst the innocent victims of the second explosion laid out on the pavement there was a body dressed in a peasant's sheepskin coat; but the face was unrecognisable, there was absolutely nothing found in the pockets of its poor clothing, and it was the only one whose identity was never established.

That day Mr. Razumov got up at his usual hour and spent the morning within the University buildings listening to the lectures and working for some time in the library. He heard the first vague rumour of something in the way of bomb-throwing at the table of the students' ordinary,[3] where he was accustomed to eat his two o'clock dinner. But this rumour was made up of mere whispers, and this was Russia, where it was not always safe, for a student especially, to appear too much interested in certain kinds of whispers. Razumov was one of those men who, living in a period of mental and political unrest, keep an instinctive hold on normal, practical, everyday life. He was aware of the emotional tension of his time; he even responded to it in an indefinite way. But his

---

1 See Appendices C, D, and E.

2 A military force of light horsemen, initially employed by Poland and later by the Russian military. Cossacks or Kazaki were originally a warlike people of Turkish origins who inhabited the northern areas around the Black Sea and Caspian Sea.

3 An eating establishment, typically where meals are served at a fixed price; in this case, something like a student cafeteria.

main concern was with his work, his studies, and with his own future.

Officially and in fact without a family (for the daughter of the Archpriest had long been dead), no home influences had shaped his opinions or his feelings. He was as lonely in the world as a man swimming in the deep sea. The word Razumov was the mere label of a solitary individuality. There were no Razumovs belonging to him anywhere. His closest parentage was defined in the statement that he was a Russian. Whatever good he expected from life would be given to or withheld from his hopes by that connexion alone. This immense parentage suffered from the throes of internal dissensions, and he shrank mentally from the fray as a good-natured man may shrink from taking definite sides in a violent family quarrel.

Razumov, going home, reflected that having prepared all the matters of the forthcoming examination, he could now devote his time to the subject of the prize essay. He hankered after the silver medal.[1] The prize was offered by the Ministry of Education; the names of the competitors would be submitted to the Minister himself. The mere fact of trying would be considered meritorious in the higher quarters; and the possessor of the prize would have a claim to an administrative appointment of the better sort after he had taken his degree. The student Razumov in an access of elation forgot the dangers menacing the stability of the institutions which give rewards and appointments. But remembering the medallist of the year before, Razumov, the young man of no parentage, was sobered. He and some others happened to be assembled in their comrade's rooms at the very time when that last received the official advice of his success. He was a quiet, unassuming young man: "Forgive me," he had said with a faint apologetic smile and taking up his cap, "I am going out to order up some wine. But I must first send a telegram to my folk at home. I say! Won't the old people make it a festive time for the neighbours for twenty miles around our place."

Razumov thought there was nothing of that sort for him in the world. His success would matter to no one. But he felt no bitterness against the nobleman his protector, who was not a provincial magnate as was generally supposed. He was in fact nobody less than Prince K——,[2] once a great and splendid figure in the world and now, his day being over, a Senator and a gouty invalid,

---

1  A fictitious award.

2  It is uncertain upon whom (if anyone) Conrad based Prince K——.

living in a still splendid but more domestic manner. He had some young children and a wife as aristocratic and proud as himself.

In all his life Razumov was allowed only once to come into personal contact with the Prince.

It had the air of a chance meeting in the little attorney's office. One day Razumov, coming in by appointment, found a stranger standing there—a tall, aristocratic-looking personage with silky, grey side-whiskers. The bald-headed, sly little lawyer-fellow called out, "Come in—come in, Mr. Razumov," with a sort of ironic heartiness. Then turning deferentially to the stranger with the grand air, "A ward of mine, your Excellency. One of the most promising students of his faculty in the St. Petersburg University."

To his intense surprise Razumov saw a white shapely hand extended to him. He took it in great confusion (it was soft and passive) and heard at the same time a condescending murmur in which he caught only the words "Satisfactory" and "Persevere." But the most amazing thing of all was to feel suddenly a distinct pressure of the white shapely hand just before it was withdrawn: a light pressure like a secret sign. The emotion of it was terrible. Razumov's heart seemed to leap into his throat. When he raised his eyes the aristocratic personage, motioning the little lawyer aside, had opened the door and was going out.

The attorney rummaged amongst the papers on his desk for a time. "Do you know who that was?" he asked suddenly.

Razumov, whose heart was thumping hard yet, shook his head in silence.

"That was Prince K——. You wonder what he could be doing in the hole of a poor legal rat like myself—eh? These awfully great people have their sentimental curiosities like common sinners. But if I were you, Kirylo Sidorovitch," he continued, leering and laying a peculiar emphasis on the patronymic,[1] "I wouldn't boast at large of the introduction. It would not be prudent, Kirylo Sidorovitch. Oh dear no! It would be in fact dangerous for your future."

The young man's ears burned like fire; his sight was dim. "That man!" Razumov was saying to himself. "He!"

Henceforth it was by this monosyllable that Mr. Razumov got into the habit of referring mentally to the stranger with grey silky

---

1   A name derived from one's father's name (in this case "son of Sidor").
    In Russia, the custom is to use the patronymic as one's middle name,
    and addressing someone by both the first name and the patronymic is
    considered polite.

side-whiskers. From that time too, when walking in the more fashionable quarters, he noted with interest the magnificent horses and carriages with Prince K——'s liveries on the box. Once he saw the Princess get out—she was shopping—followed by two girls, of which one was nearly a head taller than the other. Their fair hair hung loose down their backs in the English style; they had merry eyes, their coats, muffs, and little fur caps were exactly alike, and their cheeks and noses were tinged a cheerful pink by the frost. They crossed the pavement in front of him, and Razumov went on his way smiling shyly to himself. "His" daughters. They resembled "Him." The young man felt a glow of warm friendliness towards these girls who would never know of his existence. Presently they would marry Generals or Kammerherrs[1] and have girls and boys of their own, who perhaps would be aware of him as a celebrated old professor, decorated, possibly a Privy Councillor,[2] one of the glories of Russia—nothing more!

But a celebrated professor was a somebody. Distinction would convert the label Razumov into an honoured name. There was nothing strange in the student Razumov's wish for distinction. A man's real life is that accorded to him in the thoughts of other men by reason of respect or natural love. Returning home on the day of the attempt on Mr. de P——'s life Razumov resolved to have a good try for the silver medal.

Climbing slowly the four flights of the dark, dirty staircase in the house where he had his lodgings, he felt confident of success. The winner's name would be published in the papers on New Year's Day. And at the thought that "He" would most probably read it there, Razumov stopped short on the stairs for an instant, then went on smiling faintly at his own emotion. "This is but a shadow," he said to himself, "but the medal is a solid beginning."

With those ideas of industry in his head the warmth of his room was agreeable and encouraging. "I shall put in four hours of good work," he thought. But no sooner had he closed the door than he was horribly startled. All black against the usual tall stove of white tiles gleaming in the dusk, stood a strange figure, wearing a skirted, close-fitting, brown cloth coat strapped round the waist, in long boots, and with a little Astrakhan cap[3] on its

---

1 Chamberlains; i.e., administrators of royal or aristocratic households.
2 Confidential councillor or adviser, especially of royalty; in England and Commonwealth countries, a cabinet minister.
3 A cap made from the wool of a young lamb. Astrakhan' is a port on the Caspian Sea associated with this kind of wool.

head. It loomed lithe and martial. Razumov was utterly confounded. It was only when the figure advancing two paces asked in an untroubled, grave voice if the outer door was closed that he regained his power of speech.

"Haldin![1] . . . Victor Victorovitch! . . . Is that you? . . . Yes. The outer door is shut all right. But this is indeed unexpected."

Victor Haldin, a student older than most of his contemporaries at the University, was not one of the industrious set. He was hardly ever seen at lectures; the authorities had marked him as "restless" and "unsound"—very bad notes. But he had a great personal prestige with his comrades and influenced their thoughts. Razumov had never been intimate with him. They had met from time to time at gatherings in other students' houses. They had even had a discussion together—one of those discussions on first principles dear to the sanguine minds of youth.

Razumov wished the man had chosen some other time to come for a chat. He felt in good trim to tackle the prize essay. But as Haldin could not be slightingly dismissed Razumov adopted the tone of hospitality, asking him to sit down and smoke.

"Kirylo Sidorovitch," said the other, flinging off his cap, "we are not perhaps in exactly the same camp. Your judgment is more philosophical. You are a man of few words, but I haven't met anybody who dared to doubt the generosity of your sentiments. There is a solidity about your character which cannot exist without courage."

Razumov felt flattered and began to murmur shyly something about being very glad of his good opinion, when Haldin raised his hand.

"That is what I was saying to myself," he continued, "as I dodged in the woodyard down by the river-side. 'He has a strong character this young man,' I said to myself. 'He does not throw his soul to the winds.' Your reserve has always fascinated me, Kirylo Sidorovitch. So I tried to remember your address. But look here—it was a piece of luck. Your dvornik[2] was away from the gate talking to a sleigh-driver on the other side of the street. I met no one on the stairs, not a soul. As I came up to your floor

---

1  Modeled in part after de Pleve's assassin Egor Sazonov (1879-1909), although Sazonov was severely wounded during the assassination, captured immediately, and unlike Haldin was sentenced to 20 years hard labor, later committing suicide in prison; see Appendix C.

2  A kind of doorkeeper or porter for residences; dvorniks were often employed as police spies.

I caught sight of your landlady coming out of your rooms. But she did not see me. She crossed the landing to her own side, and then I slipped in. I have been here two hours expecting you to come in every moment."

Razumov had listened in astonishment; but before he could open his mouth Haldin added, speaking deliberately, "It was I who removed de P—— this morning."

Razumov kept down a cry of dismay. The sentiment of his life being utterly ruined by this contact with such a crime expressed itself quaintly by a sort of half derisive mental exclamation, "There goes my silver medal!"

Haldin continued after waiting a while—

"You say nothing, Kirylo Sidorovitch! I understand your silence. To be sure, I cannot expect you with your frigid English manner to embrace me. But never mind your manners. You have enough heart to have heard the sound of weeping and gnashing of teeth this man raised in the land. That would be enough to get over any philosophical hopes. He was uprooting the tender plant. He had to be stopped. He was a dangerous man—a convinced man. Three more years of his work would have put us back fifty years into bondage—and look at all the lives wasted, at all the souls lost in that time."

His curt, self-confident voice suddenly lost its ring and it was in a dull tone that he added, "Yes, brother, I have killed him. It's weary work."

Razumov had sunk into a chair. Every moment he expected a crowd of policemen to rush in. There must have been thousands of them out looking for that man walking up and down in his room. Haldin was talking again in a restrained, steady voice. Now and then he flourished an arm, slowly, without excitement.

He told Razumov how he had brooded for a year; how he had not slept properly for weeks. He and "Another" had a warning of the Minister's movements from "a certain person" late the evening before. He and that "Another" prepared their "engines" and resolved to have no sleep till "the deed" was done. They walked the streets under the falling snow with the "engines" on them, exchanging not a word the livelong night. When they happened to meet a police patrol they took each other by the arm and pretended to be a couple of peasants on the spree. They reeled and talked in drunken hoarse voices. Except for these strange outbreaks they kept silence, moving on ceaselessly. Their plans had been previously arranged. At daybreak they made their way to the spot which they knew the sledge must pass. When it appeared in sight they exchanged a muttered good-bye and separated. The "other" remained at the corner, Haldin took up a position a little farther up the street. . . .

After throwing his "engine" he ran off and in a moment was overtaken by the panic-struck people flying away from the spot after the second explosion. They were wild with terror. He was jostled once or twice. He slowed down for the rush to pass him and then turned to the left into a narrow street. There he was alone.

He marvelled at this immediate escape. The work was done. He could hardly believe it. He fought with an almost irresistible longing to lie down on the pavement and sleep. But this sort of faintness—a drowsy faintness—passed off quickly. He walked faster, making his way to one of the poorer parts of the town in order to look up Ziemianitch.

This Ziemianitch, Razumov understood, was a sort of town-peasant who had got on; owner of a small number of sledges and horses for hire. Haldin paused in his narrative to exclaim—

"A bright spirit! A hardy soul! The best driver in St. Petersburg. He has a team of three horses there. . . . Ah! He's a fellow!"

This man had declared himself willing to take out safely, at any time, one or two persons to the second or third railway station on one of the southern lines. But there had been no time to warn him the night before. His usual haunt seemed to be a low-class eating-house on the outskirts of the town. When Haldin got there the man was not to be found. He was not expected to turn up again till the evening. Haldin wandered away restlessly.

He saw the gate of a woodyard open and went in to get out of the wind which swept the bleak broad thoroughfare. The great rectangular piles of cut wood loaded with snow resembled the huts of a village. At first the watchman who discovered him crouching amongst them talked in a friendly manner. He was a dried-up old man wearing two ragged army coats one over the other; his wizened little face, tied up under the jaw and over the ears in a dirty red handkerchief, looked comical. Presently he grew sulky, and then all at once without rhyme or reason began to shout furiously.

"Aren't you ever going to clear out of this, you loafer? We know all about factory hands of your sort. A big, strong, young chap! You aren't even drunk. What do you want here? You don't frighten us. Take yourself and your ugly eyes away."

Haldin stopped before the sitting Razumov. His supple figure, with the white forehead above which the fair hair stood straight up, had an aspect of lofty daring.

"He did not like my eyes," he said. "And so . . . here I am."
Razumov made an effort to speak calmly.

"But pardon me, Victor Victorovitch. We know each other so
little. . . . I don't see why you . . ."

"Confidence," said Haldin.

This word sealed Razumov's lips as if a hand had been clapped
on his mouth. His brain seethed with arguments.

"And so—here you are," he muttered through his teeth.

The other did not detect the tone of anger. Never suspected it.

"Yes. And nobody knows I am here. You are the last person
that could be suspected—should I get caught. That's an advantage, you see. And then—speaking to a superior mind like yours
I can well say all the truth. It occurred to me that you—you have
no one belonging to you—no ties, no one to suffer for it if this
came out by some means. There have been enough ruined
Russian homes as it is. But I don't see how my passage through
your rooms can be ever known. If I should be got hold of, I'll
know how to keep silent—no matter what they may be pleased to
do to me," he added grimly.

He began to walk again while Razumov sat still appalled.

"You thought that—" he faltered out almost sick with indignation.

"Yes, Razumov. Yes, brother. Some day you shall help to build.
You suppose that I am a terrorist, now—a destructor of what is.
But consider that the true destroyers are they who destroy the
spirit of progress and truth, not the avengers who merely kill the
bodies of the persecutors of human dignity. Men like me are necessary to make room for self-contained, thinking men like you.
Well, we have made the sacrifice of our lives, but all the same I
want to escape if it can be done. It is not my life I want to save, but
my power to do. I won't live idle. Oh no! Don't make any mistake,
Razumov. Men like me are rare. And, besides, an example like this
is more awful to oppressors when the perpetrator vanishes without
a trace. They sit in their offices and palaces and quake. All I want
you to do is to help me to vanish. No great matter that. Only to go
by and by and see Ziemianitch for me at that place where I went
this morning. Just tell him, 'He whom you know wants a well-
horsed sledge to pull up half an hour after midnight at the seventh
lamp-post on the left counting from the upper end of Karabelnaya.
If nobody gets in, the sledge is to run round a block or two, so as
to come back past the same spot in ten minutes' time.'"

Razumov wondered why he had not cut short that talk and
told this man to go away long before. Was it weakness or what?

He concluded that it was a sound instinct. Haldin must have been seen. It was impossible that some people should not have noticed the face and appearance of the man who threw the second bomb. Haldin was a noticeable person. The police in their thousands must have had his description within the hour. With every moment the danger grew. Sent out to wander in the streets he could not escape being caught in the end.

The police would very soon find out all about him. They would set about discovering a conspiracy. Everybody Haldin had ever known would be in the greatest danger. Unguarded expressions, little facts in themselves innocent would be counted for crimes. Razumov remembered certain words he said, the speeches he had listened to, the harmless gatherings he had attended—it was almost impossible for a student to keep out of that sort of thing, without becoming suspect to his comrades.

Razumov saw himself shut up in a fortress,[1] worried, badgered, perhaps ill-used. He saw himself deported by an administrative order, his life broken, ruined, and robbed of all hope. He saw himself—at best—leading a miserable existence under police supervision, in some small, faraway provincial town, without friends to assist his necessities or even take any steps to alleviate his lot—as others had. Others had fathers, mothers, brothers, relations, connexions, to move heaven and earth on their behalf— he had no one. The very officials that sentenced him some morning would forget his existence before sunset.

He saw his youth pass away from him in misery and half starvation—his strength give way, his mind become an abject thing. He saw himself creeping, broken down and shabby, about the streets—dying unattended in some filthy hole of a room, or on the sordid bed of a Government hospital.

He shuddered. Then the peace of bitter calmness came over him. It was best to keep this man out of the streets till he could be got rid of with some chance of escaping. That was the best that could be done. Razumov, of course, felt the safety of his lonely existence to be permanently endangered. This evening's doings could turn up against him at any time as long as this man lived and the present institutions endured. They appeared to him rational and indestructible at that moment. They had a force of

---

1 Typically, political prisoners were detained initially at the Shliusselburg fortress in St. Petersburg where they were executed or later sent to Siberian prison camps in far eastern Russia.

harmony—in contrast with the horrible discord of this man's presence. He hated the man. He said quietly—

"Yes, of course, I will go. You must give me precise directions, and for the rest—depend on me."

"Ah! You are a fellow! Collected—cool as a cucumber. A regular Englishman. Where did you get your soul from? There aren't many like you. Look here, brother! Men like me leave no posterity, but their souls are not lost. No man's soul is ever lost. It works for itself—or else where would be the sense of self-sacrifice, of martyrdom, of conviction, of faith—the labours of the soul? What will become of my soul when I die in the way I must die—soon—very soon perhaps? It shall not perish. Don't make a mistake, Razumov. This is not murder—it is war, war. My spirit shall go on warring in some Russian body till all falsehood is swept out of the world. The modern civilization is false, but a new revelation shall come out of Russia. Ha! you say nothing. You are a sceptic. I respect your philosophical scepticism, Razumov, but don't touch the soul. The Russian soul that lives in all of us. It has a future. It has a mission, I tell you, or else why should I have been moved to do this—reckless—like a butcher—in the middle of all these innocent people—scattering death—I! I! . . . I wouldn't hurt a fly!"

"Not so loud," warned Razumov harshly.

Haldin sat down abruptly, and leaning his head on his folded arms burst into tears. He wept for a long time. The dusk had deepened in the room. Razumov, motionless in sombre wonder, listened to the sobs.

The other raised his head, got up and with an effort mastered his voice.

"Yes. Men like me leave no posterity," he repeated in a subdued tone. "I have a sister though. She's with my old mother—I persuaded them to go abroad this year—thank God. Not a bad little girl my sister. She has the most trustful eyes of any human being that ever walked this earth. She will marry well, I hope. She may have children—sons perhaps. Look at me. My father was a Government official in the provinces. He had a little land too. A simple servant of God—a true Russian in his way. His was the soul of obedience. But I am not like him. They say I resemble my mother's eldest brother, an officer. They shot him in '28. Under Nicholas,[1] you know. Haven't I told you that this is war, war. . . . But God of Justice! This is weary work."

---

1   Tsar Nikolai I (Nikolai Pavlovich) (1796-1855).

Razumov, in his chair, leaning his head on his hand, spoke as if from the bottom of an abyss.

"You believe in God, Haldin?"

"There you go catching at words that are wrung from one. What does it matter? What was it the Englishman said: 'There is a divine soul in things . . .'[1] Devil take him—I don't remember now. But he spoke the truth. When the day of you thinkers comes don't you forget what's divine in the Russian soul—and that's resignation. Respect that in your intellectual restlessness and don't let your arrogant wisdom spoil its message to the world. I am speaking to you now like a man with a rope round his neck. What do you imagine I am? A being in revolt? No. It's you thinkers who are in everlasting revolt. I am one of the resigned. When the necessity of this heavy work came to me and I understood that it had to be done—what did I do? Did I exult? Did I take pride in my purpose? Did I try to weigh its worth and consequences? No! I was resigned. I thought 'God's will be done.'"

He threw himself full length on Razumov's bed and putting the backs of his hands over his eyes remained perfectly motionless and silent. Not even the sound of his breathing could be heard. The dead stillness of the room remained undisturbed till in the darkness Razumov said gloomily—

"Haldin."

"Yes," answered the other readily, quite invisible now on the bed and without the slightest stir.

"Isn't it time for me to start?"

"Yes, brother." The other was heard, lying still in the darkness as though he were talking in his sleep. "The time has come to put fate to the test."

He paused, then gave a few lucid directions in the quiet impersonal voice of a man in a trance. Razumov made ready without a word of answer. As he was leaving the room the voice on the bed said after him—

"Go with God, thou silent soul."

---

1 Source uncertain. Paul Kirschner, in his edition of *Under Western Eyes* (Penguin 1996, 273) suggests that this may be a reference to a passage about the true reformer found in *On Heroes, Hero-Worship & the Heroic in History* (1841) by Thomas Carlyle (1795-1881): "He appeals to Heaven's invisible justice against Earth's visible force; knows that it, the invisible, is strong and alone strong. He is a believer in the divine truth of things; a *seer*, seeing through the shows of things; a worshipper, in one way or the other, of the divine truth of things" (U of California P, 1993, 100).

On the landing, moving softly, Razumov locked the door and put the key in his pocket.

## II

The words and events of that evening must have been graven as if with a steel tool on Mr. Razumov's brain since he was able to write his relation with such fullness and precision a good many months afterwards.

The record of the thoughts which assailed him in the street is even more minute and abundant. They seem to have rushed upon him with the greater freedom because his thinking powers were no longer crushed by Haldin's presence—the appalling presence of a great crime and the stunning force of a great fanaticism. On looking through the pages of Mr. Razumov's diary I own that a "rush of thoughts" is not an adequate image.

The more adequate description would be a tumult of thoughts—the faithful reflection of the state of his feelings. The thoughts in themselves were not numerous—they were like the thoughts of most human beings, few and simple—but they cannot be reproduced here in all their exclamatory repetitions which went on in an endless and weary turmoil—for the walk was long.

If to the Western reader they appear shocking, inappropriate, or even improper, it must be remembered that as to the first this may be the effect of my crude statement. For the rest I will only remark here that this is not a story of the West of Europe.

Nations it may be have fashioned their Governments, but the Governments have paid them back in the same coin. It is unthinkable that any young Englishman should find himself in Razumov's situation. This being so it would be a vain enterprise to imagine what he would think. The only safe surmise to make is that he would not think as Mr. Razumov thought at this crisis of his fate. He would not have an hereditary and personal knowledge of the means by which a historical autocracy represses ideas, guards its power, and defends its existence. By an act of mental extravagance he might imagine himself arbitrarily thrown into prison, but it would never occur to him unless he were delirious (and perhaps not even then) that he could be beaten with whips as a practical measure either of investigation or of punishment.

This is but a crude and obvious example of the different conditions of Western thought. I don't know that this danger occurred, specially to Mr. Razumov. No doubt it entered unconsciously into the general dread and the general appallingness of this crisis. Razumov, as has been seen, was aware of more subtle ways in which an individual may be undone by the proceedings of a despotic Government. A simple expulsion from the University (the very least that could happen to him), with an impossibility to continue his studies anywhere, was enough to ruin utterly a young man depending entirely upon the development of his natural abilities for his place in the world. He was a Russian: and for him to be implicated meant simply sinking into the lowest social depths amongst the hopeless and the destitute—the night birds of the city.

The peculiar circumstances of Razumov's parentage, or rather of his lack of parentage, should be taken into the account of his thoughts. And he remembered them too. He had been lately reminded of them in a peculiarly atrocious way by this fatal Haldin. "Because I haven't that, must everything else be taken away from me?" he thought.

He nerved himself for another effort to go on. Along the roadway sledges glided phantom-like and jingling through a fluttering whiteness on the black face of the night. "For it is a crime," he was saying to himself. "A murder is a murder. Though, of course, some sort of liberal institutions. . . ."

A feeling of horrible sickness came over him. "I must be courageous," he exhorted himself mentally. All his strength was suddenly gone as if taken out by a hand. Then by a mighty effort of will it came back because he was afraid of fainting in the street and being picked up by the police with the key of his lodgings in his pocket. They would find Haldin there, and then, indeed, he would be undone.

Strangely enough it was this fear which seems to have kept him up to the end. The passers-by were rare. They came upon him suddenly, looming up black in the snowflakes close by, then vanishing all at once—without footfalls.

It was the quarter of the very poor. Razumov noticed an elderly woman tied up in ragged shawls. Under the street lamp she seemed a beggar off duty. She walked leisurely in the blizzard as though she had no home to hurry to, she hugged under one arm a round loaf of black bread with an air of guarding a priceless booty: and Razumov averting his glance envied her the peace of her mind and the serenity of her fate.

To one reading Mr. Razumov's narrative it is really a wonder how he managed to keep going as he did along one interminable street after another on pavements that were gradually becoming blocked with snow. It was the thought of Haldin locked up in his rooms and the desperate desire to get rid of his presence which drove him forward. No rational determination had any part in his exertions. Thus, when on arriving at the low eating-house he heard that the man of horses, Ziemianitch, was not there, he could only stare stupidly.

The waiter, a wild-haired youth in tarred boots and a pink shirt, exclaimed, uncovering his pale gums in a silly grin, that Ziemianitch had got his skinful early in the afternoon and had gone away with a bottle under each arm to keep it up amongst the horses—he supposed.

The owner of the vile den, a bony short man in a dirty cloth caftan[1] coming down to his heels, stood by, his hands tucked into his belt, and nodded confirmation.

The reek of spirits, the greasy rancid steam of food got Razumov by the throat. He struck a table with his clenched hand and shouted violently—

"You lie."

Bleary unwashed faces were turned to his direction. A mild-eyed ragged tramp drinking tea at the next table moved farther away. A murmur of wonder arose with an undertone of uneasiness. A laugh was heard too, and an exclamation, "There! there!" jeeringly soothing. The waiter looked all round and announced to the room—

"The gentleman won't believe that Ziemianitch is drunk."

From a distant corner a hoarse voice belonging to a horrible, nondescript, shaggy being with a black face like the muzzle of a bear grunted angrily—

"The cursed driver of thieves. What do we want with his gentlemen here? We are all honest folk in this place."

Razumov, biting his lip till blood came to keep himself from bursting into imprecations, followed the owner of the den, who, whispering "Come along, little father," led him into a tiny hole of a place behind the wooden counter, whence proceeded a sound of splashing. A wet and bedraggled creature, a sort of sexless and shivering scarecrow, washed glasses in there, bending over a wooden tub by the light of a tallow dip.[2]

"Yes, little father," the man in the long caftan said plaintively. He had a brown, cunning little face, a thin greyish beard. Trying

---

1  A long tunic, usually with a belt at the waist.
2  A type of candle made from burning animal fat.

to light a tin lantern he hugged it to his breast and talked garrulously the while.

He would show Ziemianitch to the gentleman to prove there were no lies told. And he would show him drunk. His woman, it seems, ran away from him last night. "Such a hag she was! Thin! Pfui!" He spat. They were always running away from that driver of the devil—and he sixty years old too; could never get used to it. But each heart knows sorrow after its own kind and Ziemianitch was a born fool all his days. And then he would fly to the bottle. "'Who could bear life in our land without the bottle?' he says. A proper Russian man—the little pig. . . . Be pleased to follow me."

Razumov crossed a quadrangle of deep snow enclosed between high walls with innumerable windows. Here and there a dim yellow light hung within the four-square mass of darkness. The house was an enormous slum, a hive of human vermin, a monumental abode of misery towering on the verge of starvation and despair.

In a corner the ground sloped sharply down, and Razumov followed the light of the lantern through a small doorway into a long cavernous place like a neglected subterranean byre.[1] Deep within, three shaggy little horses tied up to rings hung their heads together, motionless and shadowy in the dim light of the lantern. It must have been the famous team of Haldin's escape. Razumov peered fearfully into the gloom. His guide pawed in the straw with his foot.

"Here he is. Ah! the little pigeon. A true Russian man. 'No heavy hearts for me,' he says. 'Bring out the bottle and take your ugly mug out of my sight.' Ha! ha! ha! That's the fellow he is."

He held the lantern over a prone form of a man, apparently fully dressed for outdoors. His head was lost in a pointed cloth hood. On the other side of a heap of straw protruded a pair of feet in monstrous thick boots.

"Always ready to drive," commented the keeper of the eating-house. "A proper Russian driver that. Saint or devil, night or day is all one to Ziemianitch when his heart is free from sorrow. 'I don't ask who you are, but where you want to go,' he says. He would drive Satan himself to his own abode and come back chirruping to his horses. Many a one he has driven who is clanking his chains in the Nertchinsk[2] mines by this time."

---

1 Cowshed.

2 A town in eastern Siberia, to which many convicts were sent to work in the mines.

Razumov shuddered.

"Call him, wake him up," he faltered out.

The other set down his light, stepped back and launched a kick at the prostrate sleeper. The man shook at the impact but did not move. At the third kick he grunted but remained inert as before.

The eating-house keeper desisted and fetched a deep sigh.

"You see for yourself how it is. We have done what we can for you."

He picked up the lantern. The intense black spokes of shadow swung about in the circle of light. A terrible fury—the blind rage of self-preservation—possessed Razumov.

"Ah! The vile beast," he bellowed out in an unearthly tone which made the lantern jump and tremble! "I shall wake you! Give me . . . Give me . . ."

He looked round wildly, seized the handle of a stablefork and rushing forward struck at the prostrate body with inarticulate cries. After a time his cries ceased, and the rain of blows fell in the stillness and shadows of the cellar-like stable. Razumov belaboured Ziemianitch with an insatiable fury, in great volleys of sounding thwacks. Except for the violent movements of Razumov nothing stirred, neither the beaten man nor the spoke-like shadows on the walls. And only the sound of blows was heard. It was a weird scene.

Suddenly there was a sharp crack. The stick broke and half of it flew far away into the gloom beyond the light. At the same time Ziemianitch sat up. At this Razumov became as motionless as the man with the lantern—only his breast heaved for air as if ready to burst.

Some dull sensation of pain must have penetrated at last the consoling night of drunkenness enwrapping the "bright Russian soul" of Haldin's enthusiastic praise. But Ziemianitch evidently saw nothing. His eyeballs blinked all white in the light once, twice—then the gleam went out. For a moment he sat in the straw with closed eyes with a strange air of weary meditation, then fell over slowly on his side without making the slightest sound. Only the straw rustled a little. Razumov stared wildly, fighting for his breath. After a second or two he heard a light snore.

He flung from him the piece of stick remaining in his grasp, and went off with great hasty strides without looking back once.

After going heedlessly for some fifty yards along the street he walked into a snowdrift and was up to his knees before he stopped.

This recalled him to himself; and glancing about he discovered he had been going in the wrong direction. He retraced his steps, but now at a more moderate pace. When passing before the house he had just left he flourished his fist at the sombre refuge of misery and crime rearing its sinister bulk on the white ground. It had an air of brooding. He let his arm fall by his side—discouraged.

Ziemianitch's passionate surrender to sorrow and consolation had baffled him. That was the people. A true Russian man! Razumov was glad he had beaten that brute—the "bright soul" of the other. Here they were: the people and the enthusiast.

Between the two he was done for. Between the drunkenness of the peasant incapable of action and the dream-intoxication of the idealist incapable of perceiving the reason of things, and the true character of men. It was a sort of terrible childishness. But children had their masters. "Ah! the stick, the stick, the stern hand," thought Razumov, longing for power to hurt and destroy.

He was glad he had thrashed that brute. The physical exertion had left his body in a comfortable glow. His mental agitation too was clarified as if all the feverishness had gone out of him in a fit of outward violence. Together with the persisting sense of terrible danger he was conscious now of a tranquil, unquenchable hate.

He walked slower and slower. And indeed, considering the guest he had in his rooms, it was no wonder he lingered on the way. It was like harbouring a pestilential disease that would not perhaps take your life, but would take from you all that made life worth living—a subtle pest that would convert earth into a hell.

What was he doing now? Lying on the bed as if dead, with the back of his hands over his eyes? Razumov had a morbidly vivid vision of Haldin on his bed—the white pillow hollowed by the head, the legs in long boots, the upturned feet. And in his abhorrence he said to himself, "I'll kill him when I get home." But he knew very well that that was of no use. The corpse hanging round his neck[1] would be nearly as fatal as the living man. Nothing short of complete annihilation would do. And that was impossible. What then? Must one kill oneself to escape this visitation?

Razumov's despair was too profoundly tinged with hate to accept that issue.

And yet it was despair—nothing less—at the thought of having to live with Haldin for an indefinite number of days in mortal alarm at every sound. But perhaps when he heard that this

---

1  Possibly a reference to "The Rime of the Ancient Mariner" (1798), a long narrative poem by Samuel Taylor Coleridge (1772-1834).

"bright soul" of Ziemianitch suffered from a drunken eclipse the fellow would take his infernal resignation somewhere else. And that was not likely on the face of it.

Razumov thought: "I am being crushed—and I can't even run away." Other men had somewhere a corner of the earth—some little house in the provinces where they had a right to take their troubles. A material refuge. He had nothing. He had not even a moral refuge—the refuge of confidence. To whom could he go with this tale—in all this great, great land?

Razumov stamped his foot—and under the soft carpet of snow felt the hard ground of Russia, inanimate, cold, inert, like a sullen and tragic mother hiding her face under a winding-sheet—his native soil!—his very own—without a fireside, without a heart!

He cast his eyes upwards and stood amazed. The snow had ceased to fall, and now, as if by a miracle, he saw above his head the clear black sky of the northern winter, decorated with the sumptuous fires of the stars. It was a canopy fit for the resplendent purity of the snows.

Razumov received an almost physical impression of endless space and of countless millions.

He responded to it with the readiness of a Russian who is born to an inheritance of space and numbers. Under the sumptuous immensity of the sky, the snow covered the endless forests, the frozen rivers, the plains of an immense country, obliterating the landmarks, the accidents of the ground, levelling everything under its uniform whiteness, like a monstrous blank page awaiting the record of an inconceivable history. It covered the passive land with its lives of countless people like Ziemianitch and its handful of agitators like this Haldin—murdering foolishly.

It was a sort of sacred inertia. Razumov felt a respect for it. A voice seemed to cry within him, "Don't touch it." It was a guarantee of duration, of safety, while the travail of maturing destiny went on—a work not of revolutions with their passionate levity of action and their shifting impulses—but of peace. What it needed was not the conflicting aspirations of a people, but a will strong and one: it wanted not the babble of many voices, but a man—strong and one!

Razumov stood on the point of conversion. He was fascinated by its approach, by its overpowering logic. For a train of thought is never false. The falsehood lies deep in the necessities of existence, in secret fears and half-formed ambitions, in the secret confidence combined with a secret mistrust of ourselves, in the love of hope and the dread of uncertain days.

In Russia, the land of spectral ideas and disembodied aspirations, many brave minds have turned away at last from the vain and endless conflict to the one great historical fact of the land. They turned to autocracy for the peace of their patriotic conscience as a weary unbeliever, touched by grace, turns to the faith of his fathers for the blessing of spiritual rest. Like other Russians before him, Razumov, in conflict with himself, felt the touch of grace upon his forehead.

"Haldin means disruption," he thought to himself, beginning to walk again. "What is he with his indignation, with his talk of bondage—with his talk of God's justice? All that means disruption. Better that thousands should suffer than that a people should become a disintegrated mass, helpless like dust in the wind. Obscurantism[1] is better than the light of incendiary torches. The seed germinates in the night. Out of the dark soil springs the perfect plant. But a volcanic eruption is sterile, the ruin of the fertile ground. And am I, who love my country—who have nothing but that to love and put my faith in—am I to have my future, perhaps my usefulness, ruined by this sanguinary fanatic?"

The grace entered into Razumov. He believed now in the man who would come at the appointed time.

What is a throne? A few pieces of wood upholstered in velvet. But a throne is a seat of power too. The form of government is the shape of a tool—an instrument. But twenty thousand bladders inflated by the noblest sentiments and jostling against each other in the air are a miserable incumbrance of space, holding no power, possessing no will, having nothing to give.

He went on thus, heedless of the way, holding a discourse with himself with extraordinary abundance and facility. Generally his phrases came to him slowly, after a conscious and painstaking wooing. Some superior power had inspired him with a flow of masterly argument as certain converted sinners become overwhelmingly loquacious.

He felt an austere exultation.

"What are the luridly smoky lucubrations of that fellow to the clear grasp of my intellect?" he thought. "Is not this my country? Have I not got forty million brothers?" he asked himself, unanswerably victorious in the silence of his breast. And the fearful thrashing he had given the inanimate Ziemianitch seemed to him a sign of intimate union, a pathetically severe necessity of broth-

---

1 A position opposing enlightenment, reform, or the spirit of inquiry.

erly love. "No! If I must suffer let me at least suffer for my convictions, not for a crime my reason—my cool superior reason—rejects."

He ceased to think for a moment. The silence in his breast was complete. But he felt a suspicious uneasiness, such as we may experience when we enter an unlighted strange place—the irrational feeling that something may jump upon us in the dark—the absurd dread of the unseen.

Of course he was far from being a moss-grown[1] reactionary. Everything was not for the best. Despotic bureaucracy . . . abuses . . . corruption . . . and so on. Capable men were wanted. Enlightened intelligences. Devoted hearts. But absolute power should be preserved—the tool ready for the man—for the great autocrat of the future. Razumov believed in him. The logic of history made him unavoidable. The state of the people demanded him. "What else?" he asked himself ardently, "could move all that mass in one direction? Nothing could. Nothing but a single will."

He was persuaded that he was sacrificing his personal longings of liberalism—rejecting the attractive error for the stern Russian truth. "That's patriotism," he observed mentally, and added, "There's no stopping midway on that road," and then remarked to himself, "I am not a coward."

And again there was a dead silence in Razumov's breast. He walked with lowered head, making room for no one. He walked slowly and his thoughts returning spoke within him with solemn slowness.

"What is this Haldin? And what am I? Only two grains of sand. But a great mountain is made up of just such insignificant grains. And the death of a man or of many men is an insignificant thing. Yet we combat a contagious pestilence. Do I want his death? No! I would save him if I could—but no one can do that—he is the withered member which must be cut off. If I must perish through him, let me at least not perish with him, and associated against my will with his sombre folly that understands nothing either of men or things. Why should I leave a false memory?"

It passed through his mind that there was no one in the world who cared what sort of memory he left behind him. He exclaimed to himself instantly, "Perish vainly for a falsehood! . . . What a miserable fate!"

He was now in a more animated part of the town. He did not

---

1 Literally, overgrown with moss; in this case, an expression meaning old-fashioned.

remark the crash of two colliding sledges close to the curb. The driver of one bellowed tearfully at his fellow—

"Oh, thou vile wretch!"

This hoarse yell, let out nearly in his ear, disturbed Razumov. He shook his head impatiently and went on looking straight before him. Suddenly on the snow, stretched on his back right across his path, he saw Haldin, solid, distinct, real, with his inverted hands over his eyes, clad in a brown close-fitting coat and long boots. He was lying out of the way a little, as though he had selected that place on purpose. The snow round him was untrodden.

This hallucination had such a solidity of aspect that the first movement of Razumov was to reach for his pocket to assure himself that the key of his rooms was there. But he checked the impulse with a disdainful curve of his lips. He understood. His thought, concentrated intensely on the figure left lying on his bed, had culminated in this extraordinary illusion of the sight. Razumov tackled the phenomenon calmly. With a stern face, without a check and gazing far beyond the vision, he walked on, experiencing nothing but a slight tightening of the chest. After passing he turned his head for a glance, and saw only the unbroken track of his footsteps over the place where the breast of the phantom had been lying.

Razumov walked on and after a little time whispered his wonder to himself.

"Exactly as if alive! Seemed to breathe! And right in my way too! I have had an extraordinary experience."

He made a few steps and muttered through his set teeth—

"I shall give him up."

Then for some twenty yards or more all was blank. He wrapped his cloak closer round him. He pulled his cap well forward over his eyes.

"Betray. A great word. What is betrayal? They talk of a man betraying his country, his friends, his sweetheart. There must be a moral bond first. All a man can betray is his conscience. And how is my conscience engaged here; by what bond of common faith, of common conviction, am I obliged to let that fanatical idiot drag me down with him? On the contrary—every obligation of true courage is the other way."

Razumov looked round from under his cap.

"What can the prejudice of the world reproach me with? Have I provoked his confidence? No! Have I by a single word, look, or gesture given him reason to suppose that I accepted his trust in me? No! It is true that I consented to go and see his Ziemianitch. Well, I have been to see him. And I broke a stick on his back too—the brute."

Something seemed to turn over in his head bringing uppermost a singularly hard, clear facet of his brain.

"It would be better, however," he reflected with a quite different mental accent, "to keep that circumstance altogether to myself."

He had passed beyond the turn leading to his lodgings, and had reached a wide and fashionable street. Some shops were still open, and all the restaurants. Lights fell on the pavement where men in expensive fur coats, with here and there the elegant figure of a woman, walked with an air of leisure. Razumov looked at them with the contempt of an austere believer for the frivolous crowd. It was the world—those officers, dignitaries, men of fashion, officials, members of the Yacht Club. The event of the morning affected them all. What would they say if they knew what this student in a cloak was going to do?

"Not one of them is capable of feeling and thinking as deeply as I can. How many of them could accomplish an act of conscience?"

Razumov lingered in the well-lighted street. He was firmly decided. Indeed, it could hardly be called a decision. He had simply discovered what he had meant to do all along. And yet he felt the need of some other mind's sanction.

With something resembling anguish he said to himself—

"I want to be understood." The universal aspiration with all its profound and melancholy meaning assailed heavily Razumov, who, amongst eighty millions of his kith and kin,[1] had no heart to which he could open himself.

The attorney was not to be thought of. He despised the little agent of chicane too much. One could not go and lay one's conscience before the policeman at the corner. Neither was Razumov anxious to go to the chief of his district's police—a common-looking person whom he used to see sometimes in the street in a shabby uniform and with a smouldering cigarette stuck to his lower lip. "He would begin by locking me up most probably. At any rate, he is certain to get excited and create an awful commotion," thought Razumov practically.

An act of conscience must be done with outward dignity.

---

1 Friends and relatives. Razumov's figures are off: at that time, Russia's population was roughly 130 million.

Razumov longed desperately for a word of advice, for moral support. Who knows what true loneliness is—not the conventional word, but the naked terror? To the lonely themselves it wears a mask. The most miserable outcast hugs some memory or some illusion. Now and then a fatal conjunction of events may lift the veil for an instant. For an instant only. No human being could bear a steady view of moral solitude without going mad.

Razumov had reached that point of vision. To escape from it he embraced for a whole minute the delirious purpose of rushing to his lodgings and flinging himself on his knees by the side of the bed with the dark figure stretched on it; to pour out a full confession in passionate words that would stir the whole being of that man to its innermost depths; that would end in embraces and tears; in an incredible fellowship of souls—such as the world had never seen. It was sublime!

Inwardly he wept and trembled already. But to the casual eyes that were cast upon him he was aware that he appeared as a tranquil student in a cloak, out for a leisurely stroll. He noted, too, the sidelong, brilliant glance of a pretty woman—with a delicate head, and covered in the hairy skins of wild beasts down to her feet, like a frail and beautiful savage—which rested for a moment with a sort of mocking tenderness on the deep abstraction of that good-looking young man.

Suddenly Razumov stood still. The glimpse of a passing grey whisker, caught and lost in the same instant, had evoked the complete image of Prince K——, the man who once had pressed his hand as no other man had pressed it—a faint but lingering pressure like a secret sign, like a half-unwilling caress.

And Razumov marvelled at himself. Why did he not think of him before!

"A senator, a dignitary, a great personage, the very man—He!"

A strange softening emotion came over Razumov—made his knees shake a little. He repressed it with a new-born austerity. All that sentiment was pernicious nonsense. He couldn't be quick enough; and when he got into a sledge he shouted to the driver—

"To the K—— Palace. Get on—you! Fly!"

The startled moujik,[1] bearded up to the very whites of his eyes, answered obsequiously—

"I hear, your high Nobility."

It was lucky for Razumov that Prince K—— was not a man of

---

1 Russian peasant.

timid character. On the day of Mr. de P——'s murder an extreme alarm and despondency prevailed in the high official spheres.

Prince K——, sitting sadly alone in his study, was told by his alarmed servants that a mysterious young man had forced his way into the hall, refused to tell his name and the nature of his business, and would not move from there till he had seen his Excellency in private. Instead of locking himself up and telephoning for the police, as nine out of ten high personages would have done that evening, the Prince gave way to curiosity and came quietly to the door of his study.

In the hall, the front door standing wide open, he recognised at once Razumov, pale as death, his eyes blazing, and surrounded by perplexed lackeys.

The Prince was vexed beyond measure, and even indignant. But his humane instincts and a subtle sense of self-respect could not allow him to let this young man be thrown out into the street by base menials. He retreated unseen into his room, and after a little rang his bell. Razumov heard in the hall an ominously raised harsh voice saying somewhere far away—

"Show the gentleman in here."

Razumov walked in without a tremor. He felt himself invulnerable—raised far above the shallowness of common judgment. Though he saw the Prince looking at him with black displeasure, the lucidity of his mind, of which he was very conscious, gave him an extraordinary assurance. He was not asked to sit down.

Half an hour later they appeared in the hall together. The lackeys stood up, and the Prince, moving with difficulty on his gouty feet, was helped into his furs. The carriage had been ordered before. When the great double door was flung open with a crash, Razumov, who had been standing silent with a lost gaze but with every faculty intensely on the alert, heard the Prince's voice—

"Your arm, young man."

The mobile, superficial mind of the ex-Guards[1] officer, man of showy missions, experienced in nothing but the arts of gallant intrigue and worldly success, had been equally impressed by the more obvious difficulties of such a situation and by Razumov's quiet dignity in stating them.

He had said, "No. Upon the whole I can't condemn the step you ventured to take by coming to me with your story. It is not

---

1 The Russian Imperial Guards, an elite military unit originally created by Peter the Great in the 1690s.

an affair for police understrappers. The greatest importance is attached to . . . Set your mind at rest. I shall see you through this most extraordinary and difficult situation."

Then the Prince rose to ring the bell, and Razumov, making a short bow, had said with deference—

"I have trusted my instinct. A young man having no claim upon anybody in the world has in an hour of trial involving his deepest political convictions turned to an illustrious Russian— that's all."

The Prince had exclaimed hastily—

"You have done well."

In the carriage—it was a small brougham[1] on sleigh runners— Razumov broke the silence in a voice that trembled slightly.

"My gratitude surpasses the greatness of my presumption."

He gasped, feeling unexpectedly in the dark a momentary pressure on his arm.

"You have done well," repeated the Prince.

When the carriage stopped the Prince murmured to Razumov, who had never ventured a single question—

"The house of General T——."[2]

In the middle of the snow-covered roadway blazed a great bonfire. Some Cossacks, the bridles of their horses over the arm, were warming themselves around. Two sentries stood at the door, several gendarmes[3] lounged under the great carriage gateway, and on the first-floor landing two orderlies rose and stood at attention. Razumov walked at the Prince's elbow.

A surprising quantity of hot-house plants in pots cumbered the floor of the ante-room. Servants came forward. A young man in civilian clothes arrived hurriedly, was whispered to, bowed low, and exclaiming zealously, "Certainly—this minute," fled within somewhere. The Prince signed to Razumov.

They passed through a suite of reception-rooms all barely lit and one of them prepared for dancing. The wife of the General had put off her party. An atmosphere of consternation pervaded the place. But the General's own room, with heavy sombre hangings, two massive desks, and deep armchairs, had all the lights turned on. The footman shut the door behind them and they waited.

---

1  Closed carriage drawn by one horse.

2  Perhaps based upon Dmitrii Fëdorovich Trepov (1855-1906), Governor-General of St. Petersburg and Assistant Minister of the Interior.

3  Originally of French origin, a police officer or a soldier performing police duties.

There was a coal fire in an English grate; Razumov had never before seen such a fire; and the silence of the room was like the silence of the grave; perfect, measureless, for even the clock on the mantelpiece made no sound. Filling a corner, on a black pedestal, stood a quarter-life-size smooth-limbed bronze of an adolescent figure, running. The Prince observed in an undertone—

"Spontini's. 'Flight of Youth.'[1] Exquisite."

"Admirable," assented Razumov faintly.

They said nothing more after this, the Prince silent with his grand air, Razumov staring at the statue. He was worried by a sensation resembling the gnawing of hunger.

He did not turn when he heard an inner door fly open, and a quick footstep, muffled on the carpet.

The Prince's voice immediately exclaimed, thick with excitement—

"We have got him—*ce misérable*.[2] A worthy young man came to me— No! It's incredible. . . ."

Razumov held his breath before the bronze as if expecting a crash. Behind his back a voice he had never heard before insisted politely—

"*Asseyez-vous donc.*"[3]

The Prince almost shrieked, "*Mais comprenez-vous, mon cher! L'assassin!*[4] the murderer—we have got him. . . ."

Razumov spun round. The General's smooth big cheeks rested on the stiff collar of his uniform. He must have been already looking at Razumov, because that last saw the pale blue eyes fastened on him coldly.

The Prince from a chair waved an impressive hand.

"This is a most honourable young man whom Providence itself . . . Mr. Razumov."

The General acknowledged the introduction by frowning at Razumov, who did not make the slightest movement.

Sitting down before his desk the General listened with compressed lips. It was impossible to detect any sign of emotion on his face.

---

1 A fictitious sculptor and work. Kirschner, in his edition of the novel (275), suggests that the prince mistakenly confuses the sculptor with the Italian opera composer Gaspare Luigi Pacifico Spontini (1774-1851), best known for his opera *La vestale* (1807).

2 This wretch (French). French was often spoken among the upper classes in Russian society.

3 Sit down then (French).

4 But don't you understand, my dear! The assassin! (French).

Razumov watched the immobility of the fleshy profile. But it lasted only a moment, till the Prince had finished; and when the General turned to the providential young man, his florid complexion, the blue, unbelieving eyes and the bright white flash of an automatic smile had an air of jovial, careless cruelty. He expressed no wonder at the extraordinary story—no pleasure or excitement—no incredulity either. He betrayed no sentiment whatever. Only with a politeness almost deferential suggested that "the bird might have flown while Mr.—Mr. Razumov was running about the streets."

Razumov advanced to the middle of the room and said, "The door is locked and I have the key in my pocket."

His loathing for the man was intense. It had come upon him so unawares that he felt he had not kept it out of his voice. The General looked up at him thoughtfully, and Razumov grinned.

All this went over the head of Prince K—— seated in a deep armchair, very tired and impatient.

"A student called Haldin," said the General thoughtfully.

Razumov ceased to grin.

"That is his name," he said unnecessarily loud. "Victor Victorovitch Haldin—a student."

The General shifted his position a little.

"How is he dressed? Would you have the goodness to tell me?"

Razumov angrily described Haldin's clothing in a few jerky words. The General stared all the time, then addressing the Prince—

"We were not without some indications," he said in French. "A good woman who was in the street described to us somebody wearing a dress of the sort as the thrower of the second bomb. We have detained her at the Secretariat,[1] and every one in a Tcherkess coat[2] we could lay our hands on has been brought to her to look at. She kept on crossing herself and shaking her head at them. It was exasperating. . . ."

He turned to Razumov, and in Russian, with friendly reproach—

"Take a chair, Mr. Razumov—do. Why are you standing?"

Razumov sat down carelessly and looked at the General.

---

1  A government office usually presided over by a Secretary-General.

2  A long, fitted coat, fastened by a sash (into which a sword or dagger can be inserted in the front) and often with ammunition cartridge holders across each breast, a common garment of the Cossacks. Cherkess (also Cherkes), Cherkesy, or Circassians are people from northwestern Caucasia (Kavkaz).

"This goggle-eyed imbecile understands nothing," he thought. The Prince began to speak loftily.

"Mr. Razumov is a young man of conspicuous abilities. I have it at heart that his future should not. . . ."

"Certainly," interrupted the General, with a movement of the hand. "Has he any weapons on him, do you think, Mr. Razumov?"

The General employed a gentle musical voice. Razumov answered with suppressed irritation—

"No. But my razors are lying about—you understand."

The General lowered his head approvingly.

"Precisely."

Then to the Prince, explaining courteously—

"We want that bird alive. It will be the devil if we can't make him sing a little before we are done with him."

The grave-like silence of the room with its mute clock fell upon the polite modulations of this terrible phrase. The Prince, hidden in the chair, made no sound.

The General unexpectedly developed a thought.

"Fidelity to menaced institutions on which depend the safety of a throne and of a people is no child's play. We know that, *mon Prince*, and—*tenez*—"[1] he went on with a sort of flattering harshness, "Mr. Razumov here begins to understand that too."

His eyes which he turned upon Razumov seemed to be starting out of his head. This grotesqueness of aspect no longer shocked Razumov. He said with gloomy conviction—

"Haldin will never speak."

"That remains to be seen," muttered the General.

"I am certain," insisted Razumov. "A man like this never speaks. . . . Do you imagine that I am here from fear?" he added violently. He felt ready to stand by his opinion of Haldin to the last extremity.

"Certainly not," protested the General, with great simplicity of tone. "And I don't mind telling you, Mr. Razumov, that if he had not come with his tale to such a staunch and loyal Russian as you, he would have disappeared like a stone in the water . . . which would have had a detestable effect," he added, with a bright, cruel smile under his stony stare. "So you see, there can be no suspicion of any fear here."

The Prince intervened, looking at Razumov round the back of the armchair.

---

1 ´My Prince, and—note well— (French).

"Nobody doubts the moral soundness of your action. Be at ease in that respect, pray."

He turned to the General uneasily.

"That's why I am here. You may be surprised why I should . . ."

The General hastened to interrupt.

"Not at all. Extremely natural. You saw the importance . . ."

"Yes," broke in the Prince. "And I venture to ask insistently that mine and Mr. Razumov's intervention should not become public. He is a young man of promise—of remarkable aptitudes."

"I haven't a doubt of it," murmured the General. "He inspires confidence."

"All sorts of pernicious views are so widespread nowadays— they taint such unexpected quarters—that, monstrous as it seems, he might suffer. . . . His studies. . . . His . . ."

The General, with his elbows on the desk, took his head between his hands.

"Yes. Yes. I am thinking it out. . . . How long is it since you left him at your rooms, Mr. Razumov?"

Razumov mentioned the hour which nearly corresponded with the time of his distracted flight from the big slum house. He had made up his mind to keep Ziemianitch out of the affair completely. To mention him at all would mean imprisonment for the "bright soul," perhaps cruel floggings, and in the end a journey to Siberia in chains. Razumov, who had beaten Ziemianitch, felt for him now a vague, remorseful tenderness.

The General, giving way for the first time to his secret sentiments, exclaimed contemptuously—

"And you say he came in to make you this confidence like this—for nothing—*à propos des bottes*."[1]

Razumov felt danger in the air. The merciless suspicion of despotism had spoken openly at last. Sudden fear sealed Razumov's lips. The silence of the room resembled now the silence of a deep dungeon, where time does not count, and a suspect person is sometimes forgotten for ever. But the Prince came to the rescue.

"Providence itself has led the wretch in a moment of mental aberration to seek Mr. Razumov on the strength of some old, utterly misinterpreted exchange of ideas—some sort of idle speculative conversation—months ago—I am told—and completely forgotten till now by Mr. Razumov."

"Mr. Razumov," queried the General meditatively, after a short silence, "do you often indulge in speculative conversation?"

---

1 With no good reason; without a reasonable motive (French).

"No, Excellency," answered Razumov, coolly, in a sudden access of self-confidence. "I am a man of deep convictions. Crude opinions are in the air. They are not always worth combating. But even the silent contempt of a serious mind may be misinterpreted by headlong utopists."

The General stared from between his hands. Prince K—— murmured—

"A serious young man. *Un esprit supérieur.*"[1]

"I see that, *mon cher Prince*,"[2] said the General. "Mr. Razumov is quite safe with me. I am interested in him. He has, it seems, the great and useful quality of inspiring confidence. What I was wondering at is why the other should mention anything at all—I mean even the bare fact alone—if his object was only to obtain temporary shelter for a few hours. For, after all, nothing was easier than to say nothing about it unless, indeed, he were trying, under a crazy misapprehension of your true sentiments, to enlist your assistance—eh, Mr. Razumov?"

It seemed to Razumov that the floor was moving slightly. This grotesque man in a tight uniform was terrible. It was right that he should be terrible.

"I can see what your Excellency has in your mind. But I can only answer that I don't know why."

"I have nothing in my mind," murmured the General, with gentle surprise.

"I am his prey—his helpless prey," thought Razumov. The fatigues and the disgusts of that afternoon, the need to forget, the fear which he could not keep off, reawakened his hate for Haldin.

"Then I can't help your Excellency. I don't know what he meant. I only know there was a moment when I wished to kill him. There was also a moment when I wished myself dead. I said nothing. I was overcome. I provoked no confidence—I asked for no explanations—"

Razumov seemed beside himself; but his mind was lucid. It was really a calculated outburst.

"It is rather a pity," the General said, "that you did not. Don't you know at all what he means to do?"

Razumov calmed down and saw an opening there.

"He told me he was in hopes that a sledge would meet him about half an hour after midnight at the seventh lamp-post on the left from the upper end of Karabelnaya. At any rate, he meant to

---

1 A superior spirit (French).
2 My dear Prince (French).

be there at that time. He did not even ask me for a change of clothes."

"*Ah voilà!*"[1] said the General, turning to Prince K—— with an air of satisfaction. "There is a way to keep your *protégé*, Mr. Razumov, quite clear of any connexion with the actual arrest. We shall be ready for that gentleman in Karabelnaya."

The Prince expressed his gratitude. There was real emotion in his voice. Razumov, motionless, silent, sat staring at the carpet. The General turned to him.

"Half an hour after midnight. Till then we have to depend on you, Mr. Razumov. You don't think he is likely to change his purpose?"

"How can I tell?" said Razumov. "Those men are not of the sort that ever changes its purpose."

"What men do you mean?"

"Fanatical lovers of liberty in general. Liberty with a capital L, Excellency. Liberty that means nothing precise. Liberty in whose name crimes are committed."

The General murmured—

"I detest rebels of every kind. I can't help it. It's my nature!"

He clenched a fist and shook it, drawing back his arm. "They shall be destroyed, then."

"They have made a sacrifice of their lives beforehand," said Razumov with malicious pleasure and looking the General straight in the face. "If Haldin does change his purpose to-night, you may depend on it that it will not be to save his life by flight in some other way. He would have thought then of something else to attempt. But that is not likely."

The General repeated as if to himself, "They shall be destroyed."

Razumov assumed an impenetrable expression.

The Prince exclaimed—

"What a terrible necessity!"

The General's arm was lowered slowly.

"One comfort there is. That brood leaves no posterity. I've always said it; one effort, pitiless, persistent, steady—and we are done with them for ever."

Razumov thought to himself that this man entrusted with so much arbitrary power must have believed what he said or else he could not have gone on bearing the responsibility.

The General repeated again with extreme animosity—

---

1  Ah, there it is (French).

"I detest rebels. These subversive minds! These intellectual·
*debauchés!*[1] My existence has been built on fidelity. It's a feeling.
To defend it I am ready to lay down my life—and even my
honour—if that were needed. But pray tell me what honour can
there be as against rebels—against people that deny God
Himself—perfect unbelievers! Brutes. It is horrible to think of."

During this tirade Razumov, facing the General, had nodded
slightly twice. Prince K——, standing on one side with his grand
air, murmured, casting up his eyes—

"*Hélas!*"[2]

Then lowering his glance and with great decision declared—

"This young man, General, is perfectly fit to apprehend the
bearing of your memorable words."

The General's whole expression changed from dull resentment to perfect urbanity.

"I would ask now, Mr. Razumov," he said, "to return to his
home. Note that I don't ask Mr. Razumov whether he has justified his absence to his guest. No doubt he did this sufficiently.
But I don't ask. Mr. Razumov inspires confidence. It is a great
gift. I only suggest that a more prolonged absence might awaken
the criminal's suspicions and induce him perhaps to change his
plans."

He rose and with a scrupulous courtesy escorted his visitors to
the ante-room encumbered with flower-pots.

Razumov parted with the Prince at the corner of a street. In
the carriage he had listened to speeches where natural sentiment
struggled with caution. Evidently the Prince was afraid of
encouraging any hopes of future intercourse. But there was a
touch of tenderness in the voice uttering in the dark the guarded
general phrases of goodwill. And the Prince too said—

"I have perfect confidence in you, Mr. Razumov."

"They all, it seems, have confidence in me," thought Razumov
dully. He had an indulgent contempt for the man sitting shoulder
to shoulder with him in the confined space. Probably he was
afraid of scenes with his wife. She was said to be proud and
violent.

It seemed to him bizarre that secrecy should play such a large
part in the comfort and safety of lives. But he wanted to put the
Prince's mind at ease; and with a proper amount of emphasis he
said that, being conscious of some small abilities and confident in

---

1 Degenerates (French).
2 Alas (French).

his power of work, he trusted his future to his own exertions. He expressed his gratitude for the helping hand. Such dangerous situations did not occur twice in the course of one life—he added.

"And you have met this one with a firmness of mind and correctness of feeling which give me a high idea of your worth," the Prince said solemnly. "You have now only to persevere—to persevere."

On getting out on the pavement Razumov saw an ungloved hand extended to him through the lowered window of the brougham. It detained his own in its grasp for a moment, while the light of a street lamp fell upon the Prince's long face and old-fashioned grey whiskers.

"I hope you are perfectly reassured now as to the consequences. . . ."

"After what your Excellency has condescended to do for me, I can only rely on my conscience."

"*Adieu*," said the whiskered head with feeling.

Razumov bowed. The brougham glided away with a slight swish in the snow—he was alone on the edge of the pavement.

He said to himself that there was nothing to think about, and began walking towards his home.

He walked quietly. It was a common experience to walk thus home to bed after an evening spent somewhere with his fellows or in the cheaper seats of a theatre. After he had gone a little way the familiarity of things got hold of him. Nothing was changed. There was the familiar corner; and when he turned it he saw the familiar dim light of the provision shop kept by a German woman. There were loaves of stale bread, bunches of onions and strings of sausages behind the small window-panes. They were closing it. The sickly lame fellow whom he knew so well by sight staggered out into the snow embracing a large shutter.

Nothing would change. There was the familiar gateway yawning black with feeble glimmers marking the arches of the different staircases.

The sense of life's continuity depended on trifling bodily impressions. The trivialities of daily existence were an armour for the soul. And this thought reinforced the inward quietness of Razumov as he began to climb the stairs familiar to his feet in the dark, with his hand on the familiar clammy banister. The exceptional could not prevail against the material contacts which make one day resemble another. To-morrow would be like yesterday.

It was only on the stage that the unusual was outwardly acknowledged.

"I suppose," thought Razumov, "that if I had made up my mind to blow out my brains on the landing I would be going up these stairs as quietly as I am doing it now. What's a man to do? What must be must be. Extraordinary things do happen. But when they have happened they are done with. Thus, too, when the mind is made up. That question is done with. And the daily concerns, the familiarities of our thought swallow it up—and the life goes on as before with its mysterious and secret sides quite out of sight, as they should be. Life is a public thing."

Razumov unlocked his door and took the key out; entered very quietly and bolted the door behind him carefully.

He thought, "He hears me," and after bolting the door he stood still holding his breath. There was not a sound. He crossed the bare outer room, stepping deliberately in the darkness. Entering the other, he felt all over his table for the matchbox. The silence, but for the groping of his hand, was profound. Could the fellow be sleeping so soundly?

He struck a light and looked at the bed. Haldin was lying on his back as before, only both his hands were under his head. His eyes were open. He stared at the ceiling.

Razumov held the match up. He saw the clear-cut features, the firm chin, the white forehead and the topknot of fair hair against the white pillow. There he was, lying flat on his back. Razumov thought suddenly, "I have walked over his chest."

He continued to stare till the match burnt itself out; then struck another and lit the lamp in silence without looking towards the bed any more. He had turned his back on it and was hanging his coat on a peg when he heard Haldin sigh profoundly, then ask in a tired voice—

"Well! And what have you arranged?"

The emotion was so great that Razumov was glad to put his hands against the wall. A diabolical impulse to say, "I have given you up to the police," frightened him exceedingly. But he did not say that. He said, without turning round, in a muffled voice—

"It's done."[1]

Again he heard Haldin sigh. He walked to the table, sat down with the lamp before him, and only then looked towards the bed.

---

1   The first of several appearances of this phrase (see also 94, 249, 276). This was the phrase that the eleven-year old Conrad said he kept thinking of as he led his father's funeral procession in 1868. See his essay "Poland Revisited" (*Notes on Life and Letters*, ed. J.H. Stape, Cambridge UP, 2004, 134). Young Conrad may have had in mind Christ's final words on the cross: "It is finished" (John 19:30).

In the distant corner of the large room far away from the lamp, which was small and provided with a very thick china shade, Haldin appeared like a dark and elongated shape—rigid with the immobility of death. This body seemed to have less substance than its own phantom walked over by Razumov in the street white with snow. It was more alarming in its shadowy, persistent reality than the distinct but vanishing illusion.

Haldin was heard again.

"You must have had a walk—such a walk . . ." he murmured deprecatingly. "This weather . . ."

Razumov answered with energy—

"Horrible walk. . . . A nightmare of a walk."

He shuddered audibly. Haldin sighed once more, then—

"And so you have seen Ziemianitch—brother?"

"I've seen him."

Razumov, remembering the time he had spent with the Prince, thought it prudent to add, "I had to wait some time."

"A character—eh? It's extraordinary what a sense of the necessity of freedom there is in that man. And he has sayings too—simple, to the point, such as only the people can invent in their rough sagacity. A character that . . ."

"I, you understand, haven't had much opportunity . . ." Razumov muttered through his teeth.

Haldin continued to stare at the ceiling.

"You see, brother, I have been a good deal in that house of late. I used to take there books—leaflets. Not a few of the poor people who live there can read. And, you see, the guests for the feast of freedom must be sought for in byways and hedges. The truth is, I have almost lived in that house of late. I slept sometimes in the stable. There is a stable . . ."

"That's where I had my interview with Ziemianitch," interrupted Razumov gently. A mocking spirit entered into him and he added, "It was satisfactory in a sense. I came away from it much relieved."

"Ah! he's a fellow," went on Haldin, talking slowly at the ceiling. "I came to know him in that way, you see. For some weeks now, ever since I resigned myself to do what had to be done, I tried to isolate myself. I gave up my rooms. What was the good of exposing a decent widow woman to the risk of being worried out of her mind by the police? I gave up seeing any of our comrades . . ."

Razumov drew to himself a half-sheet of paper and began to trace lines on it with a pencil.

"Upon my word," he thought angrily, "he seems to have thought of everybody's safety but mine."

Haldin was talking on.

"This morning—ah! this morning—that was different. How can I explain to you? Before the deed was done I wandered at night and lay hid in the day, thinking it out, and I felt restful. Sleepless but restful. What was there for me to torment myself about? But this morning—after! Then it was that I became restless. I could not have stopped in that big house full of misery. The miserable of this world can't give you peace. Then when that silly caretaker began to shout, I said to myself, 'There is a young man in this town head and shoulders above common prejudices.'"

"Is he laughing at me?" Razumov asked himself, going on with his aimless drawing of triangles and squares. And suddenly he thought: "My behaviour must appear to him strange. Should he take fright at my manner and rush off somewhere I shall be undone completely. That infernal General . . ."

He dropped the pencil and turned abruptly towards the bed with the shadowy figure extended full length on it—so much more indistinct than the one over whose breast he had walked without faltering. Was this, too, a phantom?

The silence had lasted a long time. "He is no longer here," was the thought against which Razumov struggled desperately, quite frightened at its absurdity. "He is already gone and this . . . only . . ."

He could resist no longer. He sprang to his feet, saying aloud, "I am intolerably anxious," and in a few headlong strides stood by the side of the bed. His hand fell lightly on Haldin's shoulder, and directly he felt its reality he was beset by an insane temptation to grip that exposed throat and squeeze the breath out of that body, lest it should escape his custody, leaving only a phantom behind.

Haldin did not stir a limb, but his overshadowed eyes moving a little gazed upwards at Razumov with wistful gratitude for this manifestation of feeling.

Razumov turned away and strode up and down the room. "It would have been possibly a kindness," he muttered to himself, and was appalled by the nature of that apology for a murderous intention his mind had found somewhere within him. And all the same he could not give it up. He became lucid about it. "What can he expect?" he thought. "The halter—in the end. And I . . ."

This argument was interrupted by Haldin's voice.

"Why be anxious for me? They can kill my body, but they

cannot exile my soul from this world. I tell you what—I believe in this world so much that I cannot conceive eternity otherwise than as a very long life. That is perhaps the reason I am so ready to die."

"H'm," muttered Razumov, and biting his lower lip he continued to walk up and down and to carry on his strange argument.

Yes, to a man in such a situation—of course it would be an act of kindness. The question, however, was not how to be kind, but how to be firm. He was a slippery customer . . .

"I too, Victor Victorovitch, believe in this world of ours," he said with force. "I too, while I live. . . . But you seem determined to haunt it. You can't seriously mean . . ."

The voice of the motionless Haldin began—

"Haunt it! Truly, the oppressors of thought which quickens the world, the destroyers of souls which aspire to perfection of human dignity, they shall be haunted. As to the destroyers of my mere body, I have forgiven them beforehand."

Razumov had stopped apparently to listen, but at the same time he was observing his own sensations. He was vexed with himself for attaching so much importance to what Haldin said.

"The fellow's mad," he thought firmly, but this opinion did not mollify him towards Haldin. It was a particularly impudent form of lunacy—and when it got loose in the sphere of public life of a country, it was obviously the duty of every good citizen . . .

This train of thought broke off short there and was succeeded by a paroxysm[1] of silent hatred towards Haldin, so intense that Razumov hastened to speak at random.

"Yes. Eternity, of course. I, too, can't very well present it to myself. . . . I imagine it, however, as something quiet and dull. There would be nothing unexpected—don't you see? The element of time would be wanting."

He pulled out his watch and gazed at it. Haldin turned over on his side and looked on intently.

Razumov got frightened at this movement. A slippery customer this fellow with a phantom. It was not midnight yet. He hastened on—

"And unfathomable mysteries! Can you conceive secret places in Eternity? Impossible. Whereas life is full of them. There are secrets of birth, for instance. One carries them on to the grave. There is something comical . . . but never mind. And there are secret motives of conduct. A man's most open actions have a

---

1 Fit or spasm.

secret side to them. That is interesting and so unfathomable! For instance, a man goes out of a room for a walk. Nothing more trivial in appearance. And yet it may be momentous. He comes back—he has seen perhaps a drunken brute, taken particular notice of the snow on the ground—and behold he is no longer the same man. The most unlikely things have a secret power over one's thoughts—the grey whiskers of a particular person—the goggle eyes of another."

Razumov's forehead was moist. He took a turn or two in the room, his head low and smiling to himself viciously.

"Have you ever reflected on the power of goggle eyes and grey whiskers? Excuse me. You seem to think I must be crazy to talk in this vein at such a time. But I am not talking lightly. I have seen instances. It has happened to me once to be talking to a man whose fate was affected by physical facts of that kind. And the man did not know it. Of course, it was a case of conscience, but the material facts such as these brought about the solution. . . . And you tell me, Victor Victorovitch, not to be anxious! Why! I am responsible for you," Razumov almost shrieked.

He avoided with difficulty a burst of Mephistophelian[1] laughter. Haldin, very pale, raised himself on his elbow.

"And the surprises of life," went on Razumov, after glancing at the other uneasily. "Just consider their astonishing nature. A mysterious impulse induces you to come here. I don't say you have done wrong. Indeed, from a certain point of view you could not have done better. You might have gone to a man with affections and family ties. You have such ties yourself. As to me, you know I have been brought up in an educational institute where they did not give us enough to eat. To talk of affection in such a connexion—you perceive yourself. . . . As to ties, the only ties I have in the world are social. I must get acknowledged in some way before I can act at all. I sit here working. . . . And don't you think I am working for progress too? I've got to find my own ideas of the true way. . . . Pardon me," continued Razumov, after drawing breath and with a short, throaty laugh, "but I haven't inherited a revolutionary inspiration together with a resemblance from an uncle."

He looked again at his watch and noticed with sickening disgust that there were yet a good many minutes to midnight. He tore watch and chain off his waistcoat and laid them on the table well in the circle of bright lamplight. Haldin, reclining on his

---

1 Mephistopheles was the spirit who tempted Dr. Faustus to sell his soul to the devil.

elbow, did not stir. Razumov was made uneasy by this attitude. "What move is he meditating over so quietly?" he thought. "He must be prevented. I must keep on talking to him."

He raised his voice.

"You are a son, a brother, a nephew, a cousin—I don't know what—to no end of people. I am just a man. Here I stand before you. A man with a mind. Did it ever occur to you how a man who had never heard a word of warm affection or praise in his life would think on matters on which you would think first with or against your class, your domestic tradition—your fireside prejudices? . . . Did you ever consider how a man like that would feel? I have no domestic tradition. I have nothing to think against. My tradition is historical. What have I to look back to but that national past from which you gentlemen want to wrench away your future? Am I to let my intelligence, my aspirations towards a better lot, be robbed of the only thing it has to go upon at the will of violent enthusiasts? You come from your province, but all this land is mine—or I have nothing. No doubt you shall be looked upon as a martyr some day—a sort of hero—a political saint. But I beg to be excused. I am content in fitting myself to be a worker. And what can you people do by scattering a few drops of blood on the snow? On this Immensity. On this unhappy Immensity! I tell you," he cried, in a vibrating, subdued voice, and advancing one step nearer the bed, "that what it needs is not a lot of haunting phantoms that I could walk through—but a man!"

Haldin threw his arms forward as if to keep him off in horror.

"I understand it all now," he exclaimed, with awestruck dismay. "I understand—at last."

Razumov staggered back against the table. His forehead broke out in perspiration while a cold shudder ran down his spine.

"What have I been saying?" he asked himself. "Have I let him slip through my fingers after all?"

He felt his lips go stiff like buckram, and instead of a reassuring smile only achieved an uncertain grimace.

"What will you have?" he began in a conciliating voice which got steady after the first trembling word or two. "What will you have? Consider—a man of studious, retired habits—and suddenly like this. . . . I am not practised in talking delicately. But . . ."

He felt anger, a wicked anger, get hold of him again.

"What were we to do together till midnight? Sit here opposite each other and think of your—your—shambles?"[1]

---

1  A place of carnage; hence, a mess or muddle.

Haldin had a subdued, heartbroken attitude. He bowed his head; his hands hung between his knees. His voice was low and pained but calm.

"I see now how it is, Razumov—brother. You are a magnanimous soul, but my action is abhorrent to you—alas . . ."

Razumov stared. From fright he had set his teeth so hard that his whole face ached. It was impossible for him to make a sound.

"And even my person, too, is loathsome to you perhaps," Haldin added mournfully, after a short pause, looking up for a moment, then fixing his gaze on the floor. "For indeed, unless one . . ."

He broke off, evidently waiting for a word. Razumov remained silent. Haldin nodded his head dejectedly twice.

"Of course. Of course," he murmured. . . . "Ah! weary work!"

He remained perfectly still for a moment, then made Razumov's leaden heart strike a ponderous blow by springing up briskly.

"So be it," he cried sadly in a low, distinct tone. "Farewell then."

Razumov started forward, but the sight of Haldin's raised hand checked him before he could get away from the table. He leaned on it heavily, listening to the faint sounds of some town clock tolling the hour. Haldin, already at the door, tall and straight as an arrow, with his pale face and a hand raised attentively, might have posed for the statue of a daring youth listening to an inner voice. Razumov mechanically glanced down at his watch. When he looked towards the door again Haldin had vanished. There was a faint rustling in the outer room, the feeble click of a bolt drawn back lightly. He was gone—almost as noiseless as a vision.

Razumov ran forward unsteadily, with parted, voiceless lips. The outer door stood open. Staggering out on the landing, he leaned far over the banister. Gazing down into the deep black shaft with a tiny glimmering flame at the bottom, he traced by ear the rapid spiral descent of somebody running down the stairs on tiptoe. It was a light, swift, pattering sound, which sank away from him into the depths: a fleeting shadow passed over the glimmer—a wink of the tiny flame. Then stillness.

Razumov hung over, breathing the cold raw air tainted by the evil smells of the unclean staircase. All quiet.

He went back into his room slowly, shutting the doors after him. The peaceful steady light of his reading-lamp shone on the watch. Razumov stood looking down at the little white dial. It wanted yet three minutes to midnight. He took the watch into his hand fumblingly.

"Slow," he muttered, and a strange fit of nervelessness came over him. His knees shook, the watch and chain slipped through his fingers in an instant and fell on the floor. He was so startled that he nearly fell himself. When at last he regained enough confidence in his limbs to stoop for it he held it to his ear at once. After a while he growled—

"Stopped," and paused for quite a long time before he muttered sourly—

"It's done. . . . And now to work."

He sat down, reached haphazard for a book, opened it in the middle and began to read; but after going conscientiously over two lines he lost his hold on the print completely and did not try to regain it. He thought—

"There was to a certainty a police agent of some sort watching the house across the street."

He imagined him lurking in a dark gateway, goggle-eyed, muffled up in a cloak to the nose and with a General's plumed, cocked hat on his head. This absurdity made him start in the chair convulsively. He literally had to shake his head violently to get rid of it. The man would be disguised perhaps as a peasant . . . a beggar. . . . Perhaps he would be just buttoned up in a dark overcoat and carrying a loaded stick—a shifty-eyed rascal, smelling of raw onions and spirits.

This evocation brought on positive nausea. "Why do I want to bother about this?" thought Razumov with disgust. "Am I a gendarme? Moreover, it is done."

He got up in great agitation. It was not done. Not yet. Not till half-past twelve. And the watch had stopped. This reduced him to despair. Impossible to know the time! The landlady and all the people across the landing were asleep. How could he go and . . . God knows what they would imagine, or how much they would guess. He dared not go into the streets to find out. "I am a suspect now. There's no use shirking that fact," he said to himself bitterly. If Haldin from some cause or another gave them the slip and failed to turn up in the Karabelnaya the police would be invading his lodging. And if he were not in he could never clear himself. Never. Razumov looked wildly about as if for some means of seizing upon time which seemed to have escaped him altogether. He had never, as far as he could remember, heard the striking of that town clock in his rooms before this night. And he was not even sure now whether he had heard it really on this night.

He went to the window and stood there with slightly bent head on the watch for the faint sound. "I will stay here till I hear something," he said to himself. He stood still, his ear turned to the panes. An atrocious aching numbness with shooting pains in his back and legs tortured him. He did not budge. His mind hovered on the borders of delirium. He heard himself suddenly saying, "I confess," as a person might do on the rack. "I am on the rack," he thought. He felt ready to swoon. The faint deep boom of the distant clock seemed to explode in his head—he heard it so clearly. . . . One!

If Haldin had not turned up the police would have been already here ransacking the house. No sound reached him. This time it was done.

He dragged himself painfully to the table and dropped into the chair. He flung the book away and took a square sheet of paper. It was like the pile of sheets covered with his neat minute handwriting, only blank. He took a pen brusquely and dipped it with a vague notion of going on with the writing of his essay—but his pen remained poised over the sheet. It hung there for some time before it came down and formed long scrawly letters.

Still-faced and his lips set hard, Razumov began to write. When he wrote a large hand his neat writing lost its character altogether—became unsteady, almost childish. He wrote five lines one under the other.

History not Theory.
Patriotism not Internationalism.
Evolution not Revolution.
Direction not Destruction.
Unity not Disruption.

He gazed at them dully. Then his eyes strayed to the bed and remained fixed there for a good many minutes, while his right hand groped all over the table for the penknife.

He rose at last, and walking up with measured steps stabbed the paper with the penknife to the lath and plaster wall at the head of the bed. This done he stepped back a pace and flourished his hand with a glance round the room.

After that he never looked again at the bed. He took his big cloak down from its peg and, wrapping himself up closely, went to lie down on the hard horse-hair sofa at the other side of his room. A leaden sleep closed his eyelids at once. Several times that night he woke up shivering from a dream of walking through drifts of snow in a Russia where he was as completely alone as any betrayed autocrat could be; an immense, wintry Russia which, somehow, his view could embrace in all its enormous expanse as if it were a map. But after each shuddering start his heavy eyelids fell over his glazed eyes and he slept again.

## III

Approaching this part of Mr. Razumov's story, my mind, the decent mind of an old teacher of languages, feels more and more the difficulty of the task.

The task is not in truth the writing in the narrative form a *précis*[1] of a strange human document, but the rendering—I perceive it now clearly—of the moral conditions ruling over a large portion of this earth's surface; conditions not easily to be understood, much less discovered in the limits of a story, till some keyword is found; a word that could stand at the back of all the words covering the pages; a word which, if not truth itself, may perchance hold truth enough to help the moral discovery which should be the object of every tale.

I turn over for the hundredth time the leaves of Mr. Razumov's record, I lay it aside, I take up the pen—and the pen being ready for its office of setting down black on white I hesitate. For the word that persists in creeping under its point is no other word than "cynicism."

For that is the mark of Russian autocracy and of Russian revolt. In its pride of numbers, in its strange pretensions of sanctity, and in the secret readiness to abase itself in suffering, the spirit of Russia is the spirit of cynicism. It informs the declarations of her statesmen, the theories of her revolutionists, and the mystic vaticinations[2] of prophets to the point of making freedom look like a form of debauch, and the Christian virtues themselves appear actually indecent. . . . But I must apologize for the digression. It proceeds from the consideration of the course taken by the story of Mr. Razumov after his conservative convictions, diluted in a vague liberalism natural to the ardour of his age, had become crystallized by the shock of his contact with Haldin.

Razumov woke up for the tenth time perhaps with a heavy shiver. Seeing the light of day in his window, he resisted the incli-

---

1 Summary (French).
2 Prophecies or foretellings.

nation to lay himself down again. He did not remember anything, but he did not think it strange to find himself on the sofa in his cloak and chilled to the bone. The light coming through the window seemed strangely cheerless, containing no promise as the light of each new day should for a young man. It was the awakening of a man mortally ill, or of a man ninety years old. He looked at the lamp which had burnt itself out. It stood there, the extinguished beacon of his labours, a cold object of brass and porcelain, amongst the scattered pages of his notes and small piles of books—a mere litter of blackened paper—dead matter—without significance or interest.

He got on his feet, and divesting himself of his cloak hung it on the peg, going through all the motions mechanically. An incredible dullness, a ditch-water stagnation was sensible to his perceptions as though life had withdrawn itself from all things and even from his own thoughts. There was not a sound in the house.

Turning away from the peg, he thought in that same lifeless manner that it must be very early yet; but when he looked at the watch on his table he saw both hands arrested at twelve o'clock.

"Ah! yes," he mumbled to himself, and as if beginning to get roused a little he took a survey of his room. The paper stabbed to the wall arrested his attention. He eyed it from the distance without approval or perplexity; but when he heard the servant-girl beginning to bustle about in the outer room with the samovar[1] for his morning tea, he walked up to it and took it down with an air of profound indifference.

While doing this he glanced down at the bed on which he had not slept that night. The hollow in the pillow made by the weight of Haldin's head was very noticeable.

Even his anger at this sign of the man's passage was dull. He did not try to nurse it into life. He did nothing all that day; he neglected even to brush his hair. The idea of going out never occurred to him—and if he did not start a connected train of thought it was not because he was unable to think. It was because he was not interested enough.

He yawned frequently. He drank large quantities of tea, he walked about aimlessly, and when he sat down he did not budge for a long time. He spent some time drumming on the window with his finger-tips quietly. In his listless wanderings round about the table he caught sight of his own face in the looking-glass and that arrested him. The eyes which returned his stare were the

---

1  Russian urn used for boiling water for tea.

most unhappy eyes he had ever seen. And this was the first thing which disturbed the mental stagnation of that day.

He was not affected personally. He merely thought that life without happiness is impossible. What was happiness? He yawned and went on shuffling about and about between the walls of his room. Looking forward was happiness—that's all—nothing more. To look forward to the gratification of some desire, to the gratification of some passion, love, ambition, hate—hate too indubitably. Love and hate. And to escape the dangers of existence, to live without fear, was also happiness. There was nothing else. Absence of fear—looking forward. "Oh! the miserable lot of humanity!" he exclaimed mentally; and added at once in his thought, "I ought to be happy enough as far as that goes." But he was not excited by that assurance. On the contrary, he yawned again as he had been yawning all day. He was mildly surprised to discover himself being overtaken by night. The room grew dark swiftly though time had seemed to stand still. How was it that he had not noticed the passing of that day? Of course, it was the watch being stopped. . . .

He did not light his lamp, but went over to the bed and threw himself on it without any hesitation. Lying on his back, he put his hands under his head and stared upward. After a moment he thought, "I am lying here like that man. I wonder if he slept while I was struggling with the blizzard in the streets. No, he did not sleep. But why should I not sleep?" and he felt the silence of the night press upon all his limbs like a weight.

In the calm of the hard frost outside, the clear-cut strokes of the town clock counting off midnight penetrated the quietness of his suspended animation.

Again he began to think. It was twenty-four hours since that man left his room. Razumov had a distinct feeling that Haldin in the fortress was sleeping that night. It was a certitude which made him angry because he did not want to think of Haldin, but he justified it to himself by physiological and psychological reasons. The fellow had hardly slept for weeks on his own confession, and now every incertitude was at an end for him. No doubt he was looking forward to the consummation of his martyrdom. A man who resigns himself to kill need not go very far for resignation to die. Haldin slept perhaps more soundly than General T——, whose task—weary work too—was not done, and over whose head hung the sword of revolutionary vengeance.

Razumov, remembering the thick-set man with his heavy jowl resting on the collar of his uniform, the champion of autocracy, who had let no sign of surprise, incredulity, or joy escape him, but whose goggle eyes could express a mortal hatred of all rebellion—Razumov moved uneasily on the bed.

"He suspected me," he thought. "I suppose he must suspect everybody. He would be capable of suspecting his own wife, if Haldin had gone to her boudoir[1] with his confession."

Razumov sat up in anguish. Was he to remain a political suspect all his days? Was he to go through life as a man not wholly to be trusted—with a bad secret police note tacked on to his record? What sort of future could he look forward to?

"I am now a suspect," he thought again; but the habit of reflection and that desire of safety, of an ordered life, which was so strong in him came to his assistance as the night wore on. His quiet, steady, and laborious existence would vouch at length for his loyalty. There were many permitted ways to serve one's country. There was an activity that made for progress without being revolutionary. The field of influence was great and infinitely varied—once one had conquered a name.

His thought like a circling bird reverted after four-and-twenty hours to the silver medal, and as it were poised itself there.

When the day broke he had not slept, not for a moment, but he got up not very tired and quite sufficiently self-possessed for all practical purposes.

He went out and attended three lectures in the morning. But the work in the library was a mere dumb show of research. He sat with many volumes open before him trying to make notes and extracts. His new tranquillity was like a flimsy garment, and seemed to float at the mercy of a casual word. Betrayal! Why! the fellow had done all that was necessary to betray himself. Precious little had been needed to deceive him.

"I have said no word to him that was not strictly true. Not one word," Razumov argued with himself.

Once engaged on this line of thought there could be no question of doing useful work. The same ideas went on passing through his mind, and he pronounced mentally the same words over and over again. He shut up all the books and rammed all his papers into his pocket with convulsive movements, raging inwardly against Haldin.

As he was leaving the library a long bony student in a threadbare overcoat joined him, stepping moodily by his side. Razumov answered his mumbled greeting without looking at him at all.

---

1  In this case, a private room where a lady may receive her close friends.

"What does he want with me?" he thought with a strange dread of the unexpected which he tried to shake off lest it should fasten itself upon his life for good and all. And the other, muttering cautiously with downcast eyes, supposed that his comrade had seen the news of de P——'s executioner—that was the expression he used—having been arrested the night before last. . . .

"I've been ill—shut up in my rooms," Razumov mumbled through his teeth.

The tall student, raising his shoulders, shoved his hands deep into his pockets. He had a hairless, square, tallowy chin which trembled slightly as he spoke, and his nose nipped bright red by the sharp air looked like a false nose of painted cardboard between the sallow cheeks. His whole appearance was stamped with the mark of cold and hunger. He stalked deliberately at Razumov's elbow with his eyes on the ground.

"It's an official statement," he continued in the same cautious mutter. "It may be a lie. But there was somebody arrested between midnight and one in the morning on Tuesday. This is certain."

And talking rapidly under the cover of his downcast air, he told Razumov that this was known through an inferior Government clerk employed at the Central Secretariat. That man belonged to one of the revolutionary circles. "The same, in fact, I am affiliated to," remarked the student.

They were crossing a wide quadrangle. An infinite distress possessed Razumov, annihilated his energy, and before his eyes everything appeared confused and as if evanescent. He dared not leave the fellow there. "He may be affiliated to the police," was the thought that passed through his mind. "Who could tell?" But eyeing the miserable frost-nipped, famine-struck figure of his companion he perceived the absurdity of his suspicion.

"But I—you know—I don't belong to any circle. I . . ."

He dared not say any more. Neither dared he mend his pace. The other, raising and setting down his lamentably shod feet with exact deliberation, protested in a low tone that it was not necessary for everybody to belong to an organization. The most valuable personalities remained outside. Some of the best work was done outside the organization. Then very fast, with whispering, feverish lips—

"The man arrested in the street was Haldin."

And accepting Razumov's dismayed silence as natural enough, he assured him that there was no mistake. That Government clerk was on night duty at the Secretariat. Hearing a great noise of footsteps in the hall and aware that political prisoners were brought over sometimes at night from the fortress, he opened the door of the room in which he was working, suddenly. Before the gendarme on duty could push him back and slam the door in his face, he had seen a prisoner being partly carried, partly dragged along the hall by a lot of policemen. He was being used very brutally. And the clerk had recognized Haldin perfectly. Less than half an hour afterwards General T—— arrived at the Secretariat to examine that prisoner personally.

"Aren't you astonished?" concluded the gaunt student.

"No," said Razumov roughly—and at once regretted his answer.

"Everybody supposed Haldin was in the provinces—with his people. Didn't you?"

The student turned his big hollow eyes upon Razumov, who said unguardedly—

"His people are abroad."

He could have bitten his tongue out with vexation. The student pronounced in a tone of profound meaning—

"So! You alone were aware . . ." and stopped.

"They have sworn my ruin," thought Razumov. "Have you spoken of this to anyone else?" he asked with bitter curiosity.

The other shook his head.

"No, only to you. Our circle thought that as Haldin had been often heard expressing a warm appreciation of your character . . ."

Razumov could not restrain a gesture of angry despair which the other must have misunderstood in some way, because he ceased speaking and turned away his black, lack-lustre eyes.

They moved side by side in silence. Then the gaunt student began to whisper again, with averted gaze—

"As we have at present no one affiliated inside the fortress so as to make it possible to furnish him with a packet of poison, we have considered already some sort of retaliatory action—to follow very soon . . ."

Razumov trudging on interrupted—

"Were you acquainted with Haldin? Did he know where you live?"

"I had the happiness to hear him speak twice," his companion answered in the feverish whisper contrasting with the gloomy apathy of his face and bearing. "He did not know where I live. . . . I am lodging poorly . . . with an artisan family. . . . I have just a corner in a room. It is not very practicable to see me there, but if you should need me for anything I am ready. . . ."

Razumov trembled with rage and fear. He was beside himself, but kept his voice low.

"You are not to come near me. You are not to speak to me. Never address a single word to me. I forbid you."

"Very well," said the other submissively, showing no surprise whatever at this abrupt prohibition. "You don't wish for secret reasons . . . perfectly . . . I understand."

He edged away at once, not looking up even; and Razumov saw his gaunt, shabby, famine-stricken figure cross the street obliquely with lowered head and that peculiar exact motion of the feet.

He watched him as one would watch a vision out of a nightmare, then he continued on his way, trying not to think. On his landing the landlady seemed to be waiting for him. She was a short, thick, shapeless woman with a large yellow face wrapped up everlastingly in a black woollen shawl. When she saw him come up the last flight of stairs she flung both her arms up excitedly, then clasped her hands before her face.

"Kirylo Sidorovitch—little father—what have you been doing? And such a quiet young man, too! The police are just gone this moment after searching your rooms."

Razumov gazed down at her with silent, scrutinizing attention. Her puffy yellow countenance was working with emotion. She screwed up her eyes at him entreatingly.

"Such a sensible young man! Anybody can see you are sensible. And now—like this—all at once. . . . What is the good of mixing yourself up with these Nihilists?[1] Do give over, little father. They are unlucky people."

Razumov moved his shoulders slightly.

"Or is it that some secret enemy has been calumniating you, Kirylo Sidorovitch? The world is full of black hearts and false denunciations nowadays. There is much fear about."

"Have you heard that I have been denounced by some one?" asked Razumov, without taking his eyes off her quivering face.

But she had not heard anything. She had tried to find out by asking the police captain while his men were turning the room upside down. The police captain of the district had known her for

---

1  People who believe in no established religious, social, or political laws. In this case, as was common for the time, the term is being used synonymously with Anarchism, which advocated a de-centralized government and the overthrow of the established order by violent or other means.

the last eleven years and was a humane person. But he said to her on the landing, looking very black and vexed—

"My good woman, do not ask questions. I don't know anything myself. The order comes from higher quarters."

And indeed there had appeared, shortly after the arrival of the policemen of the district, a very superior gentleman in a fur coat and a shiny hat, who sat down in the room and looked through all the papers himself. He came alone and went away by himself, taking nothing with him. She had been trying to put things straight a little since they left.

Razumov turned away brusquely and entered his rooms.

All his books had been shaken and thrown on the floor. His landlady followed him, and stooping painfully began to pick them up into her apron. His papers and notes which were kept always neatly sorted (they all related to his studies) had been shuffled up and heaped together into a ragged pile in the middle of the table.

This disorder affected him profoundly, unreasonably. He sat down and stared. He had a distinct sensation of his very existence being undermined in some mysterious manner, of his moral supports falling away from him one by one. He even experienced a slight physical giddiness and made a movement as if to reach for something to steady himself with.

The old woman, rising to her feet with a low groan, shot all the books she had collected in her apron on to the sofa and left the room muttering and sighing.

It was only then that he noticed that the sheet of paper which for one night had remained stabbed to the wall above his empty bed was lying on top of the pile.

When he had taken it down the day before he had folded it in four, absent-mindedly, before dropping it on the table. And now he saw it lying uppermost, spread out, smoothed out even and covering all the confused pile of pages, the record of his intellectual life for the last three years. It had not been flung there. It had been placed there—smoothed out, too! He guessed in that an intention of profound meaning—or perhaps some inexplicable mockery.

He sat staring at the piece of paper till his eyes began to smart. He did not attempt to put his papers in order, either that evening or the next day—which he spent at home in a state of peculiar irresolution. This irresolution bore upon the question whether he should continue to live—neither more nor less. But its nature was very far removed from the hesitation of a man contemplating suicide. The idea of laying violent hands upon his body did not occur to Razumov. The unrelated organism bearing that label, walking, breathing, wearing these clothes, was of no importance to anyone, unless maybe to the landlady. The true Razumov had his being in the willed, in the determined future—in that future menaced by the lawlessness of autocracy—for autocracy knows no law—and the lawlessness of revolution. The feeling that his moral personality was at the mercy of these lawless forces was so strong that he asked himself seriously if it were worth while to go on accomplishing the mental functions of that existence which seemed no longer his own.

"What is the good of exerting my intelligence, of pursuing the systematic development of my faculties and all my plans of work?" he asked himself. "I want to guide my conduct by reasonable convictions, but what security have I against something—some destructive horror—walking in upon me as I sit here? . . ."

Razumov looked apprehensively towards the door of the outer room as if expecting some shape of evil to turn the handle and appear before him silently.

"A common thief," he said to himself, "finds more guarantees in the law he is breaking, and even a brute like Ziemianitch has his consolation." Razumov envied the materialism of the thief and the passion of the incorrigible lover. The consequences of their actions were always clear and their lives remained their own.

But he slept as soundly that night as though he had been consoling himself in the manner of Ziemianitch. He dropped off suddenly, lay like a log, remembered no dream on waking. But it was as if his soul had gone out in the night to gather the flowers of wrathful wisdom. He got up in a mood of grim determination and as if with a new knowledge of his own nature. He looked mockingly on the heap of papers on his table; and left his room to attend the lectures, muttering to himself, "We shall see."

He was in no humour to talk to anybody or hear himself questioned as to his absence from lectures the day before. But it was difficult to repulse rudely a very good comrade with a smooth pink face and fair hair, bearing the nickname amongst his fellow-students of "Madcap Kostia." He was the idolized only son of a very wealthy and illiterate Government contractor, and attended the lectures only during the periodical fits of contrition following upon tearful paternal remonstrances. Noisily blundering like a retriever puppy, his elated voice and great gestures filled the bare academy corridors with the joy of thoughtless animal life, provoking indulgent smiles at a great distance. His usual discourses treated of trotting horses, wine-parties in expensive restaurants, and the merits of persons of easy virtue, with a disarming artlessness of outlook. He pounced upon Razumov about midday, somewhat less uproariously than his habit was, and led him aside.

"Just a moment, Kirylo Sidorovitch. A few words here in this quiet corner."

He felt Razumov's reluctance, and insinuated his hand under his arm caressingly.

"No—pray do. I don't want to talk to you about any of my silly scrapes. What are my scrapes? Absolutely nothing. Mere childishness. The other night I flung a fellow out of a certain place where I was having a fairly good time. A tyrannical little beast of a quill-driver from the Treasury department. . . . He was bullying the people of the house. I rebuked him. 'You are not behaving humanely to God's creatures that are a jolly sight more estimable than yourself,' I said. I can't bear to see any tyranny, Kirylo Sidorovitch. Upon my word I can't. He didn't take it in good part at all. 'Who's that impudent puppy?' he begins to shout. I was in excellent form as it happened, and he went through the closed window very suddenly. He flew quite a long way into the yard. I raged like—like a—minotaur.[1] The women clung to me and screamed, the fiddlers got under the table. . . . Such fun! My dad had to put his hand pretty deep into his pocket, I can tell you."

He chuckled.

"My dad is a very useful man. Jolly good thing it is for me, too. I do get into unholy scrapes."

His elation fell. That was just it. What was his life? Insignificant; no good to anyone; a mere festivity. It would end some fine day in his getting his skull split with a champagne bottle in a drunken brawl. At such times, too, when men were sacrificing themselves to ideas. But he could never get any ideas into his head. His head wasn't worth anything better than to be split by a champagne bottle.

Razumov, protesting that he had no time, made an attempt to get away. The other's tone changed to confidential earnestness.

"For God's sake, Kirylo, my dear soul, let me make some sort of sacrifice. It would not be a sacrifice really. I have my rich dad behind me. There's positively no getting to the bottom of his pocket."

---

1 In Greek mythology, a monstrous creature with the head of a bull and the body of a man.

And rejecting indignantly Razumov's suggestion that this was drunken raving, he offered to lend him some money to escape abroad with. He could always get money from his dad. He had only to say that he had lost it at cards or something of that sort, and at the same time promise solemnly not to miss a single lecture for three months on end. That would fetch the old man; and he, Kostia, was quite equal to the sacrifice. Though he really did not see what was the good for him to attend the lectures. It was perfectly hopeless.

"Won't you let me be of some use?" he pleaded to the silent Razumov, who with his eyes on the ground and utterly unable to penetrate the real drift of the other's intention, felt a strange reluctance to clear up the point.

"What makes you think I want to go abroad?" he asked at last very quietly.

Kostia lowered his voice.

"You had the police in your rooms yesterday. There are three or four of us who have heard of that. Never mind how we know. It is sufficient that we do. So we have been consulting together."

"Ah! You got to know that so soon," muttered Razumov negligently.

"Yes. We did. And it struck us that a man like you . . ."

"What sort of a man do you take me to be?" Razumov interrupted him.

"A man of ideas—and a man of action too. But you are very deep, Kirylo. There's no getting to the bottom of your mind. Not for fellows like me. But we all agreed that you must be preserved for our country. Of that we have no doubt whatever—I mean all of us who have heard Haldin speak of you on certain occasions. A man doesn't get the police ransacking his rooms without there being some devilry hanging over his head. . . . And so if you think that it would be better for you to bolt at once . . ."

Razumov tore himself away and walked down the corridor, leaving the other motionless with his mouth open. But almost at once he returned and stood before the amazed Kostia, who shut his mouth slowly. Razumov looked him straight in the eyes, before saying with marked deliberation and separating his words—

"I thank—you—very—much."

He went away again rapidly. Kostia, recovering from his surprise at these manoeuvres, ran up behind him pressingly.

"No! Wait! Listen. I really mean it. It would be like giving your compassion to a starving fellow. Do you hear, Kirylo? And any disguise you may think of, that too I could procure from a costumier, a Jew I know. Let a fool be made serviceable according to his folly. Perhaps also a false beard or something of that kind may be needed."

Razumov turned at bay.

"There are no false beards needed in this business, Kostia—you good-hearted lunatic, you. What do you know of my ideas? My ideas may be poison to you."

The other began to shake his head in energetic protest.

"What have you got to do with ideas? Some of them would make an end of your dad's money-bags. Leave off meddling with what you don't understand. Go back to your trotting horses and your girls, and then you'll be sure at least of doing no harm to anybody, and hardly any to yourself."

The enthusiastic youth was overcome by this disdain.

"You're sending me back to my pig's trough, Kirylo. That settles it. I am an unlucky beast—and I shall die like a beast too. But mind—it's your contempt that has done for me."

Razumov went off with long strides. That this simple and grossly festive soul should have fallen too under the revolutionary curse affected him as an ominous symptom of the time. He reproached himself for feeling troubled. Personally he ought to have felt reassured. There was an obvious advantage in this conspiracy of mistaken judgment taking him for what he was not. But was it not strange?

Again he experienced that sensation of his conduct being taken out of his hands by Haldin's revolutionary tyranny. His solitary and laborious existence had been destroyed—the only thing he could call his own on this earth. By what right? he asked himself furiously. In what name?

What infuriated him most was to feel that the "thinkers" of the University were evidently connecting him with Haldin—as a sort of confidant in the background apparently. A mysterious connexion! Ha ha! . . . He had been made a personage without knowing anything about it. How that wretch Haldin must have talked about him! Yet it was likely that Haldin had said very little. The fellow's casual utterances were caught up and treasured and pondered over by all these imbeciles. And was not all secret revolutionary action based upon folly, self-deception, and lies?

"Impossible to think of anything else," muttered Razumov to himself. "I'll become an idiot if this goes on. The scoundrels and the fools are murdering my intelligence."

He lost all hope of saving his future, which depended on the free use of his intelligence.

He reached the doorway of his house in a state of mental discouragement which enabled him to receive with apparent indifference an official-looking envelope from the dirty hand of the dvornik.

"A gendarme brought it," said the man. "He asked if you were at home. I told him 'No, he's not at home.' So he left it. 'Give it into his own hands,' says he. Now you've got it—eh?"

He went back to his sweeping, and Razumov climbed his stairs, envelope in hand. Once in his room he did not hasten to open it. Of course this official missive was from the superior direction of the police. A suspect! A suspect!

He stared in dreary astonishment at the absurdity of his position. He thought with a sort of dry, unemotional melancholy; three years of good work gone, the course of forty more perhaps jeopardized—turned from hope to terror, because events started by human folly link themselves into a sequence which no sagacity can foresee and no courage can break through. Fatality enters your rooms while your landlady's back is turned; you come home and find it in possession bearing a man's name, clothed in flesh—wearing a brown cloth coat and long boots—lounging against the stove. It asks you, "Is the outer door closed?"—and you don't know enough to take it by the throat and fling it downstairs. You don't know. You welcome the crazy fate. "Sit down," you say. And it is all over. You cannot shake it off any more. It will cling to you for ever. Neither halter nor bullet can give you back the freedom of your life and the sanity of your thought. . . . It was enough to dash one's head against a wall.

Razumov looked slowly all round the walls as if to select a spot to dash his head against. Then he opened the letter. It directed the student Kirylo Sidorovitch Razumov to present himself without delay at the General Secretariat.

Razumov had a vision of General T——'s goggle eyes waiting for him—the embodied power of autocracy, grotesque and terrible. He embodied the whole power of autocracy because he was its guardian. He was the incarnate suspicion, the incarnate anger, the incarnate ruthlessness of a political and social regime on its defence. He loathed rebellion by instinct. And Razumov reflected that the man was simply unable to understand a reasonable adherence to the doctrine of absolutism.

"What can he want with me precisely—I wonder?" he asked himself.

As if that mental question had evoked the familiar phantom, Haldin stood suddenly before him in the room with an extraordinary completeness of detail. Though the short winter day had passed already into the sinister twilight of a land buried in snow, Razumov saw plainly the narrow leather strap round the Tcherkess coat. The illusion of that hateful presence was so perfect that he half expected it to ask, "Is the outer door closed?" He looked at it with hatred and contempt. Souls do not take a shape of clothing. Moreover, Haldin could not be dead yet. Razumov stepped forward menacingly; the vision vanished—and turning short on his heel he walked out of his room with infinite disdain.

But after going down the first flight of stairs it occurred to him that perhaps the superior authorities of police meant to confront him with Haldin in the flesh. This thought struck him like a bullet, and had he not clung with both hands to the banister he would have rolled down to the next landing most likely. His legs were of no use for a considerable time. . . . But why? For what conceivable reason? To what end?

There could be no rational answer to these questions; but Razumov remembered the promise made by the General to Prince K——. His action was to remain unknown.

He got down to the bottom of the stairs, lowering himself as it were from step to step, by the banister. Under the gate he regained much of his firmness of thought and limb. He went out into the street without staggering visibly. Every moment he felt steadier mentally. And yet he was saying to himself that General T—— was perfectly capable of shutting him up in the fortress for an indefinite time. His temperament fitted his remorseless task, and his omnipotence made him inaccessible to reasonable argument.

But when Razumov arrived at the Secretariat he discovered that he would have nothing to do with General T——. It is evident from Mr. Razumov's diary that this dreaded personality was to remain in the background. A civilian of superior rank received him in a private room after a period of waiting in outer offices where a lot of scribbling went on at many tables in a heated and stuffy atmosphere.

The clerk in uniform who conducted him said in the corridor—"You are going before Gregory Matvieitch Mikulin."[1]

There was nothing formidable about the man bearing that name. His mild, expectant glance was turned on the door already

---

1 Likely modeled in part on Aleksei Aleksandrovich Lopukhin (1864-1928). In 1902, de Pleve appointed him Director of the Department of Police in the Ministry of Interior, in which position he served until his retirement in 1905.

when Razumov entered. At once, with the penholder he was holding in his hand, he pointed to a deep sofa between two windows. He followed Razumov with his eyes while that last crossed the room and sat down. The mild gaze rested on him, not curious, not inquisitive—certainly not suspicious—almost without expression. In its passionless persistence there was something resembling sympathy.

Razumov, who had prepared his will and his intelligence to encounter General T—— himself, was profoundly troubled. All the moral bracing up against the possible excesses of power and passion went for nothing before this sallow man, who wore a full unclipped beard. It was fair, thin, and very fine. The light fell in coppery gleams on the protuberances of a high, rugged forehead. And the aspect of the broad, soft physiognomy was so homely and rustic that the careful middle parting of the hair seemed a pretentious affectation.

The diary of Mr. Razumov testifies to some irritation on his part. I may remark here that the diary proper consisting of the more or less daily entries seems to have been begun on that very evening after Mr. Razumov had returned home.

Mr. Razumov, then, was irritated. His strung-up individuality had gone to pieces within him very suddenly.

"I must be very prudent with him," he warned himself in the silence during which they sat gazing at each other. It lasted some little time, and was characterized (for silences have their character) by a sort of sadness imparted to it perhaps by the mild and thoughtful manner of the bearded official. Razumov learned later that he was the chief of a department in the General Secretariat, with a rank in the civil service equivalent to that of a colonel in the army.

Razumov's mistrust became acute. The main point was, not to be drawn into saying too much. He had been called there for some reason. What reason? To be given to understand that he was a suspect—and also no doubt to be pumped. As to what precisely? There was nothing. Or perhaps Haldin had been telling lies. . . . Every alarming uncertainty beset Razumov. He could bear the silence no longer, and cursing himself for his weakness spoke first, though he had promised himself not to do so on any account.

"I haven't lost a moment's time," he began in a hoarse, provoking tone; and then the faculty of speech seemed to leave him and enter the body of Councillor Mikulin, who chimed in approvingly—

"Very proper. Very proper. Though as a matter of fact . . ."

But the spell was broken, and Razumov interrupted him boldly, under a sudden conviction that this was the safest attitude to take. With a great flow of words he complained of being totally misunderstood. Even as he talked with a perception of his own audacity he thought that the word "misunderstood" was better than the word "mistrusted," and he repeated it again with insistence. Suddenly he ceased, being seized with fright before the attentive immobility of the official. "What am I talking about?" he thought, eyeing him with a vague gaze. Mistrusted—not misunderstood—was the right symbol for these people. Misunderstood was the other kind of curse. Both had been brought on his head by that fellow Haldin. And his head ached terribly. He passed his hand over his brow—an involuntary gesture of suffering, which he was too careless to restrain. At that moment Razumov beheld his own brain suffering on the rack—a long, pale figure drawn asunder horizontally with terrific force in the darkness of a vault, whose face he failed to see. It was as though he had dreamed for an infinitesimal fraction of time of some dark print of the Inquisition. . . .[1]

It is not to be seriously supposed that Razumov had actually dozed off and had dreamed in the presence of Councillor Mikulin, of an old print of the Inquisition. He was indeed extremely exhausted, and he records a remarkably dream-like experience of anguish at the circumstance that there was no one whatever near the pale and extended figure. The solitude of the racked victim was particularly horrible to behold. The mysterious impossibility to see the face, he also notes, inspired a sort of terror. All these characteristics of an ugly dream were present. Yet he is certain that he never lost the consciousness of himself on the sofa, leaning forward with his hands between his knees and turning his cap round and round in his fingers. But everything vanished at the voice of Councillor Mikulin. Razumov felt profoundly grateful for the even simplicity of its tone.

"Yes. I have listened with interest. I comprehend in a measure your . . . But, indeed, you are mistaken in what you . . ." Councillor Mikulin uttered a series of broken sentences. Instead of finishing them he glanced down his beard. It was a deliberate curtailment which somehow made the phrases more impressive. But he could talk fluently enough, as became apparent when changing his tone to persuasiveness he went on: "By listening to

---

1   A reference to the Spanish Inquisition, which was first instituted in
    1478 by the Roman Catholic Church to identify and suppress religious
    heresies.

you as I did, I think I have proved that I do not regard our intercourse as strictly official. In fact, I don't want it to have that character at all. . . . Oh yes! I admit that the request for your presence here had an official form. But I put it to you whether it was a form which would have been used to secure the attendance of a . . ."

"Suspect," exclaimed Razumov, looking straight into the official's eyes. They were big with heavy eyelids, and met his boldness with a dim, steadfast gaze. "A suspect." The open repetition of that word which had been haunting all his waking hours gave Razumov a strange sort of satisfaction. Councillor Mikulin shook his head slightly. "Surely you do know that I've had my rooms searched by the police?"

"I was about to say a 'misunderstood person,' when you interrupted me," insinuated quietly Councillor Mikulin.

Razumov smiled without bitterness. The renewed sense of his intellectual superiority sustained him in the hour of danger. He said a little disdainfully—

"I know I am but a reed. But I beg you to allow me the superiority of the thinking reed[1] over the unthinking forces that are about to crush him out of existence. Practical thinking in the last instance is but criticism. I may perhaps be allowed to express my wonder at this action of the police being delayed for two full days during which, of course, I could have annihilated everything compromising by burning it—let us say—and getting rid of the very ashes, for that matter."

"You are angry," remarked the official, with an unutterable simplicity of tone and manner. "Is that reasonable?"

Razumov felt himself colouring with annoyance.

"I am reasonable. I am even—permit me to say—a thinker, though to be sure, this name nowadays seems to be the monopoly of hawkers of revolutionary wares, the slaves of some French or German thought[2]—devil knows what foreign notions. But I

---

1  A reference to Blaise Pascal's *Penseé* 347: "Man is but a reed, the most feeble thing in nature; but he is a thinking reed" (trans. W.F. Trotter, Dutton, 1958, 97).

2  Razumov probably has in mind such French and German thinkers as Henri de Saint-Simon (1760-1825), François-Marie-Charles Fourier (1772-1837), Étienne Cabet (1788-1856), Louis Blanc (1811-82), Louis-Auguste Blanqui (1805-81), and particularly Pierre-Joseph Proudhon (1809-65), Karl Marx (1818-83), and Friedrich Engels (1820-95), who influenced the Anarchist and Socialist movements of the nineteenth century.

am not an intellectual mongrel. I think like a Russian. I think faithfully—and I take the liberty to call myself a thinker. It is not a forbidden word, as far as I know."

"No. Why should it be a forbidden word?" Councillor Mikulin turned in his seat with crossed legs and resting his elbow on the table propped his head on the knuckles of a half-closed hand. Razumov noticed a thick forefinger clasped by a massive gold band set with a blood-red stone—a signet ring that, looking as if it could weigh half a pound, was an appropriate ornament for that ponderous man with the accurate middle-parting of glossy hair above a rugged Socratic[1] forehead.

"Could it be a wig?" Razumov detected himself wondering with an unexpected detachment. His self-confidence was much shaken. He resolved to chatter no more. Reserve! Reserve! All he had to do was to keep the Ziemianitch episode secret with absolute determination, when the questions came. Keep Ziemianitch strictly out of all the answers.

Councillor Mikulin looked at him dimly. Razumov's self-confidence abandoned him completely. It seemed impossible to keep Ziemianitch out. Every question would lead to that, because, of course, there was nothing else. He made an effort to brace himself up. It was a failure. But Councillor Mikulin was surprisingly detached too.

"Why should it be forbidden?" he repeated. "I too consider myself a thinking man, I assure you. The principal condition is to think correctly. I admit it is difficult sometimes at first for a young man abandoned to himself—with his generous impulses undisciplined, so to speak—at the mercy of every wild wind that blows. Religious belief, of course, is a great . . ."

Councillor Mikulin glanced down his beard, and Razumov, whose tension was relaxed by that unexpected and discursive turn, murmured with gloomy discontent—

"That man, Haldin, believed in God."

"Ah! You are aware," breathed out Councillor Mikulin, making the point softly, as if with discretion, but making it nevertheless plainly enough, as if he too were put off his guard by Razumov's remark. The young man preserved an impassive, moody countenance, though he reproached himself bitterly for a pernicious fool, to have given thus an utterly false impression of intimacy. He kept his eyes on the floor. "I must positively hold my tongue

---

1 A reference to the Greek philosopher Socrates (470-399 BC); a noted sculpture of him shows a broad forehead.

unless I am obliged to speak," he admonished himself. And at once against his will the question, "Hadn't I better tell him everything?" presented itself with such force that he had to bite his lower lip. Councillor Mikulin could not, however, have nourished any hope of confession. He went on—

"You tell me more than his judges were able to get out of him. He was judged by a commission of three. He would tell them absolutely nothing. I have the report of the interrogatories here, by me. After every question there stands 'Refuses to answer—refuses to answer.' It's like that page after page. You see, I have been entrusted with some further investigations around and about this affair. He has left me nothing to begin my investigations on. A hardened miscreant. And so, you say, he believed in . . ."

Again Councillor Mikulin glanced down his beard with a faint grimace; but he did not pause for long. Remarking with a shade of scorn that blasphemers also had that sort of belief, he concluded by supposing that Mr. Razumov had conversed frequently with Haldin on the subject.

"No," said Razumov loudly, without looking up. "He talked and I listened. That is not a conversation."

"Listening is a great art," observed Mikulin parenthetically.

"And getting people to talk is another," mumbled Razumov.

"Well, no—that is not very difficult," Mikulin said innocently, "except, of course, in special cases. For instance, this Haldin. Nothing could induce him to talk. He was brought four times before the delegated judges. Four secret interrogatories—and even during the last, when your personality was put forward . . ."

"My personality put forward?" repeated Razumov, raising his head brusquely. "I don't understand."

Councillor Mikulin turned squarely to the table, and taking up some sheets of grey foolscap[1] dropped them one after another, retaining only the last in his hand. He held it before his eyes while speaking.

"It was—you see—judged necessary. In a case of that gravity no means of action upon the culprit should be neglected. You understand that yourself, I am certain."

Razumov stared with enormous wide eyes at the side view of Councillor Mikulin, who now was not looking at him at all.

"So it was decided (I was consulted by General T——) that a

---

1  A sheet of writing paper roughly 16¾" x 13½," originally called such for the watermark in the shape of a fool's cap which appeared on it. Foolscap for purposes other than writing came in other sizes.

certain question should be put to the accused. But in deference to the earnest wishes of Prince K—— your name has been kept out of the documents and even from the very knowledge of the judges themselves. Prince K—— recognized the propriety, the necessity of what we proposed to do, but he was concerned for your safety. Things do leak out—that we can't deny. One cannot always answer for the discretion of inferior officials. There was, of course, the secretary of the special tribunal—one or two gendarmes in the room. Moreover, as I have said, in deference to Prince K—— even the judges themselves were to be left in ignorance. The question ready framed was sent to them by General T—— (I wrote it out with my own hand) with instructions to put it to the prisoner the very last of all. Here it is."

Councillor Mikulin threw back his head into proper focus and went on reading monotonously: "Question—Has the man well known to you, in whose rooms you remained for several hours on Monday and on whose information you have been arrested—has he had any previous knowledge of your intention to commit a political murder? . . . Prisoner refuses to reply.

"Question repeated. Prisoner preserves the same stubborn silence.

"The venerable Chaplain of the Fortress being then admitted and exhorting the prisoner to repentance, entreating him also to atone for his crime by an unreserved and full confession which should help to liberate from the sin of rebellion against the Divine laws and the sacred Majesty of the Ruler, our Christ-loving land—the prisoner opens his lips for the first time during this morning's audience and in a loud, clear voice rejects the venerable Chaplain's ministrations.

"At eleven o'clock the Court pronounces in summary form the death sentence.

"The execution is fixed for four o'clock in the afternoon, subject to further instructions from superior authorities."

Councillor Mikulin dropped the page of foolscap, glanced down his beard, and turning to Razumov, added in an easy, explanatory tone—

"We saw no object in delaying the execution. The order to carry out the sentence was sent by telegraph at noon. I wrote out the telegram myself. He was hanged at four o'clock this afternoon."

The definite information of Haldin's death gave Razumov the feeling of general lassitude which follows a great exertion or a great excitement. He kept very still on the sofa, but a murmur escaped him—

"He had a belief in a future existence."

Councillor Mikulin shrugged his shoulders slightly, and Razumov got up with an effort. There was nothing now to stay for in that room. Haldin had been hanged at four o'clock. There could be no doubt of that. He had, it seemed, entered upon his future existence, long boots, Astrakhan fur cap and all, down to the very leather strap round his waist. A flickering, vanishing sort of existence. It was not his soul, it was his mere phantom he had left behind on this earth—thought Razumov, smiling caustically to himself while he crossed the room, utterly forgetful of where he was and of Councillor Mikulin's existence. The official could have set a lot of bells ringing all over the building without leaving his chair. He let Razumov go quite up to the door before he spoke.

"Come, Kirylo Sidorovitch—what are you doing?"

Razumov turned his head and looked at him in silence. He was not in the least disconcerted. Councillor Mikulin's arms were stretched out on the table before him and his body leaned forward a little with an effort of his dim gaze.

"Was I actually going to clear out like this?" Razumov wondered at himself with an impassive countenance. And he was aware of this impassiveness concealing a lucid astonishment.

"Evidently I was going out if he had not spoken," he thought. "What would he have done then? I must end this affair one way or another. I must make him show his hand."

For a moment longer he reflected behind the mask as it were, then let go the door-handle and came back to the middle of the room.

"I'll tell you what you think," he said explosively, but not raising his voice. "You think that you are dealing with a secret accomplice of that unhappy man. No, I do not know that he was unhappy. He did not tell me. He was a wretch from my point of view, because to keep alive a false idea is a greater crime than to kill a man. I suppose you will not deny that? I hated him! Visionaries work everlasting evil on earth. Their Utopias inspire in the mass of mediocre minds a disgust of reality and a contempt for the secular logic of human development."

Razumov shrugged his shoulders and stared. "What a tirade!" he thought. The silence and immobility of Councillor Mikulin impressed him. The bearded bureaucrat sat at his post, mysteriously self-possessed like an idol with dim, unreadable eyes. Razumov's voice changed involuntarily.

"If you were to ask me where is the necessity of my hate for such as Haldin, I would answer you—there is nothing sentimental in it. I did not hate him because he had committed the crime of murder. Abhorrence is not hate. I hated him simply because I am sane. It is in that character that he outraged me. His death . . ."

Razumov felt his voice growing thick in his throat. The dimness of Councillor Mikulin's eyes seemed to spread all over his face and made it indistinct to Razumov's sight. He tried to disregard these phenomena.

"Indeed," he pursued, pronouncing each word carefully, "what is his death to me? If he were lying here on the floor I could walk over his breast. . . . The fellow is a mere phantom. . . ."

Razumov's voice died out very much against his will. Mikulin behind the table did not allow himself the slightest movement. The silence lasted for some little time before Razumov could go on again.

"He went about talking of me. . . . Those intellectual fellows sit in each other's rooms and get drunk on foreign ideas in the same way young Guards' officers treat each other with foreign wines. Merest debauchery. . . . Upon my word,"—Razumov, enraged by a sudden recollection of Ziemianitch, lowered his voice forcibly,—"upon my word, we Russians are a drunken lot. Intoxication of some sort we must have: to get ourselves wild with sorrow or maudlin with resignation; to lie inert like a log or set fire to the house. What is a sober man to do, I should like to know? To cut oneself entirely from one's kind is impossible. To live in a desert one must be a saint. But if a drunken man runs out of the grog-shop,[1] falls on your neck and kisses you on both cheeks because something about your appearance has taken his fancy, what then—kindly tell me? You may break, perhaps, a cudgel on his back and yet not succeed in beating him off. . . ."

Councillor Mikulin raised his hand and passed it down his face deliberately.

"That's . . . of course," he said in an undertone.

The quiet gravity of that gesture made Razumov pause. It was so unexpected, too. What did it mean? It had an alarming aloofness. Razumov remembered his intention of making him show his hand.

"I have said all this to Prince K——," he began with assumed indifference, but lost it on seeing Councillor Mikulin's slow nod of assent. "You know it? You've heard . . . Then why should I be called here to be told of Haldin's execution? Did you want to confront me with his silence now that the man is dead? What is

---

1 A somewhat disreputable drinking establishment.

his silence to me? This is incomprehensible. You want in some way to shake my moral balance."

"No. Not that," murmured Councillor Mikulin, just audibly. "The service you have rendered is appreciated . . ."

"Is it?" interrupted Razumov ironically.

". . . and your position too." Councillor Mikulin did not raise his voice. "But only think! You fall into Prince K——'s study as if from the sky with your startling information. . . . You are studying yet, Mr. Razumov, but we are serving already—don't forget that. . . . And naturally some curiosity was bound to . . ."

Councillor Mikulin looked down his beard. Razumov's lips trembled.

"An occurrence of that sort marks a man," the homely murmur went on. "I admit I was curious to see you. General T—— thought it would be useful, too. . . . Don't think I am incapable of understanding your sentiments. When I was young like you I studied . . ."

"Yes—you wished to see me," said Razumov in a tone of profound distaste. "Naturally you have the right—I mean the power. It all amounts to the same thing. But it is perfectly useless, if you were to look at me and listen to me for a year. I begin to think there is something about me which people don't seem able to make out. It's unfortunate. I imagine, however, that Prince K—— understands. He seemed to."

Councillor Mikulin moved slightly and spoke.

"Prince K—— is aware of everything that is being done, and I don't mind informing you that he approved my intention of becoming personally acquainted with you."

Razumov concealed an immense disappointment under the accents of railing surprise.

"So he is curious too! . . . Well—after all, Prince K—— knows me very little. It is really very unfortunate for me, but—it is not exactly my fault."

Councillor Mikulin raised a hasty deprecatory hand and inclined his head slightly over his shoulder.

"Now, Mr. Razumov—is it necessary to take it in that way? Everybody I am sure can . . ."

He glanced rapidly down his beard, and when he looked up again there was for a moment an interested expression in his misty gaze. Razumov discouraged it with a cold, repellent smile.

"No. That's of no importance to be sure—except that in respect of all this curiosity being aroused by a very simple matter. . . . What is to be done with it? It is unappeasable. I mean to say there is nothing to appease it with. I happen to have been born a Russian with patriotic instincts—whether inherited or not I am not in a position to say."

Razumov spoke consciously with elaborate steadiness.

"Yes, patriotic instincts developed by a faculty of independent thinking—of detached thinking. In that respect I am more free than any social democratic revolution[1] could make me. It is more than probable that I don't think exactly as you are thinking. Indeed, how could it be? You would think most likely at this moment that I am elaborately lying to cover up the track of my repentance."

Razumov stopped. His heart had grown too big for his breast. Councillor Mikulin did not flinch.

"Why so?" he said simply. "I assisted personally at the search of your rooms. I looked through all the papers myself. I have been greatly impressed by a sort of political confession of faith. A very remarkable document. Now may I ask for what purpose . . ."

"To deceive the police naturally," said Razumov savagely. . . . "What is all this mockery? Of course, you can send me straight from this room to Siberia. That would be intelligible. To what is intelligible I can submit. But I protest against this comedy of persecution. The whole affair is becoming too comical altogether for my taste. A comedy of errors, phantoms, and suspicions. It's positively indecent . . ."

Councillor Mikulin turned an attentive ear.

"Did you say phantoms?" he murmured.

"I could walk over dozens of them." Razumov, with an impatient wave of his hand, went on headlong, "But, really, I must claim the right to be done once for all with that man. And in order to accomplish this I shall take the liberty . . ."

Razumov on his side of the table bowed slightly to the seated bureaucrat.

". . . To retire—simply to retire," he finished with great resolution.

He walked to the door, thinking, "Now he must show his hand. He must ring and have me arrested before I am out of the building, or he must let me go. And either way . . ."

An unhurried voice said—

"Kirylo Sidorovitch."

Razumov at the door turned his head.

"To retire," he repeated.

"Where to?" asked Councillor Mikulin softly.

---

1   Perhaps a reference to the Socialist-Revolutionary Party, which was responsible for de Pleve's assassination.

# PART SECOND

## I

In the conduct of an invented story there are, no doubt, certain proprieties to be observed for the sake of clearness and effect. A man of imagination, however inexperienced in the art of narrative, has his instinct to guide him in the choice of his words, and in the development of the action. A grain of talent excuses many mistakes. But this is not a work of imagination; I have no talent; my excuse for this undertaking lies not in its art, but in its artlessness. Aware of my limitations and strong in the sincerity of my purpose, I would not try (were I able) to invent anything. I push my scruples so far that I would not even invent a transition.

Dropping then Mr. Razumov's record at the point where Councillor Mikulin's question "Where to?" comes in with the force of an insoluble problem, I shall simply say that I made the acquaintance of these ladies about six months before that time. By "these ladies" I mean, of course, the mother and the sister of the unfortunate Haldin.

By what arguments he had induced his mother to sell their little property and go abroad for an indefinite time, I cannot tell precisely. I have an idea that Mrs. Haldin, at her son's wish, would have set fire to her house and emigrated to the moon without any sign of surprise or apprehension; and that Miss Haldin—Nathalie, caressingly Natalka—would have given her assent to the scheme.

Their proud devotion to that young man became clear to me in a very short time. Following his directions they went straight to Switzerland—to Zürich[1]—where they remained the best part of a year. From Zürich, which they did not like, they came to Geneva. A friend of mine in Lausanne,[2] a lecturer in history at the University (he had married a Russian lady, a distant connection of Mrs. Haldin's), wrote to me suggesting I should call on these ladies. It was a very kindly meant business suggestion. Miss Haldin wished to go through a course of reading the best English authors with a competent teacher.

---

1  A city in northern Switzerland.
2  A city in western Switzerland, near Geneva. The University of Lausanne, founded in 1537, is one of the premier universities in Switzerland today.

Mrs. Haldin received me very kindly. Her bad French, of which she was smilingly conscious, did away with the formality of the first interview. She was a tall woman in a black silk dress. A wide brow, regular features, and delicately cut lips, testified to her past beauty. She sat upright in an easy chair and in a rather weak, gentle voice told me that her Natalka simply thirsted after knowledge. Her thin hands were lying on her lap, her facial immobility had in it something monachal.[1] "In Russia," she went on, "all knowledge was tainted with falsehood. Not chemistry and all that, but education generally," she explained. The Government corrupted the teaching for its own purposes. Both her children felt that. Her Natalka had obtained a diploma of a Superior School for Women and her son was a student at the St. Petersburg University. He had a brilliant intellect, a most noble unselfish nature, and he was the oracle of his comrades. Early next year, she hoped he would join them and they would then go to Italy together. In any other country but their own she would have been certain of a great future for a man with the extraordinary abilities and the lofty character of her son—but in Russia . . .

The young lady sitting by the window turned her head and said—

"Come, mother. Even with us things change with years."

Her voice was deep, almost harsh, and yet caressing in its harshness. She had a dark complexion, with red lips and a full figure. She gave the impression of strong vitality. The old lady sighed.

"You are both young—you two. It is easy for you to hope. But I, too, am not hopeless. Indeed, how could I be with a son like this?"

I addressed Miss Haldin, asking her what authors she wished to read. She directed upon me her grey eyes shaded by black eyelashes, and I became aware, notwithstanding my years, how attractive physically her personality could be to a man capable of appreciating in a woman something else than the mere grace of femininity. Her glance was as direct and trustful as that of a young man yet unspoiled by the world's wise lessons. And it was intrepid, but in this intrepidity there was nothing aggressive. A naïve yet thoughtful assurance is a better definition. She had reflected already (in Russia the young begin to think early), but she had never known deception as yet because obviously she had never yet fallen under the sway of passion. She was—to look at her was enough—very

1 Monkish or relating to monastic life.

capable of being roused by an idea or simply by a person. At least, so I judged with I believe an unbiassed mind; for clearly my person could not be the person—and as to my ideas! . . .

We became excellent friends in the course of our reading. It was very pleasant. Without fear of provoking a smile, I shall confess that I became very much attached to that young girl. At the end of four months I told her that now she could very well go on reading English by herself. It was time for the teacher to depart. My pupil looked unpleasantly surprised.

Mrs. Haldin, with her immobility of feature and kindly expression of the eyes, uttered from her armchair in her uncertain French, "*Mais l'ami reviendra.*"[1] And so it was settled. I returned—not four times a week as before, but pretty frequently. In the autumn we made some short excursions together in company with other Russians. My friendship with these ladies gave me a standing in the Russian colony which otherwise I could not have had.

The day I saw in the papers the news of Mr. de P——'s assassination—it was a Sunday—I met the two ladies in the street and walked with them for some distance. Mrs. Haldin wore a heavy grey cloak, I remember, over her black silk dress, and her fine eyes met mine with a very quiet expression.

"We have been to the late service," she said. "Natalka came with me. Her girl-friends, the students here, of course don't. . . . With us in Russia the church is so identified with oppression, that it seems almost necessary when one wishes to be free in this life, to give up all hope of a future existence. But I cannot give up praying for my son."

She added with a sort of stony grimness, colouring slightly, and in French, "*Ce n'est peut être qu'une habitude.*" ("It may be only habit.")

Miss Haldin was carrying two prayer-books.[2] She did not glance at her mother.

"You and Victor are both profound believers," she said.

I communicated to them the news from their country which I had just read in a café. For a whole minute we walked together fairly briskly in silence. Then Mrs. Haldin murmured—

"There will be more trouble, more persecutions for this. They may be even closing the University. There is neither peace nor rest in Russia for one but in the grave."

---

1 But the friend will return (French).
2 The first English edition has "carrying the prayer-book" (M, AS).

"Yes. The way is hard," came from the daughter, looking straight before her at the Chain of Jura[1] covered with snow, like a white wall closing the end of the street. "But concord is not so very far off."

"That is what my children think," observed Mrs. Haldin to me.

I did not conceal my feeling that these were strange times to talk of concord. Nathalie Haldin surprised me by saying, as if she had thought very much on the subject, that the occidentals[2] did not understand the situation. She was very calm and youthfully superior.

"You think it is a class conflict, or a conflict of interests, as social contests are with you in Europe. But it is not that at all. It is something quite different."

"It is quite possible that I don't understand," I admitted.

That propensity of lifting every problem from the plane of the understandable by means of some sort of mystic expression, is very Russian. I knew her well enough to have discovered her scorn for all the practical forms of political liberty known to the Western world. I suppose one must be a Russian to understand Russian simplicity, a terrible corroding simplicity in which mystic phrases clothe a naïve and hopeless cynicism. I think sometimes that the psychological secret of the profound difference of that people consists in this, that they detest life, the irremediable life of the earth as it is, whereas we Westerners cherish it with perhaps an equal exaggeration of its sentimental value. But this is a digression indeed. . . .

I helped these ladies into the tramcar[3] and they asked me to call in the afternoon. At least Mrs. Haldin asked me as she climbed up, and her Natalka smiled down at the dense Westerner indulgently from the rear platform of the moving car. The light of the clear wintry forenoon was softened in her grey eyes.

Mr. Razumov's record, like the open book of fate, revives for me the memory of that day as something startlingly pitiless in its freedom from all forebodings. Victor Haldin was still with the living, but with the living whose only contact with life is the expectation of death. He must have been already referring to the

---

1  Mountain range bordering France and Switzerland and extending into both countries.
2  Westerners or western Europeans, as opposed to those from eastern Europe.
3  Streetcar.

last of his earthly affections, the hours of that obstinate silence, which for him was to be prolonged into eternity. That afternoon the ladies entertained a good many of their compatriots—more than was usual for them to receive at one time; and the drawing-room on the ground floor of a large house on the Boulevard des Philosophes was very much crowded.

I outstayed everybody; and when I rose Miss Haldin stood up too. I took her hand and was moved to revert to that morning's conversation in the street.

"Admitting that we occidentals do not understand the character of your people . . ." I began.

It was as if she had been prepared for me by some mysterious foreknowledge. She checked me gently—

"Their impulses—their . . ." she sought the proper expression and found it, but in French . . . "their *mouvements d'âme*."[1]

Her voice was not much above a whisper.

"Very well," I said. "But still we are looking at a conflict. You say it is not a conflict of classes and not a conflict of interests. Suppose I admitted that. Are antagonistic ideas then to be reconciled more easily—can they be cemented with blood and violence into that concord which you proclaim to be so near?"

She looked at me searchingly with her clear grey eyes, without answering my reasonable question—my obvious, my unanswerable question.

"It is inconceivable," I added, with something like annoyance.

"Everything is inconceivable," she said. "The whole world is inconceivable to the strict logic of ideas. And yet the world exists to our senses, and we exist in it. There must be a necessity superior to our conceptions. It is a very miserable and a very false thing to belong to the majority. We Russians shall find some better form of national freedom than an artificial conflict of parties—which is wrong because it is a conflict and contemptible because it is artificial. It is left for us Russians to discover a better way."

Mrs. Haldin had been looking out of the window. She turned upon me the almost lifeless beauty of her face, and the living benign glance of her big dark eyes.

"That's what my children think," she declared.

"I suppose," I addressed Miss Haldin, "that you will be shocked if I tell you that I haven't understood—I won't say a single word; I've understood all the words. . . . But what can be

---

1 Movements or impulses of the soul (French).

this era of disembodied concord you are looking forward to? Life is a thing of form. It has its plastic shape and a definite intellectual aspect. The most idealistic conceptions of love and forbearance must be clothed in flesh as it were before they can be made understandable."

I took my leave of Mrs. Haldin, whose beautiful lips never stirred. She smiled with her eyes only. Nathalie Haldin went with me as far as the door, very amiable.

"Mother imagines that I am the slavish echo of my brother Victor. It is not so. He understands me better than I can understand him. When he joins us and you come to know him you will see what an exceptional soul it is." She paused. "He is not a strong man in the conventional sense, you know," she added. "But his character is without a flaw."

"I believe that it will not be difficult for me to make friends with your brother Victor."

"Don't expect to understand him quite," she said, a little maliciously. "He is not at all—at all—Western at bottom."

And on this unnecessary warning I left the room with another bow in the doorway to Mrs. Haldin in her armchair by the window. The shadow of autocracy all unperceived by me had already fallen upon the Boulevard des Philosophes, in the free, independent and democratic city of Geneva, where there is a quarter called "La Petite Russie." Whenever two Russians come together, the shadow of autocracy is with them, tinging their thoughts, their views, their most intimate feelings, their private life, their public utterances—haunting the secret of their silences.

What struck me next in the course of a week or so was the silence of these ladies. I used to meet them walking in the public garden near the University. They greeted me with their usual friendliness, but I could not help noticing their taciturnity. By that time it was generally known that the assassin of M. de P—— had been caught, judged, and executed. So much had been declared officially to the news agencies. But for the world at large he remained anonymous. The official secrecy had withheld his name from the public. I really cannot imagine for what reason.

One day I saw Miss Haldin walking alone in the main alley of the Bastions[1] under the naked trees.

"Mother is not very well," she explained.

---

1   The Parc des Bastions, a park built upon the spot of the former
    Geneva city walls. The first English edition has "valley of the Bastions"
    (AS, A1).

As Mrs. Haldin had, it seemed, never had a day's illness in her life, this indisposition was disquieting. It was nothing definite, too.

"I think she is fretting because we have not heard from my brother for rather a long time."

"No news—good news," I said cheerfully, and we began to walk slowly side by side.

"Not in Russia," she breathed out so low that I only just caught the words. I looked at her with more attention.

"You too are anxious?"

She admitted after a moment of hesitation that she was.

"It is really such a long time since we heard . . ."

And before I could offer the usual banal suggestions she confided in me.

"Oh! But it is much worse than that. I wrote to a family we know in Petersburg. They had not seen him for more than a month. They thought he was already with us. They were even offended a little that he should have left Petersburg without calling on them. The husband of the lady went at once to his lodgings. Victor had left there and they did not know his address."

I remember her catching her breath rather pitifully. Her brother had not been seen at lectures for a very long time either. He only turned up now and then at the University gate to ask the porter for his letters. And the gentleman friend was told that the student Haldin did not come to claim the last two letters for him. But the police came to inquire if the student Haldin ever received any correspondence at the University and took them away.

"My two last letters," she said.

We faced each other. A few snow-flakes fluttered under the naked boughs. The sky was dark.

"What do you think could have happened?" I asked.

Her shoulders moved slightly.

"One can never tell—in Russia."

I saw then the shadow of autocracy lying upon Russian lives in their submission or their revolt. I saw it touch her handsome open face nestled in a fur collar and darken her clear eyes that shone upon me brilliantly grey in the murky light of a beclouded, inclement afternoon.

"Let us move on," she said. "It is cold standing—to-day."

She shuddered a little and stamped her little feet. We moved briskly to the end of the alley and back to the great gates of the garden.

"Have you told your mother?" I ventured to ask.

"No. Not yet. I came out to walk off the impression of this letter."

I heard a rustle of paper somewhere. It came from her muff. She had the letter with her in there.

"What is it that you are afraid of?" I asked.

To us Europeans of the West, all ideas of political plots and conspiracies seem childish, crude inventions for the theatre or a novel. I did not like to be more definite in my inquiry.

"For us—for my mother specially, what I am afraid of is incertitude. People do disappear. Yes, they do disappear. I leave you to imagine what it is—the cruelty of the dumb weeks—months—years! This friend of ours has abandoned his inquiries when he heard of the police getting hold of the letters. I suppose he was afraid of compromising himself. He has a wife and children—and why should he, after all. . . . Moreover, he is without influential connections and not rich. What could he do? . . . Yes, I am afraid of silence—for my poor mother. She won't be able to bear it. For my brother I am afraid of . . ." she became almost indistinct, "of anything."

We were now near the gate opposite the theatre. She raised her voice.

"But lost people do turn up even in Russia. Do you know what my last hope is? Perhaps the next thing we know, we shall see him walking into our rooms."

I raised my hat and she passed out of the gardens, graceful and strong, after a slight movement of the head to me, her hands in the muff, crumpling the cruel Petersburg letter.

On returning home I opened the newspaper I receive from London, and glancing down the correspondence from Russia— not the telegrams but the correspondence—the first thing that caught my eye was the name of Haldin. Mr. de P——'s death was no longer an actuality,[1] but the enterprising correspondent was proud of having ferreted out some unofficial information about that fact of modern history. He had got hold of Haldin's name, and had picked up the story of the midnight arrest in the street. But the sensation from a journalistic point of view was already well in the past. He did not allot to it more than twenty lines out of a full column. It was quite enough to give me a sleepless night. I perceived that it would have been a sort of treason to let Miss Haldin come without preparation upon that journalistic discov-

---

1  A current event and therefore newsworthy.

ery which would infallibly be reproduced on the morrow by French and Swiss newspapers. I had a very bad time of it till the morning, wakeful with nervous worry and night-marish with the feeling of being mixed up with something theatrical and morbidly affected. The incongruity of such a complication in those two women's lives was sensible to me all night in the form of absolute anguish. It seemed due to their refined simplicity that it should remain concealed from them for ever. Arriving at an unconscionably early hour at the door of their apartment, I felt as if I were about to commit an act of vandalism. . . .

The middle-aged servant woman led me into the drawing-room where there was a duster on a chair and a broom leaning against the centre table. The motes[1] danced in the sunshine; I regretted I had not written a letter instead of coming myself, and was thankful for the brightness of the day. Miss Haldin in a plain black dress came lightly out of her mother's room with a fixed uncertain smile on her lips.

I pulled the paper out of my pocket. I did not imagine that a number of the *Standard*[2] could have the effect of Medusa's head.[3] Her face went stony in a moment—her eyes—her limbs. The most terrible thing was that being stony she remained alive. One was conscious of her palpitating heart. I hope she forgave me the delay of my clumsy circumlocution. It was not very prolonged; she could not have kept so still from head to foot for more than a second or two; and then I heard her draw a breath. As if the shock had paralysed her moral resistance, and affected the firmness of her muscles, the contours of her face seemed to have given way. She was frightfully altered. She looked aged—ruined. But only for a moment. She said with decision—

"I am going to tell my mother at once."

"Would that be safe in her state?" I objected.

"What can be worse than the state she has been in for the last month? We understand this in another way. The crime is not at his door. Don't imagine I am defending him before you."

She went to the bedroom door, then came back to ask me in a low murmur not to go till she returned. For twenty inter-

---

1 Particles of dust.
2 A London newspaper established in 1827 and still published today as the *Evening Standard*.
3 A monstrous female creature from Greek mythology, whose hair was made of live snakes and whose gaze would turn other creatures to stone.

minable minutes not a sound reached me. At last Miss Haldin came out and walked across the room with her quick light step. When she reached the armchair she dropped into it heavily as if completely exhausted.

Mrs. Haldin, she told me, had not shed a tear. She was sitting up in bed, and her immobility, her silence, were very alarming. At last she lay down gently and had motioned her daughter away.

"She will call me in presently," added Miss Haldin. "I left a bell near the bed."

I confess that my very real sympathy had no standpoint. The Western readers for whom this story is written will understand what I mean. It was, if I may say so, the want of experience. Death is a remorseless spoliator.[1] The anguish of irreparable loss is familiar to us all. There is no life so lonely as to be safe against that experience. But the grief I had brought to these two ladies had gruesome associations. It had the associations of bombs and gallows—a lurid, Russian colouring which made the complexion of my sympathy uncertain.

I was grateful to Miss Haldin for not embarrassing me by an outward display of deep feeling. I admired her for that wonderful command over herself, even while I was a little frightened at it. It was the stillness of a great tension. What if it should suddenly snap? Even the door of Mrs. Haldin's room, with the old mother alone in there, had a rather awful aspect.

Nathalie Haldin murmured sadly—

"I suppose you are wondering what my feelings are?"

Essentially that was true. It was that very wonder which unsettled my sympathy of a dense Occidental. I could get hold of nothing but of some commonplace phrases, those futile phrases that give the measure of our impotence before each other's trials. I mumbled something to the effect that, for the young, life held its hopes and compensations. It held duties too—but of that I was certain it was not necessary to remind her.

She had a handkerchief in her hands and pulled at it nervously.

"I am not likely to forget my mother," she said. "We used to be three. Now we are two—two women. She's not so very old. She may live quite a long time yet. What have we to look for in the future? For what hope and what consolation?"

"You must take a wider view," I said resolutely, thinking that with this exceptional creature this was the right note to strike. She looked at me steadily for a moment, and then the tears she

---

1 One who plunders or despoils.

had been keeping down flowed unrestrained. She jumped up and stood in the window with her back to me.

I slipped away without attempting even to approach her. Next day I was told at the door that Mrs. Haldin was better. The middle-aged servant remarked that a lot of people—Russians—had called that day, but Miss Haldin had not seen anybody. A fortnight later, when making my daily call, I was asked in and found Mrs. Haldin sitting in her usual place by the window.

At first one would have thought that nothing was changed. I saw across the room the familiar profile, a little sharper in outline and overspread by a uniform pallor as might have been expected in an invalid. But no disease could have accounted for the change in her black eyes, smiling no longer with gentle irony. She raised them as she gave me her hand. I observed the three weeks' old number of the *Standard* folded with the correspondence from Russia uppermost, lying on a little table by the side of the armchair. Mrs. Haldin's voice was startlingly weak and colourless. Her first words to me framed a question.

"Has there been anything more in your newspapers?"

I released her long emaciated hand, shook my head negatively, and sat down.

"The English press is wonderful. Nothing can be kept secret from it, and all the world must hear. Only our Russian news is not always easy to understand. Not always easy. . . . But English mothers do not look for news like that . . ."

She laid her hand on the newspaper and took it away again. I said—

"We too have had tragic times in our history."

"A long time ago. A very long time ago."

"Yes."

"There are nations that have made their bargain with fate," said Miss Haldin, who had approached us. "We need not envy them."

"Why this scorn?" I asked gently. "It may be that our bargain was not a very lofty one. But the terms men and nations obtain from Fate are hallowed by the price."

Mrs. Haldin turned her head away and looked out of the window for a time, with that new, sombre, extinct gaze of her sunken eyes which so completely made another woman of her.

"That Englishman, this correspondent," she addressed me suddenly, "do you think it is possible that he knew my son?"

To this strange question I could only say that it was possible of course. She saw my surprise.

"If one knew what sort of man he was one could perhaps write to him," she murmured.

"Mother thinks," explained Miss Haldin, standing between us, with one hand resting on the back of my chair, "that my poor brother perhaps did not try to save himself."

I looked up at Miss Haldin in sympathetic consternation, but Miss Haldin was looking down calmly at her mother. The latter said—

"We do not know the addresses[1] of any of his friends. Indeed, we know nothing of his Petersburg comrades. He had a multitude of young friends, only he never spoke much of them. One could guess that they were his disciples and that they idolized him. But he was so modest. One would think that with so many devoted . . ."

She averted her head again and looked down the Boulevard des Philosophes, a singularly arid and dusty thoroughfare, where nothing could be seen at the moment but two dogs, a little girl in a pinafore hopping on one leg, and in the distance a workman wheeling a bicycle.

"Even amongst the Apostles of Christ there was found a Judas," she whispered as if to herself, but with the evident intention to be heard by me.

The Russian visitors assembled in little knots, conversed amongst themselves meantime, in low murmurs, and with brief glances in our direction. It was a great contrast to the usual loud volubility of these gatherings. Miss Haldin followed me into the ante-room.

"People will come," she said. "We cannot shut the door in their faces."

While I was putting on my overcoat she began to talk to me of her mother. Poor Mrs. Haldin was fretting after more news. She wanted to go on hearing about her unfortunate son. She could not make up her mind to abandon him quietly to the dumb unknown. She would persist in pursuing him in there through the long days of motionless silence face to face with the empty Boulevard des Philosophes. She could not understand why he had not escaped—as so many other revolutionists and conspirators had managed to escape in other instances of that kind. It was really inconceivable that the means of secret revolutionary organisations should have failed so inexcusably to preserve her son. But in reality the inconceivable that staggered her mind was nothing

---

1  The first English edition has "address" (M, T).

but the cruel audacity of Death passing over her head to strike at that young and precious heart.

Miss Haldin mechanically, with an absorbed look, handed me my hat. I understood from her that the poor woman was possessed by the sombre and simple idea that her son must have perished because he did not want to be saved. It could not have been that he despaired of his country's future. That was impossible. Was it possible that his mother and sister had not known how to merit his confidence; and that, after having done what he was compelled to do, his spirit became crushed by an intolerable doubt, his mind distracted by a sudden mistrust?

I was very much shocked by this piece of ingenuity.

"Our three lives were like that!" Miss Haldin twined the fingers of both her hands together in demonstration, then separated them slowly, looking straight into my face. "That's what poor mother found to torment herself and me with, for all the years to come," added the strange girl. At that moment her indefinable charm was revealed to me in the conjunction of passion and stoicism. I imagined what her life was likely to be by the side of Mrs. Haldin's terrible immobility, inhabited by that fixed idea. But my concern was reduced to silence by my ignorance of her modes of feeling. Difference of nationality is a terrible obstacle for our complex Western natures. But Miss Haldin probably was too simple to suspect my embarrassment. She did not wait for me to say anything, but as if reading my thoughts on my face she went on courageously—

"At first poor mother went numb, as our peasants say; then she began to think and she will go on now thinking and thinking in that unfortunate strain. You see yourself how cruel that is. . . ."

I never spoke with greater sincerity than when I agreed with her that it would be deplorable in the highest degree. She took an anxious breath.

"But all these strange details in the English paper," she exclaimed suddenly. "What is the meaning of them? I suppose they are true. But is it not terrible that my poor brother should be caught wandering alone, as if in despair, about the streets at night? . . ."

We stood so close to each other in the dark ante-room that I could see her biting her lower lip to suppress a dry sob. After a short pause she said—

"I suggested to mother that he may have been betrayed by some false friend or simply by some cowardly creature. It may be easier for her to believe that."

I understood now the poor woman's whispered allusion to Judas.

"It may be easier," I admitted, admiring inwardly the directness and the subtlety of the girl's outlook. She was dealing with life as it was made for her by the political conditions of her country. She faced cruel realities, not morbid imaginings of her own making. I could not defend myself from a certain feeling of respect when she added simply—

"Time they say can soften every sort of bitterness. But I cannot believe that it has any power over remorse. It is better that mother should think some person guilty of Victor's death, than that she should connect it with a weakness of her son or a shortcoming of her own."

"But you, yourself, don't suppose that . . ." I began.

She compressed her lips and shook her head. She harboured no evil thoughts against any one, she declared—and perhaps nothing that happened was unnecessary. On these words, pronounced low and sounding mysterious in the half obscurity of the ante-room, we parted with an expressive and warm handshake. The grip of her strong, shapely hand had a seductive frankness, a sort of exquisite virility. I do not know why she should have felt so friendly to me. It may be that she thought I understood her much better than I was able to do. The most precise of her sayings seemed always to me to have enigmatical prolongations vanishing somewhere beyond my reach. I am reduced to suppose that she appreciated my attention and my silence. The attention she could see was quite sincere, so that the silence could not be suspected of coldness. It seemed to satisfy her. And it is to be noted that if she confided in me it was clearly not with the expectation of receiving advice, for which, indeed, she never asked.

## II

Our daily relations were interrupted at this period for something like a fortnight. I had to absent myself unexpectedly from Geneva. On my return I lost no time in directing my steps up the Boulevard des Philosophes.

Through the open door of the drawing-room I was annoyed to hear a visitor holding forth steadily in an unctuous deep voice.

Mrs. Haldin's armchair by the window stood empty. On the sofa, Nathalie Haldin raised her charming grey eyes in a glance of greeting accompanied by the merest hint of a welcoming smile.

But she made no movement. With her strong white hands lying inverted in the lap of her mourning dress she faced a man[1] who presented to me a robust back covered with black broadcloth, and well in keeping with the deep voice. He turned his head sharply over his shoulder, but only for a moment.

"Ah! your English friend. I know. I know. That's nothing."

He wore spectacles with smoked glasses, a tall silk hat stood on the floor by the side of his chair. Flourishing slightly a big soft hand he went on with his discourse, precipitating his delivery a little more.

"I have never changed the faith I held while wandering in the forests and bogs of Siberia. It sustained me then—it sustains me now. The great Powers of Europe[2] are bound to disappear—and the cause of their collapse will be very simple. They will exhaust themselves struggling against their proletariat. In Russia it is different. In Russia we have no classes to combat each other, one holding the power of wealth, and the other mighty with the strength of numbers. We have only an unclean bureaucracy in the face of a people as great and as incorruptible as the ocean. No, we have no classes. But we have the Russian woman. The admirable Russian woman! I receive most remarkable letters signed by women. So elevated in tone, so courageous, breathing such a noble ardour of service! The greatest part of our hopes rests on women. I behold their thirst for knowledge. It is admirable. Look how they absorb, how they are making it their own. It is miraculous. But what is knowledge? . . . I understand that you have not been studying anything especially—medicine[3] for instance. No? That's right. Had I been honoured by being asked to advise you on the use of your time when you arrived here I would have been strongly opposed to such a course. Knowledge in itself is mere dross."

He had one of those bearded Russian faces without shape, a mere appearance of flesh and hair with not a single feature having any sort of character. His eyes being hidden by the dark glasses there was an utter absence of all expression. I knew him by sight. He was a Russian refugee of mark. All Geneva knew his burly

---

1  Peter Ivanovitch has been associated with a number of literary and historical figures, including the Russian anarchist leader Mikhail Bakunin (1814-76) and the Russian novelists Fëdor Mikhailovich Dostoevskii (1821-81) and Leo Tolstoi (Lev Nikolaevich) (1828-1910).

2  Traditionally France, Great Britain, Prussia, Russia, and Austria.

3  Because of a lack of educational opportunities in Russia, many Russians (especially women) came to Switzerland to study. Medicine was a particularly popular course of study among them.

black-coated figure. At one time all Europe was aware of the story of his life written by himself and translated into seven or more languages. In his youth he had led an idle, dissolute life. Then a society girl he was about to marry died suddenly and thereupon he abandoned the world of fashion, and began to conspire in a spirit of repentance, and, after that, his native autocracy took good care that the usual things should happen to him. He was imprisoned in fortresses, beaten within an inch of his life, and condemned to work in mines, with common criminals. The great success of his book, however, was the chain.

I do not remember now the details of the weight and length of the fetters riveted on his limbs by an "Administrative" order, but it was in the number of pounds and the thickness of links an appalling assertion of the divine right of autocracy. Appalling and futile too, because this big man managed to carry off that simple engine of government with him into the woods. The sensational clink of these fetters is heard all through the chapters describing his escape—a subject of wonder to two continents. He had begun by concealing himself successfully from his guard in a hole on a river bank. It was the end of the day; with infinite labour he managed to free one of his legs. Meantime night fell. He was going to begin on his other leg when he was overtaken by a terrible misfortune. He dropped his file.

All this is precise yet symbolic; and the file had its pathetic history. It was given to him unexpectedly one evening, by a quiet, pale-faced girl. The poor creature had come out to the mines to join one of his fellow convicts, a delicate young man, a mechanic and a social democrat, with broad cheekbones and large staring eyes. She had worked her way across half Russia and nearly the whole of Siberia to be near him, and, as it seems, with the hope of helping him to escape. But she arrived too late. Her lover had died only a week before.

Through that obscure episode, as he says, in the history of ideas in Russia, the file came into his hands, and inspired him with an ardent resolution to regain his liberty. When it slipped through his fingers it was as if it had gone straight into the earth. He could by no manner of means put his hand on it again in the dark. He groped systematically in the loose earth, in the mud, in the water; the night was passing meantime, the precious night on which he counted to get away into the forests, his only chance of escape. For a moment he was tempted by despair to give up; but recalling the quiet, sad face of the heroic girl, he felt profoundly ashamed of his weakness. She had selected him for the gift of liberty and he must show himself worthy of the favour conferred by her feminine, indomitable soul. It appeared to be a sacred trust. To fail would have been a sort of treason against the sacredness of self-sacrifice and womanly love.

There are in his book whole pages of self-analysis whence emerges like a white figure from a dark confused sea the conviction of woman's spiritual superiority—his new faith confessed since in several volumes. His first tribute to it, the great act of his conversion, was his extraordinary existence in the endless forests of the Okhotsk[1] Province, with the loose end of the chain wound about his waist. A strip torn off his convict shirt secured the end firmly. Other strips fastened it at intervals up his left leg to deaden the clanking and to prevent the slack links from getting hooked in the bushes. He became very fierce. He developed an unsuspected genius for the arts of a wild and hunted existence. He learned to creep into villages without betraying his presence by anything more than an occasional faint jingle. He broke into outhouses with an axe he managed to purloin in a wood-cutters' camp. In the deserted tracts of country he lived on wild berries and hunted for honey. His clothing dropped off him gradually. His naked tawny figure glimpsed vaguely through the bushes with a cloud of mosquitoes and flies hovering about the shaggy head, spread tales of terror through whole districts. His temper grew savage as the days went by, and he was glad to discover that there was so much of a brute in him. He had nothing else to put his trust in. For it was as though there had been two human beings indissolubly joined in that enterprise. The civilized man, the enthusiast of advanced humanitarian ideals thirsting for the triumph of spiritual love and political liberty; and the stealthy, primeval savage, pitilessly cunning in the preservation of his freedom from day to day, like a tracked wild beast.

The wild beast was making its way instinctively eastward to the Pacific coast, and the civilized humanitarian in fearful anxious dependence watched the proceedings with awe. Through all these weeks he could never make up his mind to appeal to human compassion. In the wary primeval savage this shyness might have been natural, but the other too, the civilized creature, the thinker, the escaping "political" had developed an absurd form of morbid pessimism, a form of temporary insanity, originating perhaps in the physical worry and discomfort of the chain. These links, he

---

1   A city in the Khabarovsk territory in the far eastern part of Siberia; for Okhotsk Province, Conrad likely has in mind the Khabarovsk territory.

fancied, made him odious to the rest of mankind. It was a repugnant and suggestive load. Nobody could feel any pity at the disgusting sight of a man escaping with a broken chain. His imagination became affected by his fetters in a precise, matter-of-fact manner. It seemed to him impossible that people could resist the temptation of fastening the loose end to a staple in the wall while they went for the nearest police official. Crouching in holes or hidden in thickets, he had tried to read the faces of unsuspecting free settlers working in the clearings or passing along the paths within a foot or two of his eyes. His feeling was that no man on earth could be trusted with the temptation of the chain.

One day, however, he chanced to come upon a solitary woman. It was on an open slope of rough grass outside the forest. She sat on the bank of a narrow stream; she had a red handkerchief on her head and a small basket was lying on the ground near her hand. At a little distance could be seen a cluster of log cabins, with a water-mill over a dammed pool shaded by birch trees and looking bright as glass in the twilight. He approached her silently, his hatchet stuck in his iron belt, a thick cudgel in his hand; there were leaves and bits of twigs[1] in his tangled hair, in his matted beard; bunches of rags he had wound round the links fluttered from his waist. A faint clink of his fetters made the woman turn her head. Too terrified by this savage apparition to jump up or even to scream, she was yet too stout-hearted to faint. . . . Expecting nothing less than to be murdered on the spot she covered her eyes with her hands to avoid the sight of the descending axe. When at last she found courage to look again, she saw the shaggy wild man sitting on the bank six feet away from her. His thin, sinewy arms hugged his naked legs; the long beard covered the knees on which he rested his chin; all these clasped, folded limbs, the bare shoulders, the wild head with red staring eyes, shook and trembled violently while the bestial creature was making efforts to speak. It was six weeks since he had heard the sound of his own voice. It seemed as though he had lost the faculty of speech. He had become a dumb and despairing brute, till the woman's sudden, unexpected cry of profound pity, the insight of her feminine compassion discovering the complex misery of the man under the terrifying aspect of the monster, restored him to the ranks of humanity. This point of view is presented in his book, with a very effective eloquence. She ended, he says, by shedding tears over him, sacred, redeeming tears, while he also wept with

---

1 The first English edition has "bits of twig" (M, T).

joy in the manner of a converted sinner. Directing him to hide in the bushes and wait patiently (a police patrol was expected in the Settlement) she went away towards the houses, promising to return at night.

As if providentially appointed to be the newly wedded wife of the village blacksmith, the woman persuaded her husband to come out with her, bringing some tools of his trade, a hammer, a chisel, a small anvil. . . . "My fetters"—the book says—"were struck off on the banks of the stream, in the starlight of a calm night by an athletic, taciturn young man of the people, kneeling at my feet, while the woman like a liberating genius[1] stood by with clasped hands." Obviously a symbolic couple. At the same time they furnished his regained humanity with some decent clothing, and put heart into the new man by the information that the seacoast of the Pacific was only a very few miles away. It could be seen, in fact, from the top of the next ridge. . . .

The rest of his escape does not lend itself to mystic treatment and symbolic interpretation. He ended by finding his way to the West by the Suez Canal[2] route in the usual manner. Reaching the shores of South Europe he sat down to write his autobiography— the great literary success of its year. This book was followed by other books written with the declared purpose of elevating humanity. In these works he preached generally the cult of the woman. For his own part he practised it under the rites of special devotion to the transcendental merits of a certain Madame de S——, a lady of advanced views, no longer very young, once upon a time the intriguing wife of a now dead and forgotten diplomat. Her loud pretensions to be one of the leaders of modern thought and of modern sentiment she sheltered (like Voltaire[3] and Mme. de Staël[4]) on the republican territory of Geneva. Driving through the streets in her big landau[5] she exhibited to the indifference of the natives and the stares of the tourists a long-waisted, youthful

---

1 In the sense of a class of spirits (some good and some evil) with powers to affect human affairs (from Arabic mythology).

2 A canal in Egypt, completed in 1869, connecting the Mediterranean Sea to the Red Sea.

3 Pen name for François Marie Arouet (1694-1778), French philosopher and writer and one of the leaders of the Enlightenment movement.

4 Anne Louise Germaine de Staël (1766-1817), French author who maintained a famous intellectual salon in Paris and in Coppet, Switzerland, and strongly influenced literary tastes of the time.

5 Four-wheeled horse-drawn carriage with a top in two parts so that it can be opened or closed.

figure of hieratic[1] stiffness, with a pair of big gleaming eyes, rolling restlessly behind a short veil of black lace, which, coming down no further than her vividly red lips, resembled a mask. Usually the "heroic fugitive" (this name was bestowed upon him in a review of the English edition of his book)—the "heroic fugitive" accompanied her, sitting, portentously bearded and darkly bespectacled, not by her side, but opposite her, with his back to the horses. Thus, facing each other, with no one else in the roomy carriage, their airings suggested a conscious public manifestation. Or it may have been unconscious. Russian simplicity often marches innocently on the edge of cynicism for some lofty purpose. But it is a vain enterprise for sophisticated Europe to try and understand these doings. Considering the air of gravity extending even to the physiognomy of the coachman and the action of the showy horses, this quaint display might have possessed a mystic significance, but to the corrupt frivolity of a Western mind, like my own, it seemed hardly decent.

However, it is not becoming for an obscure teacher of languages to criticize a "heroic fugitive" of worldwide celebrity. I was aware from hearsay that he was an industrious busy-body, hunting up his compatriots in hotels, in private lodgings, and—I was told—conferring upon them the honour of his notice in public gardens when a suitable opening presented itself. I was under the impression that after a visit or two, several months before, he had given up the ladies Haldin—no doubt reluctantly, for there could be no question of his being a determined person. It was perhaps to be expected that he should reappear again on this terrible occasion, as a Russian and a revolutionist, to say the right thing, to strike the true, perhaps a comforting, note. But I did not like to see him sitting there. I trust that an unbecoming jealousy of my privileged position had nothing to do with it. I made no claim to a special standing for my silent friendship. Removed by the difference of age and nationality as if into the sphere of another existence, I produced, even upon myself, the effect of a dumb helpless ghost, of an anxious immaterial thing that could only hover about without the power to protect or guide by as much as a whisper. Since Miss Haldin with her sure instinct had refrained from introducing me to the burly celebrity, I would have retired quietly and returned later on, had I not met a peculiar expression in her eyes which I interpreted as a request to stay, with the view, perhaps, of shortening an unwelcome visit.

1  Priestly or sacred.

He picked up his hat, but only to deposit it on his knees.

"We shall meet again, Natalia Victorovna. To-day I have called only to mark those feelings towards your honoured mother and yourself, the nature of which you cannot doubt. I needed no urging, but Eleanor—Madame de S—— herself has in a way sent me. She extends to you the hand of feminine fellowship. There is positively in all the range of human sentiments no joy and no sorrow that woman cannot understand, elevate, and spiritualize by her interpretation. That young man newly arrived from St. Petersburg, I have mentioned to you, is already under the charm."

At this point Miss Haldin got up abruptly. I was glad. He did not evidently expect anything so decisive and, at first, throwing his head back, he tilted up his dark glasses with bland curiosity. At last, recollecting himself, he stood up hastily, seizing his hat off his knees with great adroitness.

"How is it, Natalia Victorovna, that you have kept aloof so long from what after all is—let disparaging tongues say what they like—a unique centre of intellectual freedom and of effort to shape a high conception of our future? In the case of your honoured mother I understand in a measure. At her age new ideas—new faces are not perhaps. . . . But you! Was it mistrust—or diffidence?[1] You must come out of your reserve. We Russians have no right to be reserved with each other. In our circumstances it is almost a crime against humanity. The luxury of private grief is not for us. Nowadays the devil is not combated by prayers and fasting. And what is fasting after all but starvation? You must not starve yourself, Natalia Victorovna. Strength is what we want. Spiritual strength, I mean. As to the other kind, what could withstand us Russians if we only put it forth? Sin is different in our day, and the way of salvation for pure souls is different too. It is no longer to be found in monasteries but in the world, in the . . ."

The deep sound seemed to rise from under the floor, and one felt steeped in it to the lips. Miss Haldin's interruption resembled the effort of a drowning person to keep above water. She struck in with an accent of impatience—

"But, Peter Ivanovitch, I don't mean to retire into a monastery. Who would look for salvation there?"

"I spoke figuratively," he boomed.

"Well, then, I am speaking figuratively too. But sorrow is sorrow and pain is pain in the old way. They make their demands

---

1  The first English edition has "indifference" (M, T).

upon people. One has got to face them the best way one can. I know that the blow which has fallen upon us so unexpectedly is only an episode in the fate of a people. You may rest assured that I don't forget that. But just now I have to think of my mother. How can you expect me to leave her to herself. . . .?"

"That is putting it in a very crude way," he protested in his great effortless voice.

Miss Haldin did not wait for the vibration to die out.

"And run about visiting amongst a lot of strange people. The idea is distasteful for me; and I do not know what else you may mean."

He towered before her, enormous, deferential, cropped as close as a convict; and this big pinkish poll[1] evoked for me the vision of a wild head with matted locks peering through parted bushes, glimpses of naked, tawny limbs slinking behind the masses of sodden foliage under a cloud of flies and mosquitoes. It was an involuntary tribute to the vigour of his writing. Nobody could doubt that he had wandered in Siberian forests, naked and girt with a chain. The black broadcloth coat invested his person with a character of austere decency—something recalling a missionary.

"Do you know what I want, Natalia Victorovna?" he uttered solemnly. "I want you to be a fanatic."

"A fanatic?"

"Yes. Faith alone won't do."

His voice dropped to a still lower tone. He raised for a moment one thick arm; the other remained hanging down against his thigh, with the fragile silk hat at the end.

"I shall tell you now something which I entreat you to ponder over carefully. Listen, we need a force that would move heaven and earth—nothing less."

The profound, subterranean note of this "nothing less" made one shudder, almost, like the deep muttering of wind in the pipes of an organ.

"And are we to find that force in the salon of Madame de S——? Excuse me, Peter Ivanovitch, if I permit myself to doubt it. Is not that lady a woman of the great world, an aristocrat?"

"Prejudice!" he cried. "You astonish me. And suppose she was all that! She is also a woman of flesh and blood. There is always something to weigh down the spiritual side in all of us. But to make of it a reproach is what I did not expect from you. No! I did

---

1  Head, especially that part on which hair grows.

not expect that. One would think you have listened to some malevolent scandal."

"I have heard no gossip, I assure you. In our province how could we? But the world speaks of her. What can there be in common in a lady of that sort and an obscure country girl like me?"

"She is a perpetual manifestation of a noble and peerless spirit," he broke in. "Her charm—no, I shall not speak of her charm. But, of course, everybody who approaches her falls under the spell. . . . Contradictions vanish, trouble falls away from one. . . . Unless I am mistaken—but I never make a mistake in spiritual matters—you are troubled in your soul, Natalia Victorovna."

Miss Haldin's clear eyes looked straight at his soft enormous face; I received the impression that behind these dark spectacles of his he could be as impudent as he chose.

"Only the other evening walking back to town from Château Borel with our latest interesting arrival from Petersburg, I could notice the powerful soothing influence—I may say reconciling influence. . . . There he was, all these kilometres along the shores of the lake,[1] silent, like a man who has been shown the way of peace. I could feel the leaven working in his soul, you understand. For one thing he listened to me patiently. I myself was inspired that evening by the firm and exquisite genius of Eleanor— Madame de S——, you know. It was a full moon and I could observe his face. I cannot be deceived. . . ."

Miss Haldin, looking down, seemed to hesitate.

"Well! I will think of what you said, Peter Ivanovitch. I shall try to call as soon as I can leave mother for an hour or two safely."

Coldly as these words were said I was amazed at the concession. He snatched her right hand with such fervour that I thought he was going to press it to his lips or his breast. But he only held it by the finger-tips in his great paw and shook it a little up and down while he delivered his last volley of words.

"That's right. That's right. I haven't obtained your full confidence as yet, Natalia Victorovna, but that will come. All in good time. The sister of Victor Haldin cannot be without importance. . . . It's simply impossible. And no woman can remain sitting on the steps. Flowers, tears, applause—that has had its time; it's a mediæval conception. The arena, the arena itself is the place for women!"

He relinquished her hand with a flourish, as if giving it to her for a gift, and remained still, his head bowed in dignified submission before her femininity.

---

1 Lake Geneva.

"The arena! . . . You must descend into the arena, Natalia."

He made one step backwards, inclined his enormous body, and was gone swiftly. The door fell to behind him. But immediately the powerful resonance of his voice was heard addressing in the ante-room the middle-aged servant woman who was letting him out. Whether he exhorted her too to descend into the arena I cannot tell. The thing sounded like a lecture, and the slight crash of the outer door cut it short suddenly.

## III

We remained looking at each other for a time.

"Do you know who he is?"

Miss Haldin, coming forward, put this question to me in English.

I took her offered hand.

"Everybody knows. He is a revolutionary feminist, a great writer, if you like, and—how shall I say it—the—the familiar guest of Madame de S——'s mystic revolutionary salon."

Miss Haldin passed her hand over her forehead.

"You know, he was with me for more than an hour before you came in. I was so glad mother was lying down. She has many nights without sleep, and then sometimes in the middle of the day she gets a rest of several hours. It is sheer exhaustion—but still, I am thankful. . . . If it were not for these intervals. . . ."

She looked at me and, with that extraordinary penetration which used to disconcert me, shook her head.

"No. She would not go mad."

"My dear young lady," I cried, by way of protest, the more shocked because in my heart I was far from thinking Mrs. Haldin quite sane.

"You don't know what a fine, lucid intellect mother had," continued Nathalie Haldin, with her calm, clear-eyed simplicity, which seemed to me always to have a quality of heroism.

"I am sure . . ." I murmured.

"I darkened mother's room and came out here. I've wanted for so long to think quietly."

She paused, then, without giving any sign of distress, added, "It's so difficult," and looked at me with a strange fixity, as if watching for a sign of dissent or surprise.

I gave neither. I was irresistibly impelled to say—

"The visit from that gentleman has not made it any easier, I fear."

Miss Haldin stood before me with a peculiar expression in her eyes.

"I don't pretend to understand Peter Ivanovitch completely. Some guide one must have, even if one does not wholly give up the direction of one's conduct to him. I am an inexperienced girl, but I am not slavish. There has been too much of that in Russia. Why should I not listen to him? There is no harm in having one's thoughts directed. But I don't mind confessing to you that I have not been completely candid with Peter Ivanovitch. I don't quite know what prevented me at the moment . . ."

She walked away suddenly from me to a distant part of the room; but it was only to open and shut a drawer in a bureau. She returned with a piece of paper in her hand. It was thin and blackened with close handwriting. It was obviously a letter.

"I wanted to read you the very words," she said. "This is one of my poor brother's letters. He never doubted. How could he doubt? They make only such a small handful, these miserable oppressors, before the unanimous will of our people."[1]

"Your brother believed in the power of a people's will to achieve anything?"

"It was his religion," declared Miss Haldin.

I looked at her calm face and her animated eyes.

"Of course the will must be awakened, inspired, concentrated," she went on. "That is the true task of real agitators. One has got to give up one's life to it. The degradation of servitude, the absolutist lies must be uprooted and swept out. Reform is impossible. There is nothing to reform. There is no legality, there are no institutions. There are only arbitrary decrees. There is only a handful of cruel—perhaps blind—officials against a nation."

The letter rustled slightly in her hand. I glanced down at the flimsy blackened pages whose very handwriting seemed cabalistic,[2] incomprehensible to the experience of Western Europe.

"Stated like this," I confessed, "the problem seems simple enough. But I fear I shall not see it solved. And if you go back to Russia I know that I shall not see you again. Yet once more I say: go back! Don't suppose that I am thinking of your preservation.

---

1  Perhaps a reference to the People's Will wing of the Land and Freedom party in Russia, which split off from the main party in 1879, with the specific idea of pursuing revolutionary force and political assassination. See Introduction, 12-13 and Appendix C6.
2  Secret or private, with sinister overtones.

No! I know that you will not be returning to personal safety. But I had much rather think of you in danger there than see you exposed to what may be met here."

"I tell you what," said Miss Haldin, after a moment of reflection. "I believe that you hate revolution; you fancy it's not quite honest. You belong to a people which has made a bargain with fate and wouldn't like to be rude to it. But we have made no bargain. It was never offered to us—so much liberty for so much hard cash. You shrink from the idea of revolutionary action for those you think well of as if it were something—how shall I say it—not quite decent."

I bowed my head.

"You are quite right," I said. "I think very highly of you."

"Don't suppose I do not know it," she began hurriedly. "Your friendship has been very valuable."

"I have done little else but look on."

She was a little flushed under the eyes.

"There is a way of looking on which is valuable. I have felt less lonely because of it. It's difficult to explain."

"Really? Well, I too have felt less lonely. That's easy to explain, though. But it won't go on much longer. The last thing I want to tell you is this: in a real revolution—not a simple dynastic change or a mere reform of institutions—in a real revolution the best characters do not come to the front. A violent revolution falls into the hands of narrow-minded fanatics and of tyrannical hypocrites at first. Afterwards comes the turn of all the pretentious intellectual failures of the time. Such are the chiefs and the leaders. You will notice that I have left out the mere rogues. The scrupulous and the just, the noble, humane, and devoted natures; the unselfish and the intelligent may begin a movement—but it passes away from them. They are not the leaders of a revolution. They are its victims: the victims of disgust, of disenchantment—often of remorse. Hopes grotesquely betrayed, ideals caricatured—that is the definition of revolutionary success. There have been in every revolution hearts broken by such successes. But enough of that. My meaning is that I don't want you to be a victim."

"If I could believe all you have said I still wouldn't think of myself," protested Miss Haldin. "I would take liberty from any hand as a hungry man would snatch at a piece of bread.[1] The true

---

1 A slightly different version of this comment appears as the epigraph to the novel.

progress must begin after. And for that the right men shall be found. They are already amongst us. One comes upon them in their obscurity, unknown, preparing themselves. . . ."

She spread out the letter she had kept in her hand all the time, and looking down at it—

"Yes! One comes upon such men!" she repeated, and then read out the words, "Unstained, lofty, and solitary existences."

Folding up the letter, while I looked at her interrogatively, she explained—

"These are the words which my brother applies to a young man he came to know in St. Petersburg. An intimate friend, I suppose. It must be. His is the only name my brother mentions in all his correspondence with me. Absolutely the only one, and—would you believe it?—the man is here. He arrived recently in Geneva."

"Have you seen him?" I inquired. "But, of course, you must have seen him."

"No! No! I haven't! I didn't know he was here. It's Peter Ivanovitch himself who told me. You have heard him yourself mentioning a new arrival from Petersburg. . . . Well, that is the man of 'unstained, lofty, and solitary existence.' My brother's friend!"

"Compromised politically, I suppose," I remarked.

"I don't know. Yes. It must be so. Who knows! Perhaps it was this very friendship with my brother which . . . But no! It is scarcely possible. Really, I know nothing except what Peter Ivanovitch told me of him. He has brought a letter of introduction from Father Zosim[1]—you know, the priest-democrat; you have heard of Father Zosim?"

"Oh yes. The famous Father Zosim was staying here in Geneva for some two months about a year ago," I said. "When he left here he seems to have disappeared from the world."

"It appears that he is at work in Russia again. Somewhere in the centre," Miss Haldin said, with animation. "But please don't mention that to any one—don't let it slip from you, because if it got into the papers it would be dangerous for him."

---

1 Probably modeled after Father Georgii Apollonovich Gapon (1870-1906), a Russian Orthodox priest who in 1905 led a peaceful march of some 200,000 workers to the Tsar's Winter Palace in St. Petersburg to petition him for reforms. In an event that came to be known as Bloody Sunday, the Russian Imperial Guards opened fire on the crowd, killing some 100 demonstrators and touching off the Russian Revolution of 1905.

"You are anxious, of course, to meet that friend of your brother?" I asked.

Miss Haldin put the letter into her pocket. Her eyes looked beyond my shoulder at the door of her mother's room.

"Not here," she murmured. "Not for the first time, at least."

After a moment of silence I said good-bye, but Miss Haldin followed me into the ante-room, closing the door behind us carefully.

"I suppose you guess where I mean to go tomorrow?"

"You have made up your mind to call on Madame de S——."

"Yes. I am going to the Château Borel. I must."

"What do you expect to hear there?" I asked, in a low voice.

I wondered if she were not deluding herself with some impossible hope. It was not that, however.

"Only think—such a friend. The only man mentioned in his letters. He would have something to give me, if nothing more than a few poor words. It may be something said and thought in those last days. Would you want me to turn my back on what is left of my poor brother—a friend?"

"Certainly not," I said. "I quite understand your pious curiosity."

"—Unstained, lofty, and solitary existences," she murmured to herself. "There are! There are! Well, let me question one of them about the loved dead."

"How do you know, though, that you will meet him there? Is he staying in the Château as a guest—do you suppose?"

"I can't really tell," she confessed. "He brought a written introduction from Father Zosim—who, it seems, is a friend of Madame de S—— too. She can't be such a worthless woman after all."

"There were all sorts of rumours afloat about Father Zosim himself," I observed.

She shrugged her shoulders.

"Calumny is a weapon of our government too. It's well known. Oh yes! It is a fact that Father Zosim had the protection of the Governor-General of a certain province. We talked on the subject with my brother two years ago, I remember. But his work was good. And now he is proscribed.[1] What better proof can one require? But no matter what that priest was or is. All that cannot affect my brother's friend. If I don't meet him there I shall ask these people for his address. And, of course, mother must see him

---

1 Officially condemned.

too, later on. There is no guessing what he may have to tell us. It would be a mercy if mamma could be soothed. You know what she imagines. Some explanation perhaps may be found, or—or even made up, perhaps. It would be no sin."

"Certainly," I said, "it would be no sin. It may be a mistake, though."

"I want her only to recover some of her old spirit. While she is like this I cannot think of anything calmly."

"Do you mean to invent some sort of pious fraud for your mother's sake?" I asked.

"Why fraud? Such a friend is sure to know something of my brother in these last days. He could tell us. . . . There is something in the facts which will not let me rest. I am certain he meant to join us abroad—that he had some plans—some great patriotic action in view; not only for himself, but for both of us. I trusted in that. I looked forward to the time! Oh! with such hope and impatience. . . . I could have helped. And now suddenly this appearance of recklessness—as if he had not cared. . . ."

She remained silent for a time, then obstinately she concluded—

"I want to know . . ."

Thinking it over, later on, while I walked slowly away from the Boulevard des Philosophes, I asked myself critically, what precisely was it that she wanted to know? What I had heard of her history was enough to give me a clue. In the educational establishment for girls where Miss Haldin finished her studies she was looked upon rather unfavourably. She was suspected of holding independent views on matters settled by official teaching. Afterwards, when the two ladies returned to their country place, both mother and daughter, by speaking their minds openly on public events, had earned for themselves a reputation of liberalism. The three-horse trap[1] of the district police-captain began to be seen frequently in their village. "I must keep an eye on the peasants"—so he explained his visits up at the house. "Two lonely ladies must be looked after a little." He would inspect the walls as though he wanted to pierce them with his eyes, peer at the photographs, turn over the books in the drawing-room negligently, and after the usual refreshments, would depart. But the old priest of the village came one evening in the greatest distress and agitation, to confess that he—the priest—had been ordered to watch and ascertain in other ways too (such as using his spir-

---

1 A small carriage on springs, typically two-wheeled.

itual power with the servants) all that was going on in the house, and especially in respect of the visitors these ladies received, who they were, the length of their stay, whether any of them were strangers to that part of the country, and so on. The poor, simple old man was in an agony of humiliation and terror. "I came to warn you. Be cautious in your conduct, for the love of God. I am burning with shame, but there is no getting out from under the net. I shall have to tell them what I see, because if I did not there is my deacon. He would make the worst of things to curry favour. And then my son-in-law, the husband of my Parasha, who is a writer in the Government Domain office; they would soon kick him out—and maybe send him away somewhere." The old man lamented the necessities of the times—"when people do not agree somehow" and wiped his eyes. He did not wish to spend the evening of his days with a shaven head in the penitent's cell of some monastery—"and subjected to all the severities of ecclesiastical discipline; for they would show no mercy to an old man," he groaned. He became almost hysterical, and the two ladies, full of commiseration, soothed him the best they could before they let him go back to his cottage. But, as a matter of fact, they had very few visitors. The neighbours—some of them old friends—began to keep away; a few from timidity, others with marked disdain, being grand people that came only for the summer—Miss Haldin explained to me—aristocrats, reactionaries. It was a solitary existence for a young girl. Her relations with her mother were of the tenderest and most open kind; but Mrs. Haldin had seen the experiences of her own generation, its sufferings, its deceptions, its apostasies too. Her affection for her children was expressed by the suppression of all signs of anxiety. She maintained a heroic reserve. To Nathalie Haldin, her brother with his Petersburg existence, not enigmatical in the least (there could be no doubt of what he felt or thought) but conducted a little mysteriously, was the only visible representative of a proscribed liberty. All the significance of freedom, its indefinite promises, lived in their long discussions, which breathed the loftiest hope of action and faith in success. Then, suddenly, the action, the hopes, came to an end with the details ferreted out by the English journalist. The concrete fact, the fact of his death remained! but it remained obscure in its deeper causes. She felt herself abandoned without explanation. But she did not suspect him. What she wanted was to learn almost at any cost how she could remain faithful to his departed spirit.

Several days elapsed before I met Nathalie Haldin again. I was crossing the place in front of the theatre when I made out her shapely figure in the very act of turning between the gate pillars of the unattractive public promenade of the Bastions. She walked away from me, but I knew we should meet as she returned down the main alley—unless, indeed, she were going home. In that case, I don't think I should have called on her yet. My desire to keep her away from these people was as strong as ever, but I had no illusions as to my power. I was but a Westerner, and it was clear that Miss Haldin would not, could not listen to my wisdom; and as to my desire of listening to her voice, it were better, I thought, not to indulge overmuch in that pleasure. No, I should not have gone to the Boulevard des Philosophes; but when at about the middle of the principal alley I saw Miss Haldin coming towards me, I was too curious, and too honest, perhaps, to run away.

There was something of the spring harshness in the air. The blue sky was hard, but the young leaves clung like soft mist about the uninteresting range of trees; and the clear sun put little points of gold into the grey of Miss Haldin's frank eyes, turned to me with a friendly greeting.

I inquired after the health of her mother.

She had a slight movement of the shoulders and a little sad sigh.

"But, you see, I did come out for a walk ... for exercise, as you English say."

I smiled approvingly, and she added an unexpected remark—

"It is a glorious day."

Her voice, slightly harsh, but fascinating with its masculine and bird-like quality, had the accent of spontaneous conviction. I was glad of it. It was as though she had become aware of her youth—for there was but little of spring-like glory in the rectangular railed space of grass and trees, framed visibly by the orderly roof-slopes of that town, comely without grace, and hospitable without sympathy. In the very air through which she moved there was but little warmth; and the sky, the sky of a land without horizons, swept and washed clean by the April showers, extended a cold cruel blue, without elevation, narrowed suddenly by the ugly, dark wall of the Jura where, here and there, lingered yet a few miserable trails and patches of snow. All the glory of the season must have been within herself—and I was glad this feeling had come into her life, if only for a little time.

"I am pleased to hear you say these words."

She gave me a quick look. Quick, not stealthy. If there was one thing of which she was absolutely incapable, it was stealthiness. Her sincerity was expressed in the very rhythm of her walk. It was I who was looking at her covertly—if I may say so. I knew where she had been, but I did not know what she had seen and heard in that nest of aristocratic conspiracies. I use the word aristocratic, for want of a better term. The Château Borel, embowered in the trees and thickets of its neglected grounds, had its fame in our day, like the residence of that other dangerous and exiled woman, Madame de Staël, in the Napoleonic era. Only the Napoleonic despotism, the booted heir of the Revolution,[1] which counted that intellectual woman for an enemy worthy to be watched, was something quite unlike the autocracy in mystic vestments, engendered by the slavery of a Tartar[2] conquest. And Madame de S—— was very far from resembling the gifted author of *Corinne*. She made a great noise about being persecuted. I don't know if she were regarded in certain circles as dangerous. As to being watched, I imagine that the Château Borel could be subjected only to a most distant observation. It was in its exclusiveness an ideal abode for hatching superior plots—whether serious or futile. But all this did not interest me. I wanted to know the effect its extraordinary inhabitants and its special atmosphere had produced on a girl like Miss Haldin, so true, so honest, but so dangerously inexperienced! Her unconsciously lofty ignorance of the baser instincts of mankind left her disarmed before her own impulses. And there was also that friend of her brother, the significant new arrival from Russia. . . . I wondered whether she had managed to meet him.

We walked for some time, slowly and in silence.

"You know," I attacked her suddenly, "if you don't intend telling me anything, you must say so distinctly, and then, of course, it shall be final. But I won't play at delicacy. I ask you point-blank for all the details."

---

1 Following the French Revolution of 1789-99, the Napoleonic era began in1799 with the *coup d'état* by Napoleon Bonaparte (1769-1821) and ended with his defeat at the Battle of Waterloo in 1815. Madame de Staël was exiled in 1807 for the publication of her novel *Corinne*.

2 Originally a Turkic-speaking people living in northeastern Mongolia, the Tatars became intermixed with the Mongols during the reign of Genghis Khan (c. 1155-1227). Under his grandson Batu Khan (c. 1205-55), the Tatars came to rule most of European Russia until the fifteenth century.

She smiled faintly at my threatening tone.

"You are as curious as a child."

"No. I am only an anxious old man," I replied earnestly.

She rested her glance on me as if to ascertain the degree of my anxiety or the number of my years. My physiognomy has never been expressive, I believe, and as to my years I am not ancient enough as yet to be strikingly decrepit. I have no long beard like the good hermit of a romantic ballad;[1] my footsteps are not tottering, my aspect not that of a slow, venerable sage. Those picturesque advantages are not mine. I am old, alas, in a brisk, commonplace way. And it seemed to me as though there were some pity for me in Miss Haldin's prolonged glance. She stepped out a little quicker.

"You ask for all the details. Let me see. I ought to remember them. It was novel enough for a—a village girl like me."

After a moment of silence she began by saying that the Château Borel was almost as neglected inside as outside. It was nothing to wonder at. A Hamburg[2] banker, I believe, retired from business, had it built to cheer his remaining days by the view of that lake whose precise, orderly, and well-to-do beauty must have been attractive to the unromantic imagination of a business man. But he died soon. His wife departed too (but only to Italy), and this house of moneyed ease, presumably unsaleable, had stood empty for several years. One went to it up a gravel drive, round a large, coarse grassplot, with plenty of time to observe the degradation of its stuccoed front. Miss Haldin said that the impression was unpleasant. It grew more depressing as one came nearer.

She observed green stains of moss on the steps of the terrace. The front door stood wide open. There was no one about. She found herself in a wide, lofty, and absolutely empty hall, with a good many doors. These doors were all shut. A broad, bare stone staircase faced her, and the effect of the whole was of an untenanted house. She stood still, disconcerted by the solitude, but after a while she became aware of a voice speaking continuously somewhere.

"You were probably being observed all the time," I suggested. "There must have been eyes."

"I don't see how that could be," she retorted. "I haven't seen even a bird in the grounds. I don't remember hearing a single

---

1  Perhaps another reference to Coleridge's poem "The Rime of the Ancient Mariner."

2  A city in north-central Germany.

twitter in the trees. The whole place appeared utterly deserted except for the voice."

She could not make out the language—Russian, French, or German. No one seemed to answer it. It was as though the voice had been left behind by the departed inhabitants to talk to the bare walls. It went on volubly, with a pause now and then. It was lonely and sad. The time seemed very long to Miss Haldin. An invincible repugnance prevented her from opening one of the doors in the hall. It was so hopeless. No one would come, the voice would never stop. She confessed to me that she had to resist an impulse to turn round and go away unseen, as she had come.

"Really? You had that impulse?" I cried, full of regret. "What a pity you did not obey it."

She shook her head.

"What a strange memory it would have been for one. Those deserted grounds, that empty hall, that impersonal, voluble voice, and—nobody, nothing, not a soul."

The memory would have been unique and harmless. But she was not a girl to run away from an intimidating impression of solitude and mystery. "No, I did not run away," she said. "I stayed where I was—and I did see a soul. Such a strange soul."

As she was gazing up the broad staircase, and had concluded that the voice came from somewhere above, a rustle of dress attracted her attention. She looked down and saw a woman crossing the hall, having issued apparently through one of the many doors. Her face was averted, so that at first she was not aware of Miss Haldin.

On turning her head and seeing a stranger, she appeared very much startled. From her slender figure Miss Haldin had taken her for a young girl; but if her face was almost childishly round, it was also sallow and wrinkled, with dark rings under the eyes. A thick crop of dusty brown hair was parted boyishly on the side with a lateral wave above the dry, furrowed forehead. After a moment of dumb blinking, she suddenly squatted down on the floor.

"What do you mean by squatted down?" I asked, astonished. "This is a very strange detail."

Miss Haldin explained the reason. This person when first seen was carrying a small bowl in her hand. She had squatted down to put it on the floor for the benefit of a large cat, which appeared then from behind her skirts, and put[1] its head into the bowl greedily. She got up, and approaching Miss Haldin asked with nervous bluntness—

---

1  The first English edition has "hid its head" (M, T, AS, A1).

"What do you want? Who are you?"

Miss Haldin mentioned her name and also the name of Peter Ivanovitch. The girlish, elderly woman nodded and puckered her face into a momentary expression of sympathy. Her black silk blouse was old and even frayed in places; the black serge[1] skirt was short and shabby. She continued to blink at close quarters, and her eyelashes and eyebrows seemed shabby too. Miss Haldin, speaking gently to her, as if to an unhappy and sensitive person, explained how it was that her visit could not be an altogether unexpected event to Madame de S——.

"Ah! Peter Ivanovitch brought you an invitation. How was I to know? A *dame de compagnie*[2] is not consulted, as you may imagine."

The shabby woman laughed a little. Her teeth, splendidly white and admirably even, looked absurdly out of place, like a string of pearls on the neck of a ragged tramp. "Peter Ivanovitch is the greatest genius of the century perhaps, but he is the most inconsiderate man living. So if you have an appointment with him you must not be surprised to hear that he is not here."

Miss Haldin explained that she had no appointment with Peter Ivanovitch. She became interested at once in that bizarre person.

"Why should he put himself out for you or any one else? Oh! these geniuses. If you only knew! Yes! And their books—I mean, of course, the books that the world admires, the inspired books. But you have not been behind the scenes. Wait till you have to sit at a table for a half a day with a pen in your hand. He can walk up and down his rooms for hours and hours. I used to get so stiff and numb that I was afraid I would lose my balance and fall off the chair all at once."

She kept her hands folded in front of her, and her eyes, fixed on Miss Haldin's face, betrayed no animation whatever. Miss Haldin, gathering that the lady who called herself a *dame de compagnie* was proud of having acted as secretary to Peter Ivanovitch, made an amiable remark.

"You could not imagine a more trying experience," declared the lady. "There is an Anglo-American journalist interviewing Madame de S—— now, or I would take you up," she continued in a changed tone and glancing towards the staircase. "I act as master of ceremonies."

---

1   A twilled fabric, very durable, made of wool or other materials.
2   Lady companion (French).

It appeared that Madame de S—— could not bear Swiss servants about her person; and, indeed, servants would not stay for very long in the Château Borel. There were always difficulties. Miss Haldin had already noticed that the hall was like a dusty barn of marble and stucco with cobwebs in the corners and faint tracks of mud on the black and white tessellated[1] floor.

"I look also after this animal," continued the *dame de compagnie*, keeping her hands folded quietly in front of her; and she bent her worn gaze upon the cat. "I don't mind a bit. Animals have their rights; though, strictly speaking, I see no reason why they should not suffer as well as human beings. Do you? But of course they never suffer so much. That is impossible. Only, in their case it is more pitiful because they cannot make a revolution. I used to be a Republican. I suppose you are a Republican?"

Miss Haldin confessed to me that she did not know what to say. But she nodded slightly, and asked in her turn—

"And are you then no longer a Republican?"[2]

"After taking down Peter Ivanovitch from dictation for two years, it is difficult for me to be anything. First of all, you have to sit perfectly motionless. The slightest movement you make puts to flight the ideas of Peter Ivanovitch. You hardly dare to breathe. And as to coughing—God forbid! Peter Ivanovitch changed the position of the table to the wall because at first I could not help raising my eyes to look out of the window, while waiting for him to go on with his dictation. That was not allowed. He said I stared so stupidly. I was likewise not permitted to look at him over my shoulder. Instantly Peter Ivanovitch stamped his foot, and would roar, 'Look down on the paper!' It seems my expression, my face, put him off. Well, I know that I am not beautiful, and that my expression is not hopeful either. He said that my air of unintelligent expectation irritated him. These are his own words."

Miss Haldin was shocked, but admitted to me that she was not altogether surprised.

"Is it possible that Peter Ivanovitch could treat any woman so rudely?" she cried.

The *dame de compagnie* nodded several times with an air of discretion, then assured Miss Haldin that she did not mind in the least. The trying part of it was to have the secret of the composition laid bare before her; to see the great author of the revolu-

---

1 Arranged to form a mosaic.
2 The first English edition has "are you no longer" (T).

tionary gospels grope for words as if he were in the dark as to what he meant to say.

"I am quite willing to be the blind instrument of higher ends. To give one's life for the cause is nothing. But to have one's illusions destroyed—that is really almost more than one can bear. I really don't exaggerate," she insisted. "It seemed to freeze my very beliefs in me—the more so that when we worked in winter Peter Ivanovitch, walking up and down the room, required no artificial heat to keep himself warm. Even when we move to the South of France there are bitterly cold days, especially when you have to sit still for six hours at a stretch. The walls of these villas on the Riviera are so flimsy. Peter Ivanovitch did not seem to be aware of anything. It is true that I kept down my shivers from fear of putting him out. I used to set my teeth till my jaws felt absolutely locked. In the moments when Peter Ivanovitch interrupted his dictation, and sometimes these intervals were very long—often twenty minutes, no less, while he walked to and fro behind my back muttering to himself—I felt I was dying by inches, I assure you. Perhaps if I had let my teeth rattle Peter Ivanovitch might have noticed my distress, but I don't think it would have had any practical effect. She's very miserly in such matters."

The *dame de compagnie* glanced up the staircase. The big cat had finished the milk and was rubbing its whiskered cheek sinuously against her skirt. She dived to snatch it up from the floor.

"Miserliness is rather a quality than otherwise, you know," she continued, holding the cat in her folded arms. "With us it is misers who can spare money for worthy objects—not the so-called generous natures. But pray don't think I am a sybarite.[1] My father was a clerk in the Ministry of Finances with no position at all. You may guess by this that our home was far from luxurious, though of course we did not actually suffer from cold. I ran away from my parents, you know, directly I began to think by myself. It is not very easy, such thinking. One has got to be put in the way of it, awakened to the truth. I am indebted for my salvation to an old apple-woman, who had her stall under the gateway of the house we lived in. She had a kind wrinkled face, and the most friendly voice imaginable. One day, casually, we began to talk about a child, a ragged little girl we had seen begging from men in the streets at dusk; and from one thing to another my eyes began to open gradually to the horrors from

---

1 Someone devoted to pleasure or luxury.

which innocent people are made to suffer in this world, only in order that governments might exist. After I once understood the crime of the upper classes, I could not go on living with my parents. Not a single charitable word was to be heard in our home from year's end to year's end; there was nothing but the talk of vile office intrigues, and of promotion and of salaries, and of courting the favour of the chiefs. The mere idea of marrying one day such another man as my father made me shudder. I don't mean that there was anyone wanting to marry me. There was not the slightest prospect of anything of the kind. But was it not sin enough to live on a Government salary while half Russia was dying of hunger? The Ministry of Finances! What a grotesque horror it is! What does the starving, ignorant people want with a Ministry of Finances? I kissed my old folks on both cheeks, and went away from them to live in cellars, with the proletariat. I tried to make myself useful to the utterly hopeless. I suppose you understand what I mean? I mean the people who have nowhere to go and nothing to look forward to in this life. Do you understand how frightful that is—nothing to look forward to! Sometimes I think that it is only in Russia that there are such people and such a depth of misery can be reached. Well, I plunged into it, and—do you know—there isn't much that one can do in there. No, indeed—at least as long as there are Ministries of Finances and such like grotesque horrors to stand in the way. I suppose I would have gone mad there just trying to fight the vermin, if it had not been for a man. It was my old friend and teacher, the poor saintly apple-woman, who discovered him for me, quite accidentally. She came to fetch me late one evening in her quiet way. I followed her where she would lead; that part of my life was in her hands altogether, and without her my spirit would have perished miserably. The man was a young workman, a lithographer[1] by trade, and he had got into trouble in connexion with that affair of temperance tracts— you remember. There was a lot of people put in prison for that. The Ministry of Finances again! What would become of it if the poor folk ceased making beasts of themselves with drink? Upon my word, I would think that finances and all the rest of it are an invention of the devil; only that a belief in a supernatural source of evil is not necessary; men alone are quite capable of every wickedness. Finances indeed!"

---

1  A type of printing from a flat surface, originally stone but later metal or
   other materials.

Hatred and contempt hissed in her utterance of the word "finances," but at the very moment she gently stroked the cat reposing in her arms. She even raised them slightly, and inclining her head rubbed her cheek against the fur of the animal, which received this caress with the complete detachment so characteristic of its kind. Then looking at Miss Haldin she excused herself once more for not taking her upstairs to Madame de S——. The interview could not be interrupted. Presently the journalist would be seen coming down the stairs. The best thing was to remain in the hall; and besides, all these rooms (she glanced all round at the many doors), all these rooms on the ground floor were unfurnished.

"Positively there is no chair down here to offer you," she continued. "But if you prefer your own thoughts to my chatter, I will sit down on the bottom step here and keep silent."

Miss Haldin hastened to assure her that, on the contrary, she was very much interested in the story of the journeyman lithographer. He was a revolutionist, of course.

"A martyr, a simple man," said the *dame de compagnie*, with a faint sigh, and gazing through the open front door dreamily. She turned her misty brown eyes on Miss Haldin.

"I lived with him for four months. It was like a nightmare."

As Miss Haldin looked at her inquisitively she began to describe the emaciated face of the man, his fleshless limbs, his destitution. The room into which the apple-woman had led her was a tiny garret, a miserable den under the roof of a sordid house. The plaster fallen off the walls covered the floor, and when the door was opened a horrible tapestry of black cobwebs waved in the draught. He had been liberated a few days before—flung out of prison into the streets. And Miss Haldin seemed to see for the first time, a name and a face upon the body of that suffering people whose hard fate had been the subject of so many conversations, between her and her brother, in the garden of their country house.

He had been arrested with scores and scores of other people in that affair of the lithographed temperance tracts. Unluckily, having got hold of a great many suspected persons, the police thought they could extract from some of them other information relating to the revolutionist propaganda.

"They beat him so cruelly in the course of investigation," went on the *dame de compagnie*, "that they injured him internally. When they had done with him he was doomed. He could do nothing for himself. I beheld him lying on a wooden bedstead without any bedding, with his head on a bundle of dirty rags, lent to him out of charity by an old rag-picker, who happened to live in the basement of the house. There he was, uncovered, burning with fever, and there was not even a jug in the room for the water to quench his thirst with. There was nothing whatever—just that bedstead and the bare floor."

"Was there no one in all that great town amongst the liberals and revolutionaries to extend a helping hand to a brother?" asked Miss Haldin indignantly.

"Yes. But you do not know the most terrible part of that man's misery. Listen. It seems that they ill-used him so atrociously that, at last, his firmness gave way, and he did let out some information. Poor soul, the flesh is weak, you know. What it was he did not tell me. There was a crushed spirit in that mangled body. Nothing I found to say could make him whole. When they let him out, he crept into that hole, and bore his remorse stoically. He would not go near anyone he knew. I would have sought assistance for him, but, indeed, where could I have gone looking for it? Where was I to look for anyone who had anything to spare or any power to help? The people living round us were all starving and drunken. They were the victims of the Ministry of Finances. Don't ask me how we lived. I couldn't tell you. It was like a miracle of wretchedness. I had nothing to sell, and I assure you my clothes were in such a state that it was impossible for me to go out in the daytime. I was indecent. I had to wait till it was dark before I ventured into the streets to beg for a crust of bread, or whatever I could get, to keep him and me alive. Often I got nothing, and then I would crawl back and lie on the floor by the side of his couch. Oh yes, I can sleep quite soundly on bare boards. That is nothing, and I am only mentioning it to you so that you should not think I am a sybarite. It was infinitely less killing than the task of sitting for hours at a table in a cold study to take the books of Peter Ivanovitch from dictation. But you shall see yourself what that is like, so I needn't say any more about it."

"It is by no means certain that I will ever take Peter Ivanovitch from dictation," said Miss Haldin.

"No!" cried the other incredulously. "Not certain? You mean to say that you have not made up your mind?"

When Miss Haldin assured her that there never had been any question of that between her and Peter Ivanovitch, the woman with the cat compressed her lips tightly for a moment.

"Oh, you will find yourself settled at the table before you know that you have made up your mind. Don't make a mistake, it is disenchanting to hear Peter Ivanovitch dictate, but at the same time there is a fascination about it. He is a man of genius. Your face is certain not to irritate him; you may perhaps even help his inspiration, make it easier for him to deliver his message. As I look at you, I feel certain that you are the kind of woman who is not likely to check the flow of his inspiration."

Miss Haldin thought it useless to protest against all these assumptions.

"But this man—this workman—did he die under your care?" she said, after a short silence.

The *dame de compagnie*, listening up the stairs where now two voices were alternating with some animation, made no answer for a time. When the loud sounds of the discussion had sunk into an almost inaudible murmur, she turned to Miss Haldin.

"Yes, he died, but not, literally speaking, in my arms, as you might suppose. As a matter of fact, I was asleep when he breathed his last. So even now I cannot say I have seen anybody die. A few days before the end, some young men found us out in our extremity. They were revolutionists, as you might guess. He ought to have trusted in his political friends when he came out of prison. He had been liked and respected before, and nobody would have dreamed of reproaching him with his indiscretion before the police. Everybody knows how they go to work, and the strongest man has his moments of weakness before pain. Why, even hunger alone is enough to give one queer ideas as to what may be done. A doctor came, our lot was alleviated as far as physical comforts go, but otherwise he could not be consoled—poor man. I assure you, Miss Haldin, that he was very lovable, but I had not the strength to weep. I was nearly dead myself. But there were kind hearts to take care of me. A dress was found to clothe my nakedness. I tell you, I was not decent—and after a time the revolutionists placed me with a Jewish family going abroad, as governess. Of course I could teach the children, I finished the sixth class of the Lyceum;[1] but the real object was that I should carry some important papers across the frontier. I was entrusted with a packet which I carried next my heart. The gendarmes at the station did not suspect the governess of a Jewish family, busy looking after three children. I don't suppose those Hebrews knew what I had on me, for I had been introduced to them in a very roundabout way by persons who did not belong to the revolutionary movement, and naturally I had been instructed to accept

1 European secondary school.

a very small salary. When we reached Germany I left that family and delivered my papers to a revolutionist in Stuttgart;[1] after this I was employed in various ways. But you do not want to hear all that. I have never felt that I was very useful, but I live in hopes of seeing all the Ministries destroyed, finances and all. The greatest joy of my life has been to hear what your brother has done."

She directed her round eyes again to the sunshine outside, while the cat reposed within her folded arms in lordly beatitude and sphinx-like meditation.

"Yes! I rejoiced," she began again. "For me there is a heroic ring about the very name of Haldin. They must have been trembling with fear in their Ministries—all those men with fiendish hearts. Here I stand talking to you, and when I think of all the cruelties, oppressions, and injustices that are going on at this very moment, my head begins to swim. I have looked closely at what would seem inconceivable if one's own eyes had not to be trusted. I have looked at things that made me hate myself for my helplessness. I hated my hands that had no power, my voice that could not be heard, my very mind that would not become unhinged. Ah! I have seen things. And you?"

Miss Haldin was moved. She shook her head slightly.

"No, I have seen nothing for myself as yet," she murmured. "We have always lived in the country. It was my brother's wish."

"It is a curious meeting—this—between you and me," continued the other. "Do you believe in chance, Miss Haldin? How could I have expected to see you, his sister, with my own eyes? Do you know that when the news came the revolutionaries here were as much surprised as pleased, every bit? No one seemed to know anything about your brother. Peter Ivanovitch himself had not foreseen that such a blow was going to be struck. I suppose your brother was simply inspired. I myself think that such deeds should be done by inspiration. It is a great privilege to have the inspiration and the opportunity. Did he resemble you at all? Don't you rejoice, Miss Haldin?"

"You must not expect too much from me," said Miss Haldin, repressing an inclination to cry which came over her suddenly. She succeeded, then added calmly, "I am not a heroic person!"

"You think you couldn't have done such a thing yourself, perhaps?"

"I don't know. I must not even ask myself till I have lived a little longer, seen more . . ."

---

1  A city in southwestern Germany.

The other moved her head appreciatively. The purring of the cat had a loud complacency in the empty hall. No sound of voices came from upstairs. Miss Haldin broke the silence.

"What is it precisely that you heard people say about my brother? You said that they were surprised. Yes, I supposed they were. Did it not seem strange to them that my brother should have failed to save himself after the most difficult part—that is, getting away from the spot—was over? Conspirators should understand these things well. There are reasons why I am very anxious to know how it is he failed to escape."

The *dame de compagnie* had advanced to the open hall-door. She glanced rapidly over her shoulder at Miss Haldin, who remained within the hall.

"Failed to escape," she repeated absently. "Didn't he make the sacrifice of his life? Wasn't he just simply inspired? Wasn't it an act of abnegation?[1] Aren't you certain?"

"What I am certain of," said Miss Haldin, "is that it was not an act of despair. Have you not heard some opinion expressed here upon his miserable capture?"

The *dame de compagnie* mused for a while in the doorway.

"Did I hear? Of course, everything is discussed here. Has not all the world been speaking about your brother? For my part, the mere mention of his achievement plunges me into an envious ecstasy. Why should a man certain of immortality think of his life at all?"

She kept her back turned to Miss Haldin. Upstairs from behind a great dingy white and gold door, visible behind the balustrade of the first floor landing, a deep voice began to drone formally, as if reading over notes or something of the sort. It paused frequently, and then ceased altogether.

"I don't think I can stay any longer now," said Miss Haldin. "I may return another day."

She waited for the *dame de compagnie* to make room for her exit; but the woman appeared lost in the contemplation of sunshine and shadows, sharing between themselves the stillness of the deserted grounds. She concealed the view of the drive from Miss Haldin. Suddenly she said—

"It will not be necessary; here is Peter Ivanovitch himself coming up. But he is not alone. He is seldom alone now."

Hearing that Peter Ivanovitch was approaching, Miss Haldin was not so pleased as she might have been expected to be.

---

1 Renunciation or self-denial.

Somehow she had lost the desire to see either the heroic captive or Madame de S——, and the reason of that shrinking which came upon her at the very last minute is accounted for by the feeling that those two people had not been treating the woman with the cat kindly.

"Would you please let me pass?" said Miss Haldin at last, touching lightly the shoulder of the *dame de compagnie*.

But the other, pressing the cat to her breast, did not budge.

"I know who is with him," she said, without even looking back.

More unaccountably than ever Miss Haldin felt a strong impulse to leave the house.

"Madame de S—— may be engaged for some time yet, and what I have got to say to Peter Ivanovitch is just a simple question which I might put to him when I meet him in the grounds on my way down. I really think I must go. I have been some time here, and I am anxious to get back to my mother. Will you let me pass, please?"

The *dame de compagnie* turned her head at last.

"I never supposed that you really wanted to see Madame de S——," she said, with unexpected insight. "Not for a moment." There was something confidential and mysterious in her tone. She passed through the door, with Miss Haldin following her, on to the terrace, and they descended side by side the moss-grown stone steps. There was no one to be seen on the part of the drive visible from the front of the house.

"They are hidden by the trees over there," explained Miss Haldin's new acquaintance, "but you shall see them directly. I don't know who that young man is to whom Peter Ivanovitch has taken such a fancy. He must be one of us, or he would not be admitted here when the others come. You know what I mean by the others. But I must say that he is not at all mystically inclined. I don't know that I have made him out yet. Naturally I am never for very long in the drawing-room. There is always something to do for me, though the establishment here is not so extensive as the villa on the Riviera.[1] But still there are plenty of opportunities for me to make myself useful."

To the left, passing by the ivy-grown end of the stables, appeared Peter Ivanovitch and his companion. They walked very slowly, conversing with some animation. They stopped for a moment, and Peter Ivanovitch was seen to gesticulate, while the young man listened motionless, with his arms hanging down and

---

1 The Mediterranean coast of Italy and France.

his head bowed a little. He was dressed in a dark brown suit and a black hat. The round eyes of the *dame de compagnie* remained fixed on the two figures, which had resumed their leisurely approach.

"An extremely polite young man," she said. "You shall see what a bow he will make; and it won't altogether be so exceptional either. He bows in the same way when he meets me alone in the hall."

She moved on a few steps, with Miss Haldin by her side, and things happened just as she had foretold. The young man took off his hat, bowed and fell back, while Peter Ivanovitch advanced quicker, his black, thick arms extended heartily, and seized hold of both Miss Haldin's hands, shook them, and peered at her through his dark glasses.

"That's right, that's right!" he exclaimed twice, approvingly. "And so you have been looked after by . . ." He frowned slightly at the *dame de compagnie*, who was still nursing the cat. "I conclude Eleanor—Madame de S—— is engaged. I know she expected somebody to-day. So the newspaper man did turn up, eh? She is engaged?"

For all answer the *dame de compagnie* turned away her head.

"It is very unfortunate—very unfortunate indeed. I very much regret that you should have been . . ." He lowered suddenly his voice. "But what is it—surely you are not departing, Natalia Victorovna? You got bored waiting, didn't you?"

"Not in the least," Miss Haldin protested. "Only I have been here some time, and I am anxious to get back to my mother."

"The time seemed long, eh? I am afraid our worthy friend here" (Peter Ivanovitch suddenly jerked his head sideways towards his right shoulder and jerked it up again),—"our worthy friend here has not the art of shortening the moments of waiting. No, distinctly she has not the art; and in that respect good intentions alone count for nothing."

The *dame de compagnie* dropped her arms, and the cat found itself suddenly on the ground. It remained quite still after alighting, one hind leg stretched backwards. Miss Haldin was extremely indignant on behalf of the lady companion.

"Believe me, Peter Ivanovitch, that the moments I have passed in the hall of this house have been not a little interesting, and very instructive too. They are memorable. I do not regret the waiting, but I see that the object of my call here can be attained without taking up Madame de S——'s time."

At this point I interrupted Miss Haldin. The above relation is founded on her narrative, which I have not so much dramatized as might be supposed. She had rendered, with extraordinary feeling and animation, the very accent almost of the disciple of the old apple-woman, the irreconcilable hater of Ministries, the voluntary servant of the poor. Miss Haldin's true and delicate humanity had been extremely shocked by the uncongenial fate of her new acquaintance, that lady companion, secretary, whatever she was. For my own part, I was pleased to discover in it one more obstacle to intimacy with Madame de S——. I had a positive abhorrence for the painted, bedizened,[1] dead-faced, glassy-eyed Egeria[2] of Peter Ivanovitch. I do not know what was her attitude to the unseen, but I know that in the affairs of this world she was avaricious, greedy, and unscrupulous. It was within my knowledge that she had been worsted in a sordid and desperate quarrel about money matters with the family of her late husband, the diplomatist. Some very august personages indeed (whom in her fury she had insisted upon scandalously involving in her affairs) had incurred her animosity. I find it perfectly easy to believe that she had come to within an ace of being spirited away, for reasons of state, into some discreet *maison de santé*[3]—a madhouse of sorts, to be plain. It appears, however, that certain other[4] high-placed personages opposed it for reasons which . . .

But it's no use to go into details.

Wonder may be expressed at a man in the position of a teacher of languages knowing all this with such definiteness. A novelist says this and that of his personages, and if only he knows how to say it earnestly enough he may not be questioned upon the inventions of his brain in which his own belief is made sufficiently manifest by a telling phrase, a poetic image, the accent of emotion. Art is great! But I have no art, and not having invented Madame de S——, I feel bound to explain how I came to know so much about her.

My informant was the Russian wife of a friend of mine already mentioned, the professor of Lausanne University. It was from her that I learned the last fact of Madame de S——'s

---

1  Dressed up to vulgar or gaudy excess.

2  A water nymph in Roman mythology, second wife and adviser to King Numa Pompilius, second king of Rome. She reputedly could make prophecies and dispense wisdom. The term is also used generically for a female counselor.

3  Literally "a house of health" (French) but understood as a mental institution.

4  The first English edition has "certain high-placed" (M, T).

history, with which I intend to trouble my readers. She told me, speaking positively, as a person who trusts her sources, of the cause of Madame de S——'s flight from Russia, some years before. It was neither more nor less than this: that she became suspect to the police in connexion with the assassination of the Emperor Alexander.[1] The ground of this suspicion was either some unguarded expressions that escaped her in public, or some talk overheard in her *salon*. Overheard, we must believe, by some guest, perhaps a friend, who hastened to play the informer, I suppose. At any rate, the overheard matter seemed to imply her foreknowledge of that event, and I think she was wise in not waiting for the investigation of such a charge. Some of my readers may remember a little book from her pen, published in Paris, a mystically bad-tempered, declamatory, and frightfully disconnected piece of writing, in which she all but admits the foreknowledge, more than hints at its supernatural origin, and plainly suggests in venomous innuendoes that the guilt of the act was not with the terrorists, but with a palace intrigue. When I observed to my friend, the professor's wife, that the life of Madame de S——, with its unofficial diplomacy, its intrigues, lawsuits, favours, disgrace, expulsions, its atmosphere of scandal, occultism, and charlatanism, was more fit for the eighteenth century than for the conditions of our own time, she assented with a smile, but a moment after went on in a reflective tone: "Charlatanism?—yes, in a certain measure. Still, times are changed. There are forces now which were non-existent in the eighteenth century. I should not be surprised if she were more dangerous than an Englishman would be willing to believe. And what's more, she is looked upon as really dangerous by certain people—*chez nous*."[2]

*Chez nous* in this connexion meant Russia in general, and the Russian political police in particular. The object of my digression from the straight course of Miss Haldin's relation (in my own words) of her visit to the Château Borel, was to bring forward that statement of my friend, the professor's wife. I wanted to bring it forward simply to make what I have to say presently of Mr. Razumov's presence in Geneva a little more credible—for

---

1 Aleksandr II was Tsar of Russia from 1855 until he was assassinated on 13 March 1881 while driving near his Winter Palace by bombs thrown by Ignacy Hryniewiecki (1856-81), a Pole, who was also killed in the explosion.

2 At our home (French).

this is a Russian story for Western ears, which, as I have observed
already, are not attuned to certain tones of cynicism and cruelty,
of moral negation, and even of moral distress already silenced at
our end of Europe. And this I state as my excuse for having left
Miss Haldin standing, one of the little group of two women and
two men who had come together below the terrace of the
Château Borel.

The knowledge which I have just stated was in my mind when,
as I have said, I interrupted Miss Haldin. I interrupted her with
the cry of profound satisfaction—

"So you never saw Madame de S——, after all?"

Miss Haldin shook her head. It was very satisfactory to me.
She had not seen Madame de S——! That was excellent, excellent! I welcomed the conviction that she would never know
Madame de S—— now. I could not explain the reason of the
conviction but by the knowledge that Miss Haldin was standing
face to face with her brother's wonderful friend. I preferred him
to Madame de S—— as the companion and guide of that young
girl, abandoned to her inexperience by the miserable end of her
brother. But, at any rate, that life now ended had been sincere,
and perhaps its thoughts might have been lofty, its moral sufferings profound, its last act a true sacrifice. It is not for us, the staid
lovers calmed by the possession of a conquered liberty, to
condemn without appeal the fierceness of thwarted desire.

I am not ashamed of the warmth of my regard for Miss
Haldin. It was, it must be admitted, an unselfish sentiment, being
its own reward. The late Victor Haldin—in the light of that sentiment—appeared to me not as a sinister conspirator, but as a pure
enthusiast. I did not wish indeed to judge him, but the very fact
that he did not escape, that fact which brought so much trouble
to both his mother and his sister, spoke to me in his favour.
Meantime, in my fear of seeing the girl surrender to the influence
of the Château Borel revolutionary feminism, I was more than
willing to put my trust in that friend of the late Victor Haldin. He
was nothing but a name, you will say. Exactly! A name! And
what's more, the only name; the only name to be found in the
correspondence between brother and sister. The young man had
turned up; they had come face to face, and, fortunately, without
the direct interference of Madame de S——. What will come of
it? what will she tell me presently? I was asking myself.

It was only natural that my thought should turn to the young
man, the bearer of the only name uttered in all the dream-talk of
a future to be brought about by a revolution. And my thought

took the shape of asking myself why this young man had not called upon these ladies. He had been in Geneva for some days before Miss Haldin heard of him first in my presence from Peter Ivanovitch. I regretted that last's presence at their meeting. I would rather have had it happen somewhere out of his spectacled sight. But I supposed that, having both these young people there, he introduced them to each other.

I broke the silence by beginning a question on that point—

"I suppose Peter Ivanovitch . . ."

Miss Haldin gave vent to her indignation. Peter Ivanovitch directly he had got his answer from her had turned upon the *dame de compagnie* in a shameful manner.

"Turned upon her?" I wondered. "What about? For what reason?"

"It was unheard of; it was shameful," Miss Haldin pursued, with angry eyes. "*Il lui a fait une scène*[1]—like this, before strangers. And for what? You would never guess. For some eggs. . . . Oh!"

I was astonished. "Eggs, did you say?"

"For Madame de S——. That lady observes a special diet, or something of the sort. It seems she complained the day before to Peter Ivanovitch that the eggs were not rightly prepared. Peter Ivanovitch suddenly remembered this against the poor woman, and flew out at her. It was most astonishing. I stood as if rooted."

"Do you mean to say that the great feminist allowed himself to be abusive to a woman?" I asked.

"Oh, not that! It was something you have no conception of. It was an odious performance. Imagine, he raised his hat to begin with. He made his voice soft and deprecatory. 'Ah! you are not kind to us—you will not deign to remember . . .' This sort of phrases, that sort of tone. The poor creature was terribly upset. Her eyes ran full of tears. She did not know where to look. I shouldn't wonder if she would have preferred abuse, or even a blow."

I did not remark that very possibly she was familiar with both on occasions when no one was by. Miss Haldin walked by my side, her head up in scornful and angry silence.

"Great men have their surprising peculiarities," I observed inanely. "Exactly like men who are not great. But that sort of thing cannot be kept up for ever. How did the great feminist wind up this very characteristic episode?"

---

1  He made a scene (French).

Miss Haldin, without turning her face my way, told me that the end was brought about by the appearance of the interviewer, who had been closeted with Madame de S——.

He came up rapidly, unnoticed, lifted his hat slightly, and paused to say in French: "The Baroness has asked me, in case I met a lady on my way out, to desire her to come in at once."

After delivering this message, he hurried down the drive. The *dame de compagnie* flew towards the house, and Peter Ivanovitch followed her hastily, looking uneasy. In a moment Miss Haldin found herself alone with the young man, who undoubtedly must have been the new arrival from Russia. She wondered whether her brother's friend had not already guessed who she was.

I am in a position to say that, as a matter of fact, he had guessed. It is clear to me that Peter Ivanovitch, for some reason or other, had refrained from alluding to these ladies' presence in Geneva. But Razumov had guessed. The trustful girl! Every word uttered by Haldin lived in Razumov's memory. They were like haunting shapes; they could not be exorcised. The most vivid amongst them was the mention of the sister. The girl had existed for him ever since. But he did not recognize her at once. Coming up with Peter Ivanovitch, he did observe her; their eyes had met, even. He had responded, as no one could help responding, to the harmonious charm of her whole person, its strength, its grace, its tranquil frankness—and then he had turned his gaze away. He said to himself that all this was not for him; the beauty of women and the friendship of men were not for him. He accepted that feeling with a purposeful sternness, and tried to pass on. It was only her outstretched hand which brought about the recognition. It stands recorded in the pages ·of his self-confession, that it nearly suffocated him physically with an emotional reaction of hate and dismay, as though her appearance had been a piece of accomplished treachery.

He faced about. The considerable elevation of the terrace concealed them from anyone lingering in the doorway of the house; and even from the upstairs windows they could not have been seen. Through the thickets run wild, and the trees of the gently sloping grounds, he had cold, placid glimpses of the lake. A moment of perfect privacy had been vouchsafed to them at this juncture. I wondered to myself what use they had made of that fortunate circumstance.

"Did you have time for more than a few words?" I asked.

That animation with which she had related to me the incidents of her visit to the Château Borel had left her completely. Strolling by my side, she looked straight before her; but I noticed a little colour on her cheek. She did not answer me.

After some little time I observed that they could not have hoped to remain forgotten for very long, unless the other two had discovered Madame de S—— swooning with fatigue, perhaps, or in a state of morbid exaltation after the long interview. Either would require their devoted ministrations. I could depict to myself Peter Ivanovitch rushing busily out of the house again, bareheaded, perhaps, and on across the terrace with his swinging gait, the black skirts of the frock-coat floating clear of his stout light grey legs. I confess to having looked upon these young people as the quarry of the "heroic fugitive." I had the notion that they would not be allowed to escape capture. But of that I said nothing to Miss Haldin, only as she still remained uncommunicative, I pressed her a little.

"Well—but you can tell me at least your impression."

She turned her head to look at me, and turned away again.

"Impression?" she repeated slowly, almost dreamily; then in a quicker tone—

"He seems to be a man who has suffered more from his thoughts than from evil fortune."

"From his thoughts, you say?"

"And that is natural enough in a Russian," she took me up. "In a young Russian; so many of them are unfit for action, and yet unable to rest."

"And you think he is that sort of man?"

"No, I do not judge him. How could I, so suddenly? You asked for my impression—I explain my impression. I—I—don't know the world, nor yet the people in it; I have been too solitary—I am too young to trust my own opinions."

"Trust your instinct," I advised her. "Most women trust to that, and make no worse mistakes than men. In this case you have your brother's letter to help you."

She drew a deep breath like a light sigh.

"Unstained, lofty, and solitary existences," she quoted as if to herself. But I caught the wistful murmur distinctly.

"High praise," I whispered to her.

"The highest possible."

"So high that, like the award of happiness, it is more fit to come only at the end of a life. But still no common or altogether unworthy personality could have suggested such a confident exaggeration of praise and . . ."

"Ah!" She interrupted me ardently. "And if you had only known the heart from which that judgment has come!"

She ceased on that note, and for a space I reflected on the character of the words which I perceived very well must tip the scale of the girl's feelings in that young man's favour. They had not the sound of a casual utterance. Vague they were to my Western mind and to my Western sentiment, but I could not forget that, standing by Miss Haldin's side, I was like a traveller in a strange country. It had also become clear to me that Miss Haldin was unwilling to enter into the details of the only material part of their visit to the Château Borel. But I was not hurt. Somehow I didn't feel it to be a want of confidence. It was some other difficulty—a difficulty I could not resent. And it was without the slightest resentment that I said—

"Very well. But on that high ground, which I will not dispute, you, like anyone else in such circumstances, you must have made for yourself a representation of that exceptional friend, a mental image of him, and—please tell me—you were not disappointed?"

"What do you mean? His personal appearance?"

"I don't mean precisely his good looks, or otherwise."

We turned at the end of the alley and made a few steps without looking at each other.

"His appearance is not ordinary," said Miss Haldin at last.

"No, I should have thought not—from the little you've said of your first impression. After all, one has to fall back on that word. Impression! What I mean is that something indescribable which is likely to mark a 'not ordinary' person."

I perceived that she was not listening. There was no mistaking her expression; and once more I had the sense of being out of it—not because of my age, which at any rate could draw inferences—but altogether out of it, on another plane whence I could only watch her from afar. And so ceasing to speak I watched her stepping out by my side.

"No," she exclaimed suddenly, "I could not have been disappointed with a man of such strong feeling."

"Aha! Strong feeling," I muttered, thinking to myself censoriously: like this, at once, all in a moment!

"What did you say?" inquired Miss Haldin innocently.

"Oh, nothing. I beg your pardon. Strong feeling. I am not surprised."

"And you don't know how abruptly I behaved to him!" she cried remorsefully.

I suppose I must have appeared surprised, for, looking at me with a still more heightened colour, she said she was ashamed to admit that she had not been sufficiently collected; she had failed to control her words and actions as the situation demanded. She lost the fortitude worthy of both the men, the dead and the living; the fortitude which should have been the note of the meeting of Victor Haldin's sister with Victor Haldin's only known friend. He was looking at her keenly, but said nothing, and she was—she confessed—painfully affected by his want of comprehension. All she could say was: "You are Mr. Razumov." A slight frown passed over his forehead. After a short, watchful pause, he made a little bow of assent, and waited.

At the thought that she had before her the man so highly regarded by her brother, the man who had known his value, spoken to him, understood him, had listened to his confidences, perhaps had encouraged him—her lips trembled, her eyes ran full of tears; she put out her hand, made a step towards him impulsively, saying with an effort to restrain her emotion, "Can't you guess who I am?" He did not take the proffered hand. He even recoiled a pace, and Miss Haldin imagined that he was unpleasantly affected. Miss Haldin excused him, directing her displeasure at herself. She had behaved unworthily, like an emotional French girl. A manifestation of that kind could not be welcomed by a man of stern, self-contained character.

He must have been stern indeed, or perhaps very timid with women, not to respond in a more human way to the advances of a girl like Nathalie Haldin—I thought to myself. Those lofty and solitary existences (I remembered the words suddenly) make a young man shy and an old man savage[1]—often.

"Well," I encouraged Miss Haldin to proceed.

She was still very dissatisfied with herself.

"I went from bad to worse," she said, with an air of discouragement very foreign to her. "I did everything foolish except actually bursting into tears. I am thankful to say I did not do that. But I was unable to speak for quite a long time."

She had stood before him, speechless, swallowing her sobs, and when she managed at last to utter something, it was only her brother's name—"Victor—Victor Haldin!" she gasped out, and again her voice failed her.

"Of course," she commented to me, "this distressed him. He

---

1 Conrad uses the word in its obsolete form: "Remote from society, solitary" (*OED*). His usage, though, probably comes from his knowledge of French.

was quite overcome. I have told you my opinion that he is a man of deep feeling—it is impossible to doubt it. You should have seen his face. He positively reeled. He leaned against the wall of the terrace. Their friendship must have been the very brotherhood of souls! I was grateful to him for that emotion, which made me feel less ashamed of my own lack of self-control. Of course I had regained the power of speech at once, almost. All this lasted not more than a few seconds. 'I am his sister,' I said. 'Maybe you have heard of me.'"

"And had he?" I interrupted.

"I don't know. How could it have been otherwise? And yet . . . But what does that matter? I stood there before him, near enough to be touched and surely not looking like an impostor. All I know is, that he put out both his hands then to me, I may say flung them out at me, with the greatest readiness and warmth, and that I seized and pressed them, feeling that I was finding again a little of what I thought was lost to me for ever, with the loss of my brother—some of that hope, inspiration, and support which I used to get from my dear dead . . ."

I understood quite well what she meant. We strolled on slowly. I refrained from looking at her. And it was as if answering my own thoughts that I murmured—

"No doubt it was a great friendship—as you say. And that young man ended by welcoming your name, so to speak, with both hands. After that, of course, you would understand each other. Yes, you would understand each other quickly."

It was a moment before I heard her voice.

"Mr. Razumov seems to be a man of few words. A reserved man—even when he is strongly moved."

Unable to forget—or even to forgive—the bass-toned expansiveness of Peter Ivanovitch, the Arch-Patron of revolutionary parties, I said that I took this for a favourable trait of character. It was associated with sincerity—in my mind.

"And, besides, we had not much time," she added.

"No, you would not have, of course." My suspicion and even dread of the feminist and his Egeria was so ineradicable that I could not help asking with real anxiety, which I made smiling—

"But you escaped all right?"

She understood me, and smiled too, at my uneasiness.

"Oh yes! I escaped, if you like to call it that. I walked away quickly. There was no need to run. I am neither frightened nor yet fascinated, like that poor woman who received me so strangely."

"And Mr.—Mr. Razumov . . . ?"

"He remained there, of course. I suppose he went into the house after I left him. You remember that he came here strongly recommended to Peter Ivanovitch—possibly entrusted with important messages for him."

"Ah yes! From that priest who . . ."

"Father Zosim—yes. Or from others, perhaps."

"You left him, then. But have you seen him since, may I ask?"

For some time Miss Haldin made no answer to this very direct question, then—

"I have been expecting to see him here to-day," she said quietly.

"You have! Do you meet, then, in this garden? In that case I had better leave you at once."

"No, why leave me? And we don't meet in this garden. I have not seen Mr. Razumov since that first time. Not once. But I have been expecting him . . ."

She paused. I wondered to myself why that young revolution-ist should show so little alacrity.

"Before we parted I told Mr. Razumov that I walked here for an hour every day at this time. I could not explain to him then why I did not ask him to come and see us at once. Mother must be prepared for such a visit. And then, you see, I do not know myself what Mr. Razumov has to tell us. He, too, must be told first how it is with poor mother. All these thoughts flashed through my mind at once. So I told him hurriedly that there was a reason why I could not ask him to see us at home, but that I was in the habit of walking here. . . . This is a public place, but there are never many people about at this hour. I thought it would do very well. And it is so near our apartments. I don't like to be very far away from mother. Our servant knows where I am in case I should be wanted suddenly."

"Yes. It is very convenient from that point of view," I agreed.

In fact, I thought the Bastions a very convenient place, since the girl did not think it prudent as yet to introduce that young man to her mother. It was here, then, I thought, looking round at that plot of ground of deplorable banality, that their acquaintance will begin and go on in the exchange of generous indignations and of extreme sentiments, too poignant, perhaps, for a non-Russian mind to con-ceive. I saw these two, escaped out of four score of millions of human beings ground between the upper and nether millstone, walking under these trees, their young heads close together. Yes, an excellent place to stroll and talk in. It even occurred to me, while we turned once more away from the wide iron gates, that when tired they would have plenty of accommodation to rest themselves. There was a quantity of tables and chairs displayed between the restaurant chalet[1] and the bandstand, a whole raft of painted deals[2] spread out under the trees. In the very middle of it I observed a solitary Swiss couple, whose fate was made secure from the cradle to the grave by the perfected mechanism of democratic institutions in a republic that could almost be held in the palm of one's hand. The man, colourlessly uncouth, was drinking beer out of a glittering glass; the woman, rustic and placid, leaning back in the rough chair, gazed idly around.

There is little logic to be expected on this earth, not only in the matter of thought, but also of sentiment. I was surprised to discover myself displeased with that unknown young man. A week had gone by since they met. Was he callous, or shy, or very stupid? I could not make it out.

"Do you think," I asked Miss Haldin, after we had gone some distance up the great alley, "that Mr. Razumov understood your intention?"

"Understood what I meant?" she wondered. "He was greatly moved. That I know! In my own agitation I could see it. But I spoke distinctly. He heard me; he seemed, indeed, to hang on my words . . ."

Unconsciously she had hastened her pace. Her utterance, too, became quicker.

I waited a little before I observed thoughtfully—

"And yet he allowed all these days to pass."

"How can we tell what work he may have to do here? He is not an idler travelling for his pleasure. His time may not be his own— nor yet his thoughts, perhaps."

She slowed her pace suddenly, and in a lowered voice added—

"Or his very life"—then paused and stood still. "For all I know, he may have had to leave Geneva the very day he saw me."

"Without telling you!" I exclaimed incredulously.

"I did not give him time. I left him quite abruptly. I behaved emotionally to the end. I am sorry for it. Even if I had given him the opportunity he would have been justified in taking me for a person not to be trusted. An emotional, tearful girl is not a person to confide in. But even if he has left Geneva for a time, I am confident that we shall meet again."

---

1  A typically Swiss style of house with noticeable structural supports.
2  Painted tables of sawn boards, usually pine or fir.

"Ah! you are confident. . . . I dare say. But on what ground?"

"Because I've told him that I was in great need of some one, a fellow-countryman, a fellow-believer, to whom I could give my confidence in a certain matter."

"I see. I don't ask you what answer he made. I confess that this is good ground for your belief in Mr. Razumov's appearance before long. But he has not turned up to-day?"

"No," she said quietly, "not to-day;" and we stood for a time in silence, like people that have nothing more to say to each other and let their thoughts run widely asunder before their bodies go off their different ways. Miss Haldin glanced at the watch on her wrist and made a brusque movement. She had already overstayed her time, it seemed.

"I don't like to be away from mother," she murmured, shaking her head. "It is not that she is very ill now. But somehow when I am not with her I am more uneasy than ever."

Mrs. Haldin had not made the slightest allusion to her son for the last week or more. She sat, as usual, in the arm-chair by the window, looking out silently on that hopeless stretch of the Boulevard des Philosophes. When she spoke, a few lifeless words, it was of indifferent, trivial things.

"For anyone who knows what the poor soul is thinking of, that sort of talk is more painful than her silence. But that is bad too; I can hardly endure it, and I dare not break it."

Miss Haldin sighed, refastening a button of her glove which had come undone. I knew well enough what a hard time of it she must be having. The stress, its causes, its nature, would have undermined the health of an Occidental girl; but Russian natures have a singular power of resistance against the unfair strains of life. Straight and supple, with a short jacket open on her black dress, which made her figure appear more slender and her fresh but colourless face more pale, she compelled my wonder and admiration.

"I can't stay a moment longer. You ought to come soon to see mother. You know she calls you '*L'ami.*' It is an excellent name, and she really means it. And now *au revoir*, I must run."

She glanced vaguely down the broad walk—the hand she put out to me eluded my grasp by an unexpected upward movement, and rested upon my shoulder. Her red lips were slightly parted, not in a smile, however, but expressing a sort of startled pleasure. She gazed towards the gates and said quickly, with a gasp—

"There! I knew it. Here he comes!"

I understood that she must mean Mr. Razumov. A young man was walking up the alley, without haste. His clothes were some dull shade of brown, and he carried a stick. When my eyes first fell on him, his head was hanging on his breast as if in deep thought. While I was looking at him he raised it sharply, and at once stopped. I am certain he did, but that pause was nothing more perceptible than a faltering check in his gait, instantaneously overcome. Then he continued his approach, looking at us steadily. Miss Haldin signed to me to remain, and advanced a step or two to meet him.

I turned my head away from that meeting, and did not look at them again till I heard Miss Haldin's voice uttering his name in the way of introduction. Mr. Razumov was informed, in a warm, low tone, that, besides being a wonderful teacher, I was a great support "in our sorrow and distress."

Of course I was described also as an Englishman. Miss Haldin spoke rapidly, faster than I have ever heard her speak, and that by contrast made the quietness of her eyes more expressive.

"I have given him my confidence," she added, looking all the time at Mr. Razumov. That young man did, indeed, rest his gaze on Miss Haldin, but certainly did not look into her eyes which were so ready for him. Afterwards he glanced backwards and forwards at us both, while the faint commencement of a forced smile, followed by the suspicion of a frown, vanished one after another; I detected them, though neither could have been noticed by a person less intensely bent upon divining him than myself. I don't know what Nathalie Haldin had observed, but my attention seized the very shades of these movements. The attempted smile was given up, the incipient frown was checked and smoothed so that there should be no sign; but I imagined him exclaiming inwardly—

"Her confidence! To this elderly person—this foreigner!"

I imagined this because he looked foreign enough to me. I was upon the whole favourably impressed. He had an air of intelligence and even some distinction quite above the average of the students and other inhabitants of the *Petite Russie*. His features were more decided than in the generality of Russian faces; he had a line of the jaw, a clean-shaven, sallow cheek; his nose was a ridge, and not a mere protuberance. He wore the hat well down over his eyes, his dark hair curled low on the nape of his neck; in the ill-fitting brown clothes there were sturdy limbs; a slight stoop brought out a satisfactory breadth of shoulders. Upon the whole I was not disappointed. Studious—robust—shy. . . .

Before Miss Haldin had ceased speaking I felt the grip of his hand on mine, a muscular, firm grip, but unexpectedly hot and dry. Not a word or even a mutter assisted this short and arid handshake.

I intended to leave them to themselves, but Miss Haldin touched me lightly on the forearm with a significant contact, conveying a distinct wish. Let him smile who likes, but I was only too ready to stay near Nathalie Haldin, and I am not ashamed to say that it was no smiling matter to me. I stayed, not as a youth would have stayed, uplifted, as it were poised in the air, but soberly, with my feet on the ground and my mind trying to penetrate her intention. She had turned to Razumov.

"Well. This is the place. Yes, it is here that I meant you to come. I have been walking every day. . . . Don't excuse yourself— I understand. I am grateful to you for coming to-day, but all the same I cannot stay now. It is impossible. I must hurry off home. Yes, even with you standing before me, I must run off. I have been too long away. . . . You know how it is?"

These last words were addressed to me. I noticed that Mr. Razumov passed the tip of his tongue over his lips just as a parched, feverish man might do. He took her hand in its black glove, which closed on his, and held it—detained it quite visibly to me against a drawing-back movement.

"Thank you once more for—for understanding me," she went on warmly. He interrupted her with a certain effect of roughness. I didn't like him speaking to this frank creature so much from under the brim of his hat, as it were. And he produced a faint, rasping voice quite like a man with a parched throat.

"What is there to thank me for? Understand you? . . . How did I understand you? . . . You had better know that I understand nothing. I was aware that you wanted to see me in this garden. I could not come before. I was hindered. And even to-day, you see . . . late."

She still held his hand.

"I can, at any rate, thank you for not dismissing me from your mind as a weak, emotional girl. No doubt I want sustaining. I am very ignorant. But I can be trusted. Indeed I can!"

"You are ignorant," he repeated thoughtfully. He had raised his head, and was looking straight into her face now, while she held his hand. They stood like this for a long moment. She released his hand.

"Yes. You did come late. It was good of you to come on the chance of me having loitered beyond my time. I was talking with this good friend here. I was talking of you. Yes, Kirylo Sidorovitch, of you. He was with me when I first heard of your being here in Geneva. He can tell you what comfort it was to my bewildered spirit to hear that news. He knew I meant to seek you out. It was the only object of my accepting the invitation of Peter Ivanovitch. . . ."

"Peter Ivanovitch talked to you of me," he interrupted, in that wavering, hoarse voice which suggested a horribly dry throat.

"Very little. Just told me your name, and that you had arrived here. Why should I have asked for more? What could he have told me that I did not know already from my brother's letter? Three lines! And how much they meant to me! I will show them to you one day, Kirylo Sidorovitch. But now I must go. The first talk between us cannot be a matter of five minutes, so we had better not begin. . . ."

I had been standing a little aside, seeing them both in profile. At that moment it occurred to me that Mr. Razumov's face was older than his age.

"If mother"—the girl had turned suddenly to me—"were to wake up in my absence (so much longer than usual) she would perhaps question me. She seems to miss me more, you know, of late. She would want to know what delayed me—and, you see, it would be painful for me to dissemble[1] before her."

I understood the point very well. For the same reason she checked what seemed to be on Mr. Razumov's part a movement to accompany her.

"No! No! I go alone, but meet me here as soon as possible." Then to me in a lower, significant tone—

"Mother may be sitting at the window at this moment, looking down the street. She must not know anything of Mr. Razumov's presence here till—till something is arranged." She paused before she added a little louder, but still speaking to me, "Mr. Razumov does not quite understand my difficulty, but you know what it is."


V


With a quick inclination of the head for us both, and an earnest, friendly glance at the young man, Miss Haldin left us covering our heads[2] and looking after her straight, supple figure receding rapidly. Her walk was not that hybrid and uncertain gliding

---

1  To feign or deceive.
2  That is, covering their heads after having taken off their hats in salutation.

affected by some women, but a frank, strong, healthy movement forward. Rapidly she increased the distance—disappeared with suddenness at last. I discovered only then that Mr. Razumov, after ramming his hat well over his brow, was looking me over from head to foot. I dare say I was a very unexpected fact for that young Russian to stumble upon. I caught in his physiognomy, in his whole bearing, an expression compounded of curiosity and scorn, tempered by alarm—as though he had been holding his breath while I was not looking. But his eyes met mine with a gaze direct enough. I saw then for the first time that they were of a clear brown colour and fringed with thick black eyelashes. They were the youngest feature of his face. Not at all unpleasant eyes. He swayed slightly, leaning on his stick and generally hung in the wind. It flashed upon me that in leaving us together Miss Haldin had an intention—that something was entrusted to me, since, by a mere accident I had been found at hand. On this assumed ground I put all possible friendliness into my manner. I cast about for some right thing to say, and suddenly in Miss Haldin's last words I perceived the clue to the nature of my mission.

"No," I said gravely, if with a smile, "you cannot be expected to understand."

His clean-shaven lip quivered ever so little before he said, as if wickedly amused—

"But haven't you heard just now? I was thanked by that young lady for understanding so well."

I looked at him rather hard. Was there a hidden and inexplicable sneer in this retort? No. It was not that. It might have been resentment. Yes. But what had he to resent? He looked as though he had not slept very well of late. I could almost feel on me the weight of his unrefreshed, motionless stare, the stare of a man who lies unwinking in the dark, angrily passive in the toils of disastrous thoughts. Now, when I know how true it was, I can honestly affirm that this *was* the effect he produced on me. It was painful in a curiously indefinite way—for, of course, the definition comes to me now while I sit writing in the fullness of my knowledge. But this is what the effect was at that time of absolute ignorance. This new sort of uneasiness which he seemed to be forcing upon me I attempted to put down by assuming a conversational, easy familiarity.

"That extremely charming and essentially admirable young girl (I am—as you see—old enough to be frank in my expressions) was referring to her own feelings. Surely you must have understood that much?"

He made such a brusque movement that he even tottered a little.

"Must understand this! Not expected to understand that! I may have other things to do. And the girl is charming and admirable. Well—and if she is! I suppose I can see that for myself."

This sally would have been insulting if his voice had not been practically extinct, dried up in his throat; and the rustling effort of his speech too painful to give real offence.

I remained silent, checked between the obvious fact and the subtle impression. It was open to me to leave him there and then; but the sense of having been entrusted with a mission, the suggestion of Miss Haldin's last glance, was strong upon me. After a moment of reflection I said—

"Shall we walk together a little?"

He shrugged his shoulders so violently that he tottered again. I saw it out of the corner of my eye as I moved on, with him at my elbow. He had fallen back a little and was practically out of my sight, unless I turned my head to look at him. I did not wish to indispose him still further by an appearance of marked curiosity. It might have been distasteful to such a young and secret refugee from under the pestilential shadow hiding the true, kindly face of his land. And the shadow, the attendant of his countrymen, stretching across the middle of Europe, was lying on him too, darkening his figure to my mental vision. "Without doubt," I said to myself, "he seems a sombre, even a desperate revolutionist; but he is young, he may be unselfish and humane, capable of compassion, of . . ."

I heard him clear gratingly his parched throat, and became all attention.

"This is beyond everything," were his first words. "It is beyond everything! I find you here, for no reason that I can understand, in possession of something I cannot be expected to understand! A confidant! A foreigner! Talking about an admirable Russian girl. Is the admirable girl a fool, I begin to wonder? What are you at? What is your object?"

He was barely audible, as if his throat had no more resonance than a dry rag, a piece of tinder. It was so pitiful that I found it extremely easy to control my indignation.

"When you have lived a little longer, Mr. Razumov, you will discover that no woman is an absolute fool. I am not a feminist, like that illustrious author, Peter Ivanovitch, who, to say the truth, is not a little suspect to me. . . ."

He interrupted me, in a surprising note of whispering astonishment.

"Suspect to you! Peter Ivanovitch suspect to you! To you! . . ."

"Yes, in a certain aspect he is," I said, dismissing my remark
lightly. "As I was saying, Mr. Razumov, when you have lived long
enough, you will learn to discriminate between the noble trust-
fulness of a nature foreign to every meanness and the flattered
credulity of some women; though even the credulous, silly as they
may be, unhappy as they are sure to be, are never absolute fools.
It is my belief that no woman is ever completely deceived. Those
that are lost leap into the abyss with their eyes open, if all the
truth were known."

"Upon my word," he cried at my elbow, "what is it to me
whether women are fools or lunatics? I really don't care what you
think of them. I—I am not interested in them. I let them be. I am
not a young man in a novel. How do you know that I want to learn
anything about women? . . . What is the meaning of all this?"

"The object, you mean, of this conversation, which I admit I
have forced upon you in a measure."

"Forced! Object!" he repeated, still keeping half a pace or so
behind me. "You wanted to talk about women, apparently. That's
a subject. But I don't care for it. I have never . . . In fact, I have
had other subjects to think about."

"I am concerned here with one woman only—a young girl—
the sister of your dead friend—Miss Haldin. Surely you can think
a little of her. What I meant from the first was that there is a situation which you cannot be expected to understand."

I listened to his unsteady footfalls by my side for the space of
several strides.

"I think that it may prepare the ground for your next interview
with Miss Haldin if I tell you of it. I imagine that she might have
had something of the kind in her mind when she left us together.
I believe myself authorized to speak. The peculiar situation I have
alluded to has arisen in the first grief and distress of Victor
Haldin's execution. There was something peculiar in the circumstances of his arrest. You no doubt know the whole truth. . . ."

I felt my arm seized above the elbow, and next instant found
myself swung so as to face Mr. Razumov.

"You spring up from the ground before me with this talk. Who
the devil are you? This is not to be borne! Why! What for? What
do you know what is or is not peculiar? What have you to do with
any confounded circumstances, or with anything that happens in
Russia, anyway?"

He leaned on his stick with his other hand, heavily; and when he let go my arm, I was certain in my mind that he was hardly able to keep on his feet.

"Let us sit down at one of these vacant tables," I proposed, disregarding this display of unexpectedly profound emotion. It was not without its effect on me, I confess. I was sorry for him.

"What tables? What are you talking about? Oh—the empty tables? The tables there. Certainly. I will sit at one of the empty tables."

I led him away from the path to the very centre of the raft of deals before the chalet. The Swiss couple were gone by that time. We were alone on the raft, so to speak. Mr. Razumov dropped into a chair, let fall his stick, and propped on his elbows, his head between his hands, stared at me persistently, openly, and continuously, while I signalled the waiter and ordered some beer. I could not quarrel with this silent inspection very well, because, truth to tell, I felt somewhat guilty of having been sprung on him with some abruptness—of having "sprung from the ground," as he expressed it.

While waiting to be served I mentioned that, born from parents settled in St. Petersburg, I had acquired the language as a child. The town I did not remember, having left it for good as a boy of nine, but in later years I had renewed my acquaintance with the language. He listened, without as much as moving his eyes the least little bit. He had to change his position when the beer came, and the instant draining of his glass revived him. He leaned back in his chair and, folding his arms across his chest, continued to stare at me squarely. It occurred to me that his clean-shaven, almost swarthy face was really of the very mobile sort, and that the absolute stillness of it was the acquired habit of a revolutionist, of a conspirator everlastingly on his guard against self-betrayal in a world of secret spies.

"But you are an Englishman—a teacher of English literature," he murmured, in a voice that was no longer issuing from a parched throat. "I have heard of you. People told me you have lived here for years."

"Quite true. More than twenty years. And I have been assisting Miss Haldin with her English studies."

"You have been reading English poetry with her," he said, immovable now, like another man altogether, a complete stranger to the man of the heavy and uncertain footfalls a little while ago—at my elbow.

"Yes, English poetry," I said. "But the trouble of which I speak was caused by an English newspaper."

He continued to stare at me. I don't think he was aware that the story of the midnight arrest had been ferreted out by an English journalist and given to the world. When I explained this to him he muttered contemptuously, "It may have been altogether a lie."

"I should think you are the best judge of that," I retorted, a little disconcerted. "I must confess that to me it looks to be true in the main."

"How can you tell truth from lies?" he queried in his new, immovable manner.

"I don't know how you do it in Russia," I began, rather nettled by his attitude. He interrupted me.

"In Russia, and in general everywhere—in a newspaper, for instance. The colour of the ink and the shapes of the letters are the same."

"Well, there are other trifles one can go by. The character of the publication, the general verisimilitude of the news, the consideration of the motive, and so on. I don't trust blindly the accuracy of special correspondents—but why should this one have gone to the trouble of concocting a circumstantial falsehood on a matter of no importance to the world?"

"That's what it is," he grumbled. "What's going on with us is of no importance—a mere sensational story to amuse the readers of the papers—the superior contemptuous Europe. It is hateful to think of. But let them wait a bit!"

He broke off on this sort of threat addressed to the Western world. Disregarding the anger in his stare, I pointed out that whether the journalist was well- or ill-informed, the concern of the friends of these ladies was with the effect the few lines of print in question had produced—the effect alone. And surely he must be counted as one of the friends—if only for the sake of his late comrade and intimate fellow-revolutionist. At that point I thought he was going to speak vehemently; but he only astounded me by the convulsive start of his whole body. He restrained himself, folded his loosened arms tighter across his chest, and sat back with a smile in which there was a twitch of scorn and malice.

"Yes, a comrade and an intimate. . . . Very well," he said.

"I ventured to speak to you on that assumption. And I cannot be mistaken. I was present when Peter Ivanovitch announced your arrival here to Miss Haldin, and I saw her relief and thankfulness when your name was mentioned. Afterwards she showed me her brother's letter, and read out the few words in which he alludes to you. What else but a friend could you have been?"

"Obviously. That's perfectly well known. A friend. Quite correct. . . . Go on. You were talking of some effect."

I said to myself: "He puts on the callousness of a stern revolutionist, the insensibility to common emotions of a man devoted to a destructive idea. He is young, and his sincerity assumes a pose before a stranger, a foreigner, an old man. Youth must assert itself. . . ." As concisely as possible I exposed to him the state of mind poor Mrs. Haldin had been thrown into by the news of her son's untimely end.

He listened—I felt it—with profound attention. His level stare deflected gradually downwards, left my face, and rested at last on the ground at his feet.

"You can enter into the sister's feelings. As you said, I have only read a little English poetry with her, and I won't make myself ridiculous in your eyes by trying to speak of her. But you have seen her. She is one of these rare human beings that do not want explaining. At least I think so. They had only that son, that brother, for a link with the wider world, with the future. The very groundwork of active existence for Nathalie Haldin is gone with him. Can you wonder then that she turns with eagerness to the only man her brother mentions in his letters? Your name is a sort of legacy."

"What could he have written of me?" he cried, in a low, exasperated tone.

"Only a few words. It is not for me to repeat them to you, Mr. Razumov; but you may believe my assertion that these words are forcible enough to make both his mother and his sister believe implicitly in the worth of your judgment and in the truth of anything you may have to say to them. It's impossible for you now to pass them by like strangers."

I paused, and for a moment sat listening to the footsteps of the few people passing up and down the broad central walk. While I was speaking his head had sunk upon his breast above his folded arms. He raised it sharply.

"Must I go then and lie to that old woman!"

It was not anger; it was something else, something more poignant, and not so simple. I was aware of it sympathetically, while I was profoundly concerned at the nature of that exclamation.

"Dear me! Won't the truth do, then? I hoped you could have told them something consoling. I am thinking of the poor mother now. Your Russia *is* a cruel country."

He moved a little in his chair.

"Yes," I repeated. "I thought you would have had something authentic to tell."

The twitching of his lips before he spoke was curious.

"What if it is not worth telling?"

"Not worth—from what point of view? I don't understand."

"From every point of view."

I spoke with some asperity.

"I should think that anything which could explain the circumstances of that midnight arrest. . . ."

"Reported by a journalist for the amusement of the civilized Europe," he broke in scornfully.

"Yes, reported. . . . But aren't they true? I can't make out your attitude in this. Either the man is a hero to you, or . . ."

He approached his face with fiercely distended nostrils close to mine so suddenly that I had the greatest difficulty in not starting back.

"You ask me! I suppose it amuses you, all this. Look here! I am a worker. I studied. Yes, I studied very hard. There is intelligence here." (He tapped his forehead with his finger-tips.) "Don't you think a Russian may have sane ambitions? Yes—I had even prospects. Certainly! I had. And now you see me here, abroad, everything gone, lost, sacrificed. You see me here—and you ask! You see me, don't you?—sitting before you."

He threw himself back violently. I kept outwardly calm.

"Yes, I see you here; and I assume you are here on account of the Haldin affair?"

His manner changed.

"You call it the Haldin affair—do you?" he observed indifferently.

"I have no right to ask you anything," I said. "I wouldn't presume. But in that case the mother and the sister of him who must be a hero in your eyes cannot be indifferent to you. The girl is a frank and generous creature, having the noblest—well— illusions. You will tell her nothing—or you will tell her everything. But speaking now of the object with which I've approached you: first, we have to deal with the morbid state of the mother. Perhaps something could be invented under your authority as a cure for a distracted and suffering soul filled with maternal affection."

His air of weary indifference was accentuated, I could not help thinking, wilfully.

"Oh yes. Something might," he mumbled carelessly.

He put his hand over his mouth to conceal a yawn. When he uncovered his lips they were smiling faintly.

"Pardon me. This has been a long conversation, and I have not had much sleep the last two nights."

This unexpected, somewhat insolent sort of apology had the merit of being perfectly true. He had had no nightly rest to speak of since that day when, in the grounds of the Château Borel, the sister of Victor Haldin had appeared before him. The perplexities and the complex terrors—I may say—of this sleeplessness are recorded in the document I was to see later—the document which is the main source of this narrative. At the moment he looked to me convincingly tired, gone slack all over, like a man who has passed through some sort of crisis.

"I have had a lot of urgent writing to do," he added.

I rose from my chair at once, and he followed my example, without haste, a little heavily.

"I must apologize for detaining you so long," I said.

"Why apologize? One can't very well go to bed before night. And you did not detain me. I could have left you at any time."

I had not stayed with him to be offended.

"I am glad you have been sufficiently interested," I said calmly. "No merit of mine, though—the commonest sort of regard for the mother of your friend was enough. . . . As to Miss Haldin herself, she at one time was disposed to think that her brother had been betrayed to the police in some way."

To my great surprise Mr. Razumov sat down again suddenly. I stared at him, and I must say that he returned my stare without winking for quite a considerable time.

"In some way," he mumbled, as if he had not understood or could not believe his ears.

"Some unforeseen event, a sheer accident might have done that," I went on. "Or, as she characteristically put it to me, the folly or weakness of some unhappy fellow-revolutionist."

"Folly or weakness," he repeated bitterly.

"She is a very generous creature," I observed after a time. The man admired by Victor Haldin fixed his eyes on the ground. I turned away and moved off, apparently unnoticed by him. I nourished no resentment of the moody brusqueness with which he had treated me. The sentiment I was carrying away from that conversation was that of hopelessness. Before I had got fairly clear of the raft of chairs and tables he had rejoined me.

"H'm, yes!" I heard him at my elbow again. "But what do you think?"

I did not look round even.

"I think that you people are under a curse."

He made no sound. It was only on the pavement outside the gate that I heard him again.

"I should like to walk with you a little."

After all, I preferred this enigmatical young man to his celebrated compatriot, the great Peter Ivanovitch. But I saw no reason for being particularly gracious.

"I am going now to the railway station, by the shortest way from here, to meet a friend from England," I said, for all answer to his unexpected proposal. I hoped that something informing could come of it. As we stood on the curbstone waiting for a tramcar to pass, he remarked gloomily—

"I like what you said just now."

"Do you?"

We stepped off the pavement together.

"The great problem," he went on, "is to understand thoroughly the nature of the curse."

"That's not very difficult, I think."

"I think so too," he agreed with me, and his readiness, strangely enough, did not make him less enigmatical in the least.

"A curse is an evil spell," I tried him again. "And the important, the great problem, is to find the means to break it."

"Yes. To find the means."

That was also an assent, but he seemed to be thinking of something else. We had crossed diagonally the open space before the theatre, and began to descend a broad, sparely frequented street in the direction of one of the smaller bridges. He kept on by my side without speaking for a long time.

"You are not thinking of leaving Geneva soon?" I asked.

He was silent for so long that I began to think I had been indiscreet, and should get no answer at all. Yet on looking at him I almost believed that my question had caused him something in the nature of positive anguish. I detected it mainly in the clasping of his hands, in which he put a great force stealthily. Once, however, he had overcome that sort of agonizing hesitation sufficiently to tell me that he had no such intention, he became rather communicative—at least relatively to the former off-hand curtness of his speeches. The tone, too, was more amiable. He informed me that he intended to study and also to write. He went even so far as to tell me he had been to Stuttgart. Stuttgart, I was aware, was one of the revolutionary centres. The directing committee of one of the Russian parties (I can't tell now which) was located in that town. It was there that he got into touch with the active work of the revolutionists outside Russia.

"I have never been abroad before," he explained, in a rather inanimate voice now. Then, after a slight hesitation, altogether different from the agonizing irresolution my first simple question "whether he meant to stay in Geneva" had aroused, he made me an unexpected confidence—

"The fact is, I have received a sort of mission from them."

"Which will keep you here in Geneva?"

"Yes. Here. In this odious . . ."

I was satisfied with my faculty for putting two and two together when I drew the inference that the mission had something to do with the person of the great Peter Ivanovitch. But I kept that surmise to myself naturally, and Mr. Razumov said nothing more for some considerable time. It was only when we were nearly on the bridge we had been making for that he opened his lips again, abruptly—

"Could I see that precious article anywhere?"

I had to think for a moment before I saw what he was referring to.

"It has been reproduced in parts by the Press here. There are files to be seen in various places. My copy of the English newspaper I have left with Miss Haldin, I remember, on the day after it reached me. I was sufficiently worried by seeing it lying on a table by the side of the poor mother's chair for weeks. Then it disappeared. It was a relief, I assure you."

He had stopped short.

"I trust," I continued, "that you will find time to see these ladies fairly often—that you will make time."

He stared at me so queerly that I hardly know how to define his aspect. I could not understand it in this connexion at all. What ailed him? I asked myself. What strange thought had come into his head? What vision of all the horrors that can be seen in his hopeless country had come suddenly to haunt his brain? If it were anything connected with the fate of Victor Haldin, then I hoped earnestly he would keep it to himself for ever. I was, to speak plainly, so shocked that I tried to conceal my impression by— Heaven forgive me—a smile and the assumption of a light manner.

"Surely," I exclaimed, "that needn't cost you a great effort."

He turned away from me and leaned over the parapet of the bridge. For a moment I waited, looking at his back. And yet, I assure you, I was not anxious just then to look at his face again.

He did not move at all. He did not mean to move. I walked on slowly on my way towards the station, and at the end of the bridge I glanced over my shoulder. No, he had not moved. He hung well over the parapet, as if captivated by the smooth rush of the blue water under the arch. The current there is swift, extremely swift; it makes some people dizzy; I myself can never look at it for any length of time without experiencing a dread of being suddenly snatched away by its destructive force. Some brains cannot resist the suggestion of irresistible power and of headlong motion.

It apparently had a charm for Mr. Razumov. I left him hanging far over the parapet of the bridge. The way he had behaved to me could not be put down to mere boorishness. There was something else under his scorn and impatience. Perhaps, I thought, with sudden approach to hidden truth, it was the same thing which had kept him over a week, nearly ten days indeed, from coming near Miss Haldin. But what it was I could not tell.

# PART THIRD

## I

The water under the bridge ran violent and deep. Its slightly undulating rush seemed capable of scouring out a channel for itself through solid granite while you looked. But had it flowed through Razumov's breast, it could not have washed away the accumulated bitterness the wrecking of his life had deposited there.

"What is the meaning of all this?" he thought, staring downwards at the headlong flow so smooth and clean that only the passage of a faint air-bubble, or a thin vanishing streak of foam like a white hair, disclosed its vertiginous rapidity, its terrible force. "Why has that meddlesome old Englishman blundered against me? And what is this silly tale of a crazy old woman?"

He was trying to think brutally on purpose, but he avoided any mental reference to the young girl. "A crazy old woman," he repeated to himself. "It is a fatality! Or ought I to despise all this as absurd? But no! I am wrong! I can't afford to despise anything. An absurdity may be the starting-point of the most dangerous complications. How is one to guard against it? It puts to rout one's intelligence. The more intelligent one is the less one suspects an absurdity."

A wave of wrath choked his thoughts for a moment. It even made his body leaning over the parapet quiver; then he resumed his silent thinking, like a secret dialogue with himself. And even in that privacy, his thought had some reservations of which he was vaguely conscious.

"After all, this is not absurd. It is insignificant. It is absolutely insignificant—absolutely. The craze of an old woman—the fussy officiousness of a blundering elderly Englishman. What devil put him in the way? Haven't I treated him cavalierly enough? Haven't I just? That's the way to treat these meddlesome persons. Is it possible that he still stands behind my back, waiting?"

Razumov felt a faint chill run down his spine. It was not fear. He was certain that it was not fear—not fear for himself—but it was, all the same, a sort of apprehension as if for another, for some one he knew without being able to put a name on the personality. But the recollection that the officious Englishman had a train to meet tranquillized him for a time. It was too stupid to suppose that he should be wasting his time in waiting. It was unnecessary to look round and make sure.

"But what did the man mean by his extraordinary rigmarole about the newspaper, and that crazy old woman?" he thought suddenly. It was a damnable presumption, anyhow, something that only an Englishman could be capable of. All this was a sort of sport for him—the sport of revolution—a game to look at from the height of his superiority. And what on earth did he mean by his exclamation, "Won't the truth do?"

Razumov pressed his folded arms to the stone coping over which he was leaning with force. "Won't the truth do? The truth for the crazy old mother of the—"

The young man shuddered again. Yes. The truth would do! Apparently it would do. Exactly. "And receive thanks," he thought, formulating the unspoken words cynically. "Fall on my neck in gratitude, no doubt," he jeered mentally. But this mood abandoned him at once. He felt sad, as if his heart had become empty suddenly. "Well, I must be cautious," he concluded, coming to himself as though his brain had been awakened from a trance. "There is nothing, no one, too insignificant, too absurd to be disregarded," he thought wearily. "I must be cautious."

Razumov pushed himself with his hands[1] away from the balustrade and, retracing his steps along the bridge, walked straight to his lodgings, where, for a few days, he led a solitary and retired existence. He neglected Peter Ivanovitch, to whom he was accredited by the Stuttgart group; he never went near the refugee revolutionists, to whom he had been introduced on his arrival. He kept out of that world altogether. And he felt that such conduct, causing surprise and arousing suspicion, contained an element of danger for himself.

This is not to say that during these few days he never went out. I met him several times in the streets, but he gave me no recognition. Once, going home after an evening call on the ladies Haldin, I saw him crossing the dark roadway of the Boulevard des Philosophes. He had a broad-brimmed soft hat, and the collar of his coat turned up. I watched him make straight for the house, but, instead of going in, he stopped opposite the still lighted windows, and after a time went away down a side-street.

I knew that he had not been to see Mrs. Haldin yet. Miss Haldin told me he was reluctant; moreover, the mental condition of Mrs. Haldin had changed. She seemed to think now that her son was living, and she perhaps awaited his arrival. Her immobility in the great arm-chair in front of the window had an air of

---

1 The first English edition has "with his hand" (M, T).

expectancy, even when the blind was down and the lamps lighted.

For my part, I was convinced that she had received her death-stroke; Miss Haldin, to whom, of course, I said nothing of my forebodings, thought that no good would come from introducing Mr. Razumov just then, an opinion which I shared fully. I knew that she met the young man on the Bastions. Once or twice I saw them strolling slowly up the main alley. They met every day for weeks. I avoided passing that way during the hour when Miss Haldin took her exercise there. One day, however, in a fit of absent-mindedness, I entered the gates and came upon her walking alone. I stopped to exchange a few words. Mr. Razumov failed to turn up, and we began to talk about him—naturally.

"Did he tell you anything definite about your brother's activities—his end?" I ventured to ask.

"No," admitted Miss Haldin, with some hesitation. "Nothing definite."

I understood well enough that all their conversations must have been referred mentally to that dead man who had brought them together. That was unavoidable. But it was in the living man that she was interested. That was unavoidable too, I suppose. And as I pushed my inquiries I discovered that he had disclosed himself to her as a by no means conventional revolutionist, contemptuous of catchwords, of theories, of men too. I was rather pleased at that—but I was a little puzzled.

"His mind goes forward, far ahead of the struggle," Miss Haldin explained. "Of course, he is an actual worker too," she added.

"And do you understand him?" I inquired point-blank.

She hesitated again. "Not altogether," she murmured.

I perceived that he had fascinated her by an assumption of mysterious reserve.

"Do you know what I think?" she went on, breaking through her reserved, almost reluctant attitude: "I think that he is observing, studying me, to discover whether I am worthy of his trust . . ."

"And that pleases you?"

She kept mysteriously silent for a moment. Then with energy, but in a confidential tone—

"I am convinced," she declared, "that this extraordinary man is meditating some vast plan, some great undertaking; he is possessed by it—he suffers from it—and from being alone in the world."

"And so he's looking for helpers?" I commented, turning away my head.

Again there was a silence.

"Why not?" she said at last.

The dead brother, the dying mother, the foreign friend, had fallen into a distant background. But, at the same time, Peter Ivanovitch was absolutely nowhere now. And this thought consoled me. Yet I saw the gigantic shadow of Russian life deepening around her like the darkness of an advancing night. It would devour her presently. I inquired after Mrs. Haldin—that other victim of the deadly shade.

A remorseful uneasiness appeared in her frank eyes. Mother seemed no worse, but if I only knew what strange fancies she had sometimes! Then Miss Haldin, glancing at her watch, declared that she could not stay a moment longer, and with a hasty hand-shake ran off lightly.

Decidedly, Mr. Razumov was not to turn up that day. Incomprehensible youth! . . .

But less than an hour afterwards, while crossing the Place Mollard, I caught sight of him boarding a South Shore tramcar.

"He's going to the Château Borel," I thought.

★★★★★

After depositing Razumov at the gates of the Château Borel, some half a mile or so from the town, the car continued its journey between two straight lines of shady trees. Across the roadway in the sunshine a short wooden pier jutted into the shallow pale water, which farther out had an intense blue tint contrasting unpleasantly with the green orderly slopes on the opposite shore. The whole view, with the harbour jetties of white stone underlining lividly the dark front of the town to the left, and the expanding space of water to the right with jutting promontories of no particular character, had the uninspiring, glittering quality of a very fresh oleograph.[1] Razumov turned his back on it with contempt. He thought it odious—oppressively odious—in its unsuggestive finish: the very perfection of mediocrity attained at last after centuries of toil and culture. And turning his back on it, he faced the entrance to the grounds of the Château Borel.

The bars of the central way and the wrought-iron arch between the dark weather-stained stone piers were very rusty;

---

1 A colored lithograph on canvas made to imitate an oil painting.

and, though fresh tracks of wheels ran under it, the gate looked as if it had not been opened for a very long time. But close against the lodge, built of the same grey stone as the piers (its windows were all boarded up), there was a small side entrance. The bars of that were rusty too; it stood ajar and looked as though it had not been closed for a long time. In fact, Razumov, trying to push it open a little wider, discovered it was immovable.

"Democratic virtue. There are no thieves here, apparently," he muttered to himself, with displeasure. Before advancing into the grounds he looked back sourly at an idle working man lounging on a bench in the clean, broad avenue. The fellow had thrown his feet up; one of his arms hung over the low back of the public seat; he was taking a day off in lordly repose, as if everything in sight belonged to him.

"Elector! Eligible! Enlightened!" Razumov muttered to himself. "A brute, all the same."

Razumov entered the grounds and walked fast up the wide sweep of the drive, trying to think of nothing—to rest his head, to rest his emotions too. But arriving at the foot of the terrace before the house he faltered, affected physically by some invisible interference. The mysteriousness of his quickened heart-beats startled him. He stopped short and looked at the brick wall of the terrace, faced with shallow arches, meagrely clothed by a few unthriving creepers, with an ill-kept narrow flower-bed along its foot.

"It is here!" he thought, with a sort of awe. "It is here—on this very spot . . ."

He was tempted to flight at the mere recollection of his first meeting with Nathalie Haldin. He confessed it to himself; but he did not move, and that not because he wished to resist an unworthy weakness, but because he knew that he had no place to fly to. Moreover, he could not leave Geneva. He recognized, even without thinking, that it was impossible. It would have been a fatal admission, an act of moral suicide. It would have been also physically dangerous. Slowly he ascended the stairs of the terrace, flanked by two stained greenish stone urns of funereal aspect.

Across the broad platform, where a few blades of grass sprouted on the discoloured gravel, the door of the house, with its ground-floor windows shuttered, faced him, wide open. He believed that his approach had been noted, because, framed in the doorway, without his tall hat, Peter Ivanovitch seemed to be waiting for his approach.

The ceremonious black frock-coat and the bared head of Europe's greatest feminist accentuated the dubiousness of his status in the house rented by Madame de S——, his Egeria. His aspect combined the formality of the caller with the freedom of the proprietor. Florid and bearded and masked by the dark blue glasses, he met the visitor, and at once took him familiarly under the arm.

Razumov suppressed every sign of repugnance by an effort which the constant necessity of prudence had rendered almost mechanical. And this necessity had settled his expression in a cast of austere, almost fanatical, aloofness. The "heroic fugitive," impressed afresh by the severe detachment of this new arrival from revolutionary Russia, took a conciliatory, even a confidential tone. Madame de S—— was resting after a bad night. She often had bad nights. He had left his hat upstairs on the landing and had come down to suggest to his young friend a stroll and a good open-hearted talk in one of the shady alleys behind the house. After voicing this proposal, the great man glanced at the unmoved face by his side, and could not restrain himself from exclaiming—

"On my word, young man, you are an extraordinary person."

"I fancy you are mistaken, Peter Ivanovitch. If I were really an extraordinary person, I would not be here, walking with you in a garden in Switzerland, Canton[1] of Geneva, Commune[2] of—what's the name of the Commune this place belongs to? . . . Never mind—the heart of democracy, anyhow. A fit heart for it; no bigger than a parched pea and about as much value. I am no more extraordinary than the rest of us Russians wandering abroad."

But Peter Ivanovitch dissented emphatically—

"No! No! You are not ordinary. I have some experience of Russians who are—well—living abroad. You appear to me, and to others too, a marked personality."

"What does he mean by this?" Razumov asked himself, turning his eyes fully on his companion. The face of Peter Ivanovitch expressed a meditative seriousness.

"You don't suppose, Kirylo Sidorovitch, that I have not heard of you from various points where you made yourself known on your way here? I have had letters."

"Oh, we are great in talking about each other," interjected Razumov, who had listened with great attention. "Gossip, tales,

---

1 Swiss equivalent of a province in Canada or a state in the United States.
2 Another administrative division, smaller than a canton. In fact, Geneva is in the Commune of Eaux-Vives.

suspicions, and all that sort of thing, we know how to deal in to perfection. Calumny, even."

In indulging in this sally, Razumov managed very well to conceal the feeling of anxiety which had come over him. At the same time he was saying to himself that there could be no earthly reason for anxiety. He was relieved by the evident sincerity of the protesting voice.

"Heavens!" cried Peter Ivanovitch. "What are you talking about? What reason can *you* have to . . . ?"

The great exile flung up his arms as if words had failed him in sober truth. Razumov was satisfied. Yet he was moved to continue in the same vein.

"I am talking of the poisonous plants which flourish in the world of conspirators, like evil mushrooms in a dark cellar."

"You are casting aspersions," remonstrated Peter Ivanovitch, "which as far as you are concerned—"

"No!" Razumov interrupted without heat. "Indeed, I don't want to cast aspersions, but it's just as well to have no illusions."

Peter Ivanovitch gave him an inscrutable glance of his dark spectacles, accompanied by a faint smile.

"The man who says that he has no illusions has at least that one," he said, in a very friendly tone. "But I see how it is, Kirylo Sidorovitch. You aim at stoicism."

"Stoicism![1] That's a pose of the Greeks and the Romans. Let's leave it to them. We are Russians, that is—children; that is—sincere; that is—cynical, if you like. But that's not a pose."

A long silence ensued. They strolled slowly under the lime-trees. Peter Ivanovitch had put his hands behind his back. Razumov felt the ungravelled ground of the deeply shaded walk damp and as if slippery under his feet. He asked himself, with uneasiness, if he were saying the right things. The direction of the conversation ought to have been more under his control, he reflected. The great man appeared to be reflecting on his side too. He cleared his throat slightly, and Razumov felt at once a painful reawakening of scorn and fear.

"I am astonished," began Peter Ivanovitch gently. "Supposing you are right in your indictment, how can you raise any question of calumny or gossip, in your case? It is unreasonable. The fact is, Kirylo Sidorovitch, there is not enough known of you to give hold

---

1 A school of philosophy emphasizing fortitude and self-control in order to become unbiased and clear-thinking. It began in ancient Greece but was also adopted in Rome.

to gossip or even calumny. Just now you are a man associated with a great deed, which had been hoped for, and tried for too, without success. People have perished for attempting that which you and Haldin have done at last. You come to us out of Russia, with that prestige. But you cannot deny that you have not been communicative, Kirylo Sidorovitch. People you have met imparted their impressions to me; one wrote this, another that, but I form my own opinions. I waited to see you first. You are a man out of the common. That's positively so. You are close, very close. This taciturnity, this severe brow, this something inflexible and secret in you, inspires hopes and a little wonder as to what you may mean. There is something of a Brutus . . ."

"Pray spare me those classical allusions!" burst out Razumov nervously. "What comes Junius Brutus[1] to do here? It is ridiculous! Do you mean to say," he added sarcastically, but lowering his voice, "that the Russian revolutionists are all patricians and that I am an aristocrat?"

Peter Ivanovitch, who had been helping himself with a few gestures, clasped his hands again behind his back, and made a few steps, pondering.

"Not *all* patricians," he muttered at last. "But you, at any rate, are one of *us*."[2]

Razumov smiled bitterly.

"To be sure my name is not Gugenheimer,"[3] he said in a

---

1 There are several prominent Roman figures of this name. It appears that Razumov is referring to Lucius Junius Brutus (d. 508? BC), founder of the Roman republic in 509 BC and a leader of the patrician revolution. Peter Ivanovitch, however, initially may be referring to Marcus Junius Brutus (85-42 BC), who betrayed and assassinated Julius Cæsar (100?-44 BC); perhaps this is why Razumov interrupts him and steers the conversation toward a different Brutus.

2 The phrase "one of us" is a common refrain in Conrad's earlier novel *Lord Jim* (1900), in which an emphasis on belonging is one of the important themes of the novel. Here, it also appears to emphasize the fact that one must belong to one side or the other and that neutrality is not an option (as Razumov has already discovered).

3 Probably a reference to Meyer Guggenheim (1828-1905). Born in Switzerland, he emigrated to the United States, where he became a self-made multi-millionaire. Despite many Jews being numbered among the revolutionaries, Razumov's anti-Semitic tone would be in keeping with typical attitudes toward Jews among many Russians of that time, particularly those in support of tsarist Russia.

sneering tone. "I am not a democratic Jew. How can I help it? Not everybody has such luck. I have no name, I have no . . ."

The European celebrity showed a great concern. He stepped back a pace and his arms flew in front of his person, extended, deprecatory, almost entreating. His deep bass voice was full of pain.

"But, my dear young friend!" he cried. "My dear Kirylo Sidorovitch . . ."

Razumov shook his head.

"The very patronymic you are so civil as to use when addressing me I have no legal right to—but what of that? I don't wish to claim it. I have no father. So much the better. But I will tell you what: my mother's grandfather was a peasant—a serf. See how much I am one of *you*. I don't want anyone to claim me. But Russia *can't* disown me. She cannot!"

Razumov struck his breast with his fist.

"I am *it*!"

Peter Ivanovitch walked on slowly, his head lowered. Razumov followed, vexed with himself. That was not the right sort of talk. All sincerity was an imprudence. Yet one could not renounce truth altogether, he thought, with despair. Peter Ivanovitch, meditating behind his dark glasses, became to him suddenly so odious that if he had had a knife, he fancied he could have stabbed him not only without compunction, but with a horrible, triumphant satisfaction. His imagination dwelt on that atrocity in spite of himself. It was as if he were becoming light-headed. "It is not what is expected of me," he repeated to himself. "It is not what is—I could get away by breaking the fastening on the little gate I see there in the back wall. It is a flimsy lock. Nobody in the house seems to know he is here with me. Oh yes. The hat! These women would discover presently the hat he has left on the landing. They would come upon him, lying dead in this damp, gloomy shade— but I would be gone and no one could ever . . . Lord! Am I going mad?" he asked himself in a fright.

The great man was heard—musing in an undertone.

"H'm, yes! That—no doubt—in a certain sense . . ." He raised his voice. "There is a deal of pride about you . . ."

The intonation of Peter Ivanovitch took on a homely, familiar ring, acknowledging, in a way, Razumov's claim to peasant descent.

"A great deal of pride, brother Kirylo. And I don't say that you have no justification for it. I have admitted you had. I have ventured to allude to the facts of your birth simply because I attach no mean importance to it. You are one of us—*un des nôtres*.[1] I reflect on that with satisfaction."

"I attach some importance to it also," said Razumov quietly. "I won't even deny that it may have some importance for you too," he continued, after a slight pause and with a touch of grimness of which he was himself aware, with some annoyance. He hoped it had escaped the perception of Peter Ivanovitch. "But suppose we talk no more about it?"

"Well, we shall not—not after this one time, Kirylo Sidorovitch," persisted the noble arch-priest of Revolution. "This shall be the last occasion. You cannot believe for a moment that I had the slightest idea of wounding your feelings. You are clearly a superior nature—that's how I read you. Quite above the common —h'm—susceptibilities. But the fact is, Kirylo Sidorovitch, I don't know your susceptibilities. Nobody, out of Russia, knows much of you—as yet!"

"You have been watching me?" suggested Razumov.

"Yes."

The great man had spoken in a tone of perfect frankness, but as they turned their faces to each other Razumov felt baffled by the dark spectacles. Under their cover, Peter Ivanovitch hinted that he had felt for some time the need of meeting a man of energy and character, in view of a certain project. He said nothing more precise, however; and after some critical remarks upon the personalities of the various members of the committee of revolutionary action in Stuttgart, he let the conversation lapse for quite a long while. They paced the alley from end to end. Razumov, silent too, raised his eyes from time to time to cast a glance at the back of the house. It offered no sign of being inhabited. With its grimy, weather-stained walls and all the windows shuttered from top to bottom, it looked damp and gloomy and deserted. It might very well have been haunted in traditional style by some doleful, groaning, futile ghost of a middle-class order. The shades evoked, as worldly rumour had it, by Madame de S—— to meet statesmen, diplomatists, deputies of various European Parliaments, must have been of another sort. Razumov had never seen Madame de S—— but in the carriage.

Peter Ivanovitch came out of his abstraction.

"Two things I may say to you at once. I believe, first, that neither a leader nor any decisive action can come out of the dregs

---

1  One of us (French).

of a people. Now, if you ask me what are the dregs of a people—h'm—it would take too long to tell. You would be surprised at the variety of ingredients that for me go to the making up of these dregs—of that which ought, *must* remain at the bottom. Moreover, such a statement might be subject to discussion. But I can tell you what is *not* the dregs. On that it is impossible for us to disagree. The peasantry of a people is not the dregs; neither is its highest class—well—the nobility. Reflect on that, Kirylo Sidorovitch! I believe you are well fitted for reflection. Everything in a people that is not genuine, not its own by origin or development, is—well—dirt! Intelligence in the wrong place is that. Foreign-bred doctrines are that. Dirt! Dregs! The second thing I would offer to your meditation is this: that for us at this moment there yawns a chasm between the past and the future. It can never be bridged by foreign liberalism. All attempts at it are either folly or cheating. Bridged it can never be! It has to be filled up."

A sort of sinister jocularity had crept into the tones of the burly feminist. He seized Razumov's arm above the elbow, and gave it a slight shake.

"Do you understand, enigmatical young man? It has got to be just filled up."

Razumov kept an unmoved countenance.

"Don't you think that I have already gone beyond meditation on that subject?" he said, freeing his arm by a quiet movement which increased the distance a little between himself and Peter Ivanovitch, as they went on strolling abreast. And he added that surely whole cartloads of words and theories could never fill that chasm. No meditation was necessary. A sacrifice of many lives could alone— He fell silent without finishing the phrase.

Peter Ivanovitch inclined his big hairy head slowly. After a moment he proposed that they should go and see if Madame de S—— was now visible.

"We shall get some tea," he said, turning out of the shaded gloomy walk with a brisker step.

The lady companion had been on the look out. Her dark skirt whisked into the doorway as the two men came in sight round the corner. She ran off somewhere altogether, and had disappeared when they entered the hall. In the crude light falling from the dusty glass skylight upon the black and white tessellated floor, covered with muddy tracks, their footsteps echoed faintly. The great feminist led the way up the stairs. On the balustrade of the first-floor landing a shiny tall hat reposed, rim upwards, opposite the double door of the drawing-room, haunted, it was said, by evoked ghosts, and frequented, it was to be supposed, by fugitive revolutionists. The cracked white paint of the panels, the tarnished gilt of the mouldings, permitted one to imagine nothing but dust and emptiness within. Before turning the massive brass handle, Peter Ivanovitch gave his young companion a sharp, partly critical, partly preparatory glance.

"No one is perfect," he murmured discreetly. Thus, the possessor of a rare jewel might, before opening the casket, warn the profane that no gem perhaps is flawless.

He remained with his hand on the door-handle so long that Razumov assented by a moody "No."

"Perfection itself would not produce that effect," pursued Peter Ivanovitch, "in a world not meant for it. But you shall find there a mind—no!—the quintessence of feminine intuition which will understand any perplexity you may be suffering from by the irresistible, enlightening force of sympathy. Nothing can remain obscure before that—that—inspired, yes, inspired penetration, this true light of femininity."

The gaze of the dark spectacles in its glossy steadfastness gave his face an air of absolute conviction. Razumov felt a momentary shrinking before that closed door.

"Penetration? Light," he stammered out. "Do you mean some sort of thought-reading?"

Peter Ivanovitch seemed shocked.

"I mean something utterly different," he retorted, with a faint, pitying smile.

Razumov began to feel angry, very much against his wish.

"This is very mysterious," he muttered through his teeth.

"You don't object to being understood, to being guided?" queried the great feminist.

Razumov exploded in a fierce whisper.

"In what sense? Be pleased to understand that I am a serious person. Who do you take me for?"

They looked at each other very closely. Razumov's temper was cooled by the impenetrable earnestness of the blue glasses meeting his stare. Peter Ivanovitch turned the handle at last.

"You shall know directly," he said, pushing the door open.

A low-pitched grating voice was heard within the room.

"*Enfin. Vous voilà.*"[1]

In the doorway, his black-coated bulk blocking the view, Peter Ivanovitch boomed in a hearty tone with something boastful in it.

---

1 Finally. There you are (French).

"Yes. Here I am!"

He glanced over his shoulder at Razumov, who waited for him to move on.

"And I am bringing you a proved conspirator—a real one this time. *Un vrai celui là.*"[1]

This pause in the doorway gave the "proved conspirator" time to make sure that his face did not betray his angry curiosity and his mental disgust.

These sentiments stand confessed in Mr. Razumov's memorandum of his first interview with Madame de S——. The very words I use in my narrative are written where their sincerity cannot be suspected. The record, which could not have been meant for anyone's eyes but his own, was not, I think, the outcome of that strange impulse of indiscretion common to men who lead secret lives, and accounting for the invariable existence of "compromising documents" in all the plots and conspiracies of history. Mr. Razumov looked at it, I suppose, as a man looks at himself in a mirror, with wonder, perhaps with anguish, with anger or despair. Yes, as a threatened man may look fearfully at his own face in the glass, formulating to himself reassuring excuses for his appearance marked by the taint of some insidious hereditary disease.

## II

The Egeria of the "Russian Mazzini"[2] produced, at first view, a strong effect by the death-like immobility of an obviously painted face. The eyes appeared extraordinarily brilliant. The figure, in a close-fitting dress, admirably made, but by no means fresh, had an elegant stiffness. The rasping voice inviting him to sit down; the rigidity of the upright attitude with one arm extended along the back of the sofa, the white gleam of the big eyeballs setting off the black, fathomless stare of the enlarged pupils, impressed Razumov more than anything he had seen since his hasty and secret departure from St. Petersburg. A witch in Parisian clothes, he thought. A portent! He actually hesitated in his advance, and did not even comprehend, at first, what the rasping voice was saying.

---

1  A real one, that one there (French).

2  Guiseppe Mazzini (1805-72) was an Italian revolutionary who favored the unification of Italy by means of popular uprisings. He lived in exile in France, Switzerland, and then England from 1831 until 1848.

"Sit down. Draw your chair nearer me. There—"

He sat down. At close quarters the rouged cheek-bones, the wrinkles, the fine lines on each side of the vivid lips, astounded him. He was being received graciously, with a smile which made him think of a grinning skull.

"We have been hearing about you for some time."

He did not know what to say, and murmured some disconnected words. The grinning skull effect vanished.

"And do you know that the general complaint is that you have shown yourself very reserved everywhere?"

Razumov remained silent for a time, thinking of his answer.

"I, don't you see, am a man of action," he said huskily, glancing upwards.

Peter Ivanovitch stood in portentous expectant silence by the side of his chair. A slight feeling of nausea came over Razumov. What could be the relations of these two people to each other? She like a galvanized corpse out of some Hoffman's Tale[1]—he the preacher of feminist gospel for all the world, and a super-revolutionist besides! This ancient, painted mummy with unfathomable eyes, and this burly, bull-necked, deferential . . . what was it? Witchcraft, fascination. . . . "It's for her money," he thought. "She has millions!"

The walls, the floor of the room were bare like a barn. The few pieces of furniture had been discovered in the garrets and dragged down into service without having been properly dusted, even. It was the refuse the banker's widow had left behind her. The windows without curtains had an indigent, sleepless look. In two of them the dirty yellowy-white blinds had been pulled down. All this spoke, not of poverty, but of sordid penuriousness.[2]

The hoarse voice on the sofa uttered angrily—

"You are looking round, Kirylo Sidorovitch. I have been shamefully robbed, positively ruined."

A rattling laugh, which seemed beyond her control, interrupted her for a moment.

"A slavish nature would find consolation in the fact that the principal robber was an exalted and almost a sacrosanct person— a Grand Duke, in fact. Do you understand, Mr. Razumov? A Grand Duke—No! You have no idea what thieves those people are! Downright thieves!"

---

1  E.T.A. Hoffman (1776-1822), a German artist, composer, and author who is particularly known for his tales of the supernatural.

2  Miserliness.

Her bosom heaved, but her left arm remained rigidly extended along the back of the couch.

"You will only upset yourself," breathed out a deep voice, which, to Razumov's startled glance, seemed to proceed from under the steady spectacles of Peter Ivanovitch, rather than from his lips, which had hardly moved.

"What of that? I say thieves! *Voleurs! Voleurs!*"[1]

Razumov was quite confounded by this unexpected clamour, which had in it something of wailing and croaking, and more than a suspicion of hysteria.

"*Voleurs! Voleurs! Vol . . .*"

"No power on earth can rob you of your genius," shouted Peter Ivanovitch in an overpowering bass, but without stirring, without a gesture of any kind. A profound silence fell.

Razumov remained outwardly impassive. "What is the meaning of this performance?" he was asking himself. But with a preliminary sound of bumping outside some door behind him, the lady companion, in a threadbare black skirt and frayed blouse, came in rapidly, walking on her heels, and carrying in both hands a big Russian samovar, obviously too heavy for her. Razumov made an instinctive movement to help, which startled her so much that she nearly dropped her hissing burden. She managed, however, to land it on the table, and looked so frightened that Razumov hastened to sit down. She produced then, from an adjacent room, four glass tumblers, a teapot, and a sugar-basin, on a black iron tray.

The rasping voice asked from the sofa abruptly—

"*Les gâteaux?*[2] Have you remembered to bring the cakes?"

Peter Ivanovitch, without a word, marched out on to the landing, and returned instantly with a parcel wrapped up in white glazed paper, which he must have extracted from the interior of his hat. With imperturbable gravity he undid the string and smoothed the paper open on a part of the table within reach of Madame de S——'s hand. The lady companion poured out the tea, then retired into a distant corner out of everybody's sight. From time to time Madame de S—— extended a claw-like hand, glittering with costly rings, towards the paper of cakes, took up one and devoured it, displaying her big false teeth ghoulishly. Meantime she talked in a hoarse tone of the political situation in

---

1 Thieves! Thieves! (French).
2 The cakes (French).

the Balkans.[1] She built great hopes on some complication in the peninsula for arousing a great movement of national indignation in Russia against "these thieves—thieves—thieves."

"You will only upset yourself," Peter Ivanovitch interposed, raising his glassy gaze. He smoked cigarettes and drank tea in silence, continuously. When he had finished a glass, he flourished his hand above his shoulder. At that signal the lady companion, ensconced in her corner, with round eyes like a watchful animal, would dart out to the table and pour him out another tumblerful.

Razumov looked at her once or twice. She was anxious, tremulous, though neither Madame de S—— nor Peter Ivanovitch paid the slightest attention to her. "What have they done between them to that forlorn creature?" Razumov asked himself. "Have they terrified her out of her senses with ghosts, or simply have they only been beating her?" When she gave him his second glass of tea, he noticed that her lips trembled in the manner of a scared person about to burst into speech. But of course she said nothing, and retired into her corner, as if hugging to herself the smile of thanks he gave her.

"She may be worth cultivating," thought Razumov suddenly.

He was calming down, getting hold of the actuality into which he had been thrown—for the first time perhaps since Victor Haldin had entered his room . . . and had gone out again. He was distinctly aware of being the object of the famous—or notorious—Madame de S——'s ghastly graciousness.

Madame de S—— was pleased to discover that this young man was different from the other types of revolutionist members of committees, secret emissaries, vulgar and unmannerly fugitive professors, rough students, ex-cobblers with apostolic faces, consumptive and ragged enthusiasts, Hebrew youths, common fellows of all sorts that used to come and go around Peter Ivanovitch—fanatics, pedants, proletarians all. It was pleasant to talk to this young man of notably good appearance—for Madame de S—— was not always in a mystical state of mind. Razumov's taciturnity only excited her to a quicker, more voluble utterance. It still dealt with the Balkans. She knew all the statesmen of that

---

1   A peninsula in southeastern Europe comprising the present-day countries of Albania, Bosnia and Herzegovina, Bulgaria, Croatia, Montenegro, Greece, Macedonia, Serbia, Romania, and Slovenia. During the nineteenth century, Russia continually sought to extend its influence into this region.

region, Turks, Bulgarians, Montenegrins,[1] Roumanians, Greeks, Armenians,[2] and nondescripts, young and old, the living and the dead. With some money an intrigue could be started which would set the Peninsula in a blaze and outrage the sentiment of the Russian people. A cry of abandoned brothers could be raised, and then, with the nation seething with indignation, a couple of regiments or so would be enough to begin a military revolution in St. Petersburg and make an end of these thieves. . . .

"Apparently I've got only to sit still and listen," the silent Razumov thought to himself. "As to that hairy and obscene brute" (in such terms did Mr. Razumov refer mentally to the popular expounder of a feministic conception of social state), "as to him, for all his cunning he too shall speak out some day."

Razumov ceased to think for a moment. Then a sombre-toned reflection formulated itself in his mind, ironical and bitter. "I have the gift of inspiring confidence." He heard himself laughing aloud. It was like a goad to the painted, shiny-eyed harridan[3] on the sofa.

"You may well laugh!" she cried hoarsely. "What else can one do! Perfect swindlers—and what base swindlers at that! Cheap Germans—Holstein-Gottorps![4] Though, indeed, it's hardly safe to say who and what they are. A family that counts a creature like Catherine the Great[5] in its ancestry—you understand!"

"You are only upsetting yourself," said Peter Ivanovitch, patiently but in a firm tone. This admonition had its usual effect on the Egeria. She dropped her thick, discoloured eyelids and changed her position on the sofa. All her angular and lifeless movements seemed completely automatic now that her eyes were

---

1 Inhabitants of Montenegro, which is located on the Mediterranean Sea, north of Albania and south of Bosnia-Herzegovina.

2 Inhabitants of Armenia, which is located west of Turkey, east of Azerbaijan, and south of Georgia.

3 Haggard or ill-tempered old woman.

4 A duchy in an area of present-day Germany and Denmark. Members of the House of Holstein-Gottorps ascended to the thrones of several European countries, including Russia with Peter III (Pëtr Fëdorovich) (1728-62). Madame de S—— refers to this latter branch of the family.

5 Catherine (Ekaterina Alekseevna) II of Russia (1729-96), or Catherine the Great, was of German descent and married Peter III. She was noted for her many lovers and aided in forcing her husband's abdication in 1762, reigning in his stead until her death. Some have also suspected her of having a role in her husband's death.

closed. Presently she opened them very full. Peter Ivanovitch drank tea steadily, without haste.

"Well, I declare!" She addressed Razumov directly. "The people who have seen you on your way here are right. You are very reserved. You haven't said twenty words altogether since you came in. You let nothing of your thoughts be seen in your face either."

"I have been listening, Madame," said Razumov, using French for the first time, hesitatingly, not being certain of his accent. But. it seemed to produce an excellent impression. Madame de S—— looked meaningly into Peter Ivanovitch's spectacles, as if to convey her conviction of this young man's merit. She even nodded the least bit in his direction, and Razumov heard her murmur under her breath the words, "Later on in the diplomatic service," which could not but refer to the favourable impression he had made. The fantastic absurdity of it revolted him because it seemed to outrage his ruined hopes with the vision of a mock-career. Peter Ivanovitch, impassive as though he were deaf, drank some more tea. Razumov felt that he must say something.

"Yes," he began deliberately, as if uttering a meditated opinion. "Clearly. Even in planning a purely military revolution the temper of the people should be taken into account."

"You have understood me perfectly. The discontent should be spiritualized. That is what the ordinary heads of revolutionary committees will not understand. They aren't capable of it. For instance, Mordatiev was in Geneva last month. Peter Ivanovitch brought him here. You know Mordatiev? Well, yes—you have heard of him. They call him an eagle—a hero! He has never done half as much as you have. Never attempted—not half. . . ."

Madame de S—— agitated herself angularly on the sofa.

"We, of course, talked to him. And do you know what he said to me? 'What have we to do with Balkan intrigues? We must simply extirpate[1] the scoundrels.' Extirpate is all very well—but what then? The imbecile! I screamed at him, 'But you must spiritualize—don't you understand?—spiritualize the discontent.' . . ."

She felt nervously in her pocket for a handkerchief; she pressed it to her lips.

"Spiritualize?" said Razumov interrogatively, watching her heaving breast. The long ends of an old black lace scarf she wore over her head slipped off her shoulders and hung down on each side of her ghastly rosy cheeks.

---

1  Destroy, root out.

"An odious creature," she burst out again. "Imagine a man who takes five lumps of sugar in his tea.... Yes, I said spiritualize! How else can you make discontent effective and universal?"

"Listen to this, young man." Peter Ivanovitch made himself heard solemnly. "Effective and universal."

Razumov looked at him suspiciously.

"Some say hunger will do that," he remarked.

"Yes. I know. Our people are starving in heaps. But you can't make famine universal. And it is not despair that we want to create. There is no moral support to be got out of that. It is indignation. . . ."

Madame de S—— let her thin, extended arm sink on her knees.

"I am not a Mordatiev," began Razumov.

"*Bien sûr!*"[1] murmured Madame de S——.

"Though I too am ready to say extirpate, extirpate! But in my ignorance of political work, permit me to ask: A Balkan—well—intrigue, wouldn't that take a very long time?"

Peter Ivanovitch got up and moved off quietly, to stand with his face to the window. Razumov heard a door close; he turned his head and perceived that the lady companion had scuttled out of the room.

"In matters of politics I am a supernaturalist." Madame de S—— broke the silence harshly.

Peter Ivanovitch moved away from the window and struck Razumov lightly on the shoulder. This was a signal for leaving, but at the same time he addressed Madame de S—— in a peculiar reminding tone—

"Eleanor!"

Whatever it meant, she did not seem to hear him. She leaned back in the corner of the sofa like a wooden figure. The immovable peevishness of the face, framed in the limp, rusty lace, had a character of cruelty.

"As to extirpating," she croaked at the attentive Razumov, "there is only one class in Russia which must be extirpated. Only one. And that class consists of only one family. You understand me? That one family must be extirpated."

Her rigidity was frightful, like the rigor of a corpse galvanized into harsh speech and glittering stare by the force of murderous hate. The sight fascinated Razumov—yet he felt more self-possessed than at any other time since he had entered this weirdly

---

1  Of course! (French).

bare room. He was interested. But the great feminist by his side again uttered his appeal—

"Eleanor!"

She disregarded it. Her carmine lips vaticinated[1] with an extraordinary rapidity. The liberating spirit would use arms before which rivers would part like Jordan, and ramparts fall down like the walls of Jericho. The deliverance from bondage would be effected by plagues and by signs, by wonders[2] and by war. The women . . .

"Eleanor!"

She ceased; she had heard him at last. She pressed her hand to her forehead.

"What is it? Ah yes! That girl—the sister of . . ."

It was Miss Haldin that she meant. That young girl and her mother had been leading a very retired life. They were provincial ladies—were they not? The mother had been very beautiful—traces were left yet. Peter Ivanovitch, when he called there for the first time, was greatly struck. . . . But the cold way they received him was really surprising.

"He is one of our national glories," Madame de S—— cried out, with sudden vehemence. "All the world listens to him."

"I don't know these ladies," said Razumov loudly rising from his chair.

"What are you saying, Kirylo Sidorovitch? I understand that she was talking to you here, in the garden, the other day."

"Yes, in the garden," said Razumov gloomily. Then, with an effort, "She made herself known to me."

"And then ran away from us all," Madame de S—— continued, with ghastly vivacity. "After coming to the very door! What a peculiar proceeding! Well, I have been a shy little provincial girl at one time. Yes, Razumov" (she fell into this familiarity intentionally, with an appalling grimace of graciousness. Razumov gave a perceptible start), "yes, that's my origin. A simple provincial family."

"You are a marvel," Peter Ivanovitch uttered in his deepest voice.

But it was to Razumov that she gave her death's-head smile. Her tone was quite imperious.

"You must bring the wild young thing here. She is wanted. I reckon upon your success—mind!"

---

1 Prophesied.
2 Allusions to Joshua 5:13-6:23, 3:11-17, and Exodus chapters 7-14 respectively.

"She is not a wild young thing," muttered Razumov, in a surly voice.

"Well, then—that's all the same. She may be one of these young conceited democrats. Do you know what I think? I think she is very much like you in character. There is a smouldering fire of scorn in you. You are darkly self-sufficient, but I can see your very soul."

Her shiny eyes had a dry, intense stare, which, missing Razumov, gave him an absurd notion that she was looking at something which was visible to her behind him. He cursed himself for an impressionable fool, and asked with forced calmness—

"What is it you see? Anything resembling me?"

She moved her rigidly set face from left to right, negatively.

"Some sort of phantom in my image?" pursued Razumov slowly. "For, I suppose, a soul when it is seen is just that. A vain thing. There are phantoms of the living as well as of the dead."

The tenseness of Madame de S——'s stare had relaxed, and now she looked at Razumov in a silence that became disconcerting.

"I myself have had an experience," he stammered out, as if compelled. "I've seen a phantom once."

The unnaturally red lips moved to frame a question harshly.

"Of a dead person?"

"No. Living."

"A friend?"

"No."

"An enemy?"

"I hated him."

"Ah! It was not a woman, then?"

"A woman!" repeated Razumov, his eyes looking straight into the eyes of Madame de S——. "Why should it have been a woman? And why this conclusion? Why should I not have been able to hate a woman?"

As a matter of fact, the idea of hating a woman was new to him. At that moment he hated Madame de S——. But it was not exactly hate. It was more like the abhorrence that may be caused by a wooden or plaster figure of a repulsive kind. She moved no more than if she were such a figure; even her eyes, whose unwinking stare plunged into his own, though shining, were lifeless, as though they were as artificial as her teeth. For the first time Razumov became aware of a faint perfume, but faint as it was it nauseated him exceedingly. Again Peter Ivanovitch tapped him slightly on the shoulder. Thereupon he bowed, and was about to turn away when he received the unexpected favour of a bony, inanimate hand extended to him, with the two words in hoarse French—

"*Au revoir!*"

He bowed over the skeleton hand and left the room, escorted by the great man, who made him go out first. The voice from the sofa cried after them—

"You remain here, *Pierre*."

"Certainly, *ma chère amie*."[1]

But he left the room with Razumov, shutting the door behind him. The landing was prolonged into a bare corridor, right and left, desolate perspectives of white and gold decoration without a strip of carpet. The very light, pouring through a large window at the end, seemed dusty; and a solitary speck reposing on the balustrade of white marble—the silk top-hat of the great feminist—asserted itself extremely, black and glossy in all that crude whiteness.

Peter Ivanovitch escorted the visitor without opening his lips. Even when they had reached the head of the stairs Peter Ivanovitch did not break the silence. Razumov's impulse to continue down the flight and out of the house without as much as a nod abandoned him suddenly. He stopped on the first step and leaned his back against the wall. Below him the great hall with its chequered floor of black and white seemed absurdly large and like some public place where a great power of resonance awaits the provocation of footfalls and voices. As if afraid of awakening the loud echoes of that empty house, Razumov adopted a low tone.

"I really have no mind to turn into a dilettante spiritualist."

Peter Ivanovitch shook his head slightly, very serious.

"Or spend my time in spiritual ecstasies or sublime meditations upon the gospel of feminism," continued Razumov. "I made my way here for my share of action—action, most respected Peter Ivanovitch! It was not the great European writer who attracted me, here, to this odious town of liberty. It was somebody much greater. It was the idea of the chief which attracted me. There are starving young men in Russia who believe in you so much that it seems the only thing that keeps them alive in their misery. Think of that, Peter Ivanovitch! No! But only think of that!"

The great man, thus entreated, perfectly motionless and silent, was the very image of patient, placid respectability.

---

1  My dear friend (French).

"Of course I don't speak of the people. They are brutes," added Razumov, in the same subdued but forcible tone. At this, a protesting murmur issued from the "heroic fugitive's" beard. A murmur of authority.

"Say—children."

"No! Brutes!" Razumov insisted bluntly.

"But they are sound, they are innocent," the great man pleaded in a whisper.

"As far as that goes, a brute is sound enough." Razumov raised his voice at last. "And you can't deny the natural innocence of a brute. But what's the use of disputing about names? You just try to give these children the power and stature of men and see what they will be like. You just give it to them and see. . . . But never mind. I tell you, Peter Ivanovitch, that half a dozen young men do not come together nowadays in a shabby student's room without your name being whispered, not as a leader of thought, but as a centre of revolutionary energies—the centre of action. What else has drawn me near you, do you think? It is not what all the world knows of you, surely. It's precisely what the world at large does not know. I was irresistibly drawn—let us say impelled, yes, impelled; or, rather, compelled, driven—driven," repeated Razumov loudly, and ceased, as if startled by the hollow reverberation of the word "driven" along two bare corridors and in the great empty hall.

Peter Ivanovitch did not seem startled in the least. The young man could not control a dry, uneasy laugh. The great revolutionist remained unmoved with an effect of commonplace, homely superiority.

"Curse him," said Razumov to himself, "he is waiting behind his spectacles for me to give myself away." Then aloud, with a satanic enjoyment of the scorn prompting him to play with the greatness of the great man—

"Ah, Peter Ivanovitch, if you only knew the force which drew—no, which *drove* me towards you! The irresistible force."

He did not feel any desire to laugh now. This time Peter Ivanovitch moved his head sideways, knowingly, as much as to say, "Don't I?" This expressive movement was almost imperceptible. Razumov went on in secret derision—

"All these days you have been trying to read me, Peter Ivanovitch. That is natural. I have perceived it and I have been frank. Perhaps you may think I have not been very expansive? But with a man like you it was not needed; it would have looked like an impertinence, perhaps. And besides, we Russians are prone to talk too much as a rule. I have always felt that. And yet, as a nation, we are dumb. I assure you that I am not likely to talk to you so much again—ha! ha!—"

Razumov, still keeping on the lower step, came a little nearer to the great man.

"You have been condescending enough. I quite understood it was to lead me on. You must render me the justice that I have not tried to please. I have been impelled, compelled, or rather sent—let us say sent—towards you for a work that no one but myself can do. You would call it a harmless delusion: a ridiculous delusion at which you don't even smile. It is absurd of me to talk like this, yet some day you shall remember these words, I hope. Enough of this. Here I stand before you—confessed! But one thing more I must add to complete it: a mere blind tool I can never consent to be."

Whatever acknowledgment Razumov was prepared for, he was not prepared to have both his hands seized in the great man's grasp. The swiftness of the movement was aggressive enough to startle. The burly feminist could not have been quicker had his purpose been to jerk Razumov treacherously up on the landing and bundle him behind one of the numerous closed doors near by. This idea actually occurred to Razumov; his hands being released after a darkly eloquent squeeze, he smiled, with a beating heart, straight at the beard and the spectacles hiding that impenetrable man.

He thought to himself (it stands confessed in his handwriting), "I won't move from here till he either speaks or turns away. This is a duel." Many seconds passed without a sign or sound.

"Yes, yes," the great man said hurriedly, in subdued tones, as if the whole thing had been a stolen, breathless interview. "Exactly. Come to see us here in a few days. This must be gone into deeply—deeply, between you and me. Quite to the bottom. To the . . . And, by the by, you must bring along Natalia Victorovna—you know, the Haldin girl . . ."

"Am I to take this as my first instruction from you?" inquired Razumov stiffly.

Peter Ivanovitch seemed perplexed by this new attitude.

"Ah! h'm! You are naturally the proper person—*la personne indiquée*.[1] Every one shall be wanted presently. Every one."

He bent down from the landing over Razumov, who had lowered his eyes.

---

1 The appropriate (or proper) person; the one singled out (French).

"The moment of action approaches," he murmured.

Razumov did not look up. He did not move till he heard the door of the drawing-room close behind the greatest of feminists returning to his painted Egeria. Then he walked down slowly into the hall. The door stood open, and the shadow of the house was lying aslant over the greatest part of the terrace. While crossing it slowly, he lifted his hat and wiped his damp forehead, expelling his breath with force to get rid of the last vestiges of the air he had been breathing inside. He looked at the palms of his hands, and rubbed them gently against his thighs.

He felt, bizarre as it may seem, as though another self, an independent sharer of his mind, had been able to view his whole person very distinctly indeed. "This is curious," he thought. After a while he formulated his opinion of it in the mental ejaculation: "Beastly!" This disgust vanished before a marked uneasiness. "This is an effect of nervous exhaustion," he reflected with weary sagacity. "How am I to go on day after day if I have no more power of resistance—moral resistance?"

He followed the path at the foot of the terrace. "Moral resistance, moral resistance;" he kept on repeating these words mentally. Moral endurance. Yes, that was the necessity of the situation. An immense longing to make his way out of these grounds and to the other end of the town, of throwing himself on his bed and going to sleep for hours, swept everything clean out of his mind for a moment. "Is it possible that I am but a weak creature after all?" he asked himself, in sudden alarm. "Eh! What's that?"

He gave a start as if awakened from a dream. He even swayed a little before recovering himself.

"Ah! You stole away from us quietly to walk about here," he said.

The lady companion stood before him, but how she came there he had not the slightest idea. Her folded arms were closely cherishing the cat.

"I have been unconscious as I walked, it's a positive fact," said Razumov to himself in wonder. He raised his hat with marked civility.

The sallow woman blushed duskily. She had her invariably scared expression, as if somebody had just disclosed to her some terrible news. But she held her ground, Razumov noticed, without timidity. "She is incredibly shabby," he thought. In the sunlight her black costume looked greenish, with here and there threadbare patches where the stuff seemed decomposed by age into a velvety, black, furry state. Her very hair and eyebrows looked shabby. Razumov wondered whether she were sixty years old. Her figure, though, was young enough. He observed that she did not appear starved, but rather as if she had been fed on unwholesome scraps and leavings of plates.

Razumov smiled amiably and moved out of her way. She turned her head to keep her scared eyes on him.

"I know what you have been told in there," she affirmed, without preliminaries. Her tone, in contrast with her manner, had an unexpectedly assured character which put Razumov at his ease.

"Do you? You must have heard all sorts of talk on many occasions in there."

She varied her phrase, with the same incongruous effect of positiveness.

"I know to a certainty what you have been told to do."

"Really?" Razumov shrugged his shoulders a little. He was about to pass on with a bow, when a sudden thought struck him. "Yes. To be sure! In your confidential position you are aware of many things," he murmured, looking at the cat.

That animal got a momentary convulsive hug from the lady companion.

"Everything was disclosed to me a long time ago," she said.

"Everything," Razumov repeated absently.

"Peter Ivanovitch is an awful despot," she jerked out.

Razumov went on studying the stripes on the grey fur of the cat.

"An iron will is an integral part of such a temperament. How else could he be a leader? And I think that you are mistaken in—"

"There!" she cried. "You tell me that I am mistaken. But I tell you all the same that he cares for no one." She jerked her head up. "Don't you bring that girl here. That's what you have been told to do—to bring that girl here. Listen to me; you had better tie a stone round her neck and throw her into the lake."[1]

Razumov had a sensation of chill and gloom, as if a heavy cloud had passed over the sun.

"The girl?" he said. "What have I to do with her?"

"But you have been told to bring Nathalie Haldin here. Am I not right? Of course I am right. I was not in the room, but I know.

---

1 Perhaps an oblique allusion to Matthew 18:6: "But whoso shall offend one of these little ones which believe in me, it were better for him that a millstone were hanged about his neck, and that he were drowned in the depth of the sea." (See also Mark 9:42 and Luke 17:2.)

I know Peter Ivanovitch sufficiently well. He is a great man. Great men are horrible. Well, that's it. Have nothing to do with her. That's the best you can do, unless you want her to become like me—disillusioned! Disillusioned!"

"Like you," repeated Razumov, glaring at her face, as devoid of all comeliness of feature and complexion as the most miserable beggar is of money. He smiled, still feeling chilly: a peculiar sensation which annoyed him. "Disillusioned as to Peter Ivanovitch! Is that all you have lost?"

She declared, looking frightened, but with immense conviction, "Peter Ivanovitch stands for everything." Then she added, in another tone, "Keep the girl away from this house."

"And are you absolutely inciting me to disobey Peter Ivanovitch just because—because you are disillusioned?"

She began to blink.

"Directly I saw you for the first time I was comforted. You took your hat off to me. You looked as if one could trust you. Oh!"

She shrank before Razumov's savage snarl of, "I have heard something like this before."

She was so confounded that she could do nothing but blink for a long time.

"It was your humane manner," she explained plaintively. "I have been starving for, I won't say kindness, but just for a little civility, for I don't know how long. And now you are angry . . ."

"But no, on the contrary," he protested. "I am very glad you trust me. It's possible that later on I may . . ."

"Yes, if you were to get ill," she interrupted eagerly, "or meet some bitter trouble, you would find I am not a useless fool. You have only to let me know. I will come to you. I will indeed. And I will stick to you. Misery and I are old acquaintances—but this life here is worse than starving."

She paused anxiously, then in a voice for the first time sounding really timid, she added—

"Or if you were engaged in some dangerous work. Sometimes a humble companion—I would not want to know anything. I would follow you with joy. I could carry out orders. I have the courage."

Razumov looked attentively at the scared round eyes, at the withered, sallow, round cheeks. They were quivering about the corners of the mouth.

"She wants to escape from here," he thought.

"Suppose I were to tell you that I am engaged in dangerous work?" he uttered slowly.

She pressed the cat to her threadbare bosom with a breathless exclamation. "Ah!" Then not much above a whisper: "Under Peter Ivanovitch?"

"No, not under Peter Ivanovitch."

He read admiration in her eyes, and made an effort to smile.

"Then—alone?"

He held up his closed hand with the index raised.

"Like this finger," he said.

She was trembling slightly. But it occurred to Razumov that they might have been observed from the house, and he became anxious to be gone. She blinked, raising up to him her puckered face, and seemed to beg mutely to be told something more, to be given a word of encouragement for her starving, grotesque, and pathetic devotion.

"Can we be seen from the house?" asked Razumov confidentially.

She answered, without showing the slightest surprise at the question—

"No, we can't, on account of this end of the stables." And she added, with an acuteness which surprised Razumov, "But anybody looking out of an upstairs window would know that you have not passed through the gates yet."

"Who's likely to spy out of the window?" queried Razumov. "Peter Ivanovitch?"

She nodded.

"Why should he trouble his head?"

"He expects somebody this afternoon."

"You know the person?"

"There's more than one."

She had lowered her eyelids. Razumov looked at her curiously.

"Of course. You hear everything they say."

She murmured without any animosity—

"So do the tables and chairs."

He understood that the bitterness accumulated in the heart of that helpless creature had got into her veins, and, like some subtle poison, had decomposed her fidelity to that hateful pair. It was a great piece of luck for him, he reflected; because women are seldom venal after the manner of men, who can be bought for material considerations. She would be a good ally, though it was not likely that she was allowed to hear as much as the tables and chairs of the Château Borel. That could not be expected. But still . . . And, at any rate, she could be made to talk.

When she looked up her eyes met the fixed stare of Razumov, who began to speak at once.

"Well, well, dear . . . but upon my word, I haven't the pleasure of knowing your name yet. Isn't it strange?"

For the first time she made a movement of the shoulders.

"Is it strange? No one is told my name. No one cares. No one talks to me, no one writes to me. My parents don't even know if I'm alive. I have no use for a name, and I have almost forgotten it myself."

Razumov murmured gravely, "Yes, but still . . ."

She went on much slower, with indifference—

"You may call me Tekla, then. My poor Andrei called me so. I was devoted to him. He lived in wretchedness and suffering, and died in misery. That is the lot of all us Russians, nameless Russians. There is nothing else for us, and no hope anywhere, unless . . ."

"Unless what?"

"Unless all these people with names are done away with," she finished, blinking and pursing up her lips.

"It will be easier to call you Tekla, as you direct me," said Razumov, "if you consent to call me Kirylo, when we are talking like this—quietly—only you and me."

And he said to himself, "Here's a being who must be terribly afraid of the world, else she would have run away from this situation before." Then he reflected that the mere fact of leaving the great man abruptly would make her a suspect. She could expect no support or countenance from anyone. This revolutionist was not fit for an independent existence.

She moved with him a few steps, blinking and nursing the cat with a small balancing movement of her arms.

"Yes—only you and I. That's how I was with my poor Andrei, only he was dying, killed by these official brutes—while you! You are strong. You kill the monsters. You have done a great deed. Peter Ivanovitch himself must consider you. Well—don't forget me—especially if you are going back to work in Russia. I could follow you, carrying anything that was wanted—at a distance, you know. Or I could watch for hours at the corner of a street if necessary,—in wet or snow—yes, I could—all day long. Or I could write for you dangerous documents, lists of names or instructions, so that in case of mischance the handwriting could not compromise you. And you need not be afraid if they were to catch me. I would know how to keep dumb. We women are not so easily daunted by pain. I heard Peter Ivanovitch say it is our blunt nerves or something. We can stand it better. And it's true; I would just as soon bite my tongue out and throw it at them as not. What's the good of speech to me? Who would ever want to hear what I could say? Ever since I closed the eyes of my poor Andrei I haven't met a man who seemed to care for the sound of my voice. I should never have spoken to you if the very first time you appeared here you had not taken notice of me so nicely. I could not help speaking of you to that charming dear girl. Oh, the sweet creature! And strong! One can see that at once. If you have a heart don't let her set her foot in here. Good-bye!"

Razumov caught her by the arm. Her emotion at being thus seized manifested itself by a short struggle, after which she stood still, not looking at him.

"But you can tell me," he spoke in her ear, "why they—these people in that house there—are so anxious to get hold of her?"

She freed herself to turn upon him, as if made angry by the question.

"Don't you understand that Peter Ivanovitch must direct, inspire, influence? It is the breath of his life. There can never be too many disciples. He can't bear thinking of anyone escaping him. And a woman, too! There is nothing to be done without women, he says. He has written it. He—"

The young man was staring at her passion when she broke off suddenly and ran away behind the stable.

## III

Razumov, thus left to himself, took the direction of the gate. But on this day of many conversations, he discovered that very probably he could not leave the grounds without having to hold another one.

Stepping in view from beyond the lodge appeared the expected visitors of Peter Ivanovitch: a small party composed of two men and a woman. They noticed him too, immediately, and stopped short as if to consult. But in a moment the woman, moving aside, motioned with her arm to the two men, who, leaving the drive at once, struck across the large neglected lawn, or rather grass-plot, and made directly for the house. The woman remained on the path waiting for Razumov's approach. She had recognized him. He, too, had recognized her at the first glance. He had been made known to her at Zürich, where he had broken his journey while on his way from Dresden.[1] They had been much together for the three days of his stay.

She was wearing the very same costume in which he had seen her first. A blouse of crimson silk made her noticeable at a distance. With that she wore a short brown skirt and a leather belt. Her complexion was the colour of coffee and milk, but very clear; her eyes black and glittering, her figure erect. A lot of thick hair, nearly white, was done up loosely under a dusty Tyrolese hat[2] of dark cloth, which seemed to have lost some of its trimmings.

The expression of her face was grave, intent; so grave that Razumov, after approaching her close, felt obliged to smile. She greeted him with a manly hand-grasp.

"What! Are you going away?" she exclaimed. "How is that, Razumov?"

"I am going away because I haven't been asked to stay," Razumov answered, returning the pressure of her hand with much less force than she had put into it.

She jerked her head sideways like one who understands. Meantime Razumov's eyes had strayed after the two men. They were crossing the grass-plot obliquely, without haste. The shorter of the two was buttoned up in a narrow overcoat of some thin grey material, which came nearly to his heels. His companion, much taller and broader, wore a short, close-fitting jacket and tight trousers tucked into shabby top-boots.

The woman, who had sent them out of Razumov's way apparently, spoke in a businesslike voice.

"I had to come rushing from Zürich on purpose to meet the train and take these two along here to see Peter Ivanovitch. I've just managed it."

"Ah! indeed," Razumov said perfunctorily, and very vexed at her staying behind to talk to him. "From Zürich—yes, of course. And these two, they come from . . ."

She interrupted, without emphasis—

"From quite another direction. From a distance, too. A considerable distance."

Razumov shrugged his shoulders. The two men from a distance, after having reached the wall of the terrace, disappeared suddenly at its foot as if the earth had opened to swallow them up.

"Oh, well, they have just come from America." The woman in the crimson blouse shrugged her shoulders too a little before

---

1 A city in eastern Germany.
2 A soft hat made of felt with a brim with upturned sides.

making that statement. "The time is drawing near," she interjected, as if speaking to herself. "I did not tell them who you were. Yakovlitch would have wanted to embrace you."

"Is that he with the wisp of hair hanging from his chin, in the long coat?"

"You've guessed aright. That's Yakovlitch."

"And they could not find their way here from the station without you coming on purpose from Zürich to show it to them? Verily, without women we can do nothing. So it stands written, and apparently so it is."

He was conscious of an immense lassitude under his effort to be sarcastic. And he could see that she had detected it with those steady, brilliant black eyes.

"What is the matter with you?"

"I don't know. Nothing. I've had a devil of a day."

She waited, with her black eyes fixed on his face. Then—

"What of that? You men are so impressionable and self-conscious. One day is like another, hard, hard—and there's an end of it, till the great day comes. I came over for a very good reason. They wrote to warn Peter Ivanovitch of their arrival. But where from? Only from Cherbourg[1] on a bit of ship's notepaper. Anybody could have done that. Yakovlitch has lived for years and years in America. I am the only one at hand who had known him well in the old days. I knew him very well indeed. So Peter Ivanovitch telegraphed, asking me to come. It's natural enough, is it not?"

"You came to vouch for his identity?" inquired Razumov.

"Yes. Something of the kind. Fifteen years of a life like his make changes in a man. Lonely, like a crow in a strange country. When I think of Yakovlitch before he went to America—"

The softness of the low tone caused Razumov to glance at her sideways. She sighed; her black eyes were looking away; she had plunged the fingers of her right hand deep into the mass of nearly white hair, and stirred them there absently. When she withdrew her hand the little hat perched on top of her head[2] remained slightly tilted, with a queer inquisitive effect, contrasting strongly with the reminiscent murmur that escaped her.

"We were not in our first youth even then. But a man is a child always."

Razumov thought suddenly, "They have been living together." Then aloud—

---

1 A seaport in northwestern France.
2 The first English edition has "perched on the top of her head" (M, T).

"Why didn't you follow him to America?" he asked point-blank.

She looked up at him with a perturbed air.

"Don't you remember what was going on fifteen years ago? It was a time of activity. The Revolution has its history by this time. You are in it and yet you don't seem to know it. Yakovlitch went away then on a mission; I went back to Russia. It had to be so. Afterwards there was nothing for him to come back to."

"Ah! indeed," muttered Razumov, with affected surprise. "Nothing!"

"What are you trying to insinuate?" she exclaimed quickly. "Well, and what then if he did get discouraged a little . . ."

"He looks like a Yankee, with that goatee hanging from his chin. A regular Uncle Sam," growled Razumov. "Well, and you? You who went to Russia? You did not get discouraged."

"Never mind. Yakovlitch is a man who cannot be doubted. He, at any rate, is the right sort."

Her black, penetrating gaze remained fixed upon Razumov while she spoke, and for a moment afterwards.

"Pardon me," Razumov inquired coldly, "but does it mean that you, for instance, think that I am not the right sort?"

She made no protest, gave no sign of having heard the question; she continued looking at him in a manner which he judged not to be absolutely unfriendly. In Zürich when he passed through she had taken him under her charge, in a way, and was with him from morning till night during his stay of two days. She took him round to see several people. At first she talked to him a great deal and rather unreservedly, but always avoiding all reference to herself; towards the middle of the second day she fell silent, attending him zealously as before, and even seeing him off at the railway station, where she pressed his hand firmly through the lowered carriage window, and, stepping back without a word, waited till the train moved. He had noticed that she was treated with quiet regard. He knew nothing of her parentage, nothing of her private history or political record; he judged her from his own private point of view, as being a distinct danger in his path. "Judged" is not perhaps the right word. It was more of a feeling, the summing up of slight impressions aided by the discovery that he could not despise her as he despised all the others. He had not expected to see her again so soon.

No, decidedly; her expression was not unfriendly. Yet he perceived an acceleration in the beat of his heart. The conversation could not be abandoned at that point. He went on in accents of scrupulous inquiry—

"Is it perhaps because I don't seem to accept blindly every development of the general doctrine—such for instance as the feminism of our great Peter Ivanovitch? If that is what makes me suspect, then I can only say I would scorn to be a slave even to an idea."

She had been looking at him all the time, not as a listener looks at one, but as if the words he chose to say were only of secondary interest. When he finished she slipped her hand, by a sudden and decided movement, under his arm and impelled him gently towards the gate of the grounds. He felt her firmness and obeyed the impulsion at once, just as the other two men had, a moment before, obeyed unquestioningly the wave of her hand.

They made a few steps like this.

"No, Razumov, your ideas are probably all right," she said. "You may be valuable—very valuable. What's the matter with you is that you don't like us."

She released him. He met her with a frosty smile.

"Am I expected then to have love as well as convictions?"

She shrugged her shoulders.

"You know very well what I mean. People have been thinking you not quite whole-hearted. I have heard that opinion from one side and another. But I have understood you at the end of the first day . . ."

Razumov interrupted her, speaking steadily.

"I assure you that your perspicacity is at fault here."

"What phrases he uses!" she exclaimed parenthetically. "Ah! Kirylo Sidorovitch, you like other men are fastidious, full of self-love and afraid of trifles. Moreover, you had no training. What you want is to be taken in hand by some woman. I am sorry I am not staying here a few days. I am going back to Zürich to-morrow, and shall take Yakovlitch with me most likely."

This information relieved Razumov.

"I am sorry too," he said. "But, all the same, I don't think you understand me."

He breathed more freely; she did not protest, but asked, "And how did you get on with Peter Ivanovitch? You have seen a good deal of each other. How is it between you two?"

Not knowing what answer to make, the young man inclined his head slowly.

Her lips had been parted in expectation. She pressed them together, and seemed to reflect.

"That's all right."

This had a sound of finality, but she did not leave him. It was impossible to guess what she had in her mind. Razumov muttered—

"It is not of me that you should have asked that question. In a moment you shall see Peter Ivanovitch himself, and the subject will come up naturally. He will be curious to know what has delayed you so long in this garden."

"No doubt Peter Ivanovitch will have something to say to me. Several things. He may even speak of you—question me. Peter Ivanovitch is inclined to trust me generally."

"Question you? That's very likely."

She smiled, half serious.

"Well—and what shall I say to him?"

"I don't know. You may tell him of your discovery."

"What's that?"

"Why—my lack of love for . . ."

"Oh! That's between ourselves," she interrupted, it was hard to say whether in jest or earnest.

"I see that you want to tell Peter Ivanovitch something in my favour," said Razumov, with grim playfulness. "Well, then, you can tell him that I am very much in earnest about my mission. I mean to succeed."

"You have been given a mission!" she exclaimed quickly.

"It amounts to that. I have been told to bring about a certain event."

She looked at him searchingly.

"A mission," she repeated, very grave and interested all at once. "What sort of mission?"

"Something in the nature of propaganda work."

"Ah! Far away from here?"

"No. Not very far," said Razumov, restraining a sudden desire to laugh, though he did not feel joyous in the least.

"So!" she said thoughtfully. "Well, I am not asking questions. It's sufficient that Peter Ivanovitch should know what each of us is doing. Everything is bound to come right in the end."

"You think so?"

"I don't think, young man. I just simply believe it."

"And is it to Peter Ivanovitch that you owe that faith?"

She did not answer the question, and they stood idle, silent, as if reluctant to part with each other.

"That's just like a man," she murmured at last. "As if it were possible to tell how a belief comes to one." Her thin Mephistophelian eyebrows moved a little. "Truly there are millions of people in Russia who would envy the life of dogs in this country. It is a horror and a shame to confess this even between ourselves. One must believe for very pity. This can't go on. No! It can't go on. For twenty years I have been coming and going, looking neither to the left nor to the right. . . . What are you smiling to yourself for? You are only at the beginning. You have begun well, but you just wait till you have trodden every particle of yourself under your feet in your comings and goings. For that is what it comes to. You've got to trample down every particle of your own feelings; for stop you cannot, you must not. I have been young, too—but perhaps you think that I am complaining—eh?"

"I don't think anything of the sort," protested Razumov indifferently.

"I dare say you don't, you dear superior creature. You don't care."

She plunged her fingers into the bunch of hair on the left side, and that brusque movement had the effect of setting the Tyrolese hat straight on her head. She frowned under it without animosity, in the manner of an investigator. Razumov averted his face carelessly.

"You men are all alike. You mistake luck for merit. You do it in good faith too! I would not be too hard on you. It's masculine nature. You men are ridiculously pitiful in your aptitude to cherish childish illusions down to the very grave. There are a lot of us who have been at work for fifteen years—I mean constantly—trying one way after another, underground and above ground, looking neither to the right nor to the left! I can talk about it. I have been one of these that never rested. . . . There! What's the use of talking. . . . Look at my grey hairs! And here two babies come along—I mean you and Haldin—you come along and manage to strike a blow at the very first try."

At the name of Haldin falling from the rapid and energetic lips of the woman revolutionist, Razumov had the usual brusque consciousness of the irrevocable. But in all the months which had passed over his head he had become hardened to the experience. The consciousness was no longer accompanied by the blank dismay and the blind anger of the early days. He had argued himself into new beliefs; and he had made for himself a mental atmosphere of gloomy and sardonic reverie, a sort of murky medium through which the event appeared like a featureless shadow having vaguely the shape of a man; a shape extremely familiar, yet utterly inexpressive, except for its air of discreet waiting in the dusk. It was not alarming.

"What was _he_ like?" the woman revolutionist asked unexpectedly.

"What was he like?" echoed Razumov, making a painful effort not to turn upon her savagely. But he relieved himself by laughing a little while he stole a glance at her out of the corners of his eyes. This reception of her inquiry disturbed her.

"How like a woman," he went on. "What is the good of concerning yourself with his appearance? Whatever it was, he is removed beyond all feminine influences now."

A frown, making three folds at the root of her nose, accentuated the Mephistophelian slant of her eyebrows.

"You suffer, Razumov," she suggested, in her low, confident voice.

"What nonsense!" Razumov faced the woman fairly. "But now I think of it, I am not sure that he is beyond the influence of one woman at least; the one over there—Madame de S——, you know. Formerly the dead were allowed to rest, but now it seems they are at the beck and call of a crazy old harridan. We revolutionists make wonderful discoveries. It is true that they are not exactly our own. We have nothing of our own. But couldn't the friend of Peter Ivanovitch satisfy your feminine curiosity? Couldn't she conjure him up for you?"—he jested like a man in pain.

Her concentrated frowning expression relaxed, and she said, a little wearily, "Let us hope she will make an effort and conjure up some tea for us. But that is by no means certain. I am tired, Razumov."

"You tired! What a confession! Well, there has been tea up there. I had some. If you hurry on after Yakovlitch, instead of wasting your time with such an unsatisfactory sceptical person as myself, you may find the ghost of it—the cold ghost of it—still lingering in the temple. But as to you being tired I can hardly believe it. We are not supposed to be. We mustn't. We can't. The other day I read in some paper or other an alarmist article on the tireless activity of the revolutionary parties. It impresses the world. It's our prestige."

"He flings out continually these flouts and sneers;" the woman in the crimson blouse spoke as if appealing quietly to a third person, but her black eyes never left Razumov's face. "And what for, pray? Simply because some of his conventional notions are shocked, some of his petty masculine standards. You might think he was one of these nervous sensitives that come to a bad end.

And yet," she went on, after a short, reflective pause and changing the mode of her address, "and yet I have just learned something which makes me think that you are a man of character, Kirylo Sidorovitch. Yes! indeed—you are."

The mysterious positiveness of this assertion startled Razumov. Their eyes met. He looked away and, through the bars of the rusty gate, stared at the clean, wide road shaded by the leafy trees. An electric tramcar, quite empty, ran along the avenue with a metallic rustle. It seemed to him he would have given anything to be sitting inside all alone. He was inexpressibly weary, weary in every fibre of his body, but he had a reason for not being the first to break off the conversation. At any instant, in the visionary and criminal babble of revolutionists, some momentous words might fall on his ear; from her lips, from anybody's lips. As long as he managed to preserve a clear mind and to keep down his irritability there was nothing to fear. The only condition of success and safety was indomitable will-power, he reminded himself.

He longed to be on the other side of the bars, as though he were actually a prisoner within the grounds of this centre of revolutionary plots, of this house of folly, of blindness, of villainy and crime. Silently he indulged his wounded spirit in a feeling of immense moral and mental remoteness. He did not even smile when he heard her repeat the words—

"Yes! A strong character."

He continued to gaze through the bars like a moody prisoner, not thinking of escape, but merely pondering upon the faded memories of freedom.

"If you don't look out," he mumbled, still looking away, "you shall certainly miss seeing as much as the mere ghost of that tea."

She was not to be shaken off in such a way. As a matter of fact he had not expected to succeed.

"Never mind, it will be no great loss. I mean the missing of her tea and only the ghost of it at that. As to the lady, you must understand that she has her positive uses. See *that*, Razumov."

He turned his head at this imperative appeal and saw the woman revolutionist making the motions of counting money into the palm of her hand.

"That's what it is. You see?"

Razumov uttered a slow "I see," and returned to his prisoner-like gazing upon the neat and shady road.

"Material means must be obtained in some way, and this is

easier than breaking into banks. More certain too. There! I am joking . . . What is he muttering to himself now?" she cried under her breath.

"My admiration of Peter Ivanovitch's devoted self-sacrifice that's all. It's enough to make one sick."

"Oh, you squeamish, masculine creature. Sick! Makes him sick! And what do you know of the truth of it? There's no looking into the secrets of the heart. Peter Ivanovitch knew her years ago, in his worldly days, when he was a young officer in the Guards. It is not for us to judge an inspired person. That's where you men have an advantage. You are inspired sometimes both in thought and action. I have always admitted that when you *are* inspired, when you manage to throw off your masculine cowardice and prudishness you are not to be equalled by us. Only, how seldom . . . Whereas the silliest woman can always be made of use. And why? Because we have passion, unappeasable passion . . . I should like to know what he is smiling at?"

"I am not smiling," protested Razumov gloomily.

"Well! How is one to call it? You made some sort of face. Yes, I know! You men can love here and hate there and desire something or other—and you make a great to-do about it, and you call it passion! Yes! While it lasts. But we women are in love with love, and with hate, with these very things I tell you, and with desire itself. That's why we can't be bribed off so easily as you men. In life, you see, there is not much choice. You have either to rot or to burn. And there is not one of us, painted or unpainted, that would not rather burn than rot."

She spoke with energy, but in a matter-of-fact tone. Razumov's attention had wandered away on a track of its own— outside the bars of the gate—but not out of earshot. He stuck his hands into the pockets of his coat.

"Rot or burn! Powerfully stated. Painted or unpainted. Very vigorous. Painted or . . . Do tell me—she would be infernally jealous of him, wouldn't she?"

"Who? What? The Baroness? Eleanor Maximovna? Jealous of Peter Ivanovitch? Heavens! Are these the questions the man's mind is running on? Such a thing is not to be thought of."

"Why? Can't a wealthy old woman be jealous? Or, are they all pure spirits together?"

"But what put it into your head to ask such a question?" she wondered.

"Nothing. I just asked. Masculine frivolity, if you like."

"I don't like," she retorted at once. "It is not the time to be frivolous. What are you flinging your very heart against? Or, perhaps, you are only playing a part."

Razumov had felt that woman's observation of him like a physical contact, like a hand resting lightly on his shoulder. At that moment he received the mysterious impression of her having made up her mind for a closer grip. He stiffened himself inwardly to bear it without betraying himself.

"Playing a part," he repeated, presenting to her an unmoved profile. "It must be done very badly since you see through the assumption."

She watched him, her forehead drawn into perpendicular folds, the thin black eyebrows diverging upwards like the antennæ of an insect. He added hardly audibly—

"You are mistaken. I am doing it no more than the rest of us."

"Who is doing it?" she snapped out.

"Who? Everybody," he said impatiently. "You are a materialist, aren't you?"

"Eh! My dear soul, I have outlived all that nonsense."

"But you must remember the definition of Cabanis:[1] 'Man is a digestive tube.' I imagine now . . ."

"I spit on him."

"What? On Cabanis? All right. But you can't ignore the importance of a good digestion. The joy of life—you know the joy of life?—depends on a sound stomach, whereas a bad digestion inclines one to scepticism, breeds black fancies and thoughts of death. These are facts ascertained by physiologists. Well, I assure you that ever since I came over from Russia I have been stuffed with indigestible foreign concoctions of the most nauseating kind—pah!"

"You are joking," she murmured incredulously. He assented in a detached way.

"Yes. It is all a joke. It's hardly worth while talking to a man like me. Yet for that very reason men have been known to take their own life."

"On the contrary, I think it *is* worth while talking to you."

He kept her in the corner of his eye. She seemed to be thinking out some scathing retort, but ended by only shrugging her shoulders slightly.

---

1   Pierre Jean George Cabanis (1757-1808), physician and materialist philosopher, believed that the brain experiences phenomena, digests them (as the stomach does food), and then secretes thought (as the liver secretes bile).

"Shallow talk! I suppose one must pardon this weakness in you," she said, putting a special accent on the last word. There was something anxious in her indulgent conclusion.

Razumov noted the slightest shades in this conversation, which he had not expected, for which he was not prepared. That was it. "I was not prepared," he said to himself. "It has taken me unawares." It seemed to him that if he only could allow himself to pant openly like a dog for a time this oppression would pass away. "I shall never be found prepared," he thought, with despair. He laughed a little, saying as lightly as he could—

"Thanks. I don't ask for mercy." Then affecting a playful uneasiness, "But aren't you afraid Peter Ivanovitch might suspect us of plotting something unauthorized together by the gate here?"

"No, I am not afraid. You are quite safe from suspicions while you are with me, my dear young man." The humorous gleam in her black eyes went out. "Peter Ivanovitch trusts me," she went on, quite austerely. "He takes my advice. I am his right hand, as it were, in certain most important things. . . . That amuses you—what? Do you think I am boasting?"

"God forbid. I was just only saying to myself that Peter Ivanovitch seems to have solved the woman question pretty completely."

Even as he spoke he reproached himself for his words, for his tone. All day long he had been saying the wrong things. It was folly, worse than folly. It was weakness; it was this disease of perversity overcoming his will. Was this the way to meet speeches which certainly contained the promise of future confidences from that woman who apparently had a great store of secret knowledge and so much influence? Why give her this puzzling impression? But she did not seem inimical.[1] There was no anger in her voice. It was strangely speculative.

"One does not know what to think, Razumov. You must have bitten something bitter in your cradle."

Razumov gave her a sidelong glance.

"H'm! Something bitter? That's an explanation," he muttered. "Only it was much later. And don't you think, Sophia Antonovna, that you and I come from the same cradle?"

The woman, whose name he had forced himself at last to pronounce (he had experienced a strong repugnance in letting it pass his lips), the woman revolutionist murmured, after a pause—

---

1 Hostile.

"You mean—Russia?"

He disdained even to nod. She seemed softened, her black eyes very still, as though she were pursuing the simile in her thoughts to all its tender associations. But suddenly she knitted her brows in a Mephistophelian frown.

"Yes. Perhaps no wonder, then. Yes. One lies there lapped up in evils, watched over by beings that are worse than ogres, ghouls, and vampires. They must be driven away, destroyed utterly. In regard of that task nothing else matters if men and women are determined and faithful. That's how I came to feel in the end. The great thing is not to quarrel amongst ourselves about all sorts of conventional trifles. Remember that, Razumov."

Razumov was not listening. He had even lost the sense of being watched in a sort of heavy tranquillity. His uneasiness, his exasperation, his scorn were blunted at last by all these trying hours. It seemed to him that now they were blunted for ever. "I am a match for them all," he thought, with a conviction too firm to be exulting. The woman revolutionist had ceased speaking; he was not looking at her; there was no one passing along the road. He almost forgot that he was not alone. He heard her voice again, curt, businesslike, and yet betraying the hesitation which had been the real reason of her prolonged silence.

"I say, Razumov!"

Razumov, whose face was turned away from her, made a grimace like a man who hears a false note.

"Tell me: is it true that on the very morning of the deed you actually attended the lectures at the University?"

An appreciable fraction of a second elapsed before the real import of the question reached him, like a bullet which strikes some time after the flash of the fired shot. Luckily his disengaged hand was ready to grip a bar of the gate. He held it with a terrible force, but his presence of mind was gone. He could make only a sort of gurgling, grumpy sound.

"Come, Kirylo Sidorovitch!" she urged him. "I know you are not a boastful man. *That* one must say for you. You are a silent man. Too silent, perhaps. You are feeding on some bitterness of your own. You are not an enthusiast. You are, perhaps, all the stronger for that. But you might tell me. One would like to understand you a little more. I was so immensely struck . . . Have you really done it?"

He got his voice back. The shot had missed him. It had been fired at random, altogether, more like a signal for coming to close quarters. It was to be a plain struggle for self-preservation. And she was a dangerous adversary too. But he was ready for battle; he was so ready that when he turned towards her not a muscle of his face moved.

"Certainly," he said, without animation, secretly strung up but perfectly sure of himself. "Lectures—certainly. But what makes you ask?"

It was she who was animated.

"I had it in a letter, written by a young man in Petersburg; one of us, of course. You were seen—you were observed with your notebook, impassible,[1] taking notes . . ."

He enveloped her with his fixed stare.

"What of that?"

"I call such coolness superb—that's all. It is a proof of uncommon strength of character. The young man writes that nobody could have guessed from your face and manner the part you had played only some two hours before—the great, momentous, glorious part . . ."

"Oh no. Nobody could have guessed," assented Razumov gravely, "because, don't you see, nobody at that time . . ."

"Yes, yes. But all the same you are a man of exceptional fortitude, it seems. You looked exactly as usual. It was remembered afterwards with wonder . . ."

"It cost me no effort," Razumov declared, with the same staring gravity.

"Then it's almost more wonderful still!" she exclaimed, and fell silent while Razumov asked himself whether he had not said there something utterly unnecessary—or even worse.

She raised her head eagerly.

"Your intention was to stay in Russia? You had planned . . ."

"No," interrupted Razumov without haste. "I had made no plans of any sort."

"You just simply walked away?" she struck in.

He bowed his head in slow assent. "Simply—yes." He had gradually released his hold on the bar of the gate, as though he had acquired the conviction that no random shot could knock him over now. And suddenly he was inspired to add, "The snow was coming down very thick, you know."

She had a slight appreciative movement of the head, like an expert in such enterprises, very interested, capable of taking every point professionally. Razumov remembered something he had heard.

---

1 Incapable of feeling or emotion.

"I turned into a narrow side street, you understand," he went on negligently, and paused as if it were not worth talking about. Then he remembered another detail and dropped it before her, like a disdainful dole to her curiosity.

"I felt inclined to lie down and go to sleep there."

She clicked her tongue at that symptom, very struck indeed. Then—

"But the notebook! The amazing notebook, man. You don't mean to say you had put it in your pocket beforehand!" she cried.

Razumov gave a start. It might have been a sign of impatience.

"I went home. Straight home to my rooms," he said distinctly.

"The coolness of the man! You dared?"

"Why not? I assure you I was perfectly calm. Ha! Calmer than I am now perhaps."

"I like you much better as you are now than when you indulge that bitter vein of yours, Razumov. And nobody in the house saw you return—eh? That might have appeared queer."

"No one," Razumov said firmly. "Dvornik, landlady, girl, all out of the way. I went up like a shadow. It was a murky morning. The stairs were dark. I glided up like a phantom. Fate? Luck? What do you think?"

"I just see it!" The eyes of the woman revolutionist snapped darkly. "Well—and then you considered . . ."

Razumov had it all ready in his head.

"No. I looked at my watch, since you want to know. There was just time. I took that notebook, and ran down the stairs on tiptoe. Have you ever listened to the pit-pat of a man running round and round the shaft of a deep staircase? They have a gaslight at the bottom burning night and day. I suppose it's gleaming down there now . . . The sound dies out—the flame winks . . ."

He noticed the vacillation of surprise passing over the steady curiosity of the black eyes fastened on his face as if the woman revolutionist received the sound of his voice into her pupils instead of her ears. He checked himself, passed his hand over his forehead, confused, like a man who has been dreaming aloud.

"Where could a student be running if not to his lectures in the morning? At night it's another matter. I did not care if all the house had been there to look at me. But I don't suppose there was anyone. It's best not to be seen or heard. Aha! The people that are neither seen nor heard are the lucky ones—in Russia. Don't you admire my luck?"

"Astonishing," she said. "If you have luck as well as determination, then indeed you are likely to turn out an invaluable acquisition for the work in hand."

Her tone was earnest; and it seemed to Razumov that it was speculative, even as though she were already apportioning him, in her mind, his share of the work. Her eyes were cast down. He waited, not very alert now, but with the grip of the ever-present danger giving him an air of attentive gravity. Who could have written about him in that letter from Petersburg? A fellow-student, surely—some imbecile victim of revolutionary propaganda, some foolish slave of foreign, subversive ideals. A long, famine-stricken, red-nosed figure presented itself to his mental search. That must have been the fellow!

He smiled inwardly at the absolute wrong-headedness of the whole thing, the self-deception of a criminal idealist shattering his existence like a thunder-clap out of a clear sky, and re-echoing amongst the wreckage in the false assumptions of those other fools. Fancy that hungry and piteous imbecile furnishing to the curiosity of the revolutionist refugees this utterly fantastic detail! He appreciated it as by no means constituting a danger. On the contrary. As things stood it was for his advantage rather, a piece of sinister luck which had only to be accepted with proper caution.

"And yet, Razumov," he heard the musing voice of the woman, "you have not the face of a lucky man." She raised her eyes with renewed interest. "And so that was the way of it. After doing your work you simply walked off and made for your rooms. That sort of thing succeeds sometimes. I suppose it was agreed beforehand that, once the business over, each of you would go his own way?"

Razumov preserved the seriousness of his expression and the deliberate, if cautious, manner of speaking.

"Was not that the best thing to do?" he asked, in a dispassionate tone. "And anyway," he added, after waiting a moment, "we did not give much thought to what would come after. We never discussed formally any line of conduct. It was understood, I think."

She approved his statement with slight nods.

"You, of course, wished to remain in Russia?"

"In St. Petersburg itself," emphasized Razumov. "It was the only safe course for me. And, moreover, I had nowhere else to go."

"Yes! Yes! I know. Clearly. And the other—this wonderful

Haldin appearing only to be regretted[1]—you don't know what he intended?"

Razumov had foreseen that such a question would certainly come to meet him sooner or later. He raised his hands a little and let them fall helplessly by his side—nothing more.

It was the white-haired woman conspirator who was the first to break the silence.

"Very curious," she pronounced slowly. "And you did not think, Kirylo Sidorovitch, that he might perhaps wish to get in touch with you again?"

Razumov discovered that he could not suppress the trembling of his lips. But he thought that he owed it to himself to speak. A negative sign would not do again. Speak he must, if only to get at the bottom of what that St. Petersburg letter might have contained.

"I stayed at home next day," he said, bending down a little and plunging his glance into the black eyes of the woman so that she should not observe the trembling of his lips. "Yes, I stayed at home. As my actions are remembered and written about, then perhaps you are aware that I was *not* seen at the lectures next day. Eh? You didn't know? Well, I stopped at home—the live-long day."

As if moved by his agitated tone, she murmured a sympathetic "I see! It must have been trying enough."

"You seem to understand one's feelings," said Razumov steadily. "It was trying. It was horrible; it was an atrocious day. It was not the last."

"Yes, I understand. Afterwards, when you heard they had got him. Don't I know how one feels after losing a comrade in the good fight? One's ashamed of being left. And I can remember so many. Never mind. They shall be avenged before long. And what is death? At any rate, it is not a shameful thing like some kinds of life."

Razumov felt something stir in his breast, a sort of feeble and unpleasant tremor.

"Some kinds of life?" he repeated, looking at her searchingly.

"The subservient, submissive life. Life? No! Vegetation on the filthy heap of iniquity which the world is. Life, Razumov, not to be vile must be a revolt—a pitiless protest—all the time."

She calmed down, the gleam of suffused tears in her eyes dried

---

1  Conrad uses the transitive form of the verb, meaning to think of or remember with grief or sorrow.

out instantly by the heat of her passion, and it was in her capable, businesslike manner that she went on—

"You understand me, Razumov. You are not an enthusiast, but there is an immense force of revolt in you. I felt it from the first, directly I set my eyes on you—you remember—in Zürich. Oh! You are full of bitter revolt. That is good. Indignation flags sometimes, revenge itself may become a weariness, but that uncompromising sense of necessity and justice which armed your and Haldin's hands to strike down that fanatical brute . . . for it was that—nothing but that! I have been thinking it out. It could have been nothing else but that."

Razumov made a slight bow, the irony of which was concealed by an almost sinister immobility of feature.

"I can't speak for the dead. As for myself, I can assure you that my conduct was dictated by necessity and by the sense of—well—retributive justice."

"Good, that," he said to himself, while her eyes rested upon him, black and impenetrable like the mental caverns where revolutionary thought should sit plotting the violent way of its dream of changes. As if anything could be changed! In this world of men nothing can be changed—neither happiness nor misery. They can only be displaced at the cost of corrupted consciences and broken lives—a futile game for arrogant philosophers and sanguinary triflers. Those thoughts darted through Razumov's head while he stood facing the old revolutionary hand, the respected, trusted, and influential Sophia Antonovna, whose word had such a weight in the "active" section of every party. She was much more representative than the great Peter Ivanovitch. Stripped of rhetoric, mysticism, and theories, she was the true spirit of destructive revolution. And she was the personal adversary he had to meet. It gave him a feeling of triumphant pleasure to deceive her out of her own mouth. The epigrammatic saying that speech has been given to us for the purpose of concealing our thoughts came into his mind.[1] Of that cynical theory this was a very subtle and a very scornful application, flouting in its own words the very spirit of ruthless revolution, embodied in that woman with her white hair and black eyebrows, like slightly

---

1  In an August 1891 letter to Conrad, his uncle Tadeusz Bobrowski quotes: "Speech (in this case the written word) was given to us to conceal our thoughts." Bobrowski attributes this statement (perhaps erroneously) to the Prince of Benevento (*Conrad's Polish Background*, ed. Zdzisław Najder, trans. Halina Carroll, Oxford UP, 1964, 149).

sinuous lines of Indian ink,[1] drawn together by the perpendicular folds of a thoughtful frown.

"That's it. Retributive. No pity!" was the conclusion of her silence. And this once broken, she went on impulsively in short, vibrating sentences—

"Listen to my story, Razumov! . . ." Her father was a clever but unlucky artisan. No joy had lighted up his laborious days. He died at fifty; all the years of his life he had panted under the thumb of masters whose rapacity exacted from him the price of the water, of the salt, of the very air he breathed; taxed the sweat of his brow and claimed the blood of his sons. No protection, no guidance! What had society to say to him? Be submissive and be honest. If you rebel I shall kill you. If you steal I shall imprison you. But if you suffer I have nothing for you—nothing except perhaps a beggarly dole of bread—but no consolation for your trouble, no respect for your manhood, no pity for the sorrows of your miserable life.

And so he laboured, he suffered, and he died. He died in the hospital. Standing by the common grave she thought of his tormented existence—she saw it whole. She reckoned the simple joys of life, the birthright of the humblest, of which his gentle heart had been robbed by the crime of a society which nothing can absolve.

"Yes, Razumov," she continued, in an impressive, lowered voice, "it was like a lurid light in which I stood, still almost a child, and cursed not the toil, not the misery which had been his lot, but the great social iniquity of the system resting on unrequited toil and unpitied sufferings. From that moment I was a revolutionist."

Razumov, trying to raise himself above the dangerous weaknesses of contempt or compassion, had preserved an impassive countenance. She, with an unaffected touch of mere bitterness, the first he could notice since he had come in contact with the woman, went on—

"As I could not go to the Church where the priests of the system exhorted such unconsidered vermin as I to resignation, I went to the secret societies as soon as I knew how to find my way. I was sixteen years old—no more, Razumov! And—look at my white hair."

In these last words there was neither pride nor sadness. The bitterness too was gone.

"There is a lot of it. I had always magnificent hair, even as a

---

1 A black ink made in Japan and China in the form of solid sticks.

chit[1] of a girl. Only, at that time we were cutting it short and thinking that there was the first step towards crushing the social infamy. Crush the Infamy![2] A fine watchword! I would placard it on the walls of prisons and palaces, carve it on hard rocks, hang it out in letters of fire on that empty sky for a sign of hope and terror—a portent of the end . . ."

"You are eloquent, Sophia Antonovna," Razumov interrupted suddenly. "Only, so far you seem to have been writing it in water . . ."[3]

She was checked but not offended. "Who knows? Very soon it may become a fact written all over that great land of ours," she hinted meaningly. "And then one would have lived long enough. White hair won't matter."

Razumov looked at her white hair: and this mark of so many uneasy years seemed nothing but a testimony to the invincible vigour of revolt. It threw out into an astonishing relief the unwrinkled face, the brilliant black glance, the upright compact figure, the simple, brisk self-possession of the mature personality—as though in her revolutionary pilgrimage she had discovered the secret, not of everlasting youth, but of everlasting endurance.

How un-Russian she looked, thought Razumov. Her mother might have been a Jewess or an Armenian or—devil knew what. He reflected that a revolutionist is seldom true to the settled type. All revolt is the expression of strong individualism—ran his thought vaguely. One can tell them a mile off in any society, in any surroundings. It was astonishing that the police . . .

"We shall not meet again very soon, I think," she was saying. "I am leaving to-morrow."

"For Zürich?" Razumov asked casually, but feeling relieved, not from any distinct apprehension, but from a feeling of stress as if after a wrestling match.

"Yes, Zürich—and farther on, perhaps, much farther. Another

---

1 A somewhat derogatory term for a young girl; also a forward or pert young woman.
2 This quotation (*Ecrasez l'infâme*) appears in a letter from Voltaire to Jean le Rond d'Alembert (1717-83)dated 28 November 1762. For Voltaire, the infamy was the Christian religion, particularly what he saw as its intolerance.
3 Perhaps a reference to the epitaph of the English Romantic poet John Keats (1795-1821): "Here lies one whose name was writ in water." The phrase also appears in *Henry VIII* (1613) by William Shakespeare (1564-1616): "We write in water" (4.2.46); and *Philaster* (1608-09) by Francis Beaumont (1584-1616) and John Fletcher (1579-1625): "All your better deeds / Shall be in water writ" (5.3.81-82).

journey. When I think of all my journeys! The last must come some day. Never mind, Razumov. We had to have a good long talk. I would have certainly tried to see you if we had not met. Peter Ivanovitch knows where you live? Yes. I meant to have asked him—but it's better like this. You see, we expect two more men; and I had much rather wait here talking with you than up there at the house with . . ."

Having cast a glance beyond the gate, she interrupted herself. "Here they are," she said rapidly. "Well, Kirylo Sidorovitch, we shall have to say good-bye, presently."


## IV

In his incertitude of the ground on which he stood Razumov felt perturbed. Turning his head quickly, he saw two men on the opposite side of the road. Seeing themselves noticed by Sophia Antonovna, they crossed over at once, and passed one after another through the little gate by the side of the empty lodge. They looked hard at the stranger, but without mistrust, the crimson blouse being a flaring safety signal. The first, great white hairless face, double chin, prominent stomach, which he seemed to carry forward consciously within a strongly distended overcoat, only nodded and averted his eyes peevishly; his companion—lean, flushed cheekbones, a military red moustache below a sharp, salient nose—approached at once Sophia Antonovna, greeting her warmly. His voice was very strong but inarticulate. It sounded like a deep buzzing. The woman revolutionist was quietly cordial. . . .

"This is Razumov," she announced in a clear voice.

The lean new-comer made an eager half-turn. "He will want to embrace me," thought our young man with a deep recoil of all his being, while his limbs seemed too heavy to move. But it was a groundless alarm. He had to do now with a generation of conspirators who did not kiss each other on both cheeks; and raising an arm that felt like lead he dropped his hand into a largely-outstretched palm, fleshless and hot as if dried up by fever, giving a bony pressure, expressive, seeming to say, "Between us there's no need of words."

The man had big, wide-open eyes. Razumov fancied he could see a smile behind their sadness.

"This is Razumov," Sophia Antonovna repeated loudly for the benefit of the fat man, who at some distance displayed the profile of his stomach.

No one moved. Everything, sounds, attitudes, movements, and immobility seemed to be part of an experiment, the result of which was a thin voice piping with comic peevishness—

"Oh yes! Razumov. We have been hearing of nothing but Mr. Razumov for months. For my part, I confess I would rather have seen Haldin on this spot instead of Mr. Razumov."

The squeaky stress put on the name "Razumov—Mr. Razumov" pierced the ear ridiculously, like the falsetto of a circus clown beginning an elaborate joke. Astonishment was Razumov's first response, followed by sudden indignation.

"What's the meaning of this?" he asked in a stern tone.

"Tut! Silliness. He's always like that." Sophia Antonovna was obviously vexed. But she dropped the information, "Necator," from her lips just loud enough to be heard by Razumov. The abrupt squeaks of the fat man seemed to proceed from that thing like a balloon he carried under his overcoat. The stolidity of his attitude, the big feet, the lifeless, hanging hands, the enormous bloodless cheek, the thin wisps of hair straggling down the fat nape of the neck, fascinated Razumov into a stare on the verge of horror and laughter.

Nikita,[1] surnamed Necator, with a sinister aptness of alliteration! Razumov had heard of him. He had heard so much since crossing the frontier of these celebrities of the militant revolution; the legends, the stories, the authentic chronicle, which now and then peeps out before a half-incredulous world. Razumov had heard of him. He was supposed to have killed more gendarmes and police agents than any revolutionist living. He had been entrusted with executions.

The paper with the letters N.N., the very pseudonym of murder, found pinned on the stabbed breast of a certain notorious spy (this picturesque detail of a sensational murder case had got into the newspapers), was the mark of his handiwork. "By order of the Committee.—N.N." A corner of the curtain lifted to strike the imagination of the gaping world. He was said to have been innumerable times in and out of Russia, the Necator of bureaucrats, of provincial governors, of obscure informers. He lived between whiles, Razumov had heard, on the shores of the

---

1 Nikita is modeled in part on Evno Filippovich Azef (1869-1918), a member of the Socialist-Revolutionary Party and responsible in part for the assassinations of de Pleve and other Russian officials, as well as the execution of Father Gapon.

Lake of Como,[1] with a charming wife, devoted to the cause, and two young children. But how could that creature, so grotesque as to set town dogs barking at its mere sight, go about on those deadly errands and slip through the meshes of the police?

"What now? what now?" the voice squeaked. "I am only sincere. It's not denied that the other was the leading spirit. Well, it would have been better if he had been the one spared to us. More useful. I am not a sentimentalist. Say what I think . . . only natural."

Squeak, squeak, squeak, without a gesture, without a stir—the horrible squeaky burlesque of professional jealousy—this man of a sinister alliterative nickname, this executioner of revolutionary verdicts, the terrifying N.N. exasperated like a fashionable tenor by the attention attracted to the performance of an obscure amateur. Sophia Antonovna shrugged her shoulders. The comrade with the martial red moustache hurried towards Razumov full of conciliatory intentions in his strong buzzing voice.

"Devil take it! And in this place, too, in the public street, so to speak. But you can see yourself how it is. One of his fantastic sallies. Absolutely of no consequence."

"Pray don't concern yourself," cried Razumov, going off into a long fit of laughter. "Don't mention it."

The other, his hectic flush like a pair of burns on his cheek-bones, stared for a moment and burst out laughing too. Razumov, whose hilarity died out all at once, made a step forward.

"Enough of this," he began in a clear, incisive voice, though he could hardly control the trembling of his legs. "I will have no more of it. I shall not permit anyone. . . . I can see very well what you are at with those allusions. . . . Inquire, investigate! I defy you, but I will not be played with."

He had spoken such words before. He had been driven to cry them out in the face of other suspicions. It was an infernal cycle bringing round that protest like a fatal necessity of his existence. But it was no use. He would be always played with. Luckily life does not last for ever.

"I won't have it!" he shouted, striking his fist into the palm of his other hand.

"Kirylo Sidorovitch—what has come to you?" The woman revolutionist interfered with authority. They were all looking at

---

1  A lake in northern Italy.

Razumov now; the slayer of spies and gendarmes had turned about, presenting his enormous stomach in full, like a shield.

"Don't shout. There are people passing." Sophia Antonovna was apprehensive of another outburst. A steam-launch from Monrepos[1] had come to the landing-stage opposite the gate, its hoarse whistle and the churning noise alongside all unnoticed, had landed a small bunch of local passengers who were dispersing their several ways. Only a specimen of early tourist in knicker-bockers, conspicuous by a brand-new yellow leather glass-case,[2] hung about for a moment, scenting something unusual about these four people within the rusty iron gates of what looked the grounds run wild of an unoccupied private house. Ah! If he had only known what the chance of commonplace travelling had suddenly put in his way! But he was a well-bred person; he averted his gaze and moved off with short steps along the avenue, on the watch for a tramcar.

A gesture from Sophia Antonovna, "Leave him to me," had sent the two men away—the buzzing of the inarticulate voice growing fainter and fainter, and the thin pipe of "What now? what's the matter?" reduced to the proportions of a squeaking toy by the distance. They had left him to her. So many things could be left safely to the experience of Sophia Antonovna. And at once, her black eyes turned to Razumov, her mind tried to get at the heart of that outburst. It had some meaning. No one is born an active revolutionist. The change comes disturbingly, with the force of a sudden vocation, bringing in its train agonizing doubts, assertive violences, an unstable state of the soul, till the final appeasement of the convert in the perfect fierceness of conviction. She had seen—often had only divined—scores of these young men and young women going through an emotional crisis. This young man looked like a moody egotist. And besides, it was a special—a unique case. She had never met an individuality which interested and puzzled her so much.

"Take care, Razumov, my good friend. If you carry on like this you will go mad. You are angry with everybody and bitter with

---

1   Probably a reference to the small park, Parc Mon Repos ("my rest" in French), on the shore of Lake Geneva, a little north of Rue de France. The little pier for steam launches still exists; in fact steam launches still circulate between there and the Parc la Grange and Parc des Eaux-Vives on the opposite shore. There was also a Hôtel Mon-Repos on Rue de Lausanne in this same area that is still in operation.

2   A case for binoculars.

yourself, and on the look out for something to torment yourself with."

"It's intolerable!" Razumov could only speak in gasps. "You must admit that I can have no illusions on the attitude which . . . it isn't clear . . . or rather . . . only too clear."

He made a gesture of despair. It was not his courage that failed him. The choking fumes of falsehood had taken him by the throat—the thought of being condemned to struggle on and on in that tainted atmosphere without the hope of ever renewing his strength by a breath of fresh air.

"A glass of cold water is what you want." Sophia Antonovna glanced up the grounds at the house and shook her head, then out of the gate at the brimful placidity of the lake. With a half-comical shrug of the shoulders, she gave the remedy up in the face of that abundance.

"It is you, my dear soul, who are flinging yourself at something which does not exist. What is it? Self-reproach, or what? It's absurd. You couldn't have gone and given yourself up because your comrade was taken."

She remonstrated with him reasonably, at some length too. He had nothing to complain of in his reception. Every new-comer was discussed more or less. Everybody had to be thoroughly understood before being accepted. No one that she could remember had been shown from the first so much confidence. Soon, very soon, perhaps sooner than he expected, he would be given an opportunity of showing his devotion to the sacred task of crushing the Infamy.

Razumov, listening quietly, thought: "It may be that she is trying to lull my suspicions to sleep. On the other hand, it is obvious that most of them are fools." He moved aside a couple of paces and, folding his arms on his breast, leaned back against the stone pillar of the gate.

"As to what remains obscure in the fate of that poor Haldin," Sophia Antonovna dropped into a slowness of utterance which was to Razumov like the falling of molten lead drop by drop; "as to that—though no one ever hinted that either from fear or neglect your conduct has not been what it should have been—well, I have a bit of intelligence . . ."

Razumov could not prevent himself from raising his head, and Sophia Antonovna nodded slightly.

"I have. You remember that letter from St. Petersburg I mentioned to you a moment ago?"

"The letter? Perfectly. Some busybody has been reporting my

conduct on a certain day. It's rather sickening. I suppose our police are greatly edified when they open these interesting and—and—superfluous letters."

"Oh dear no! The police do not get hold of our letters as easily as you imagine. The letter in question did not leave St. Petersburg till the ice broke up. It went by the first English steamer which left the Neva[1] this spring. They have a fireman on board—one of us, in fact. It has reached me from Hull . . ."[2]

She paused as if she were surprised at the sullen fixity of Razumov's gaze, but went on at once, and much faster.

"We have some of our people there who . . . but never mind. The writer of the letter relates an incident which he thinks may possibly be connected with Haldin's arrest. I was just going to tell you when those two men came along."

"That also was an incident," muttered Razumov, "of a very charming kind—for me."

"Leave off that!" cried Sophia Antonovna. "Nobody cares for Nikita's barking. There's no malice in him. Listen to what I have to say. You may be able to throw a light. There was in St. Petersburg a sort of town peasant—a man who owned horses. He came to town years ago to work for some relation as a driver and ended by owning a cab or two."

She might well have spared herself the slight effort of the gesture: "Wait!" Razumov did not mean to speak; he could not have interrupted her now, not to save his life. The contraction of his facial muscles had been involuntary, a mere surface stir, leaving him sullenly attentive as before.

"He was not a quite ordinary man of his class—it seems," she went on. "The people of the house—my informant talked with many of them—you know, one of those enormous houses of shame and misery . . ."

Sophia Antonovna need not have enlarged on the character of the house. Razumov saw clearly, towering at her back, a dark mass of masonry veiled in snowflakes, with the long row of windows of the eating-shop shining greasily very near the ground. The ghost of that night pursued him. He stood up to it with rage and with weariness.

"Did the late Haldin ever by chance speak to you of that house?" Sophia Antonovna was anxious to know.

"Yes." Razumov, making that answer, wondered whether he

---

1  A river in northwestern Russia; St. Petersburg lies at its mouth.
2  A seaport in northeastern England, at the mouth of the Hull River.

were falling into a trap. It was so humiliating to lie to these people that he probably could not have said no. "He mentioned to me once," he added, as if making an effort of memory, "a house of that sort. He used to visit some workmen there."

"Exactly."

Sophia Antonovna triumphed. Her correspondent had discovered that fact quite accidentally from the talk of the people of the house, having made friends with a workman who occupied a room there. They described Haldin's appearance perfectly. He brought comforting words of hope into their misery. He came irregularly, but he came very often, and—her correspondent wrote—sometimes he spent a night in the house, sleeping, they thought, in a stable which opened upon the inner yard.

"Note that, Razumov! In a stable."

Razumov had listened with a sort of ferocious but amused acquiescence.

"Yes. In the straw. It was probably the cleanest spot in the whole house."

"No doubt," assented the woman with that deep frown which seemed to draw closer together her black eyes in a sinister fashion. No four-footed beast could stand the filth and wretchedness so many human beings were condemned to suffer from in Russia. The point of this discovery was that it proved Haldin to have been familiar with that horse-owning peasant—a reckless, independent, free-living fellow not much liked by the other inhabitants of the house. He was believed to have been the associate of a band of housebreakers. Some of these got captured. Not while he was driving them, however; but still there was a suspicion against the fellow of having given a hint to the police and . . .

The woman revolutionist checked herself suddenly.

"And you? Have you ever heard your friend refer to a certain Ziemianitch?"

Razumov was ready for the name. He had been looking out for the question. "When it comes I shall own up," he had said to himself. But he took his time.

"To be sure!" he began slowly. "Ziemianitch, a peasant owning a team of horses. Yes. On one occasion. Ziemianitch! Certainly! Ziemianitch of the horses. . . . How could it have slipped my memory like this? One of the last conversations we had together."

"That means,"—Sophia Antonovna looked very grave,—"that means, Razumov, it was very shortly before—eh?"

"Before what?" shouted Razumov, advancing at the woman,

who looked astonished but stood her ground. "Before . . . Oh! Of course, it was before! How could it have been after? Only a few hours before."

"And he spoke of him favourably?"

"With enthusiasm! The horses of Ziemianitch! The free soul of Ziemianitch!"

Razumov took a savage delight in the loud utterance of that name, which had never before crossed his lips audibly. He fixed his blazing eyes on the woman till at last her fascinated expression recalled him to himself.

"The late Haldin," he said, holding himself in, with downcast eyes, "was inclined to take sudden fancies to people, on—on— what shall I say—insufficient grounds."

"There!" Sophia Antonovna clapped her hands. "That, to my mind, settles it. The suspicions of my correspondent were aroused . . ."

"Aha! Your correspondent," Razumov said in an almost openly mocking tone. "What suspicions? How aroused? By this Ziemianitch? Probably some drunken, gabbling, plausible . . ."

"You talk as if you had known him."

Razumov looked up.

"No. But I knew Haldin."

Sophia Antonovna nodded gravely.

"I see. Every word you say confirms to my mind the suspicion communicated to me in that very interesting letter. This Ziemianitch was found one morning hanging from a hook in the stable—dead."

Razumov felt a profound trouble. It was visible, because Sophia Antonovna was moved to observe vivaciously—

"Aha! You begin to see."

He saw it clearly enough—in the light of a lantern casting spokes of shadow in a cellar-like stable, the body in a sheepskin coat and long boots hanging against the wall. A pointed hood, with the ends wound about up to the eyes, hid the face. "But that does not concern me," he reflected. "It does not affect my position at all. He never knew who had thrashed him. He could not have known." Razumov felt sorry for the old lover of the bottle and women.

"Yes. Some of them end like that," he muttered. "What is your idea, Sophia Antonovna?"

It was really the idea of her correspondent, but Sophia Antonovna had adopted it fully. She stated it in one word— "Remorse." Razumov opened his eyes very wide at that. Sophia

Antonovna's informant, by listening to the talk of the house, by putting this and that together, had managed to come very near to the truth of Haldin's relation to Ziemianitch.

"It is I who can tell you what you were not certain of—that your friend had some plan for saving himself afterwards, for getting out of St. Petersburg, at any rate. Perhaps that and no more, trusting to luck for the rest. And that fellow's horses were part of the plan."

"They have actually got at the truth," Razumov marvelled to himself, while he nodded judicially. "Yes, that's possible, very possible." But the woman revolutionist was very positive that it was so. First of all, a conversation about horses between Haldin and Ziemianitch had been partly overheard. Then there were the suspicions of the people in the house when their "young gentleman" (they did not know Haldin by his name) ceased to call at the house. Some of them used to charge Ziemianitch with knowing something of this absence. He denied it with exasperation; but the fact was that ever since Haldin's disappearance he was not himself, growing moody and thin. Finally, during a quarrel with some woman (to whom he was making up), in which most of the inmates of the house took part apparently, he was openly abused by his chief enemy, an athletic pedlar, for an informer, and for having driven "our young gentleman to Siberia, the same as you did those young fellows who broke into houses." In consequence of this there was a fight, and Ziemianitch got flung down a flight of stairs. Thereupon he drank and moped for a week, and then hanged himself.

Sophia Antonovna drew her conclusions from the tale. She charged Ziemianitch either with drunken indiscretion as to a driving job on a certain date, overheard by some spy in some low grog-shop—perhaps in the very eating-shop on the ground floor of the house—or, maybe, a downright denunciation, followed by remorse. A man like that would be capable of anything. People said he was a flighty old chap. And if he had been once before mixed up with the police—as seemed certain, though he always denied it—in connexion with these thieves, he would be sure to be acquainted with some police underlings, always on the look out for something to report. Possibly at first his tale was not made anything of till the day that scoundrel de P—— got his deserts. Ah! But then every bit and scrap of hint and information would be acted on, and fatally they were bound to get Haldin.

Sophia Antonovna spread out her hands—"Fatally."

Fatality—chance! Razumov meditated in silent astonishment

upon the queer verisimilitude of these inferences. They were obviously to his advantage.

"It is right now to make this conclusive evidence known generally." Sophia Antonovna was very calm and deliberate again. She had received the letter three days ago, but did not write at once to Peter Ivanovitch. She knew then that she would have the opportunity presently of meeting several men of action assembled for an important purpose.

"I thought it would be more effective if I could show the letter itself at large. I have it in my pocket now. You understand how pleased I was to come upon you."

Razumov was saying to himself, "She won't offer to show the letter to me. Not likely. Has she told me everything that correspondent of hers has found out?" He longed to see the letter, but he felt he must not ask.

"Tell me, please, was this an investigation ordered, as it were?"

"No, no," she protested. "There you are again with your sensitiveness. It makes you stupid. Don't you see, there was no starting-point for an investigation even if any one had thought of it. A perfect blank! That's exactly what some people were pointing out as the reason for receiving you cautiously. It was all perfectly accidental, arising from my informant striking an acquaintance with an intelligent skindresser lodging in that particular slum-house. A wonderful coincidence!"

"A pious person," suggested Razumov, with a pale smile, "would say that the hand of God has done it all."

"My poor father would have said that." Sophia Antonovna did not smile. She dropped her eyes. "Not that his God ever helped him. It's a long time since God has done anything for the people. Anyway, it's done."

"All this would be quite final," said Razumov, with every appearance of reflective impartiality, "if there was any certitude that the 'our young gentleman' of these people was Victor Haldin. Have we got that?"

"Yes. There's no mistake. My correspondent was as familiar with Haldin's personal appearance as with your own," the woman affirmed decisively.

"It's the red-nosed fellow beyond a doubt," Razumov said to himself, with reawakened uneasiness. Had his own visit to that accursed house passed unnoticed? It was barely possible. Yet it was hardly probable. It was just the right sort of food for the popular gossip that gaunt busybody had been picking up. But the letter did not seem to contain any allusion to that. Unless she had suppressed it. And, if so, why? If it had really escaped the prying of that hunger-stricken democrat with a confounded genius for recognizing people from description, it could only be for a time. He would come upon it presently and hasten to write another letter—and then!

For all the envenomed recklessness of his temper, fed on hate and disdain, Razumov shuddered inwardly. It guarded him from common fear, but it could not defend him from disgust at being dealt with in any way by these people. It was a sort of superstitious dread. Now, since his position had been made more secure by their own folly at the cost of Ziemianitch, he felt the need of perfect safety, with its freedom from direct lying, with its power of moving amongst them silent, unquestioning, listening, impenetrable, like the very fate of their crimes and their folly. Was this advantage his already? Or not yet? Or never would be?

"Well, Sophia Antonovna," his air of reluctant concession was genuine in so far that he was really loath to part with her without testing her sincerity by a question it was impossible to bring about in any way; "well, Sophia Antonovna, if that is so, then—"

"The creature has done justice to himself," the woman observed, as if thinking aloud.

"What? Ah yes! Remorse," Razumov muttered, with equivocal contempt.

"Don't be harsh, Kirylo Sidorovitch, if you have lost a friend." There was no hint of softness in her tone, only the black glitter of her eyes seemed detached for an instant from vengeful visions. "He was a man of the people. The simple Russian soul is never wholly impenitent. It's something to know that."

"Consoling?" insinuated Razumov, in a tone of inquiry.

"Leave off railing," she checked him explosively. "Remember, Razumov, that women, children, and revolutionists hate irony, which is the negation of all saving instincts, of all faith, of all devotion, of all action. Don't rail! Leave off. . . . I don't know how it is, but there are moments when you are abhorrent to me. . . ."

She averted her face. A languid silence, as if all the electricity of the situation had been discharged in this flash of passion, lasted for some time. Razumov had not flinched. Suddenly she laid the tips of her fingers on his sleeve.

"Don't mind."

"I don't mind," he said very quietly.

He was proud to feel that she could read nothing on his face. He was really mollified, relieved, if only for a moment, from an obscure oppression. And suddenly he asked himself,

"Why the devil did I go to that house? It was an imbecile thing to do."

A profound disgust came over him. Sophia Antonovna lingered, talking in a friendly manner with an evident conciliatory intention. And it was still about the famous letter, referring to various minute details given by her informant, who had never seen Ziemianitch. The "victim of remorse" had been buried several weeks before her correspondent began frequenting the house. It—the house—contained very good revolutionary material. The spirit of the heroic Haldin had passed through these dens of black wretchedness with a promise of universal redemption from all the miseries that oppress mankind. Razumov listened without hearing, gnawed by the newborn desire of safety with its independence from that degrading method of direct lying which at times he found it almost impossible to practice.

No. The point he wanted to hear about could never come into this conversation. There was no way of bringing it forward. He regretted not having composed a perfect story for use abroad, in which his fatal connexion with the house might have been owned up to. But when he left Russia he did not know that Ziemianitch had hanged himself. And, anyway, who could have foreseen this woman's "informant" stumbling upon that particular slum, of all the slums awaiting destruction in the purifying flame of social revolution? Who could have foreseen? Nobody! "It's a perfect, diabolic surprise," thought Razumov, calm-faced in his attitude of inscrutable superiority, nodding assent to Sophia Antonovna's remarks upon the psychology of "the people," "Oh yes—certainly," rather coldly, but with a nervous longing in his fingers to tear some sort of confession out of her throat.

Then, at the very last, on the point of separating, the feeling of relaxed tension already upon him, he heard Sophia Antonovna allude to the subject of his uneasiness. How it came about he could only guess, his mind being absent at the moment, but it must have sprung from Sophia Antonovna's complaints of the illogical absurdity of the people. For instance—that Ziemianitch was notoriously irreligious, and yet, in the last weeks of his life, he suffered from the notion that he had been beaten by the devil.

"The devil," repeated Razumov, as though he had not heard aright.

"The actual devil. The devil in person. You may well look astonished, Kirylo Sidorovitch. Early on the very night poor Haldin was taken, a complete stranger turned up and gave Ziemianitch a most fearful thrashing while he was lying dead-drunk in the stable. The wretched creature's body was one mass of bruises. He showed them to the people in the house."

"But you, Sophia Antonovna, you don't believe in the actual devil?"

"Do you?" retorted the woman curtly. "Not but that there are plenty of men worse than devils to make a hell of this earth," she muttered to herself.

Razumov watched her, vigorous and white-haired, with the deep fold between her thin eyebrows, and her black glance turned idly away. It was obvious that she did not make much of the story—unless, indeed, this was the perfection of duplicity. "A dark young man," she explained further. "Never seen there before, never seen afterwards. Why are you smiling, Razumov?"

"At the devil being still young after all these ages," he answered composedly. "But who was able to describe him, since the victim, you say, was dead-drunk at the time?"

"Oh! The eating-house keeper has described him. An over-bearing, swarthy young man in a student's cloak, who came rushing in, demanded Ziemianitch, beat him furiously, and rushed away without a word, leaving the eating-house keeper paralysed with astonishment."

"Does he, too, believe it was the devil?"

"That I can't say. I am told he's very reserved on the matter. Those sellers of spirits are great scoundrels generally. I should think he knows more of it than anybody."

"Well, and you, Sophia Antonovna, what's your theory?" asked Razumov in a tone of great interest. "Yours and your informant's, who is on the spot."

"I agree with him. Some police-hound in disguise. Who else could beat a helpless man so unmercifully? As for the rest, if they were out that day on every trail, old and new, it is probable enough that they might have thought it just as well to have Ziemi-anitch at hand for more information, or for identification, or what not. Some scoundrelly detective was sent to fetch him along, and being vexed at finding him so drunk broke a stable fork over his ribs. Later on, after they had the big game safe in the net, they troubled their heads no more about that peasant."

Such were the last words of the woman revolutionist in this conversation, keeping so close to the truth, departing from it so far in the verisimilitude of thoughts and conclusions as to give one the notion of the invincible nature of human error, a glimpse into the utmost depths of self-deception. Razumov, after shaking hands with Sophia Antonovna, left the grounds, crossed the road, and walking out on the little steamboat pier leaned over the rail.

His mind was at ease; ease such as he had not known for many days, ever since that night . . . the night. The conversation with the woman revolutionist had given him the view of his danger at the very moment this danger vanished, characteristically enough. "I ought to have foreseen the doubts that would arise in those people's minds," he thought. Then his attention being attracted by a stone of peculiar shape, which he could see clearly lying at the bottom, he began to speculate as to the depth of water in that spot. But very soon, with a start of wonder at this extraordinary instance of ill-timed detachment, he returned to his train of thought. "I ought to have told very circumstantial lies from the first," he said to himself, with a mortal distaste of the mere idea which silenced his mental utterance for quite a perceptible interval. "Luckily, that's all right now," he reflected, and after a time spoke to himself, half aloud, "Thanks to the devil," and laughed a little.

The end of Ziemianitch then arrested his wandering thoughts. He was not exactly amused at the interpretation, but he could not help detecting in it a certain piquancy. He owned to himself that, had he known of that suicide before leaving Russia, he would have been incapable of making such excellent use of it for his own purposes. He ought to be infinitely obliged to the fellow with the red nose for his patience and ingenuity, "A wonderful psychologist apparently," he said to himself sarcastically. Remorse, indeed! It was a striking example of your true conspirator's blindness, of the stupid subtlety of people with one idea. This was a drama of love, not of conscience, Razumov continued to himself mockingly. A woman the old fellow was making up to! A robust pedlar, clearly a rival, throwing him down a flight of stairs. . . . And at sixty, for a lifelong lover, it was not an easy matter to get over. That was a feminist of a different stamp from Peter Ivanovitch. Even the comfort of the bottle might conceivably fail him in this supreme crisis. At such an age nothing but a halter could cure the pangs of an unquenchable passion. And, besides, there was the wild exasperation aroused by the unjust aspersions and the contumely[1] of the house, with the maddening impossibility to account for that mysterious thrashing, added to these simple and bitter sorrows. "Devil, eh?" Razumov exclaimed, with mental excitement, as if he had made an interesting discovery. "Ziemianitch ended by falling into mysticism. So many of our true

---

1   Insolent or reproachful language or treatment.

Russian souls end in that way! Very characteristic." He felt pity for Ziemianitch, a large neutral pity, such as one may feel for an unconscious multitude, a great people seen from above—like a community of crawling ants working out its destiny. It was as if this Ziemianitch could not possibly have done anything else. And Sophia Antonovna's cocksure and contemptuous "some police-hound" was characteristically Russian in another way. But there was no tragedy there. This was a comedy of errors. It was as if the devil himself were playing a game with all of them in turn. First with him, then with Ziemianitch, then with those revolutionists. The devil's own game this. . . . He interrupted his earnest mental soliloquy with a jocular thought at his own expense. "Hallo! I am falling into mysticism too."

His mind was more at ease than ever. Turning about he put his back against the rail comfortably. "All this fits with marvellous aptness," he continued to think. "The brilliance of my reputed exploit is no longer darkened by the fate of my supposed colleague. The mystic Ziemianitch accounts for that. An incredible chance has served me. No more need of lies. I shall have only to listen and to keep my scorn from getting the upper hand of my caution."

He sighed, folded his arms, his chin dropped on his breast, and it was a long time before he started forward from that pose, with the recollection that he had made up his mind to do something important that day. What it was he could not immediately recall, yet he made no effort of memory, for he was uneasily certain that he would remember presently.

He had not gone more than a hundred yards towards the town when he slowed down, almost faltered in his walk, at the sight of a figure walking in the contrary direction, draped in a cloak, under a soft, broad-brimmed hat, picturesque but diminutive, as if seen through the big end of an opera-glass. It was impossible to avoid that tiny man, for there was no issue for retreat.

"Another one going to that mysterious meeting," thought Razumov. He was right in his surmise, only *this* one, unlike the others who came from a distance, was known to him personally. Still, he hoped to pass on with a mere bow, but it was impossible to ignore the little thin hand with hairy wrist and knuckles protruded in a friendly wave from under the folds of the cloak, worn Spanish-wise, in disregard of a fairly warm day, a corner flung over the shoulder.

"And how is Herr Razumov?" sounded the greeting in German, by that alone made more odious to the object of the affable recognition. At closer quarters the diminutive personage looked like a reduction of an ordinary-sized man, with a lofty brow bared for a moment by the raising of the hat, the great pepper-and-salt full beard spread over the proportionally broad chest. A fine bold nose jutted over a thin mouth hidden in the mass of fine hair. All this, accented features, strong limbs in their relative smallness, appeared delicate without the slightest sign of debility. The eyes alone, almond-shaped and brown, were too big, with the whites slightly bloodshot by much pen labour under a lamp. The obscure celebrity of the tiny man was well known to Razumov. Polyglot,[1] of unknown parentage, of indefinite nationality, anarchist, with a pedantic and ferocious temperament, and an amazingly inflammatory capacity for invective, he was a power in the background, this violent pamphleteer clamouring for revolutionary justice, this Julius Laspara, editor of the *Living Word*, confidant of conspirators, inditer of sanguinary menaces and manifestos, suspected of being in the secret of every plot. Laspara lived in the old town in a sombre, narrow house presented to him by a naïve middle-class admirer of his humanitarian eloquence. With him lived his two daughters, who overtopped him head and shoulders, and a pasty-faced, lean boy of six, languishing in the dark rooms in blue cotton overalls and clumsy boots, who might have belonged to either one of them or to neither. No stranger could tell. Julius Laspara no doubt knew which of his girls it was who, after casually vanishing for a few years, had as casually returned to him possessed of that child; but, with admirable pedantry, he had refrained from asking her for details—no, not so much as the name of the father, because maternity should be an anarchist function. Razumov had been admitted twice to that suite of several small dark rooms on the top floor: dusty window-panes, litter of all sorts of sweepings all over the place, half-full glasses of tea forgotten on every table, the two Laspara daughters prowling about enigmatically silent, sleepy-eyed, corsetless,[2] and generally, in their want of shape and the disorder of their rumpled attire, resembling old dolls; the great but obscure Julius, his feet twisted round his three-legged stool, always ready to receive the visitors, the pen instantly dropped, the body screwed round with a striking display of the lofty brow and of the great austere beard.

---

1 A person with a knowledge of several languages.
2 I.e., not fully dressed. At that time, in public at least, women generally wore a corset, which was a tight undergarment, reinforced with bone and fitted from hips to bust, that emphasized the female figure.

When he got down from his stool it was as though he had descended from the heights of Olympus.[1] He was dwarfed by his daughters, by the furniture, by any caller of ordinary stature. But he very seldom left it, and still more rarely was seen walking in broad daylight.

It must have been some matter of serious importance which had driven him out in that direction that afternoon. Evidently he wished to be amiable to that young man whose arrival had made some sensation in the world of political refugees. In Russian now, which he spoke, as he spoke and wrote four or five other European languages, without distinction and without force (other than that of invective), he inquired if Razumov had taken his inscriptions[2] at the University as yet. And the young man, shaking his head negatively—

"There's plenty of time for that. But, meantime, are you not going to write something for us?"

He could not understand how any one could refrain from writing on anything, social, economic, historical—anything. Any subject could be treated in the right spirit, and for the ends of social revolution. And, as it happened, a friend of his in London had got in touch with a review of advanced ideas. "We must educate, educate everybody—develop the great thought of absolute liberty and of revolutionary justice."

Razumov muttered rather surlily that he did not even know English.

"Write in Russian. We'll have it translated. There can be no difficulty. Why, without seeking further, there is Miss Haldin. My daughters go to see her sometimes." He nodded significantly. "She does nothing, has never done anything in her life. She would be quite competent, with a little assistance. Only write. You know you must. And so good-bye for the present."

He raised his arm and went on. Razumov backed against the low wall, looked after him, spat violently, and went on his way with an angry mutter—

"Cursed Jew!"

He did not know anything about it. Julius Laspara might have been a Transylvanian, a Turk, an Andalusian, or a citizen of one

---

1 Mount Olympus, the traditional home of the main gods in ancient Greek mythology, is the highest mountain in Greece.

2 Conrad appears to have in mind the French phrase *prendre son inscription*, "to take his inscription," meaning to enter one's name in a register etc.—in this case to enroll in the university.

of the Hanse towns[1] for anything he could tell to the contrary. But this is not a story of the West, and this exclamation must be recorded, accompanied by the comment that it was merely an expression of hate and contempt, best adapted to the nature of the feelings Razumov suffered from at the time. He was boiling with rage, as though he had been grossly insulted. He walked as if blind, following instinctively the shore of the diminutive harbour along the quay, through a pretty, dull garden, where dull people sat on chairs under the trees, till, his fury abandoning him, he discovered himself in the middle of a long, broad bridge. He slowed down at once. To his right, beyond the toy-like jetties, he saw the green slopes framing the Petit Lac[2] in all the marvellous banality of the picturesque made of painted cardboard, with the more distant stretch of water inanimate and shining like a piece of tin.

He turned his head away from that view for the tourists, and walked on slowly, his eyes fixed on the ground. One or two persons had to get out of his way, and then turned round to give a surprised stare to his profound absorption. The insistence of the celebrated subversive journalist rankled in his mind strangely. Write. Must write! He! Write! A sudden light flashed upon him. To write was the very thing he had made up his mind to do that day. He had made up his mind irrevocably to that step and then had forgotten all about it. That incorrigible tendency to escape from the grip of the situation was fraught with serious danger. He was ready to despise himself for it. What was it? Levity, or deep-seated weakness? Or an unconscious dread?

"Is it that I am shrinking? It can't be! It's impossible. To shrink now would be worse than moral suicide; it would be nothing less than moral damnation," he thought. "Is it possible that I have a conventional conscience?"

He rejected that hypothesis with scorn, and, checked on the edge of the pavement, made ready to cross the road and proceed up the wide street facing the head of the bridge; and that for no other reason except that it was there before him. But at the moment a couple of carriages and a slow-moving cart interposed,

---

1 Transylvania is a region in central and western Romania; Andalucía is a region in southern Spain; the phrase "Hanse towns" refers to the Hanseatic League, a trading alliance consisting of some 100 towns and 80 cities in northern Europe that formed a monopoly that existed from the twelfth century to the seventeenth century.
2 The western part of Lake Geneva, along which shore the city of Geneva is located.

and suddenly he turned sharp to the left, following the quay again, but now away from the lake.

"It may be just my health," he thought, allowing himself a very unusual doubt of his soundness; for, with the exception of a childish ailment or two, he had never been ill in his life. But that was a danger, too. Only, it seemed as though he were being looked after in a specially remarkable way. "If I believed in an active Providence," Razumov said to himself, amused grimly, "I would see here the working of an ironical finger. To have a Julius Laspara put in my way as if expressly to remind me of my purpose is—Write, he had said. I must write—I must, indeed! I shall write—never fear. Certainly. That's why I am here. And for the future I shall have something to write about."

He was exciting himself by this mental soliloquy. But the idea of writing evoked the thought of a place to write in, of shelter, of privacy, and naturally of his lodgings, mingled with a distaste for the necessary exertion of getting there, with a mistrust as of some hostile influence awaiting him within those odious four walls.

"Suppose one of these revolutionists," he asked himself, "were to take a fancy to call on me while I am writing?" The mere prospect of such an interruption made him shudder. One could lock one's door, or ask the tobacconist downstairs (some sort of a refugee himself) to tell inquirers that one was not in. Not very good precautions those. The manner of his life, he felt, must be kept clear of every cause for suspicion or even occasion for wonder, down to such trifling occurrences as a delay in opening a locked door. "I wish I were in the middle of some field miles away from everywhere," he thought.

He had unconsciously turned to the left once more and now was aware of being on a bridge again. This one was much narrower than the other, and instead of being straight, made a sort of elbow or angle. At the point of that angle a short arm joined it to a hexagonal islet with a soil of gravel and its shores faced with dressed stone, a perfection of puerile neatness. A couple of tall poplars and a few other trees stood grouped on the clean, dark gravel, and under them a few garden benches and a bronze effigy of Jean Jacques Rousseau[1] seated on its pedestal.

---

1 Swiss-French philosopher (1712-78) of the Enlightenment, born in Geneva. He is best known for his books *The Social Contract* (1762) and *The Confessions of Jean-Jacques Rousseau* (1782) and is often credited with the concept of the "noble savage"—that is, that humanity is essentially good when in a state of nature but becomes corrupt through contact with society.

On setting his foot on it Razumov became aware that, except for the woman in charge of the refreshment chalet, he would be alone on the island. There was something of naïve, odious, and inane simplicity about that unfrequented tiny crumb of earth named after Jean Jacques Rousseau. Something pretentious and shabby, too. He asked for a glass of milk, which he drank standing, at one draught (nothing but tea had passed his lips since the morning), and was going away with a weary, lagging step when a thought stopped him short. He had found precisely what he needed. If solitude could ever be secured in the open air in the middle of a town, he would have it there on this absurd island, together with the faculty of watching the only approach.

He went back heavily to a garden seat, dropped into it. This was the place for making a beginning of that writing which had to be done. The materials he had on him. "I shall always come here," he said to himself, and afterwards sat for quite a long time motionless, without thought and sight and hearing, almost without life. He sat long enough for the declining sun to dip behind the roofs of the town at his back, and throw the shadow of the houses on the lake front over the islet, before he pulled out of his pocket a fountain pen, opened a small notebook on his knee, and began to write quickly, raising his eyes now and then at the connecting arm of the bridge. These glances were needless; the people crossing over in the distance seemed unwilling even to look at the islet where the exiled effigy of the author of the *Social Contract*[1] sat enthroned above the bowed head of Razumov in the sombre immobility of bronze. After finishing his scribbling, Razumov, with a sort of feverish haste, put away the pen, then rammed the notebook into his pocket, first tearing out the written pages with an almost convulsive brusqueness. But the folding of the flimsy batch on his knee was executed with thoughtful nicety. That done, he leaned back in his seat and remained motionless, the papers holding in his left hand. The twilight had deepened. He got up and began to pace to and fro slowly under the trees.

"There can be no doubt that now I am safe," he thought. His fine ear could detect the faintly accentuated murmurs of the current breaking against the point of the island, and he forgot

---

1  *The Social Contract: Or Principles of Political Right* (1762), an influential book of Enlightenment political philosophy by Rousseau that famously begins by asserting, "Man is born free, but everywhere he is in chains" (trans. H.J. Tozer [Wordsworth, 1998], 5).

himself in listening to them with interest. But even to his acute sense of hearing the sound was too elusive.

"Extraordinary occupation I am giving myself up to," he murmured. And it occurred to him that this was about the only sound he could listen to innocently, and for his own pleasure, as it were. Yes, the sound of water, the voice of the wind—completely foreign to human passions. All the other sounds of this earth brought contamination to the solitude of a soul.

This was Mr. Razumov's feeling, the soul, of course, being his own, and the word being used not in the theological sense, but standing, as far as I can understand it, for that part of Mr. Razumov which was not his body, and more specially in danger from the fires of this earth. And it must be admitted that in Mr. Razumov's case the bitterness of solitude from which he suffered was not an altogether morbid phenomenon.

# PART FOURTH

## I

That I should, at the beginning of this retrospect, mention again that Mr. Razumov's youth had no one in the world, as literally no one as it can be honestly affirmed of any human being, is but a statement of fact from a man who believes in the psychological value of facts. There is also, perhaps, a desire of punctilious fairness. Unidentified with anyone in this narrative where the aspects of honour and shame are remote from the ideas of the Western world, and taking my stand on the ground of common humanity, it is for that very reason that I feel a strange reluctance to state baldly here what every reader has most likely already discovered himself. Such reluctance may appear absurd if it were not for the thought that because of the imperfection of language there is always something ungracious (and even disgraceful) in the exhibition of naked truth. But the time has come when Councillor of State Mikulin can no longer be ignored. His simple question "Where to?" on which we left Mr. Razumov in St. Petersburg, throws a light on the general meaning of this individual case.

"Where to?" was the answer in the form of a gentle question to what we may call Mr. Razumov's declaration of independence. The question was not menacing in the least and, indeed, had the ring of innocent inquiry. Had it been taken in a merely topographical sense, the only answer to it would have appeared sufficiently appalling to Mr. Razumov. Where to? Back to his rooms, where the Revolution had sought him out to put to a sudden test his dormant instincts, his half-conscious thoughts and almost wholly unconscious ambitions, by the touch as of some furious and dogmatic religion, with its call to frantic sacrifices, its tender resignations, its dreams and hopes uplifting the soul by the side of the most sombre moods of despair. And Mr. Razumov had let go the door-handle and had come back to the middle of the room, asking Councillor Mikulin angrily, "What do you mean by it?"

As far as I can tell, Councillor Mikulin did not answer that question. He drew Mr. Razumov into familiar conversation. It is the peculiarity of Russian natures that, however strongly engaged in the drama of action, they are still turning their ear to the murmur of abstract ideas. This conversation (and others later on) need not be recorded. Suffice it to say that it brought Mr. Razumov as we know him to the test of another faith. There was nothing official in its expression, and Mr. Razumov was led to defend his attitude of detachment. But Councillor Mikulin would have none of his arguments. "For a man like you," were his last weighty words in the discussion, "such a position is impossible. Don't forget that I have seen that interesting piece of paper. I understand your liberalism. I have an intellect of that kind myself. Reform for me is mainly a question of method. But the principle of revolt is a physical intoxication, a sort of hysteria which must be kept away from the masses. You agree to this without reserve, don't you? Because, you see, Kirylo Sidorovitch, abstention, reserve, in certain situations, come very near to political crime. The ancient Greeks[1] understood that very well."

Mr. Razumov, listening with a faint smile, asked Councillor Mikulin point-blank if this meant that he was going to have him watched.

The high official took no offence at the cynical inquiry.

"No, Kirylo Sidorovitch," he answered gravely. "I don't mean to have you watched."

Razumov, suspecting a lie, affected yet the greatest liberty of mind during the short remainder of that interview. The older man expressed himself throughout in familiar terms, and with a sort of shrewd simplicity. Razumov concluded that to get to the bottom of that mind was an impossible feat. A great disquiet made his heart beat quicker. The high official, issuing from behind the desk, was actually offering to shake hands with him.

"Good-bye, Mr Razumov. An understanding between intelligent men is always a satisfactory occurrence. Is it not? And, of course, these rebel gentlemen have not the monopoly of intelligence."

"I presume that I shall not be wanted any more?" Razumov brought out that question while his hand was still being grasped. Councillor Mikulin released it slowly.

"That, Mr. Razumov," he said with great earnestness, "is as it

---

1 Likely a reference to the view of Pericles (c. 495-429 BC): "We are unique in considering the man who takes no part in these [public affairs] to be not apolitical but useless" (2.40.2; trans. Steven Lattimore [Hackett 1998] 93), as it appears in *The History of the Peloponnesian War* by Thucydides (c. 460-c. 400 BC)—although this view may have been as much that of Thucydides as it was that of Pericles. This opinion was not universal among the ancient Greeks: in contrast, Plato (c. 428-c. 347 BC) suggests in *The Republic* that one ought to take shelter from politics when nothing good can be accomplished (6.496.d), and the Epicureans actively advocated withdrawing from public life.

may be. God alone knows the future. But you may rest assured that I never thought of having you watched. You are a young man of great independence. Yes. You are going away free as air, but you shall end by coming back to us."

"I! I!" Razumov exclaimed in an appalled murmur of protest. "What for?" he added feebly.

"Yes! You yourself, Kirylo Sidorovitch," the high police functionary insisted in a low, severe tone of conviction. "You shall be coming back to us. Some of our greatest minds[1] had to do that in the end."

"Our greatest minds," repeated Razumov in a dazed voice.

"Yes, indeed! Our greatest minds. . . . Good-bye."

Razumov, shown out of the room, walked away from the door. But before he got to the end of the passage he heard heavy footsteps, and a voice calling upon him to stop. He turned his head and was startled to see Councillor Mikulin pursuing him in person. The high functionary hurried up, very simple, slightly out of breath.

"One minute. As to what we were talking about just now, it shall be as God wills it. But I may have occasion to require you again. You look surprised, Kirylo Sidorovitch. Yes, again . . . to clear up any further point that may turn up."

"But I don't know anything," stammered out Razumov. "I couldn't possibly know anything."

"Who can tell? Things are ordered in a wonderful manner. Who can tell what *may* become disclosed to you before this day is out? You have been already the instrument of Providence. You smile, Kirylo Sidorovitch; you are an *esprit fort*."[2] (Razumov was

---

1 Mikulin probably has a number of figures in mind here. Nikolai Ivanovich Novikov (1743-1818) published satirical journals critical of Catherine the Great and was later imprisoned; upon his release from prison after four years, Novikov gave up his journalist career. Aleksandr Nikolaevich Radishchev (1749-1802) published a book, *A Journey from St. Petersburg to Moscow* (1790), criticizing Russian autocracy, for which he was exiled for ten years; on his return, the government hired him to write legal reforms. Nikolai Vasil'evich Gogol' (1809-52) fled Russia after the 1836 performance of his satirical comedy *The Government Inspector* only to return to Russia some years later espousing conservative political views. Dostoevskii became involved in a revolutionary circle for which he was exiled to Siberia for ten years in 1849; by the time he returned to St. Petersburg in 1859, he had left behind his revolutionary activities.

2 Strong spirit (French).

not conscious of having smiled.) "But I believe firmly in Providence. Such a confession on the lips of an old hardened official like me may sound to you funny. But you yourself yet some day shall recognize . . . Or else what happened to you cannot be accounted for at all. Yes, decidedly I shall have occasion to see you again, but not here. This wouldn't be quite—h'm . . . Some convenient place shall be made known to you. And even the written communications between us in *that* respect or in any other had better pass through the intermediacy of our—if I may express myself so—common friend, Prince K——. Now I beg you, Kirylo Sidorovitch—don't! I am certain he'll consent. You must give me the credit of being aware of what I am saying. You have no better friend than Prince K——, and as to myself it is a long time now since I've been honoured by his . . ."

He glanced down his beard.

"I won't detain you any longer. We live in difficult times, in times of monstrous chimeras[1] and evil dreams and criminal follies. We shall certainly meet once more. It may be some little time, though, before we do. Till then may Heaven send you fruitful reflections!"

Once in the street, Razumov started off rapidly, without caring for the direction. At first he thought of nothing; but in a little while the consciousness of his position presented itself to him as something so ugly, dangerous, and absurd, the difficulty of ever freeing himself from the toils of that complication so insoluble, that the idea of going back and, as he termed it to himself, *confessing* to Councillor Mikulin flashed through his mind.

Go back! What for? Confess! To what? "I have been speaking to him with the greatest openness," he said to himself with perfect truth. "What else could I tell him? That I have undertaken to carry a message to that brute Ziemianitch? Establish a false complicity and destroy what chance of safety I have won for nothing—what folly!"

Yet he could not defend himself from fancying that Councillor Mikulin was, perhaps, the only man in the world able to understand his conduct. To be understood appeared extremely fascinating.

On the way home he had to stop several times; all the strength[2] seemed to run out of his limbs; and in the movement of the busy

---

1  In Greek mythology, a fire-breathing monster with the head of a lion, body of a goat, and tail of a serpent; used here metaphorically.

2  The first English edition has "all his strength" (M).

streets, isolated as if in a desert, he remained suddenly motionless for a minute or so before he could proceed on his way. He reached his rooms at last.

Then came an illness, something in the nature of a low fever, which all at once removed him to a great distance from the perplexing actualities, from his very room, even. He never lost consciousness; he only seemed to himself to be existing languidly somewhere very far away from everything that had ever happened to him. He came out of this state slowly, with an effect, that is to say, of extreme slowness, though the actual number of days was not very great. And when he had got back into the middle of things they were all changed, subtly and provokingly in their nature: inanimate objects, human faces, the landlady, the rustic servant-girl, the staircase, the streets, the very air. He tackled these changed conditions in a spirit of severity. He walked to and fro to the University, ascended stairs, paced the passages, listened to lectures, took notes, crossed courtyards in angry aloofness, his teeth set hard till his jaws ached.

He was perfectly aware of madcap Kostia gazing like a young retriever from a distance, of the famished student with the red drooping nose keeping scrupulously away as desired; of twenty others, perhaps, he knew well enough to speak to. And they all had an air of curiosity and concern as if they expected something to happen. "This can't last much longer," thought Razumov more than once. On certain days he was afraid that anyone addressing him suddenly in a certain way would make him scream out insanely a lot of filthy abuse. Often, after returning home, he would drop into a chair in his cap and cloak and remain still for hours holding some book he had got from the library in his hand; or he would pick up the little penknife and sit there scraping his nails endlessly and feeling furious all the time— simply furious. "This is impossible," he would mutter suddenly to the empty room.

Fact to be noted: this room might conceivably have become physically repugnant to him, emotionally intolerable, morally uninhabitable. But no. Nothing of the sort (and he had himself dreaded it at first), nothing of the sort happened. On the contrary, he liked his lodgings better than any other shelter he, who had never known a home, had ever hired before. He liked his lodgings so well that often, on that very account, he found a certain difficulty in making up his mind to go out. It resembled a physical seduction such as, for instance, makes a man reluctant to leave the neighbourhood of a fire on a cold day.

For as, at that time, he seldom stirred except to go to the University (what else was there to do?) it followed that whenever he went abroad he felt himself at once closely involved in the moral consequences of his act. It was there that the dark prestige of the Haldin mystery fell on him, clung to him like a poisoned robe[1] it was impossible to fling off. He suffered from it exceedingly, as well as from the conversational, commonplace, unavoidable intercourse with the other kind of students. "They must be wondering at the change in me," he reflected anxiously. He had an uneasy recollection of having savagely told one or two innocent, nice enough fellows to go to the devil. Once a married professor he used to call upon formerly addressed him in passing: "How is it we never see you at our Wednesdays now, Kirylo Sidorovitch?" Razumov was conscious of meeting this advance with odious, muttering boorishness. The professor was obviously too astonished to be offended. All this was bad. And all this was Haldin, always Haldin—nothing but Haldin—everywhere Haldin: a moral spectre infinitely more effective than any visible apparition of the dead. It was only the room through which that man had blundered on his way from crime to death that his spectre did not seem to be able to haunt. Not, to be exact, that he was ever completely absent from it, but that there he had no sort of power. There it was Razumov who had the upper hand, in a composed sense of his own superiority. A vanquished phantom—nothing more. Often in the evening, his repaired watch faintly ticking on the table by the side of the lighted lamp, Razumov would look up from his writing and stare at the bed with an expectant, dispassionate attention. Nothing was to be seen there. He never really supposed that anything ever could be seen there. After a while he would shrug his shoulders slightly and bend again over his work. For he had gone to work and, at first, with some success. His unwillingness to leave that place where he was safe from Haldin grew so strong that at last he ceased to go out at all. From early morning till far into the night he wrote, he wrote for nearly a week; never looking at the time, and only throwing himself on the bed when he could keep his eyes open no longer. Then, one after-

---

1  In Greek mythology, afraid that her husband, Heracles, was falling in love with another woman, Deianeira gave him a robe to wear that had been soaked in the blood of the centaur Nessus, whom Heracles had killed. Deianeira thought that the garment would make Heracles love her forever, but instead it clung to Heracles's body and acted as a powerful poison, bringing about his eventual death.

noon, quite casually, he happened to glance at his watch. He laid down his pen slowly.

"At this very hour," was his thought, "the fellow stole unseen into this room while I was out. And there he sat quiet as a mouse—perhaps in this very chair."

Razumov got up and began to pace the floor steadily, glancing at the watch now and then. "This is the time when I returned and found him standing against the stove," he observed to himself. When it grew dark he lit his lamp. Later on he interrupted his tramping once more, only to wave away angrily the girl who attempted to enter the room with tea and something to eat on a tray. And presently he noted the watch pointing at the hour of his own going forth into the falling snow on that terrible errand.

"Complicity," he muttered faintly, and resumed his pacing, keeping his eye on the hands as they crept on slowly to the time of his return.

"And, after all," he thought suddenly, "I might have been the chosen instrument of Providence. This is a manner of speaking, but there may be truth in every manner of speaking. What if that absurd saying were true in its essence?"

He meditated for a while, then sat down, his legs stretched out, with stony eyes, and with his arms hanging down on each side of the chair like a man totally abandoned by Providence—desolate.

He noted the time of Haldin's departure and continued to sit still for another half-hour; then muttering, "And now to work," drew up to the table, seized the pen and instantly dropped it under the influence of a profoundly disquieting reflection: "There's three weeks gone by and no word from Mikulin."

What did it mean? Was he forgotten? Possibly. Then why not remain forgotten—creep in somewhere? Hide. But where? How? With whom? In what hole? And was it to be for ever, or what?

But a retreat was big with shadowy dangers. The eye of the social revolution was on him, and Razumov for a moment felt an unnamed and despairing dread, mingled with an odious sense of humiliation. Was it possible that he no longer belonged to himself? This was damnable. But why not simply keep on as before? Study. Advance. Work hard as if nothing had happened (and first of all win the silver medal), acquire distinction, become a great reforming servant of the greatest of States. Servant, too, of the mightiest homogeneous mass of mankind with a capability for logical, guided development in a brotherly solidarity of force and aim such as the world had never dreamt of . . . the Russian nation! . . .

Calm, resolved, steady in his great purpose, he was stretching his hand towards the pen when he happened to glance towards the bed. He rushed at it, enraged, with a mental scream: "It's you, crazy fanatic, who stands in the way!" He flung the pillow on the floor violently, tore the blankets aside. . . . Nothing there.

And, turning away, he caught for an instant in the air, like a vivid detail in a dissolving view of two heads, the eyes of General T—— and of Privy-Councillor Mikulin[1] side by side fixed upon him, quite different in character, but with the same unflinching and weary and yet purposeful expression. . . . servants of the nation!

Razumov tottered to the washstand very alarmed about himself, drank some water and bathed his forehead. "This will pass and leave no trace," he thought confidently. "I am all right." But as to supposing that he had been forgotten it was perfect nonsense. He was a marked man on that side. And that was nothing. It was what that miserable phantom stood for which had to be got out of the way. . . . "If one only could go and spit it all out at some of them—and take the consequences."

He imagined himself accosting the red-nosed student and suddenly shaking his fist in his face. "From that one, though," he reflected, "there's nothing to be got, because he has no mind of his own. He's living in a red democratic trance. Ah! you want to smash your way into universal happiness, my boy. I will give you universal happiness, you silly, hypnotized ghoul, you! And what about my own happiness, eh? Haven't I got any right to it, just because I can think for myself? . . ."

And again, but with a different mental accent, Razumov said to himself, "I am young. Everything can be lived down." At that moment he was crossing the room slowly, intending to sit down on the sofa and try to compose his thoughts. But before he had got so far everything abandoned him—hope, courage, belief in himself, trust in men. His heart had, as it were, suddenly emptied itself. It was no use struggling on. Rest, work, solitude, and the frankness of intercourse with his kind were alike forbidden to him. Everything was gone. His existence was a great cold blank, something like the enormous plain of the whole of Russia levelled with snow and fading gradually on all sides into shadows and mists.

He sat down, with swimming head, closed his eyes, and remained like that, sitting bolt upright on the sofa and perfectly

---

1 Earlier Mikulin had been referred to as having the rank of Councillor of State (261).

awake for the rest of the night; till the girl bustling into the outer room with the samovar thumped with her fist on the door, calling out, "Kirylo Sidorovitch, please! It is time for you to get up!"

Then, pale like a corpse obeying the dread summons of judgment, Razumov opened his eyes and got up.

*****

Nobody will be surprised to hear, I suppose, that when the summons came he went to see Councillor Mikulin. It came that very morning, while, looking white and shaky, like an invalid just out of bed, he was trying to shave himself. The envelope was addressed in the little attorney's handwriting. That envelope contained another, superscribed[1] to Razumov, in Prince K——'s hand, with the request "Please forward under cover at once" in a corner. The note inside was an autograph[2] of Councillor Mikulin. The writer stated candidly that nothing had arisen which needed clearing up, but nevertheless appointed a meeting with Mr. Razumov at a certain address in town which seemed to be that of an oculist.[3]

Razumov read it, finished shaving, dressed, looked at the note again, and muttered gloomily, "Oculist." He pondered over it for a time, lit a match, and burned the two envelopes and the enclosure carefully. Afterwards he waited, sitting perfectly idle and not even looking at anything in particular till the appointed hour drew near—and then went out.

Whether, looking at the unofficial character of the summons, he might have refrained from attending to it is hard to say. Probably not. At any rate, he went; but, what's more, he went with a certain eagerness, which may appear incredible till it is remembered that Councillor Mikulin was the only person on earth with whom Razumov could talk, taking the Haldin adventure for granted. And Haldin, when once taken for granted, was no longer a haunting, falsehood-breeding spectre. Whatever troubling power he exercised in all the other places of the earth, Razumov knew very well that at this oculist's address he would be merely the hanged murderer of M. de P—— and nothing more. For the dead can live only with the exact intensity and quality of the life imparted to them by the living. So Mr. Razumov, certain of relief,

---

1  Addressed to or directed to.
2  Letter in Mikulin's handwriting.
3  Eye doctor.

went to meet Councillor Mikulin with the eagerness of a pursued person welcoming any sort of shelter.

This much said, there is no need to tell anything more of that first interview and of the several others. To the morality of a Western reader an account of these meetings would wear perhaps the sinister character of old legendary tales where the Enemy of Mankind is represented holding subtly mendacious dialogues with some tempted soul. It is not my part to protest. Let me but remark that the Evil One, with his single passion of satanic pride for the only motive, is yet, on a larger, modern view, allowed to be not quite so black as he used to be painted. With what greater latitude, then, should we appraise the exact shade of mere mortal man, with his many passions and his miserable ingenuity in error, always dazzled by the base glitter of mixed motives, everlastingly betrayed by a short-sighted wisdom.

Councillor Mikulin was one of those powerful officials who, in a position not obscure, not occult, but simply inconspicuous, exercise a great influence over the methods rather than over the conduct of affairs. A devotion to Church and Throne is not in itself a criminal sentiment; to prefer the will of one to the will of many does not argue the possession of a black heart or prove congenital idiocy. Councillor Mikulin was not only a clever but also a faithful official. Privately he was a bachelor with a love of comfort, living alone in an apartment of five rooms luxuriously furnished; and was known by his intimates to be an enlightened patron of the art of female dancing. Later on the larger world first heard of him in the very hour of his downfall, during one of those State trials which astonish and puzzle the average plain man who reads the newspapers, by a glimpse of unsuspected intrigues. And in the stir of vaguely seen monstrosities, in that momentary, mysterious disturbance of muddy waters, Councillor Mikulin went under, dignified, with only a calm, emphatic protest of his innocence—nothing more.[1] No disclosures damaging to a harassed autocracy, complete fidelity to the secrets of the miserable *arcana imperii*[2] deposited in his patriotic breast, a display of bureaucratic stoicism in a Russian official's ineradicable, almost sublime con-

---

1   Mikulin's model Aleksei Aleksandrovich Lopukhin also was eventually discredited and exiled to Minusinsk, Eniseisk in Siberia in 1909. He was later pardoned and allowed to return to St. Petersburg in 1913.
2   "Secrets of the empire" or "secrets of power" (Latin), a common Latin phrase probably originating in *The Annals* (2:36) by Publius (Gaius) Cornelius Tacitus (AD c. 56-c. 120).

tempt for truth; stoicism of silence understood only by the very few of the initiated, and not without a certain cynical grandeur of self-sacrifice on the part of a sybarite. For the terribly heavy sentence turned Councillor Mikulin civilly into a corpse, and actually into something very much like a common convict.

It seems that the savage autocracy, no more than the divine democracy, does not limit its diet exclusively to the bodies of its enemies. It devours its friends and servants as well. The downfall of His Excellency Gregory Gregorievitch Mikulin[1] (which did not occur till some years later) completes all that is known of the man. But at the time of M. de P——'s murder (or execution) Councillor Mikulin, under the modest style of Head of Department at the General Secretariat, exercised a wide influence as the confidant and right-hand man of his former schoolfellow and lifelong friend, General T——. One can imagine them talking over the case of Mr. Razumov, with the full sense of their unbounded power over all the lives in Russia, with cursory disdain, like two Olympians[2] glancing at a worm. The relationship with Prince K—— was enough to save Razumov from some carelessly arbitrary proceeding, and it is also very probable that after the interview at the Secretariat he would have been left alone. Councillor Mikulin would have not[3] forgotten him (he forgot no one who ever fell under his observation), but would have simply dropped him for ever. Councillor Mikulin was a good-natured man and wished no harm to anyone. Besides (with his own reforming tendencies) he was favourably impressed by that young student, the son of Prince K——, and apparently no fool.

But as fate would have it, while Mr. Razumov was finding that no way of life was possible to him, Councillor Mikulin's discreet abilities were rewarded by a very responsible post—nothing less than the direction of the general police supervision over Europe. And it was then, and then only, when taking in hand the perfecting of the service which watches the revolutionist activities abroad, that he thought again of Mr. Razumov. He saw great possibilities of special usefulness in that uncommon young man on whom he had a hold already, with his peculiar temperament, his

---

1  When first introduced, Mikulin's name appears as Gregory Matvieitch Mikulin; see 109.
2  Greek gods.
3  The first English edition has "would not have forgotten him" (M, T, ES, A1).

unsettled mind and shaken conscience, and struggling[1] in the toils of a false position. . . . It was as if the revolutionists themselves had put into his hand that tool so much finer than the common base instruments, so perfectly fitted, if only vested with sufficient credit, to penetrate into places inaccessible to common informers. Providential! Providential! And Prince K——, taken into the secret, was ready enough to adopt that mystical view too. "It will be necessary, though, to make a career for him afterwards," he had stipulated anxiously. "Oh! absolutely. We shall make that our affair," Mikulin had agreed. Prince K——'s mysticism was of an artless kind; but Councillor Mikulin was astute enough for two.

Things and men have always a certain sense, a certain side by which they must be got hold of if one wants to obtain a solid grasp and a perfect command. The power of Councillor Mikulin consisted in the ability to seize upon that sense, that side in the men he used. It did not matter to him what it was—vanity, despair, love, hate, greed, intelligent pride or stupid conceit, it was all one to him as long as the man could be made to serve. The obscure, unrelated young student Razumov, in the moment of great moral loneliness, was allowed to feel that he was an object of interest to a small group of people of high position. Prince K—— was persuaded to intervene personally, and on a certain occasion gave way to a manly emotion which, all unexpected as it was, quite upset Mr. Razumov. The sudden embrace of that man, agitated by his loyalty to a throne and by suppressed paternal affection, was a revelation to Mr. Razumov of something within his own breast.

"So that was it!" he exclaimed to himself. A sort of contemptuous tenderness softened the young man's grim view of his position as he reflected upon that agitated interview with Prince K——. This simple-minded, worldly ex-Guardsman and senator whose soft grey official whiskers had brushed against his cheek, his aristocratic and convinced father, was he a whit less estimable or more absurd than that famine-stricken, fanatical revolutionist, the red-nosed student?

And there was some pressure, too, besides the persuasiveness. Mr. Razumov was always being made to feel that he had committed himself. There was no getting away from that feeling, from that soft, unanswerable, "Where to?" of Councillor Mikulin. But no susceptibilities were ever hurt. It was to be a

---

1  The first English edition has "a struggling" (M, T, ES, AS, A1).

dangerous mission to Geneva for obtaining, at a critical moment, absolutely reliable information from a very inaccessible quarter of the inner revolutionary circle. There were indications that a very serious plot was being matured. . . . The repose indispensable to a great country was at stake. . . . A great scheme of orderly reforms would be endangered. . . . The highest personages in the land were patriotically uneasy, and so on. In short, Councillor Mikulin knew what to say. This skill is to be inferred clearly from the mental and psychological self-confession, self-analysis of Mr. Razumov's written journal—the pitiful resource of a young man who had near him no trusted intimacy, no natural affection to turn to.

How all this preliminary work was concealed from observation need not be recorded. The expedient of the oculist gives a sufficient instance. Councillor Mikulin was resourceful, and the task not very difficult. Any fellow-student, even the red-nosed one, was perfectly welcome to see Mr. Razumov entering a private house to consult an oculist. Ultimate success depended solely on the revolutionary self-delusion which credited Razumov with a mysterious complicity in the Haldin affair. To be compromised in it was credit enough—and it was their own doing. It was precisely *that* which stamped Mr. Razumov as a providential man, wide as poles apart from the usual type of agent for "European supervision."

And it was *that* which the Secretariat set itself the task to foster by a course of calculated and false indiscretions.

It came at last to this, that one evening Mr. Razumov was unexpectedly called upon by one of the "thinking" students whom formerly, before the Haldin affair, he used to meet at various private gatherings; a big fellow with a quiet, unassuming manner and a pleasant voice.

Recognizing his voice raised in the ante-room, "May one come in?" Razumov, lounging idly on his couch, jumped up. "Suppose he were coming to stab me?" he thought sardonically, and, assuming a green shade over his left eye, said in a severe tone, "Come in."

The other was embarrassed; hoped he was not intruding.

"You haven't been seen for several days, and I've wondered." He coughed a little. "Eye better?"

"Nearly well now."

"Good. I won't stop a minute; but you see I, that is, we—anyway, I have undertaken the duty to warn you, Kirylo Sidorovitch, that you are living in false security maybe."

Razumov sat still with his head leaning on his hand, which nearly concealed the unshaded eye.

"I have that idea, too."

"That's all right, then. Everything seems quiet now, but those people are preparing some move of general repression. That's of course. But it isn't that I came to tell you." He hitched his chair closer, dropped his voice. "You will be arrested before long—we fear."

An obscure scribe in the Secretariat had overheard a few words of a certain conversation, and had caught a glimpse of a certain report. This intelligence was not to be neglected.

Razumov laughed a little, and his visitor became very anxious.

"Ah! Kirylo Sidorovitch, this is no laughing matter. They have left you alone for a while, but . . . ! Indeed, you had better try to leave the country, Kirylo Sidorovitch, while there's yet time."

Razumov jumped up and began to thank him for the advice with mocking effusiveness, so that the other, colouring up, took himself off with the notion that this mysterious Razumov was not a person to be warned or advised by inferior mortals.

Councillor Mikulin, informed the next day of the incident, expressed his satisfaction. "H'm. Ha! Exactly what was wanted to . . ." and glanced down his beard.

"I conclude," said Razumov, "that the moment has come for me to start on my mission."

"The psychological moment," Councillor Mikulin insisted softly—very gravely—as if awed.

All the arrangements to give verisimilitude to the appearance of a difficult escape were made. Councillor Mikulin did not expect to see Mr. Razumov again before his departure. These meetings were a risk, and there was nothing more to settle.

"We have said everything to each other by now, Kirylo Sidorovitch," said the high official feelingly, pressing Razumov's hand with that unreserved heartiness a Russian can convey in his manner. "There is nothing obscure between us. And I will tell you what! I consider myself fortunate in having—h'm—your . . ."

He glanced down his beard, and, after a moment of thoughtful silence, handed to Razumov a half-sheet of notepaper—an abbreviated note of matters already discussed, certain points of inquiry, the line of conduct agreed on, a few hints as to personalities, and so on. It was the only compromising document in the case, but, as Councillor Mikulin observed, it could be easily destroyed. Mr. Razumov had better not see any one now—till on

the other side of the frontier, when, of course, it will be just that
. . . See and hear and . . .

He glanced down his beard; but when Razumov declared his intention to see one person at least before leaving St. Petersburg, Councillor Mikulin failed to conceal a sudden uneasiness. The young man's studious, solitary, and austere existence was well known to him. It was the greatest guarantee of fitness. He became deprecatory. Had his dear Kirylo Sidorovitch considered whether, in view of such a momentous enterprise, it wasn't really advisable to sacrifice every sentiment . . .

Razumov interrupted the remonstrance scornfully. It was not a young woman, it was a young fool he wished to see for a certain purpose. Councillor Mikulin was relieved, but surprised.

"Ah! And what for—precisely?"

"For the sake of improving the aspect of verisimilitude," said Razumov curtly, in a desire to affirm his independence. "I must be trusted in what I do."

Councillor Mikulin gave way tactfully, murmuring, "Oh, certainly, certainly. Your judgment . . ."

And with another handshake they parted.

The fool of whom Mr. Razumov had thought was the rich and festive student known as madcap Kostia. Feather-headed, loquacious, excitable, one could make certain of his utter and complete indiscretion. But that riotous youth, when reminded by Razumov of his offers of service some time ago, passed from his usual elation into boundless dismay.

"Oh, Kirylo Sidorovitch, my dearest friend—my saviour— what shall I do? I've blown last night every rouble I had from my dad the other day. Can't you give me till Thursday? I shall rush round to all the usurers I know . . . No, of course, you can't! Don't look at me like that. What shall I do? No use asking the old man. I tell you he's given me a fistful of big notes three days ago. Miserable wretch that I am."

He wrung his hands in despair. Impossible to confide in the old man. "They" had given him a decoration, a cross on the neck only last year, and he had been cursing the modern tendencies ever since. Just then he would see all the intellectuals in Russia hanged in a row rather than part with a single rouble.

"Kirylo Sidorovitch, wait a moment. Don't despise me. I have it. I'll, yes—I'll do it—I'll break into his desk. There's no help for it. I know the drawer where he keeps his plunder, and I can buy a chisel on my way home. He will be terribly upset, but, you know, the dear old duffer really loves me. He'll have to get over it—and I, too. Kirylo, my dear soul, if you can only wait for a few hours—till this evening—I shall steal all the blessed lot I can lay my hands on! You doubt me! Why? You've only to say the word."

"Steal, by all means," said Razumov, fixing him stonily.

"To the devil with the ten commandments!" cried the other, with the greatest animation. "It's the new future now."

But when he entered Razumov's room late in the evening it was with an unaccustomed soberness of manner, almost solemnly.

"It's done," he said.

Razumov sitting bowed, his clasped hands hanging between his knees, shuddered at the familiar sound of these words. Kostia deposited slowly in the circle of lamplight a small brown-paper parcel tied with a piece of string.

"As I've said—all I could lay my hands on. The old boy'll think the end of the world has come."

Razumov nodded from the couch, and contemplated the hare-brained fellow's gravity with a feeling of malicious pleasure.

"I've made my little sacrifice," sighed mad Kostia. "And I've to thank you, Kirylo Sidorovitch, for the opportunity."

"It has cost you something?"

"Yes, it has. You see, the dear old duffer really loves me. He'll be hurt."

"And you believe all they tell you of the new future and the sacred will of the people?"[1]

"Implicitly. I would give my life . . . Only, you see, I am like a pig at a trough. I am no good. It's my nature."

Razumov, lost in thought, had forgotten his existence till the youth's voice, entreating him to fly without loss of time, roused him unpleasantly.

"All right. Well—good-bye."

"I am not going to leave you till I've seen you out of St. Petersburg," declared Kostia unexpectedly, with calm determination. "You can't refuse me that now. For God's sake, Kirylo, my soul, the police may be here any moment, and when they get you they'll immure you somewhere for ages—till your hair turns grey. I have down there the best trotter of dad's stables and a light sledge.[2] We shall do thirty miles before the moon sets, and find some roadside station . . . "

---

1 Perhaps another reference to the revolutionary People's Will party in Russia; see Appendix C6.

2 A carriage on runners for traveling over ice and snow.

Razumov looked up amazed. The journey was decided—unavoidable. He had fixed the next day for his departure on the mission. And now he discovered suddenly that he had not believed in it. He had gone about listening, speaking, thinking, planning his simulated flight, with the growing conviction that all this was preposterous. As if anybody ever did such things! It was like a game of make-believe. And now he was amazed! Here was somebody who believed in it with desperate earnestness. "If I don't go now, at once," thought Razumov, with a start of fear, "I shall never go." He rose without a word, and the anxious Kostia thrust his cap on him, helped him into his cloak, or else he would have left the room bareheaded as he stood. He was walking out silently when a sharp cry arrested him.

"Kirylo!"

"What?" He turned reluctantly in the doorway. Upright, with a stiffly extended arm, Kostia, his face set and white, was pointing an eloquent forefinger at the brown little packet lying forgotten in the circle of bright light on the table. Razumov hesitated, came back for it under the severe eyes of his companion, at whom he tried to smile. But the boyish, mad youth was frowning. "It's a dream," thought Razumov, putting the little parcel into his pocket and descending the stairs; "nobody does such things." The other held him under the arm, whispering of dangers ahead, and of what he meant to do in certain contingencies. "Preposterous," murmured Razumov, as he was being tucked up in the sledge. He gave himself up to watching the development of the dream with extreme attention. It continued on foreseen lines, inexorably logical—the long drive, the wait at the small station sitting by a stove. They did not exchange half a dozen words altogether. Kostia, gloomy himself, did not care to break the silence. At parting they embraced twice—it had to be done; and then Kostia vanished out of the dream.

When dawn broke, Razumov, very still in a hot, stuffy railway-car full of bedding and of sleeping people in all its dimly lighted length, rose quietly, lowered the glass a few inches, and flung out on the great plain of snow a small brown-paper parcel. Then he sat down again muffled up and motionless. "For the people," he thought, staring out of the window. The great white desert of frozen, hard earth glided past his eyes without a sign of human habitation.

That had been a waking act; and then the dream had him

again: Prussia, Saxony, Würtemberg,[1] faces, sights, words—all a dream, observed with an angry, compelled attention. Zürich, Geneva—still a dream, minutely followed, wearing one into harsh laughter, to fury, to death—with the fear of awakening at the end. . . .

## II

"Perhaps life is just that," reflected Razumov, pacing to and fro under the trees of the little island, all alone with the bronze statue of Rousseau. "A dream and a fear." The dusk deepened. The pages written over and torn out of his notebook were the first-fruit of his "mission." No dream that. They contained the assurance that he was on the eve of real discoveries. "I think there is no longer anything in the way of my being completely accepted."

He had resumed his impressions in those pages, some of the conversations. He even went so far as to write: "By the by, I have discovered the personality of that terrible N.N. A horrible, paunchy brute. If I hear anything of his future movements I shall send a warning."

The futility of all this overcame him like a curse. Even then he could not believe in the reality of his mission. He looked round despairingly, as if for some way to redeem his existence from that unconquerable feeling. He crushed angrily in his hand the pages of the notebook. "This must be posted," he thought.

He gained the bridge and returned to the north shore, where he remembered having seen in one of the narrower streets a little obscure shop stocked with cheap wood carvings, its walls lined with extremely dirty cardboard-bound volumes of a small circulating library. They sold stationery there, too. A morose, shabby old man dozed behind the counter. A thin woman in black, with a sickly face, produced the envelope he had asked for without even looking at him. Razumov thought that these people were safe to deal with because they no longer cared for anything in the

---

1 Prussia was a kingdom in northern Europe and a state of the German empire; at its height, it extended from the Netherlands, Belgium, and Luxembourg on the west to Lithuania and the Russian empire on the east. Saxony is a large region in central Germany, bordering the Czech Republic on the south and Poland on the east. Württemberg comprised the eastern and central parts of present-day Baden-Württemberg in southwestern Germany.

world. He addressed the envelope on the counter with the German name of a certain person living in Vienna. But Razumov knew that this, his first communication for Councillor Mikulin, would find its way to the Embassy there, be copied in cypher by somebody trustworthy, and sent on to its destination, all safe, along with the diplomatic correspondence. That was the arrangement contrived to cover up the track of the information from all unfaithful eyes, from all indiscretions, from all mishaps and treacheries. It was to make him safe—absolutely safe.

He wandered out of the wretched shop and made for the post office. It was then that I saw him for the second time that day. He was crossing the Rue Mont Blanc with every appearance of an aimless stroller. He did not recognize me, but I made him out at some distance. He was very good-looking, I thought, this remarkable friend of Miss Haldin's brother. I watched him go up to the letter-box and then retrace his steps. Again he passed me very close, but I am certain he did not see me that time, either. He carried his head well up, but he had the expression of a somnambulist[1] struggling with the very dream which drives him forth to wander in dangerous places. My thoughts reverted to Natalia Haldin, to her mother. He was all that was left to them of their son and brother.

The Westerner in me was discomposed. There was something shocking in the expression of that face. Had I been myself a conspirator, a Russian political refugee, I could have perhaps been able to draw some practical conclusion from this chance glimpse. As it was, it only discomposed me strongly, even to the extent of awakening an indefinite apprehension in regard to Natalia Haldin. All this is rather inexplicable, but such was the origin of the purpose I formed there and then to call on these ladies in the evening, after my solitary dinner. It was true that I had met Miss Haldin only a few hours before, but Mrs. Haldin herself I had not seen for some considerable time. The truth is, I had shirked calling of late.

Poor Mrs. Haldin! I confess she frightened me a little. She was one of those natures, rare enough, luckily, in which one cannot help being interested, because they provoke both terror and pity.[2] One dreads their contact for oneself, and still more for those one

---

1 Sleepwalker.
2 A reference to Aristotle's *Poetics* and the idea that terror and pity, as they are evoked by literature or drama, can produce a cathartic effect in the reader or spectator.

cares for, so clear it is that they are born to suffer and to make others suffer, too. It is strange to think that, I won't say liberty, but the mere liberalism of outlook which for us is a matter of words, of ambitions, of votes (and if of feeling at all, then of the sort of feeling which leaves our deepest affections untouched), may be for other beings very much like ourselves and living under the same sky, a heavy trial of fortitude, a matter of tears and anguish and blood. Mrs. Haldin had felt the pangs of her own generation. There was that enthusiast brother of hers—the officer they shot under Nicholas. A faintly ironic resignation is no armour for a vulnerable heart. Mrs. Haldin, struck at through her children, was bound to suffer afresh from the past, and to feel the anguish of the future. She was of those who do not know how to heal themselves, of those who are too much aware of their heart, who, neither cowardly nor selfish, look passionately at its wounds—and count the cost.

Such thoughts as these seasoned my modest, lonely bachelor's meal. If anybody wishes to remark that this was a roundabout way of thinking of Natalia Haldin, I can only retort that she was well worth some concern. She had all her life before her. Let it be admitted, then, that I was thinking of Natalia Haldin's life in terms of her mother's character, a manner of thinking about a girl permissible for an old man, not too old yet to have become a stranger to pity. There was almost all her youth before her; a youth robbed arbitrarily of its natural lightness and joy, over-shadowed by an un-European despotism; a terribly sombre youth given over to the hazards of a furious strife between equally ferocious antagonisms.

I lingered over my thoughts more than I should have done. One felt so helpless, and even worse—so unrelated, in a way. At the last moment I hesitated as to going there at all. What was the good?

The evening was already advanced when, turning into the Boulevard des Philosophes, I saw the light in the window at the corner. The blind was down, but I could imagine behind it Mrs. Haldin seated in the chair, in her usual attitude, looking out for some one, which had lately acquired the poignant quality of mad expectation.

I thought that I was sufficiently authorized by the light to knock at the door. The ladies had not retired as yet. I only hoped they would not have any visitors of their own nationality. A broken-down, retired Russian official was to be found there sometimes in the evening. He was infinitely forlorn and wearisome by his mere dismal presence. I think these ladies tolerated his frequent visits because of an ancient friendship with Mr. Haldin, the father, or something of that sort. I made up my mind that if I found him prosing away there in his feeble voice I should remain but a very few minutes.

The door surprised me by swinging open before I could ring the bell. I was confronted by Miss Haldin, in hat and jacket, obviously on the point of going out. At that hour! For the doctor, perhaps?

Her exclamation of welcome reassured me. It sounded as if I had been the very man she wanted to see. My curiosity was awakened. She drew me in, and the faithful Anna, the elderly German maid, closed the door, but did not go away afterwards. She remained near it as if in readiness to let me out presently. It appeared that Miss Haldin had been on the point of going out to find me.

She spoke in a hurried manner very unusual with her. She would have gone straight and rung at Mrs. Ziegler's door, late as it was, for Mrs. Ziegler's habits . . .

Mrs. Ziegler, the widow of a distinguished professor who was an intimate friend of mine, lets me have three rooms out of her very large and fine apartment, which she didn't give up after her husband's death; but I have my own entrance opening on the same landing. It was an arrangement of at least ten years' standing. I said that I was very glad that I had the idea to . . .

Miss Haldin made no motion to take off her outdoor things. I observed her heightened colour, something pronouncedly resolute in her tone. Did I know where Mr. Razumov lived?

Where Mr. Razumov lived? Mr. Razumov? At this hour—so urgently? I threw my arms up in sign of utter ignorance. I had not the slightest idea where he lived. If I could have foreseen her question only three hours ago, I might have ventured to ask him on the pavement before the new post office building, and possibly he would have told me, but very possibly, too, he would have dismissed me rudely to mind my own business. And possibly, I thought, remembering that extraordinary hallucined, anguished, and absent expression, he might have fallen down in a fit from the shock of being spoken to. I said nothing of all this to Miss Haldin, not even mentioning that I had a glimpse of the young man so recently. The impression had been so extremely unpleasant that I would have been glad to forget it myself.

"I don't see where I could make inquiries," I murmured helplessly. I would have been glad to be of use in any way, and would have set off to fetch any man, young or old, for I had the greatest confidence in her common sense. "What made you think of coming to me for that information?" I asked.

"It wasn't exactly for that," she said, in a low voice. She had the air of some one confronted by an unpleasant task.

"Am I to understand that you must communicate with Mr. Razumov this evening?"

Natalia Haldin moved her head affirmatively; then, after a glance at the door of the drawing-room, said in French—

"*C'est maman,*"[1] and remained perplexed for a moment. Always serious, not a girl to be put out by any imaginary difficulties, my curiosity was suspended on her lips, which remained closed for a moment. What was Mr. Razumov's connexion with this mention of her mother? Mrs. Haldin had not been informed of her son's friend's arrival in Geneva.

"May I hope to see your mother this evening?" I inquired.

Miss Haldin extended her hand as if to bar the way.

"She is in a terrible state of agitation. Oh, you would not be able to detect. . . . It's inward, but I who know mother, I am appalled. I haven't the courage to face it any longer. It's all my fault; I suppose I cannot play a part; I've never before hidden anything from mother. There has never been an occasion for anything of that sort between us. But you know yourself the reason why I refrained from telling her at once of Mr. Razumov's arrival here. You understand, don't you? Owing to her unhappy state. And—there—I am no actress. My own feelings being strongly engaged, I somehow . . . I don't know. She noticed something in my manner. She thought I was concealing something from her. She noticed my longer absences, and, in fact, as I have been meeting Mr. Razumov daily, I used to stay away longer than usual when I went out. Goodness knows what suspicions arose in her mind. You know that she has not been herself ever since. . . . So this evening she—who has been so awfully silent for weeks—began to talk all at once. She said that she did not want to reproach me; that I had my character as she had her own; that she did not want to pry into my affairs or even into my thoughts; for her part, she had never had anything to conceal from her children . . . cruel things to listen to. And all this in her quiet voice, with that poor, wasted face as calm as a stone. It was unbearable."

Miss Haldin talked in an undertone and more rapidly than I had ever heard her speak before. That in itself was disturbing. The

---

1 It's mama (French).

ante-room being strongly lighted, I could see under the veil the heightened colour of her face. She stood erect, her left hand was resting lightly on a small table. The other hung by her side without stirring. Now and then she caught her breath slightly.

"It was too startling. Just fancy! She thought that I was making preparations to leave her without saying anything. I knelt by the side of her chair and entreated her to think of what she was saying! She put her hand on my head, but she persists in her delusion all the same. She had always thought that she was worthy of her children's confidence, but apparently it was not so. Her son could not trust her love nor yet her understanding—and now I was planning to abandon her in the same cruel and unjust manner, and so on, and so on. Nothing I could say. . . . It is morbid obstinacy. . . . She said that she felt there was something, some change in me. . . . If my convictions were calling me away, why this secrecy, as though she had been a coward or a weakling not safe to trust? 'As if my heart could play traitor to my children,' she said. . . . It was hardly to be borne. And she was smoothing my head all the time. . . . It was perfectly useless to protest. She is ill. Her very soul is . . ."

I did not venture to break the silence which fell between us. I looked into her eyes, glistening through the veil.

"I! Changed!" she exclaimed in the same low tone. "My convictions calling me away! It was cruel to hear this, because my trouble is that I am weak and cannot see what I ought to do. You know that. And to end it all I did a selfish thing. To remove her suspicions of myself I told her of Mr. Razumov. It was selfish of me. You know we were completely right in agreeing to keep the knowledge away from her. Perfectly right. Directly I told her of our poor Victor's friend being here I saw how right we have been. She ought to have been prepared; but in my distress I just blurted it out. Mother got terribly excited at once. How long has he been here? What did he know, and why did he not come to see us at once, this friend of her Victor? What did that mean? Was she not to be trusted even with such memories as there were left of her son? . . . Just think how I felt seeing her, white like a sheet, perfectly motionless, with her thin hands gripping the arms of the chair. I told her it was all my fault."

I could imagine the motionless dumb figure of the mother in her chair, there, behind the door, near which the daughter was talking to me. The silence in there seemed to call aloud for vengeance against an historical fact and the modern instances of its working. That view flashed through my mind, but I could not doubt that Miss Haldin had had an atrocious time of it. I quite understood when she said that she could not face the night upon the impression of that scene. Mrs. Haldin had given way to most awful imaginings, to most fantastic and cruel suspicions. All this had to be lulled at all costs and without loss of time. It was no shock to me to learn that Miss Haldin had said to her, "I will go and bring him here at once." There was nothing absurd in that cry, no exaggeration of sentiment. I was not even doubtful in my "Very well, but how?"

It was perfectly right that she should think of me, but what could I do in my ignorance of Mr. Razumov's quarters?

"And to think he may be living near by, within a stone's-throw, perhaps!" she exclaimed.

I doubted it; but I would have gone off cheerfully to fetch him from the other end of Geneva. I suppose she was certain of my readiness, since her first thought was to come to me. But the service she meant to ask of me really was to accompany her to the Château Borel.

I had an unpleasant mental vision of the dark road, of the sombre grounds, and the desolately suspicious aspect of that home of necromancy[1] and intrigue and feminist adoration. I objected that Madame de S—— most likely would know nothing of what we wanted to find out. Neither did I think it likely that the young man would be found there. I remembered my glimpse of his face, and somehow gained the conviction that a man who looked worse than if he had seen the dead would want to shut himself up somewhere where he could be alone. I felt a strange certitude that Mr. Razumov was going home when I saw him.

"It is really of Peter Ivanovitch that I was thinking," said Miss Haldin quietly.

Ah! He, of course, would know. I looked at my watch. It was twenty minutes past nine only. . . . Still.

"I would try his hotel, then," I advised. "He has rooms at the Cosmopolitan, somewhere on the top floor."

I did not offer to go by myself, simply from mistrust of the reception I should meet with. But I suggested the faithful Anna, with a note asking for the information.

Anna was still waiting by the door at the other end of the room, and we two discussed the matter in whispers. Miss Haldin thought she must go herself. Anna was timid and slow. Time would be lost in bringing back the answer, and from that point of

---

1 Witchcraft or sorcery.

view it was getting late, for it was by no means certain that Mr. Razumov lived near by.

"If I go myself," Miss Haldin argued, "I can go straight to him from the hotel. And in any case I should have to go out, because I must explain to Mr. Razumov personally—prepare him in a way. You have no idea of mother's state of mind."

Her colour came and went. She even thought that both for her mother's sake and for her own it was better that they should not be together for a little time. Anna, whom her mother liked, would be at hand.

"She could take her sewing into the room," Miss Haldin continued, leading the way to the door. Then, addressing in German the maid who opened it before us, "You may tell my mother that this gentleman called and is gone with me to find Mr. Razumov. She must not be uneasy if I am away for some length of time."

We passed out quickly into the street, and she took deep breaths of the cool night air. "I did not even ask you," she murmured.

"I should think not," I said, with a laugh. The manner of my reception by the great feminist could not be considered now. That he would be annoyed to see me, and probably treat me to some solemn insolence, I had no doubt, but I supposed that he would not absolutely dare to throw me out. And that was all I cared for. "Won't you take my arm?" I asked.

She did so in silence, and neither of us said anything worth recording till I let her go first into the great hall of the hotel. It was brilliantly lighted, and with a good many people lounging about.

"I could very well go up there without you," I suggested.

"I don't like to be left waiting in this place," she said in a low voice. "I will come too."

I led her straight to the lift then. At the top floor the attendant directed us to the right: "End of the corridor."

The walls were white, the carpet red, electric lights blazed in profusion, and the emptiness, the silence, the closed doors all alike and numbered, made me think of the perfect order of some severely luxurious model penitentiary on the solitary confinement principle. Up there under the roof of that enormous pile for housing travellers no sound of any kind reached us, the thick crimson felt muffled our footsteps completely. We hastened on, not looking at each other till we found ourselves before the very last door of that long passage. Then our eyes met, and we stood thus for a moment lending ear to a faint murmur of voices inside.

"I suppose this is it," I whispered unnecessarily. I saw Miss Haldin's lips move without a sound, and after my sharp knock the murmur of voices inside ceased. A profound stillness lasted for a few seconds, and then the door was brusquely opened by a short, black-eyed woman in a red blouse, with a great lot of nearly white hair, done up negligently in an untidy and unpicturesque manner. Her thin, jetty eyebrows were drawn together. I learned afterwards with interest that she was the famous—or the notorious—Sophia Antonovna, but I was struck then by the quaint Mephistophelian character of her inquiring glance, because it was so curiously evil-less, so—I may say—un-devilish. It got softened still more as she looked up at Miss Haldin, who stated, in her rich, even voice, her wish to see Peter Ivanovitch for a moment.

"I am Miss Haldin," she added.

At this, with her brow completely smoothed out now, but without a word in answer, the woman in the red blouse walked away to a sofa and sat down, leaving the door wide open.

And from the sofa, her hands lying on her lap, she watched us enter, with her black, glittering eyes.

Miss Haldin advanced into the middle of the room; I, faithful to my part of mere attendant, remained by the door after closing it behind me. The room, quite a large one, but with a low ceiling, was scantily furnished, and an electric bulb with a porcelain shade pulled low down over a big table (with a very large map spread on it) left its distant parts in a dim, artificial twilight. Peter Ivanovitch was not to be seen, neither was Mr. Razumov present. But, on the sofa, near Sophia Antonovna, a bony-faced man with a goatee beard leaned forward with his hands on his knees, staring hard with a kindly expression. In a remote corner a broad, pale face and a bulky shape could be made out, uncouth, and as if insecure on the low seat on which it rested. The only person known to me was little Julius Laspara, who seemed to have been poring over the map, his feet twined tightly round the chair-legs. He got down briskly and bowed to Miss Haldin, looking absurdly like a hook-nosed boy with a beautiful false pepper-and-salt beard. He advanced, offering his seat, which Miss Haldin declined. She had only come in for a moment to say a few words to Peter Ivanovitch.

His high-pitched voice became painfully audible in the room.

"Strangely enough, I was thinking of you this very afternoon, Natalia Victorovna. I met Mr. Razumov. I asked him to write me an article on anything he liked. You could translate it into English—with such a teacher."

He nodded complimentarily in my direction. At the name of Razumov an indescribable sound, a sort of feeble squeak, as of some angry small animal, was heard in the corner occupied by the man who seemed much too large for the chair on which he sat. I did not hear what Miss Haldin said. Laspara spoke again.

"It's time to do something, Natalia Victorovna. But I suppose you have your own ideas. Why not write something yourself? Suppose you came to see us soon? We could talk it over. Any advice . . ."

Again I did not catch Miss Haldin's words. It was Laspara's voice once more.

"Peter Ivanovitch? He's retired for a moment into the other room. We are all waiting for him."

The great man, entering at that moment, looked bigger, taller, quite imposing in a long dressing-gown of some dark stuff. It descended in straight lines down to his feet. He suggested a monk or a prophet, a robust figure of some desert-dweller—something Asiatic; and the dark glasses in conjunction with this costume made him more mysterious than ever in the subdued light.

Little Laspara went back to his chair to look at the map, the only brilliantly lit object in the room. Even from my distant position by the door I could make out, by the shape of the blue part representing the water, that it was a map of the Baltic provinces.[1] Peter Ivanovitch exclaimed slightly, advancing towards Miss Haldin, checked himself on perceiving me, very vaguely no doubt, and peered with his dark, bespectacled stare. He must have recognized me by my grey hair, because, with a marked shrug of his broad shoulders, he turned to Miss Haldin in benevolent indulgence. He seized her hand in his thick cushioned palm, and put his other big paw over it like a lid.

While those two standing in the middle of the floor were exchanging a few inaudible phrases no one else moved in the room: Laspara, with his back to us, kneeling on the chair, his elbows propped on the big-scale map, the shadowy enormity in the corner, the frankly staring man with the goatee on the sofa, the woman in the red blouse by his side—not one of them stirred. I suppose that really they had no time, for Miss Haldin withdrew her hand immediately from Peter Ivanovitch and before I was ready for her was moving to the door. A disregarded Westerner, I threw it open hurriedly and followed her out, my last glance

---

1  Areas on the Baltic Sea, particularly Lithuania, Estonia, Latvia, and Russian Kaliningrad.

leaving them all motionless in their varied poses: Peter Ivanovitch alone standing up, with his dark glasses like an enormous blind teacher, and behind him the vivid patch of light on the coloured map, pored over by the diminutive Laspara.

Later on, much later on, at the time of the newspaper rumours (they were vague and soon died out) of an abortive military conspiracy in Russia, I remembered the glimpse I had of that motionless group with its central figure. No details ever came out, but it was known that the revolutionary parties abroad had given their assistance, had sent emissaries in advance, that even money was found to dispatch a steamer with a cargo of arms and conspirators to invade the Baltic provinces.[1] And while my eyes scanned the imperfect disclosures (in which the world was not much interested) I thought that the old, settled Europe had been given in my person attending that Russian girl something like a glimpse behind the scenes. A short, strange glimpse on the top floor of a great hotel of all places in the world: the great man himself; the motionless great bulk in the corner of the slayer of spies and gendarmes; Yakovlitch, the veteran of ancient terrorist campaigns; the woman, with her hair as white as mine and the lively black eyes, all in a mysterious half-light, with the strongly lighted map of Russia on the table. The woman I had the opportunity to see again. As we were waiting for the lift she came hurrying along the corridor, with her eyes fastened on Miss Haldin's face, and drew her aside as if for a confidential communication. It was not long. A few words only.

Going down in the lift, Natalia Haldin did not break the silence. It was only when out of the hotel and as we moved along the quay in the fresh darkness spangled by the quay lights, reflected in the black water of the little port on our left hand, and with lofty piles of hotels on our right, that she spoke.

"That was Sophia Antonovna—you know the woman? . . ."

"Yes, I know—the famous . . ."

"The same. It appears that after we went out Peter Ivanovitch told them why I had come. That was the reason she ran out after us. She named herself to me, and then she said, 'You are the sister of a brave man who shall be remembered. You may see better times.' I told her I hoped to see the time when all this would be

---

1  Conrad probably refers here to the attempt in 1905 to smuggle arms into Russia aboard the steamer *John Grafton*, a plot in which Father Gapon was involved. The steamer ran aground, however, off the coast of Finland in the Gulf of Bothnia and was discovered by the authorities.

forgotten, even if the name of my brother were to be forgotten too. Something moved me to say that, but you understand?"

"Yes," I said. "You think of the era of concord and justice."

"Yes. There is too much hate and revenge in that work. It must be done. It is a sacrifice—and so let it be all the greater. Destruction is the work of anger. Let the tyrants and the slayers be forgotten together, and only the reconstructors be remembered."

"And did Sophia Antonovna agree with you?" I asked sceptically.

"She did not say anything except, 'It is good for you to believe in love.' I should think she understood me. Then she asked me if I hoped to see Mr. Razumov presently. I said I trusted I could manage to bring him to see my mother this evening, as my mother had learned of his being here and was morbidly impatient to learn if he could tell us something of Victor. He was the only friend of my brother we knew of, and a great intimate. She said, 'Oh! Your brother—yes. Please tell Mr. Razumov that I have made public the story which came to me from St. Petersburg. It concerns your brother's arrest,' she added. 'He was betrayed by a man of the people who has since hanged himself. Mr. Razumov will explain it all to you. I gave him the full information this afternoon. And please tell Mr. Razumov that Sophia Antonovna sends him her greetings. I am going away early in the morning—far away.'"

And Miss Haldin added, after a moment of silence—

"I was so moved by what I heard so unexpectedly that I simply could not speak to you before. . . . A man of the people! Oh, our poor people!"

She walked slowly, as if tired out suddenly. Her head drooped; from the windows of a building with terraces and balconies came the banal sound of hotel music; before the low mean portals of the Casino two red posters blazed under the electric lamps, with a cheap provincial effect.—and the emptiness of the quays, the desert aspect of the streets, had an air of hypocritical respectability and of inexpressible dreariness.

I had taken for granted she had obtained the address, and let myself be guided by her. On the Mont Blanc bridge, where a few dark figures seemed lost in the wide and long perspective defined by the lights, she said—

"It isn't very far from our house. I somehow thought it couldn't be. The address is Rue de Carouge. I think it must be one of those big new houses for artisans."

She took my arm confidingly, familiarly, and accelerated her pace. There was something primitive in our proceedings. We did not think of the resources of civilization. A late tramcar overtook us; a row of *fiacres*[1] stood by the railing of the gardens. It never entered our heads to make use of these conveyances. She was too hurried, perhaps, and as to myself—well, she had taken my arm confidingly. As we were ascending the easy incline of the Corraterie,[2] all the shops shuttered and no light in any of the windows (as if all the mercenary population had fled at the end of the day), she said tentatively—

"I could run in for a moment to have a look at mother. It would not be much out of the way."

I dissuaded her. If Mrs. Haldin really expected to see Razumov that night it would have been unwise to show herself without him. The sooner we got hold of the young man and brought him along to calm her mother's agitation the better. She assented to my reasoning, and we crossed diagonally the Place du Théâtre, bluish grey with its floor of slabs of stone, under the electric light, and the lonely equestrian statue all black in the middle. In the Rue de Carouge we were in the poorer quarters and approaching the outskirts of the town. Vacant building plots alternated with high, new houses. At the corner of a side street the crude light of a whitewashed shop fell into the night, fan-like, through a wide doorway. One could see from a distance the inner wall with its scantily furnished shelves, and the deal counter painted brown. That was the house. Approaching it along the dark stretch of a fence of tarred planks, we saw the narrow pallid face of the cut angle, five single windows high, without a gleam in them, and crowned by the heavy shadow of a jutting roof slope.

"We must inquire in the shop," Miss Haldin directed me.

A sallow, thinly whiskered man, wearing a dingy white collar and a frayed tie, laid down a newspaper, and, leaning familiarly on both elbows far over the bare counter, answered that the person I was inquiring for was indeed his *locataire*[3] on the third floor, but that for the moment he was out.

"For the moment," I repeated, after a glance at Miss Haldin. "Does this mean that you expect him back at once?"

He was very gentle, with ingratiating eyes and soft lips. He smiled faintly as though he knew all about everything. Mr. Razumov, after being absent all day, had returned early in the

---

1  Cabs or carriages (French).
2  Rue de la Corraterie, a street in Geneva.
3  Tenant (French).

evening. He was very surprised about half an hour or a little more since to see him come down again. Mr. Razumov left his key, and in the course of some words which passed between them had remarked that he was going out because he needed air.

From behind the bare counter he went on smiling at us, his head held between his hands. Air. Air. But whether that meant a long or a short absence it was difficult to say. The night was very close, certainly.

After a pause, his ingratiating eyes turned to the door, he added—

"The storm shall drive him in."

"There's going to be a storm?" I asked.

"Why, yes!"

As if to confirm his words we heard a very distant, deep rumbling noise.

Consulting Miss Haldin by a glance, I saw her so reluctant to give up her quest that I asked the shopkeeper, in case Mr. Razumov came home within half an hour, to beg him to remain downstairs in the shop. We would look in again presently.

For all answer he moved his head imperceptibly. The approval of Miss Haldin was expressed by her silence. We walked slowly down the street, away from the town; the low garden walls of the modest villas doomed to demolition were overhung by the boughs of trees and masses of foliage, lighted from below by gas lamps. The violent and monotonous noise of the icy waters of the Arve[1] falling over a low dam swept towards us with a chilly draught of air across a great open space, where a double line of lamp-lights outlined a street as yet without houses. But on the other shore, overhung by the awful blackness of the thunder-cloud, a solitary dim light seemed to watch us with a weary stare. When we had strolled as far as the bridge, I said—

"We had better get back. . . ."

In the shop the sickly man was studying his smudgy newspaper, now spread out largely on the counter. He just raised his head when I looked in and shook it negatively, pursing up his lips. I rejoined Miss Haldin outside at once, and we moved off at a brisk pace. She remarked that she would send Anna with a note the first thing in the morning. I respected her taciturnity, silence being perhaps the best way to show my concern.

The semi-rural street we followed on our return changed

---

1 The Arve River, which flows for approximately 62 miles through eastern France and Switzerland.

gradually to the usual town thoroughfare, broad and deserted. We did not meet four people altogether, and the way seemed interminable, because my companion's natural anxiety had communicated itself sympathetically to me. At last we turned into the Boulevard des Philosophes, more wide, more empty, more dead —the very desolation of slumbering respectability. At the sight of the two lighted windows, very conspicuous from afar, I had the mental vision of Mrs. Haldin in her armchair keeping a dreadful, tormenting vigil under the evil spell of an arbitrary rule: a victim of tyranny and revolution, a sight at once cruel and absurd.

## III

"You will come in for a moment?" said Natalia Haldin.

I demurred on account of the late hour. "You know mother likes you so much," she insisted.

"I will just come in to hear how your mother is."

She said, as if to herself, "I don't even know whether she will believe that I could not find Mr. Razumov, since she has taken it into her head that I am concealing something from her. You may be able to persuade her. . . ."

"Your mother may mistrust me too," I observed.

"You! Why? What could you have to conceal from her? You are not a Russian nor a conspirator."

I felt profoundly my European remoteness, and said nothing, but I made up my mind to play my part of helpless spectator to the end. The distant rolling of thunder in the valley of the Rhone[1] was coming nearer to the sleeping town of prosaic virtues and universal hospitality. We crossed the street opposite the great dark gateway, and Miss Haldin rang at the door of the apartment. It was opened almost instantly, as if the elderly maid had been waiting in the ante-room for our return. Her flat physiognomy had an air of satisfaction. The gentleman was there, she declared, while closing the door.

Neither of us understood. Miss Haldin turned round brusquely to her. "Who?"

"Herr Razumov," she explained.

She had heard enough of our conversation before we left to

---

1　The Rhône River, which flows for some 505 miles through southern Switzerland and France before emptying into the Mediterranean Sea.

know why her young mistress was going out. Therefore, when the gentleman gave his name at the door, she admitted him at once.

"No one could have foreseen that," Miss Haldin murmured, with her serious grey eyes fixed upon mine. And, remembering the expression of the young man's face seen not much more than four hours ago, the look of a haunted somnambulist, I wondered with a sort of awe.

"You asked my mother first?" Miss Haldin inquired of the maid.

"No. I announced the gentleman," she answered, surprised at our troubled faces.

"Still," I said in an undertone, "your mother was prepared."

"Yes. But he has no idea . . ."

It seemed to me she doubted his tact. To her question how long the gentleman had been with her mother, the maid told us that Der Herr[1] had been in the drawing-room no more than a short quarter of an hour.

She waited a moment, then withdrew, looking a little scared. Miss Haldin gazed at me in silence.

"As things have turned out," I said, "you happen to know exactly what your brother's friend has to tell your mother. And surely after that . . ."

"Yes," said Natalia Haldin slowly. "I only wonder, as I was not here when he came, if it wouldn't be better not to interrupt now."

We remained silent, and I suppose we both strained our ears, but no sound reached us through the closed door. The features of Miss Haldin expressed a painful irresolution; she made a movement as if to go in, but checked herself. She had heard footsteps on the other side of the door. It came open, and Razumov, without pausing, stepped out into the ante-room. The fatigue of that day and the struggle with himself had changed him so much that I would have hesitated to recognize that face which, only a few hours before, when he brushed against me in front of the post office, had been startling enough but quite different. It had been not so livid then, and its eyes not so sombre. They certainly looked more sane now, but there was upon them the shadow of something consciously evil.

I speak of that, because, at first, their glance fell on me, though without any sort of recognition or even comprehension. I was simply in the line of his stare. I don't know if he had heard the bell or expected to see anybody. He was going out, I believe, and

1 The gentleman (German).

I do not think that he saw Miss Haldin till she advanced towards him a step or two. He disregarded the hand she put out.

"It's you, Natalia Victorovna. . . . Perhaps you are surprised . . . at this late hour. But, you see, I remembered our conversations in that garden. I thought really it was your wish that I should—without loss of time . . . so I came. No other reason. Simply to tell . . ."

He spoke with difficulty. I noticed that, and remembered his declaration to the man in the shop that he was going out because he "needed air." If that was his object, then it was clear that he had miserably failed. With downcast eyes and lowered head he made an effort to pick up the strangled phrase.

"To tell what I have heard myself only to-day—to-day . . ."

Through the door he had not closed I had a view of the drawing-room. It was lighted only by a shaded lamp—Mrs. Haldin's eyes could not support either gas or electricity. It was a comparatively big room, and in contrast with the strongly lighted ante-room its length was lost in semi-transparent gloom backed by heavy shadows; and on that ground I saw the motionless figure of Mrs. Haldin, inclined slightly forward, with a pale hand resting on the arm of the chair.

She did not move. With the window before her she had no longer that attitude suggesting expectation. The blind was down; and outside there was only the night sky harbouring a thunder-cloud, and the town indifferent and hospitable in its cold, almost scornful, toleration—a respectable town of refuge to which all these sorrows and hopes were nothing. Her white head was bowed.

The thought that the real drama of autocracy is not played on the great stage of politics came to me as, fated to be a spectator, I had this other glimpse behind the scenes, something more profound than the words and gestures of the public play. I had the certitude that this mother refused in her heart to give her son up after all. It was more than Rachel's inconsolable mourning,[1] it was something deeper, more inaccessible in its frightful tranquillity. Lost in the ill-defined mass of the high-backed chair, her white, inclined profile suggested the contemplation of something in her lap, as though a beloved head were resting there.

---

1  A reference to Jeremiah 31:15: "Thus saith the Lord; A voice was heard in Ramah, lamentation, and bitter weeping; Rachel weeping for her children refused to be comforted for her children, because they were not." (See also Matthew 2:18.)

I had this glimpse behind the scenes, and then Miss Haldin, passing by the young man, shut the door. It was not done without hesitation. For a moment I thought that she would go to her mother, but she sent in only an anxious glance. Perhaps if Mrs. Haldin had moved . . . but no. There was in the immobility of that bloodless face the dreadful aloofness of suffering without remedy.

Meantime the young man kept his eyes fixed on the floor. The thought that he would have to repeat the story he had told already was intolerable to him. He had expected to find the two women together. And then, he had said to himself, it would be over for all time—for all time. "It's lucky I don't believe in another world," he had thought cynically.

Alone in his room after having posted his secret letter, he had regained a certain measure of composure by writing in his secret diary. He was aware of the danger of that strange self-indulgence. He alludes to it himself, but he could not refrain. It calmed him—it reconciled him to his existence. He sat there scribbling by the light of a solitary candle, till it occurred to him that having heard the explanation of Haldin's arrest, as put forward by Sophia Antonovna, it behoved him to tell these ladies himself. They were certain to hear the tale through some other channel, and then his abstention would look strange, not only to the mother and sister of Haldin, but to other people also. Having come to this conclusion, he did not discover in himself any marked reluctance to face the necessity, and very soon an anxiety to be done with it began to torment him. He looked at his watch. No; it was not absolutely too late.

The fifteen minutes with Mrs. Haldin were like the revenge of the unknown: that white face, that weak, distinct voice; that head, at first turned to him eagerly, then, after a while, bowed again and motionless—in the dim, still light of the room in which his words which he tried to subdue resounded so loudly—had troubled him like some strange discovery. And there seemed to be a secret obstinacy in that sorrow, something he could not understand; at any rate, something he had not expected. Was it hostile? But it did not matter. Nothing could touch him now; in the eyes of the revolutionists there was now no shadow on his past. The phantom of Haldin had been indeed walked over, was left behind lying powerless and passive on the pavement covered with snow. And this was the phantom's mother consumed with grief and white as a ghost. He had felt a pitying surprise. But that, of course, was of no importance. Mothers did not matter. He could not shake off the poignant impression of that silent, quiet, white-haired woman, but a sort of sternness crept into his thoughts. These were the consequences. Well, what of it? "Am I then on a bed of roses?" he had exclaimed to himself, sitting at some distance with his eyes fixed upon that figure of sorrow. He had said all he had to say to her, and when he had finished she had not uttered a word. She had turned away her head while he was speaking. The silence which had fallen on his last words had lasted for five minutes or more. What did it mean? Before its incomprehensible character he became conscious of anger in his stern mood, the old anger against Haldin reawakened by the contemplation of Haldin's mother. And was it not something like enviousness which gripped his heart, as if of a privilege denied to him alone of all the men that had ever passed through this world? It was the other who had attained to repose and yet continued to exist in the affection of that mourning old woman, in the thoughts of all these people posing for lovers of humanity. It was impossible to get rid of him. "It's myself whom I have given up to destruction," thought Razumov. "He has induced me to do it. I can't shake him off."

Alarmed by that discovery, he got up and strode out of the silent, dim room with its silent old woman in the chair, that mother! He never looked back. It was frankly a flight. But on opening the door he saw his retreat cut off. There was the sister. He had never forgotten the sister, only he had not expected to see her then—or ever any more, perhaps. Her presence in the ante-room was as unforeseen as the apparition of her brother had been. Razumov gave a start as though he had discovered himself cleverly trapped. He tried to smile, but could not manage it, and lowered his eyes. "Must I repeat that silly story now?" he asked himself, and felt a sinking sensation. Nothing solid had passed his lips since the day before, but he was not in a state to analyse the origins of his weakness. He meant to take up his hat and depart with as few words as possible, but Miss Haldin's swift movement to shut the door took him by surprise. He half turned after her, but without raising his eyes, passively, just as a feather might stir in the disturbed air. The next moment she was back in the place she had started from, with another half-turn on his part, so that they came again into the same relative positions.

"Yes, yes," she said hurriedly. "I am very grateful to you, Kirylo Sidorovitch, for coming at once—like this. . . . Only, I wish I had . . . Did mother tell you?"

"I wonder what she could have told me that I did not know

before," he said, obviously to himself, but perfectly audible. "Because I always *did* know it," he added louder, as if in despair.

He hung his head. He had such a strong sense of Natalia Haldin's presence that to look at her he felt would be a relief. It was she who had been haunting him now. He had suffered that persecution ever since she had suddenly appeared before him in the garden of the Villa Borel with an extended hand and the name of her brother on her lips. . . . The ante-room had a row of hooks on the wall nearest to the outer door, while against the wall opposite there stood a small dark table and one chair. The paper, bearing a very faint design, was all but white. The light of an electric bulb high up under the ceiling searched that clear square box into its four bare corners, crudely, without shadows—a strange stage for an obscure drama.

"What do you mean?" asked Miss Haldin. "What is it that you knew always?"

He raised his face, pale, full of unexpressed suffering. But that look in his eyes of dull, absent obstinacy, which struck and surprised everybody he was talking to, began to pass away. It was as though he were coming to himself in the awakened consciousness of that marvellous harmony of feature, of lines, of glances, of voice, which made of the girl before him a being so rare, outside, and, as it were, above the common notion of beauty. He looked at her so long that she coloured slightly.

"What is it that you knew?" she repeated vaguely.

That time he managed to smile.

"Indeed, if it had not been for a word of greeting or two, I would doubt whether your mother was aware at all of my existence. You understand?"

Natalia Haldin nodded; her hands moved slightly by her side.

"Yes. Is it not heart-breaking? She has not shed a tear yet—not a single tear."

"Not a tear! And you, Natalia Victorovna? You have been able to cry?"

"I have. And then I am young enough, Kirylo Sidorovitch, to believe in the future. But when I see my mother so terribly distracted, I almost forget everything. I ask myself whether one should feel proud—or only resigned. We had such a lot of people coming to see us. There were utter strangers who wrote asking for permission to call to present their respects. It was impossible to keep our door shut for ever. You know that Peter Ivanovitch himself . . . Oh yes, there was much sympathy, but there were persons who exulted openly at that death. Then, when I was left alone with poor mother, all this seemed so wrong in spirit, something not worth the price she is paying for it. But directly I heard you were here in Geneva, Kirylo Sidorovitch, I felt that you were the only person who could assist me . . ."

"In comforting a bereaved mother? Yes!" he broke in in a manner which made her open her clear unsuspecting eyes. "But there is a question of fitness. Has this occurred to you?"

There was a breathlessness in his utterance which contrasted with the monstrous hint of mockery in his intention.

"Why!" whispered Natalia Haldin with feeling. "Who more fit than you?"

He had a convulsive movement of exasperation, but controlled himself.

"Indeed! Directly you heard that I was in Geneva, before even seeing me? It is another proof of that confidence which . . ."

All at once his tone changed, became more incisive and more detached.

"Men are poor creatures, Natalia Victorovna. They have no intuition of sentiment. In order to speak fittingly to a mother of her lost son one must have had some experience of the filial relation. It is not the case with me—if you must know the whole truth. Your hopes have to deal here with 'a breast unwarmed by any affection,' as the poet says. . . .[1] That does not mean it is insensible," he added in a lower tone.

"I am certain your heart is not unfeeling," said Miss Haldin softly.

"No. It is not as hard as a stone," he went on in the same introspective voice, and looking as if his heart were lying as heavy as a stone in that unwarmed breast of which he spoke. "No, not so hard. But how to prove what you give me credit for—ah! that's another question. No one has ever expected such a thing from me before. No one whom my tenderness would have been of any use to. And now you come. You! Now! No, Natalia Victorovna. It's too late. You come too late. You must expect nothing from me."

She recoiled from him a little, though he had made no movement, as if she had seen some change in his face, charging his words with the significance of some hidden sentiment they shared together. To me, the silent spectator, they looked like two people becoming conscious of a spell which had been lying on them ever since they first set eyes on each other. Had either of them cast a glance then in my direction, I would have opened the

---

1  The poet and poem (if such exist) are unidentified.

door quietly and gone out. But neither did; and I remained, every fear of indiscretion lost in the sense of my enormous remoteness from their captivity within the sombre horizon of Russian problems, the boundary of their eyes, of their feelings—the prison of their souls.

Frank, courageous, Miss Haldin controlled her voice in the midst of her trouble.

"What can this mean?" she asked, as if speaking to herself.

"It may mean that you have given yourself up to vain imaginings while I have managed to remain amongst the truth of things and the realities of life—our Russian life—such as they are."

"They are cruel," she murmured.

"And ugly. Don't forget that—and ugly. Look where you like. Look near you, here abroad where you are, and then look back at home, whence you came."

"One must look beyond the present." Her tone had an ardent conviction.

"The blind can do that best. I have had the misfortune to be born clear-eyed. And if you only knew what strange things I have seen! What amazing and unexpected apparitions! . . . But why talk of all this?"

"On the contrary, I want to talk of all this with you," she protested with earnest serenity. The sombre humours of her brother's friend left her unaffected, as though that bitterness, that suppressed anger, were the signs of an indignant rectitude. She saw that he was not an ordinary person, and perhaps she did not want him to be other than he appeared to her trustful eyes. "Yes, with you especially," she insisted. "With you of all the Russian people in the world. . . ." A faint smile dwelt for a moment on her lips. "I am like poor mother in a way. I too seem unable to give up our beloved dead, who, don't forget, was all in all to us. I don't want to abuse your sympathy, but you must understand that it is in you that we can find all that is left of his generous soul."

I was looking at him; not a muscle of his face moved in the least. And yet, even at the time, I did not suspect him of insensibility. It was a sort of rapt thoughtfulness. Then he stirred slightly.

"You are going, Kirylo Sidorovitch?" she asked.

"I! Going? Where? Oh yes, but I must tell you first . . ." His voice was muffled and he forced himself to produce it with visible repugnance, as if speech were something disgusting or deadly. "That story, you know—the story I heard this afternoon . . ."

"I know the story already," she said sadly.

"You know it! Have you correspondents in St. Petersburg too?"

"No. It's Sophia Antonovna. I have seen her just now. She sends you her greetings. She is going away to-morrow."

He had lowered at last his fascinated glance; she too was looking down, and standing thus before each other in the glaring light, between the four bare walls, they seemed brought out from the confused immensity of the Eastern borders to be exposed cruelly to the observation of my Western eyes. And I observed them. There was nothing else to do. My existence seemed so utterly forgotten by these two that I dared not now make a movement. And I thought to myself that, of course, they had to come together, the sister and the friend of that dead man. The ideas, the hopes, the aspirations, the cause of Freedom, expressed in their common affection for Victor Haldin, the moral victim of autocracy,—all this must draw them to each other fatally. Her very ignorance and his loneliness to which he had alluded so strangely must work to that end. And, indeed, I saw that the work was done already. Of course. It was manifest that they must have been thinking of each other for a long time before they met. She had the letter from that beloved brother kindling her imagination by the severe praise attached to that one name; and for him to see that exceptional girl was enough. The only cause for surprise was his gloomy aloofness before her clearly expressed welcome. But he was young, and however austere and devoted to his revolutionary ideals, he was not blind. The period of reserve was over; he was coming forward in his own way. I could not mistake the significance of this late visit, for in what he had to say there was nothing urgent. The true cause dawned upon me: he had discovered that he needed her—and she was moved by the same feeling. It was the second time that I saw them together, and I knew that next time they met I would not be there, either remembered or forgotten. I would have virtually ceased to exist for both these young people.

I made this discovery in a very few moments. Meantime, Natalia Haldin was telling Razumov briefly of our peregrinations from one end of Geneva to the other. While speaking she raised her hands above her head to untie her veil, and that movement displayed for an instant the seductive grace of her youthful figure, clad in the simplest of mourning. In the transparent shadow the hat rim threw on her face her grey eyes had an enticing lustre. Her voice, with its unfeminine yet exquisite timbre, was steady, and she spoke quickly, frank, unembarrassed. As she justified her action by the mental state of her mother, a spasm of pain marred the generously confiding harmony of her features. I perceived that with his downcast eyes he had the air of a man who is listening to a strain of music rather than to articulated speech. And in the same way, after she had ceased, he seemed to listen yet, motionless, as if under the spell of suggestive sound. He came to himself, muttering—

"Yes, yes. She has not shed a tear. She did not seem to hear what I was saying. I might have told her anything. She looked as if no longer belonging to this world."

Miss Haldin gave signs of profound distress. Her voice faltered. "You don't know how bad it has come to be. She expects now to *see him!*" The veil dropped from her fingers and she clasped her hands in anguish. "It shall end by her seeing him," she cried.

Razumov raised his head sharply and attached on her a prolonged thoughtful glance.

"H'm. That's very possible," he muttered in a peculiar tone, as if giving his opinion on a matter of fact. "I wonder what . . ." He checked himself.

"That would be the end. Her mind shall be gone then, and her spirit will follow."

Miss Haldin unclasped her hands and let them fall by her side.

"You think so?" he queried profoundly. Miss Haldin's lips were slightly parted. Something unexpected and unfathomable in that young man's character had fascinated her from the first. "No! There's neither truth nor consolation to be got from the phantoms of the dead," he added after a weighty pause. "I might have told her something true; for instance, that your brother meant to save his life—to escape. There can be no doubt of that. But I did not."

"You did not! But why?"

"I don't know. Other thoughts came into my head," he answered. He seemed to me to be watching himself inwardly, as though he were trying to count his own heart-beats, while his eyes never for a moment left the face of the girl. "You were not there," he continued. "I had made up my mind never to see you again."

This seemed to take her breath away for a moment.

"You . . . How is it possible?"

"You may well ask. . . . However, I think that I refrained from telling your mother from prudence. I might have assured her that in the last conversation he held as a free man he mentioned you both . . ."

"That last conversation was with you," she struck in her deep, moving voice. "Some day you must . . ."

"It was with me. Of you he said that you had trustful eyes. And why I have not been able to forget that phrase I don't know. It meant that there is in you no guile, no deception, no falsehood, no suspicion—nothing in your heart that could give you a conception of a living, acting, speaking lie, if ever it came in your way. That you are a predestined victim . . . Ha! what a devilish suggestion!"

The convulsive, uncontrolled tone of the last words disclosed the precarious hold he had over himself. He was like a man defying his own dizziness in high places and tottering suddenly on the very edge of the precipice. Miss Haldin pressed her hand to her breast. The dropped black veil lay on the floor between them. Her movement steadied him. He looked intently on that hand till it descended slowly, and then raised again his eyes to her face. But he did not give her time to speak.

"No? You don't understand? Very well." He had recovered his calm by a miracle of will. "So you talked with Sophia Antonovna?"

"Yes. Sophia Antonovna told me . . ." Miss Haldin stopped, wonder growing in her wide eyes.

"H'm. That's the respectable enemy," he muttered, as though he were alone.

"The tone of her references to you was extremely friendly," remarked Miss Haldin, after waiting for a while.

"Is that your impression? And she the most intelligent of the lot, too. Things then are going as well as possible. Everything conspires to . . . Ah! these conspirators," he said slowly, with an accent of scorn; "they would get hold of you in no time! You know, Natalia Victorovna, I have the greatest difficulty in saving myself from the superstition of an active Providence. It's irresistible. . . . The alternative, of course, would be the personal Devil of our simple ancestors. But, if so, he has overdone it altogether—the old Father of Lies[1]—our national patron—our domestic god, whom we take with us when we go abroad. He has overdone it. It seems that I am not simple enough . . . That's it! I ought to have known . . . And I did know it," he added in a tone of poignant distress which overcame my astonishment.

"This man is deranged," I said to myself, very much frightened.

---

1 Satan; see John 8:44.

The next moment he gave me a very special impression beyond the range of commonplace definitions. It was as though he had stabbed himself outside and had come in there to show it; and more than that—as though he were turning the knife in the wound and watching the effect. That was the impression, rendered in physical terms. One could not defend oneself from a certain amount of pity. But it was for Miss Haldin, already so tried in her deepest affections, that I felt a serious concern. Her attitude, her face, expressed compassion struggling with doubt on the verge of terror.

"What is it, Kirylo Sidorovitch?" There was a hint of tenderness in that cry. He only stared at her in that complete surrender of all his faculties which in a happy lover would have had the name of ecstasy.

"Why are you looking at me like this, Kirylo Sidorovitch? I have approached you frankly. I need at this time to see clearly in myself . . ." She ceased for a moment as if to give him an opportunity to utter at last some word worthy of her exalted trust in her brother's friend. His silence became impressive, like a sign of a momentous resolution.

In the end Miss Haldin went on, appealingly—

"I have waited for you anxiously. But now that you have been moved to come to us in your kindness, you alarm me. You speak obscurely. It seems as if you were keeping back something from me."

"Tell me, Natalia Victorovna," he was heard at last in a strange unringing voice, "whom did you see in that place?"

She was startled, and as if deceived in her expectations.

"Where? In Peter Ivanovitch's rooms? There was Mr. Laspara and three other people."

"Ha! The vanguard—the forlorn hope of the great plot," he commented to himself. "Bearers of the spark to start an explosion[1]

---

1   Possibly a reference to *Iskra*, a revolutionary newspaper founded in Geneva in 1900 by Vladimir Il'ich Lenin (Vladimir Il'ich Ul'ianov)(1870-1924), Georgii Valentinovich Plekhanov (1856-1918), and Aleksandr Nikolaevich Potresev (1869-1934). The newspaper's motto was "The spark will kindle a flame," a quote taken from a letter to the Russian poet Aleksandr Sergeevich Pushkin (1799-1837) from an exiled Russian convict of the Decembrist revolt of 1825. This line also bears similarities to the revolutionary lines from Percy Bysshe Shelley's "Ode to the West Wind": "Scatter, as from an unextinguished hearth / Ashes and sparks, my words among mankind! / Be through my lips to unawakened earth / The trumpet of a prophecy! (ll. 66-69)." Conrad uses a similar line early in *Heart of Darkness* (1899): "bearers of a spark from the sacred fire" (*Youth and Two Other Stories* [Doubleday, 1928], 47).

which is meant to change fundamentally the lives of so many millions in order that Peter Ivanovitch should be the head of a State."

"You are testing[1] me," she said. "Our dear one told me once to remember that men serve always something greater than themselves—the idea."

"Our dear one," he repeated slowly. The effort he made to appear unmoved absorbed all the force of his soul. He stood before her like a being with hardly a breath of life. His eyes, even as under great physical suffering, had lost all their fire. "Ah! your brother . . . But on your lips, in your voice, it sounds . . . and indeed in you everything is divine. . . . I wish I could know the innermost depths of your thoughts, of your feelings."

"But why, Kirylo Sidorovitch?" she cried, alarmed by these words coming out of strangely lifeless lips.

"Have no fear. It is not to betray you. So you went there? . . . And Sophia Antonovna, what did she tell you, then?"

"She said very little, really. She knew that I should hear everything from you. She had no time for more than a few words." Miss Haldin's voice dropped and she became silent for a moment. "The man, it appears, has taken his life," she said sadly.

"Tell me, Natalia Victorovna," he asked after a pause, "do you believe in remorse."

"What a question!"

"What can *you* know of it?" he muttered thickly. "It is not for such as you . . . What I meant to ask was whether you believed in the efficacy of remorse?"

She hesitated as though she had not understood, then her face lighted up.

"Yes," she said firmly.

"So he is absolved. Moreover, that Ziemianitch was a brute, a drunken brute."

A shudder passed through Natalia Haldin.

"But a man of the people," Razumov went on, "to whom they, the revolutionists, tell a tale of sublime hopes. Well, the people must be forgiven. . . . And you must not believe all you've heard from that source, either," he added, with a sort of sinister reluctance.

"You are concealing something from me," she exclaimed.

"Do you, Natalia Victorovna, believe in the duty of revenge?"

"Listen, Kirylo Sidorovitch. I believe that the future shall be merciful to us all. Revolutionist and reactionary, victim and exe-

---

1   The first English edition has "You are teasing me" (M, T, AS, ES, A1).

cutioner, betrayer and betrayed, they shall all be pitied together when the light breaks on our black sky at last. Pitied and forgotten; for without that there can be no union and no love."

"I hear. No revenge for you, then? Never? Not the least bit?" He smiled bitterly with his colourless lips. "You yourself are like the very spirit of that merciful future. Strange that it does not make it easier. . . . No! But suppose that the real betrayer of your brother—Ziemianitch had a part in it too, but insignificant and quite involuntary—suppose that he was a young man, educated, an intellectual worker, thoughtful, a man your brother might have trusted lightly, perhaps, but still—suppose . . . But there's a whole story there."

"And you know the story! But why, then—"

"I have heard it. There is a staircase in it, and even phantoms, but that does not matter if a man always serves something greater than himself—the idea. I wonder who is the greatest victim in that tale?"

"In that tale!" Miss Haldin repeated. She seemed turned into stone.

"Do you know why I came to you? It is simply because there is no one anywhere in the whole great world I could go to. Do you understand what I say? Not one to go to. Do you conceive the desolation of the thought—no one—to—go—to?"

Utterly misled by her own enthusiastic interpretation of two lines in the letter of a visionary, under the spell of her own dread of lonely days, in their overshadowed world of angry strife, she was unable to see the truth struggling on his lips. What she was conscious of was the obscure form of his suffering. She was on the point of extending her hand to him impulsively when he spoke again.

"An hour after I saw you first I knew how it would be. The terrors of remorse, revenge, confession, anger, hate, fear, are like nothing to the atrocious temptation which you put in my way the day you appeared before me with your voice, with your face, in the garden of that accursed villa."

She looked utterly bewildered for a moment; then, with a sort of despairing insight went straight to the point.

"The story, Kirylo Sidorovitch, the story!"

"There is no more to tell!" He made a movement forward, and she actually put her hand on his shoulder to push him away; but her strength failed her, and he kept his ground, though trembling in every limb. "It ends here—on this very spot." He pressed a denunciatory finger to his breast with force, and became perfectly still.

I ran forward, snatching up the chair, and was in time to catch hold of Miss Haldin and lower her down. As she sank into it she swung half round on my arm, and remained averted from us both, drooping over the back. He looked at her with an appalling expressionless tranquillity. Incredulity, struggling with astonishment, anger, and disgust, deprived me for a time of the power of speech. Then I turned on him, whispering from very rage—

"This is monstrous. What are you staying for? Don't let her catch sight of you again. Go away! . . ." He did not budge. "Don't you understand that your presence is intolerable—even to me? If there's any sense of shame in you. . . ."

Slowly his sullen eyes moved in my direction. "How did this old man come here?" he muttered, astounded.

Suddenly Miss Haldin sprang up from the chair, made a few steps, and tottered. Forgetting my indignation, and even the man himself, I hurried to her assistance. I took her by the arm, and she let me lead her into the drawing-room. Away from the lamp, in the deeper dusk of the distant end, the profile of Mrs. Haldin, her hands, her whole figure had the stillness of a sombre painting. Miss Haldin stopped, and pointed mournfully at the tragic immobility of her mother, who seemed to watch a beloved head lying in her lap.

That gesture had an unequalled force of expression, so far-reaching in its human distress that one could not believe that it pointed out merely the ruthless working of political institutions. After assisting Miss Haldin to the sofa, I turned round to go back and shut the door. Framed in the opening, in the searching glare of the white anteroom, my eyes fell on Razumov, still there, standing before the empty chair, as if rooted for ever to the spot of his atrocious confession. A wonder came over me that the mysterious force which had torn it out of him had failed to destroy his life, to shatter his body. It was there unscathed. I stared at the broad line of his shoulders, his dark head, the amazing immobility of his limbs. At his feet the veil dropped by Miss Haldin looked intensely black in the white crudity of the light. He was gazing at it spell-bound. Next moment, stooping with an incredible, savage swiftness, he snatched it up and pressed it to his face with both hands. Something, extreme astonishment perhaps, dimmed my eyes, so that he seemed to vanish before he moved.

The slamming of the outer door restored my sight, and I went on contemplating the empty chair in the empty ante-room. The meaning of what I had seen reached my mind with a staggering shock. I seized Natalia Haldin by the shoulder.

"That miserable wretch has carried off your veil!" I cried, in the scared, deadened voice of an awful discovery. "He . . ."

The rest remained unspoken. I stepped back and looked down at her, in silent horror. Her hands were lying lifelessly, palms upwards, on her lap. She raised her grey eyes slowly. Shadows seemed to come and go in them as if the steady flame of her soul had been made to vacillate at last in the cross-currents of poisoned air from the corrupted dark immensity claiming her for its own, where virtues themselves fester into crimes in the cynicism of oppression and revolt.

"It is impossible to be more unhappy. . . ." The languid whisper of her voice struck me with dismay. "It is impossible. . . . I feel my heart becoming like ice."[1]


# IV


Razumov walked straight home on the wet glistening pavement. A heavy shower passed over him; distant lightning played faintly against the fronts of the dumb houses with the shuttered shops all along the Rue de Carouge; and now and then, after the faint flash, there was a faint, sleepy rumble; but the main forces of the thunderstorm remained massed down the Rhone valley as if loath to attack the respectable and passionless abode of democratic liberty, the serious-minded town of dreary hotels, tendering the same indifferent, hospitality to tourists of all nations and to international conspirators of every shade.

The owner of the shop was making ready to close when Razumov entered and without a word extended his hand for the key of his room. On reaching it for him, from a shelf, the man was about to pass a small joke as to taking the air in a thunderstorm, but, after looking at the face of his lodger, he only observed, just to say something—

"You've got very wet."

"Yes, I am washed clean," muttered Razumov, who was dripping from head to foot, and passed through the inner door towards the staircase leading to his room.

He did not change his clothes, but, after lighting the candle,

---

1 Yves Hervouet argues that this is an allusion to *Le Rouge et le noir* (1830) by Stendhal, pen name for Marie-Henri Beyle (1783-1842): "*Il est impossible d'être plus malheureuse . . . Je sens mon coeur se glacer*" (196); see *The French Face of Joseph Conrad* (Cambridge UP, 1990), 107.

took off his watch and chain, laid them on the table, and sat down at once to write. The book of his compromising record was kept in a locked drawer, which he pulled out violently, and did not even trouble to push back afterwards.

In this queer pedantism of a man who had read, thought, lived, pen in hand, there is the sincerity of the attempt to grapple by the same means with another profounder knowledge. After some passages which have been already made use of in the building up of this narrative, or add nothing new to the psychological side of this disclosure (there is even one more allusion to the silver medal in this last entry), comes a page and a half of incoherent writing where his expression is baffled by the novelty and the mysteriousness of that side of our emotional life to which his solitary existence had been a stranger. Then only he begins to address directly the reader he had in his mind, trying to express in broken sentences, full of wonder and awe, the sovereign (he uses that very word) power of her person over his imagination, in which lay the dormant seed of her brother's words.

"... The most trustful eyes in the world—your brother said of you when he was as well as a dead man already. And when you stood before me with your hand extended, I remembered the very sound of his voice, and I looked into your eyes—and that was enough. I knew that something had happened, but I did not know then what. . . . But don't be deceived, Natalia Victorovna. I believed that I had in my breast nothing but an inexhaustible fund of anger and hate for you both. I remembered that he had looked to you for the perpetuation of his visionary soul. He, this man who had robbed me of my hard-working, purposeful existence. I, too, had my guiding idea; and remember that, amongst us, it is more difficult to lead a life of toil and self-denial than to go out in the street and kill from conviction. But enough of that. Hate or no hate, I felt at once that, while shunning the sight of you, I could never succeed in driving away your image. I would say, addressing that dead man, 'Is this the way you are going to haunt me?' It is only later on that I understood—only to-day, only a few hours ago. What could I have known of what was tearing me to pieces and dragging the secret for ever to my lips? You were appointed to undo the evil by making me betray myself back into truth and peace. You! And you have done it in the same way, too, in which he ruined me: by forcing upon me your confidence. Only what I detested him for, in you ended by appearing noble and exalted. But, I repeat, be not deceived. I was given up to evil. I exulted in having induced that silly innocent fool to steal his father's money. He was a fool, but not a thief. I made him one. It was necessary. I had to confirm myself in my contempt and hate for what I betrayed. I have suffered from as many vipers in my heart as any social democrat of them all—vanity, ambitions, jealousies, shameful desires, evil passions of envy and revenge. I had my security stolen from me, years of good work, my best hopes. Listen—now comes the true confession. The other was nothing. To save me, your trustful eyes had to entice my thought to the very edge of the blackest treachery. I could see them constantly looking at me with the confidence of your pure heart which had not been touched by evil things. Victor Haldin had stolen the truth of my life from me, who had nothing else in the world, and he boasted of living on through you on this earth where I had no place to lay my head on. She will marry some day, he had said— and your eyes were trustful. And do you know what I said to myself? I shall steal his sister's soul from her. When we met that first morning in the gardens, and you spoke to me confidingly in the generosity of your spirit, I was thinking, 'Yes, he himself by talking of her trustful eyes has delivered her into my hands!' If you could have looked then into my heart, you would have cried out aloud with terror and disgust.

"Perhaps no one will believe the baseness of such an intention to be possible. It's certain that, when we parted that morning, I gloated over it. I brooded upon the best way. The old man you introduced me to insisted on walking with me. I don't know who he is. He talked of you, of your lonely, helpless state, and every word of that friend of yours was egging me on to the unpardonable sin of stealing a soul. Could he have been the devil himself in the shape of an old Englishman? Natalia Victorovna, I was possessed! I returned to look at you every day, and drink in your presence the poison of my infamous intention. But I foresaw difficulties. Then Sophia Antonovna, of whom I was not thinking— I had forgotten her existence—appears suddenly with that tale from St. Petersburg. . . . The only thing needed to make me safe— a trusted revolutionist for ever.

"It was as if Ziemianitch had hanged himself to help me on to further crime. The strength of falsehood seemed irresistible. These people stood doomed by the folly and the illusion that was in them—they being themselves the slaves of lies. Natalia Victorovna, I embraced the might of falsehood, I exulted in it—I gave myself up to it for a time. Who could have resisted! You yourself were the prize of it. I sat alone in my room, planning a life, the very thought of which makes me shudder now, like a believer who had been tempted to an atrocious sacrilege. But I brooded ardently over its images. The only thing was that there seemed to be no air in it. And also I was afraid of your mother. I never knew mine. I've never known any kind of love. There is something in the mere word. . . . Of you, I was not afraid—forgive me for telling you this. No, not of you. You were truth itself. You could not suspect me. As to your mother, you yourself feared already that her mind had given way from grief. Who could believe anything against me? Had not Ziemianitch hanged himself from remorse? I said to myself, 'Let's put it to the test, and be done with it once for all.' I trembled when I went in; but your mother hardly listened to what I was saying to her, and, in a little while, seemed to have forgotten my very existence. I sat looking at her. There was no longer anything between you and me. You were defenceless—and soon, very soon, you would be alone. . . . I thought of you. Defenceless. For days you have talked with me—opening your heart. I remembered the shadow of your eyelashes over your grey trustful eyes. And your pure forehead! It is low like the forehead of statues—calm, unstained. It was as if your pure brow bore a light which fell on me, searched my heart and saved me from ignominy, from ultimate undoing. And it saved you too. Pardon my presumption. But there was that in your glances which seemed to tell me that you . . . Your light! your truth! I felt that I must tell you that I had ended by loving you. And to tell you that I must first confess. Confess, go out—and perish.

"Suddenly you stood before me! You alone in all the world to whom I must confess. You fascinated me—you have freed me from the blindness of anger and hate—the truth shining in you drew the truth out of me. Now I have done it; and as I write here, I am in the depths of anguish, but there is air to breathe at last—air! And, by the by, that old man sprang up from somewhere as I was speaking to you, and raged at me like a disappointed devil. I suffer horribly, but I am not in despair. There is only one more thing to do for me. After that—if they let me—I shall go away and bury myself in obscure misery. In giving Victor Haldin up, it was myself, after all, whom I have betrayed most basely. You must believe what I say now, you can't refuse to believe this. Most basely. It is through you that I came to feel this so deeply. After all, it is they and not I who have the right on their side!—theirs is the strength of invisible powers. So be it. Only don't be deceived, Natalia Victorovna, I am not converted. Have I then the soul of a slave? No! I am independent—and therefore perdition is my lot."

On these words, he stopped writing, shut the book, and

wrapped it in the black veil he had carried off. He then ransacked the drawers for paper and string, made up a parcel which he addressed to Miss Haldin, Boulevard des Philosophes, and then flung the pen away from him into a distant corner.

This done, he sat down with the watch before him. He could have gone out at once, but the hour had not struck yet. The hour would be midnight. There was no reason for that choice except that the facts and the words of a certain evening in his past were timing his conduct in the present. The sudden power Natalia Haldin had gained over him he ascribed to the same cause. "You don't walk with impunity over a phantom's breast," he heard himself mutter. "Thus he saves me," he thought suddenly. "He himself, the betrayed man." The vivid image of Miss Haldin seemed to stand by him, watching him relentlessly. She was not disturbing. He had done with life, and his thought even in her presence tried to take an impartial survey. Now his scorn extended to himself. "I had neither the simplicity nor the courage nor the self-possession to be a scoundrel, or an exceptionally able man. For who, with us in Russia, is to tell a scoundrel from an exceptionally able man? . . ."

He was the puppet of his past, because at the very stroke of midnight he jumped up and ran swiftly downstairs as if confident that, by the power of destiny, the house door would fly open before the absolute necessity of his errand. And as a matter of fact, just as he got to the bottom of the stairs, it was opened for him by some people of the house coming home late—two men and a woman. He slipped out through them into the street, swept then by a fitful gust of wind. They were, of course, very much startled. A flash of lightning enabled them to observe him walking away quickly. One of the men shouted, and was starting in pursuit, but the woman had recognized him. "It's all right. It's only that young Russian from the third floor." The darkness returned with a single clap of thunder, like a gun fired for a warning of his escape from the prison of lies.

He must have heard at some time or other and now remembered unconsciously that there was to be a gathering of revolutionists at the house of Julius Laspara that evening. At any rate, he made straight for the Laspara house, and found himself without surprise ringing at its street door, which, of course, was closed. By that time the thunderstorm had attacked in earnest. The steep incline of the street ran with water, the thick fall of rain enveloped him like a luminous veil in the play of lightning. He was perfectly calm, and, between the crashes, listened attentively to the delicate tinkling of the doorbell somewhere within the house.

There was some difficulty before he was admitted. His person was not known to that one of the guests who had volunteered to go downstairs and see what was the matter. Razumov argued with him patiently. There could be no harm in admitting a caller. He had something to communicate to the company upstairs.

"Something of importance?"

"That'll be for the hearers to judge."

"Urgent?"

"Without a moment's delay."

Meantime, one of the Laspara daughters descended the stairs, small lamp in hand, in a grimy and crumpled gown, which seemed to hang on her by a miracle, and looking more than ever like an old doll with a dusty brown wig, dragged from under a sofa. She recognized Razumov at once.

"How do you do? Of course you may come in."

Following her light, Razumov climbed two flights of stairs from the lower darkness. Leaving the lamp on a bracket on the landing, she opened a door, and went in, accompanied by the sceptical guest. Razumov entered last. He closed the door behind him, and stepping on one side, put his back against the wall.

The three little rooms *en suite*,[1] with low, smoky ceilings and lit by paraffin lamps, were crammed with people. Loud talking was going on in all three, and tea-glasses, full, half-full, and empty, stood everywhere, even on the floor. The other Laspara girl sat, dishevelled and languid, behind an enormous samovar. In the inner doorway Razumov had a glimpse of the protuberance of a large stomach, which he recognized. Only a few feet from him Julius Laspara was getting down hurriedly from his high stool.

The appearance of the midnight visitor caused no small sensation. Laspara is very summary in his version of that night's happenings. After some words of greeting, disregarded by Razumov, Laspara (ignoring purposely his guest's soaked condition and his extraordinary manner of presenting himself) mentioned something about writing an article. He was growing uneasy, and Razumov appeared absent-minded. "I have written already all I shall ever write," he said at last, with a little laugh.

The whole company's attention was riveted on the newcomer, dripping with water, deadly pale, and keeping his position

---

1  As a suite; a group of rooms connected to one another (French).

against the wall. Razumov put Laspara gently aside, as though he wished to be seen from head to foot by everybody. By then the buzz of conversations had died down completely, even in the most distant of the three rooms. The doorway facing Razumov became blocked by men and women, who craned their necks and certainly seemed to expect something startling to happen.

A squeaky, insolent declaration was heard from that group.

"I know this ridiculously conceited individual."

"What individual?" asked Razumov, raising his bowed head, and searching with his eyes all the eyes fixed upon him. An intense surprised silence lasted for a time. "If it's me . . ."

He stopped, thinking over the form of his confession, and found it suddenly, unavoidably suggested by the fateful evening of his life.

"I am come here," he began, in a clear voice, "to talk of an individual called Ziemianitch. Sophia Antonovna has informed me that she would make public a certain letter from St. Petersburg . . ."

"Sophia Antonovna has left us early in the evening," said Laspara. "It's quite correct. Everybody here has heard . . ."

"Very well," Razumov interrupted, with a shade of impatience, for his heart was beating strongly. Then, mastering his voice so far that there was even a touch of irony in his clear, forcible enunciation—

"In justice to that individual, the much ill-used peasant, Ziemianitch, I now declare solemnly that the conclusions of that letter calumniate a man of the people—a bright Russian soul. Ziemianitch had nothing to do with the actual arrest of Victor Haldin."

Razumov dwelt on the name heavily, and then waited till the faint, mournful murmur which greeted it had died out.

"Victor Victorovitch Haldin," he began again, "acting with, no doubt, noble-minded imprudence, took refuge with a certain student of whose opinions he knew nothing but what his own illusions suggested to his generous heart. It was an unwise display of confidence. But I am not here to appreciate the actions of Victor Haldin. Am I to tell you of the feelings of that student, sought out in his obscure solitude, and menaced by the complicity forced upon him? Am I to tell you what he did? It's a rather complicated story. In the end the student went to General T—— himself, and said, 'I have the man who killed de P—— locked up in my room, Victor Haldin—a student like myself.'"

A great buzz arose, in which Razumov raised his voice.

"Observe—that man had certain honest ideals in view. But I didn't come here to explain him."

"No. But you must explain how you know all this," came in grave tones from somebody.

"A vile coward!" This simple cry vibrated with indignation. "Name him!" shouted other voices.

"What are you clamouring for?" said Razumov disdainfully, in the profound silence which fell on the raising of his hand. "Haven't you all understood that I am that man?"

Laspara went away brusquely from his side and climbed upon his stool. In the first forward surge of people towards him, Razumov expected to be torn to pieces, but they fell back without touching him, and nothing came of it but noise. It was bewildering. His head ached terribly. In the confused uproar he made out several times the name of Peter Ivanovitch, the word "judgment," and the phrase, "But this is a confession," uttered by somebody in a desperate shriek. In the midst of the tumult, a young man, younger than himself, approached him with blazing eyes.

"I must beg you," he said, with venomous politeness, "to be good enough not to move from this spot till you are told what you are to do."

Razumov shrugged his shoulders.

"I came in voluntarily."

"Maybe. But you won't go out till you are permitted," retorted the other.

He beckoned with his hand, calling out, "Louisa! Louisa! come here, please"; and, presently, one of the Laspara girls (they had been staring at Razumov from behind the samovar) came along, trailing a bedraggled tail of dirty flounces, and dragging with her a chair, which she set against the door, and, sitting down on it, crossed her legs. The young man thanked her effusively, and rejoined a group carrying on an animated discussion in low tones. Razumov lost himself for a moment.

A squeaky voice screamed, "Confession or no confession, you are a police spy!"

The revolutionist Nikita had pushed his way in front of Razumov, and faced him with his big, livid cheeks, his heavy paunch, bull neck, and enormous hands. Razumov looked at the famous slayer of gendarmes in silent disgust.

"And what are you?" he said, very low, then shut his eyes, and rested the back of his head against the wall.

"It would be better for you to depart now." Razumov heard a mild, sad voice, and opened his eyes. The gentle speaker was an elderly man, with a great brush of fine hair making a silvery halo all round his keen, intelligent face. "Peter Ivanovitch shall be informed of your confession—and you shall be directed . . ."

Then, turning to Nikita, nicknamed Necator, standing by, he appealed to him in a murmur—

"What else can we do? After this piece of sincerity he cannot be dangerous any longer."

The other muttered, "Better make sure of that before we let him go. Leave that to me. I know how to deal with such gentlemen."

He exchanged meaning glances with two or three men, who nodded slightly, then turning roughly to Razumov, "You have heard? You are not wanted here. Why don't you get out?"

The Laspara girl on guard rose, and pulled the chair out of the way unemotionally. She gave a sleepy stare to Razumov, who started, looked round the room and passed slowly by her as if struck by some sudden thought.

"I beg you to observe," he said, already on the landing, "that I had only to hold my tongue. To-day, of all days since I came amongst you, I was made safe, and to-day I made myself free from falsehood, from remorse—independent of every single human being on this earth."

He turned his back on the room, and walked towards the stairs, but, at the violent crash of the door behind him, he looked over his shoulder and saw that Nikita, with three others, had followed him out. "They are going to kill me, after all," he thought.

Before he had time to turn round and confront them fairly, they set on him with a rush. He was driven headlong against the wall. "I wonder how," he completed his thought. Nikita cried, with a shrill laugh right in his face, "We shall make you harmless. You wait a bit."

Razumov did not struggle. The three men held him pinned against the wall, while Nikita, taking up a position a little on one side, deliberately swung off his enormous arm. Razumov, looking for a knife in his hand, saw it come at him open, unarmed, and received a tremendous blow on the side of his head over his ear. At the same time he heard a faint, dull detonating sound, as if some one had fired a pistol on the other side of the wall. A raging fury awoke in him at this outrage. The people in Laspara's rooms, holding their breath, listened to the desperate scuffling of four men all over the landing; thuds against the walls, a terrible crash against the very door, then all of them went down together with a violence which seemed to shake the whole house. Razumov, overpowered, breathless, crushed under the weight of his assailants, saw the monstrous Nikita squatting on his heels near his head, while the others held him down, kneeling on his chest, gripping his throat, lying across his legs.

"Turn his face the other way," the paunchy terrorist directed, in an excited, gleeful squeak.

Razumov could struggle no longer. He was exhausted; he had to watch passively the heavy open hand of the brute descend again in a degrading blow over his other ear. It seemed to split his head in two, and all at once the men holding him became perfectly silent—soundless as shadows. In silence they pulled him brutally to his feet, rushed with him noiselessly down the staircase, and, opening the door, flung him out into the street.

He fell forward, and at once rolled over and over helplessly, going down the short slope together with the rush of running rain water. He came to rest in the roadway of the street at the bottom, lying on his back, with a great flash of lightning over his face—a vivid, silent flash of lightning which blinded him utterly. He picked himself up, and put his arm over his eyes to recover his sight. Not a sound reached him from anywhere, and he began to walk, staggering, down a long, empty street. The lightning waved and darted round him its silent flames, the water of the deluge fell, ran, leaped, drove—noiseless like the drift of mist. In this unearthly stillness his footsteps fell silent on the pavement, while a dumb wind drove him on and on, like a lost mortal in a phantom world ravaged by a soundless thunderstorm. God only knows where his noiseless feet took him to that night, here and there, and back again without pause or rest. Of one place, at least, where they did lead him, we heard afterwards; and, in the morning, the driver of the first south-shore tramcar, clanging his bell desperately, saw a bedraggled, soaked man without a hat, and walking in the roadway unsteadily with his head down, step right in front of his car, and go under.

When they picked him up, with two broken limbs and a crushed side, Razumov had not lost consciousness. It was as though he had tumbled, smashing himself, into a world of mutes. Silent men, moving unheard, lifted him up, laid him on the sidewalk, gesticulating and grimacing round him their alarm, horror, and compassion. A red face with moustaches stooped close over him, lips moving, eyes rolling. Razumov tried hard to understand the reason of this dumb show. To those who stood around him, the features of that stranger, so grievously hurt, seemed composed in meditation. Afterwards his eyes sent out at them a look of fear and closed slowly. They stared at him. Razumov made an effort to remember some French words.

"*Je suis sourd*,"[1] he had time to utter feebly, before he fainted.

"He is deaf," they exclaimed to each other. "That's why he did not hear the car."

They carried him off in that same car. Before it started on its journey, a woman in a shabby black dress, who had run out of the iron gate of some private grounds up the road, clambered on to the rear platform and would not be put off.

"I am a relation," she insisted, in bad French. "This young man is a Russian, and I am his relation."

On this plea they let her have her way. She sat down calmly, and took his head on her lap; her scared faded eyes avoided looking at his deathlike face. At the corner of a street, on the other side of the town, a stretcher met the car. She followed it to the door of the hospital, where they let her come in and see him laid on a bed. Razumov's new-found relation never shed a tear, but the officials had some difficulty in inducing her to go away. The porter observed her lingering on the opposite pavement for a long time. Suddenly, as though she had remembered something, she ran off.

The ardent hater of all Finance ministers, the slave of Madame de S——, had made up her mind to offer her resignation as lady companion to the Egeria of Peter Ivanovitch. She had found work to do after her own heart.

But hours before, while the thunderstorm still raged in the night, there had been in the rooms of Julius Laspara a great sensation. The terrible Nikita, coming in from the landing, uplifted his squeaky voice in horrible glee before all the company—

"Razumov! Mr. Razumov! The wonderful Razumov! He shall never be any use as a spy on any one. He won't talk, because he will never hear anything in his life—not a thing! I have burst the drums of his ears for him. Oh, you may trust me. I know the trick. Ha! Ha! Ha! I know the trick."


## V


It was nearly a fortnight after her mother's funeral that I saw Natalia Haldin for the last time.

In those silent, sombre days the doors of the *appartement* on the Boulevard des Philosophes were closed to every one but

---

1  I am deaf (French).

myself. I believe I was of some use, if only in this, that I alone was aware of the incredible part of the situation. Miss Haldin nursed her mother alone to the last moment. If Razumov's visit had anything to do with Mrs. Haldin's end (and I cannot help thinking that it hastened it considerably), it is because the man, trusted impulsively by the ill-fated Victor Haldin, had failed to gain the confidence of Victor Haldin's mother. What tale, precisely, he told her cannot be known—at any rate, I do not know it—but to me she seemed to die from the shock of an ultimate disappointment borne in silence. She had not believed him. Perhaps she could no longer believe any one, and consequently had nothing to say to any one—not even to her daughter. I suspect that Miss Haldin lived the heaviest hours of her life by that silent death-bed. I confess I was angry with the broken-hearted old woman passing away in the obstinacy of her mute distrust of her daughter.

When it was all over I stood aside. Miss Haldin had her compatriots round her then. A great number of them attended the funeral. I was there too, but afterwards managed to keep away from Miss Haldin, till I received a short note rewarding my self-denial. "It is as you would have it. I am going back to Russia at once. My mind is made up. Come and see me."

Verily, it was a reward of discretion. I went without delay to receive it. The *appartement* of the Boulevard des Philosophes presented the dreary signs of impending abandonment. It looked desolate and as if already empty to my eyes.

Standing, we exchanged a few words about her health, mine, remarks as to some people of the Russian colony, and then Natalia Haldin, establishing me on the sofa, began to talk openly of her future work, of her plans. It was all to be as I had wished it. And it was to be for life. We should never see each other again. Never!

I gathered this success to my breast. Natalia Haldin looked matured by her open and secret experiences. With her arms folded she walked up and down the whole length of the room, talking slowly, smooth-browed, with a resolute profile. She gave me a new view of herself, and I marvelled at that something grave and measured in her voice, in her movements, in her manner. It was the perfection of collected independence. The strength of her nature had come to surface because the obscure depths had been stirred.

"We two can talk of it now," she observed, after a silence and stopping short before me. "Have you been to inquire at the hospital lately?"

"Yes, I have." And as she looked at me fixedly, "He will live, the doctors say. But I thought that Tekla . . ."

"Tekla has not been near me for several days," explained Miss Haldin quickly. "As I never offered to go to the hospital with her, she thinks that I have no heart. She is disillusioned about me."

And Miss Haldin smiled faintly.

"Yes. She sits with him as long and as often as they will let her," I said. "She says she must never abandon him—never as long as she lives. He'll need somebody—a hopeless cripple, and stone deaf with that."

"Stone deaf? I didn't know," murmured Natalia Haldin.

"He is. It seems strange. I am told there were no apparent injuries to the head. They say, too, that it is not very likely that he will live so very long for Tekla to take care of him."

Miss Haldin shook her head.

"While there are travellers ready to fall by the way our Tekla shall never be idle. She is a good Samaritan by an irresistible vocation. The revolutionists didn't understand her. Fancy a devoted creature like that being employed to carry about documents sewn in her dress, or made to write from dictation."

"There is not much perspicacity in the world."

No sooner uttered, I regretted that observation. Natalia Haldin, looking me straight in the face, assented by a slight movement of her head. She was not offended, but turning away began to pace the room again. To my Western eyes she seemed to be getting farther and farther from me, quite beyond my reach now, but undiminished in the increasing distance. I remained silent as though it were hopeless to raise my voice. The sound of hers, so close to me, made me start a little.

"Tekla saw him picked up after the accident. The good soul never explained to me really how it came about. She affirms that there was some understanding between them—some sort of compact—that in any sore need, in misfortune, or difficulty, or pain, he was to come to her."

"Was there?" I said. "It is lucky for him that there was, then. He'll need all the devotion of the good Samaritan."

It was a fact that Tekla, looking out of her window at five in the morning, for some reason or other, had beheld Razumov in the grounds of the Château Borel, standing stockstill, bare-headed in the rain, at the foot of the terrace. She had screamed out to him, by name, to know what was the matter. He never even raised his head. By the time she had dressed herself sufficiently to run downstairs he was gone. She started in pursuit, and rushing out into the road, came almost directly upon the arrested tramcar and the small knot of people picking up Razumov. That much Tekla had told me herself one afternoon we happened to meet at the door of the hospital, and without any kind of comment. But I did not want to meditate very long on the inwardness of this peculiar episode.

"Yes, Natalia Victorovna, he shall need somebody when they dismiss him, on crutches and stone deaf from the hospital. But I do not think that when he rushed like an escaped madman into the grounds of the Château Borel it was to seek the help of that good Tekla."

"No," said Natalia, stopping short before me, "perhaps not." She sat down and leaned her head on her hand thoughtfully. The silence lasted for several minutes. During that time I remembered the evening of his atrocious confession—the plaint she seemed to have hardly enough life left in her to utter, "It is impossible to be more unhappy. . . ." The recollection would have given me a shudder if I had not been lost in wonder at her force and her tranquillity. There was no longer any Natalia Haldin, because she had completely ceased to think of herself. It was a great victory, a characteristically Russian exploit in self-suppression.

She recalled me to myself by getting up suddenly like a person who has come to a decision. She walked to the writing-table, now stripped of all the small objects associated with her by daily use— a mere piece of dead furniture; but it contained something living, still, since she took from a recess a flat parcel which she brought to me.

"It's a book," she said rather abruptly. "It was sent to me wrapped up in my veil. I told you nothing at the time, but now I've decided to leave it with you. I have the right to do that. It was sent to me. It is mine. You may preserve it, or destroy it after you have read it. And while you read it, please remember that I *was* defenceless. And that he . . ."

"Defenceless!" I repeated, surprised, looking hard at her.

"You'll find the very word written there," she whispered. "Well, it's true! I *was* defenceless—but perhaps you were able to see that for yourself." Her face coloured, then went deadly pale. "In justice to the man, I want you to remember that I was. Oh, I was, I was!"

I rose, a little shakily.

"I am not likely to forget anything you say at this our last parting."

Her hand fell into mine.

"It's difficult to believe that it must be good-bye with us."

She returned my pressure and our hands separated.

"Yes. I am leaving here to-morrow. My eyes are open at last and my hands are free now. As for the rest—which of us can fail to hear the stifled cry of our great distress? It may be nothing to the world."

"The world is more conscious of your discordant voices," I said. "It is the way of the world."

"Yes." She bowed her head in assent, and hesitated for a moment. "I must own to you that I shall never give up looking forward to the day when all discord shall be silenced. Try to imagine its dawn! The tempest of blows and of execrations is over; all is still; the new sun is rising, and the weary men united at last, taking count in their conscience of the ended contest, feel saddened by their victory, because so many ideas have perished for the triumph of one, so many beliefs have abandoned them without support. They feel alone on the earth and gather close together. Yes, there must be many bitter hours! But at last the anguish of hearts shall be extinguished in love."

And on this last word of her wisdom, a word so sweet, so bitter, so cruel sometimes, I said good-bye to Natalia Haldin. It is hard to think I shall never look any more into the trustful eyes of that girl—wedded to an invincible belief in the advent of loving concord springing like a heavenly flower from the soil of men's earth, soaked in blood, torn by struggles, watered with tears.

★★★★★

It must be understood that at that time I didn't know anything of Mr. Razumov's confession to the assembled revolutionists. Natalia Haldin might have guessed what was the "one thing more" which remained for him to do; but this my Western eyes had failed to see.

Tekla, the ex-lady companion of Madame de S——, haunted his bedside at the hospital. We met once or twice at the door of that establishment, but on these occasions she was not communicative. She gave me news of Mr. Razumov as concisely as possible. He was making a slow recovery, but would remain a hopeless cripple all his life. Personally, I never went near him: I never saw him again, after the awful evening when I stood by, a watchful but ignored spectator of his scene with Miss Haldin. He was in due course discharged from the hospital, and his "relative"— so I was told—had carried him off somewhere.

My information was completed nearly two years later. The opportunity, certainly, was not of my seeking; it was quite accidentally that I met a much-trusted woman revolutionist at the house of a distinguished Russian gentleman of liberal convictions, who came to live in Geneva for a time.

He was a quite different sort of celebrity from Peter Ivanovitch—a dark-haired man with kind eyes, high-shouldered, courteous, and with something hushed and circumspect in his manner. He approached me, choosing the moment when there was no one near, followed by a grey-haired, alert lady in a crimson blouse.

"Our Sophia Antonovna wishes to be made known to you," he addressed me, in his guarded voice. "And so I leave you two to have a talk together."

"I would never have intruded myself upon your notice," the grey-haired lady began at once, "if I had not been charged with a message for you."

It was a message of a few friendly words from Natalia Haldin. Sophia Antonovna had just returned from a secret excursion into Russia, and had seen Miss Haldin. She lived in a town "in the centre," sharing her compassionate labours between the horrors of overcrowded jails, and the heartrending misery of bereaved homes. She did not spare herself in good service, Sophia Antonovna assured me.

"She has a faithful soul, an undaunted spirit and an indefatigable body," the woman revolutionist summed it all up, with a touch of enthusiasm.

A conversation thus engaged was not likely to drop from want of interest on my side. We went to sit apart in a corner where no one interrupted us. In the course of our talk about Miss Haldin, Sophia Antonovna remarked suddenly—

"I suppose you remember seeing me before? That evening when Natalia came to ask Peter Ivanovitch for the address of a certain Razumov, that young man who . . ."

"I remember perfectly," I said. When Sophia Antonovna learned that I had in my possession that young man's journal given me by Miss Haldin she became intensely interested. She did not conceal her curiosity to see the document.

I offered to show it to her, and she at once volunteered to call on me next day for that purpose.

She turned over the pages greedily for an hour or more, and then handed me the book with a faint sigh. While moving about

Russia, she had seen Razumov too. He lived, not "in the centre," but "in the south." She described to me a little two-roomed wooden house, in the suburb of some very small town, hiding within the high plank-fence of a yard overgrown with nettles. He was crippled, ill, getting weaker every day, and Tekla the Samaritan tended him unweariedly with the pure joy of unselfish devotion. There was nothing in that task to become disillusioned about.

I did not hide from Sophia Antonovna my surprise that she should have visited Mr. Razumov. I did not even understand the motive. But she informed me that she was not the only one.

"Some of *us* always go to see him when passing through. He is intelligent. He has ideas. . . . He talks well, too."

Presently I heard for the first time of Razumov's public confession in Laspara's house. Sophia Antonovna gave me a detailed relation of what had occurred there. Razumov himself had told her all about it, most minutely.

Then, looking hard at me with her brilliant black eyes—

"There are evil moments in every life. A false suggestion enters one's brain, and then fear is born—fear of oneself, fear for oneself. Or else a false courage—who knows? Well, call it what you like; but tell me, how many of them would deliver themselves up deliberately to perdition (as he himself says in that book) rather than go on living, secretly debased in their own eyes? How many? . . . And please mark this—he was safe when he did it. It was just when he believed himself safe and more—infinitely more—when the possibility of being loved by that admirable girl first dawned upon him, that he discovered that his bitterest railings, the worst wickedness, the devil work of his hate and pride, could never cover up the ignominy of the existence before him. There's character in such a discovery."

I accepted her conclusion in silence. Who would care to question the grounds of forgiveness or compassion? However, it appeared later on that there was some compunction, too, in the charity extended by the revolutionary world to Razumov the betrayer. Sophia Antonovna continued uneasily—

"And then, you know, he was the victim of an outrage. It was not authorized. Nothing was decided as to what was to be done with him. He had confessed voluntarily. And that Nikita who burst the drums of his ears purposely, out on the landing, you know, as if carried away by indignation—well, he has turned out to be a scoundrel of the worst kind—a traitor himself, a betrayer—a spy![1] Razumov told me he had charged him with it by a sort of inspiration . . ."

"I had a glimpse of that brute," I said. "How any of you could have been deceived for half a day passes my comprehension!"

She interrupted me.

"There! There! Don't talk of it. The first time I saw him, I, too, was appalled. They cried me down. We were always telling each other, 'Oh! you mustn't mind his appearance.' And then he was always ready to kill. There was no doubt of it. He killed—yes! in both camps. The fiend . . ."

Then Sophia Antonovna, after mastering the angry trembling of her lips, told me a very queer tale. It went that Councillor Mikulin, travelling in Germany (shortly after Razumov's disappearance from Geneva), happened to meet Peter Ivanovitch in a railway carriage. Being alone in the compartment, these two talked together half the night, and it was then that Mikulin the Police Chief gave a hint to the Arch-Revolutionist as to the true character of the arch-slayer of gendarmes. It looks as though Mikulin had wanted to get rid of that particular agent of his own! He might have grown tired of him, or frightened of him. It must also be said that Mikulin had inherited the sinister Nikita from his predecessor in office.

And this story, too, I received without comment in my character of a mute witness of things Russian, unrolling their Eastern logic under my Western eyes. But I permitted myself a question—

"Tell me, please, Sophia Antonovna, did Madame de S—— leave all her fortune to Peter Ivanovitch?"

"Not a bit of it." The woman revolutionist shrugged her shoulders in disgust. "She died without making a will. A lot of nephews and nieces came down from St. Petersburg, like a flock of vultures, and fought for her money amongst themselves. All beastly Kammerherrs and Maids of Honour[2]—abominable court flunkeys. Tfui!"

"One does not hear much of Peter Ivanovitch now," I remarked, after a pause.

"Peter Ivanovitch," said Sophia Antonovna gravely, "has united himself to a peasant girl."

---

1 Nikita's model Azef was also a double agent who worked for both the Russian secret police organization Okhrana (hired by Aleksei Aleksandrovich Lopukhin) and for the Socialist-Revolutionary Party.

2 Unmarried females of the nobility who were attendants to the royal family.

I was truly astonished.

"What! On the Riviera?"

"What nonsense! Of course not."

Sophia Antonovna's tone was slightly tart.

"Is he, then, living actually in Russia? It's a tremendous risk—isn't it?" I cried. "And all for the sake of a peasant girl. Don't you think it's very wrong of him?"

Sophia Antonovna preserved a mysterious silence for a while, then made a statement.

"He just simply adores her."

"Does he? Well, then, I hope that she won't hesitate to beat him."

Sophia Antonovna got up and wished me good-bye, as though she had not heard a word of my impious hope; but, in the very doorway, where I attended her, she turned round for an instant, and declared in a firm voice—

"Peter Ivanovitch is an inspired man."

# Appendix A: Selected Letters

[This appendix contains letters by Conrad regarding the writing of *Under Western Eyes*, taken from his *Collected Letters*.[1] With the exception of the last letter reprinted here, they cover the four-year period 1908-11, from the novel's earliest conception through Conrad's struggles in writing it to his emotional collapse after its completion. These letters provide a unique window on Conrad's creative process.]

## 1. To John Galsworthy[2]

[letterhead: Someries[3]]
6th Jan of the New Year 1908

Dearest Jack

[I am] writing now a story the title of which is *Razumov*. Isn't it expressive. I think that I am trying to capture the very soul of things Russian—Cosas de Russia [*sic*].[4] It is not an easy work but it may be rather good when it's done. It may also be worth a hundred £ if the good Pinker[5] flies round with it actively enough to become crimson . . . But there's no heart in my jokes. Listen to the theme: The Student Razumov (a natural son of a Prince K——) gives up secretly to the police his fellow Student Haldin who seeks refuge in his rooms after com[m]itting a political crime (supposed to be the murder of de Plehve). First movement in S$^t$ Petersburg. (Haldin is hanged of course).

2$^d$ in Geneva: The Student Razumov meeting abroad the mother and sister of Haldin falls in love with that last, marries her and after a time confesses to her the part he played in the arrest and death of her brother.

The psychological developments leading to Razumov's betrayal of Haldin, to his confession of the fact to his wife and to the death of

---

1  *The Collected Letters of Joseph Conrad*, ed. Laurence Davies et al., 9 vols. Cambridge: Cambridge UP, 1983-2008.

2  John Galsworthy, English novelist, playwright, and winner of the Nobel Prize for literature in 1932. One of Conrad's first literary acquaintances, Galsworthy was a close friend from the time they met in 1893, while Conrad was first mate aboard the *Torrens*, until Conrad's death in 1924.

3  Someries was the Conrads' house in the town of Bedford in Bedfordshire in southeastern England. They lived there from September 1907 to March 1909.

4  Things of Russia (Spanish).

5  James B. Pinker, Conrad's literary agent and long-time friend and supporter.

these people (brought about mainly by the resemblance of their child to the late Haldin) form the real subject of the story.

And perhaps no magazine will touch it. B'wood[1] since the old man[2] has retired do not care much to have my work. I think of trying the Fort[y].[3] Ah my dear You don't know what an inspiration-killing anxiety it is to think:—is it saleable? There's nothing more cruel than to be caught between one's impulse, one's art and that question which for me simply is a question of life and death. There are moments when the unholy fear sweeps my head clean of every thought. It is agonizing— no less. And—you know—that pressure grows from day to day instead of getting less.

But I had to write it. I had to get away from *Chance*[4] with which I was making no serious progress....

> Yours ever
> J Conrad.

## 2. To J.B. Pinker

> [letterhead: Someries]
> Wednesday. 6pm. 7 Jan. 08

My dear Pinker.

I have just sent off 8 or 10 pp of Razumov. I have more in hand and shall start writing again about 9 o'clock till one in the morning. I am anxious to throw that story off my chest.

You may let any Editor know that C. would shorten it (in reason) for serial publication. But I think that L.W. [*sic*] Courtney[5] might be approached on the ground of the story's essential seriousness—a contribution to and a reading of the Russian character. It is just the fiction for a review of the Fort[y]'s standing. In the States I've no doubt it will

---

1 *Blackwood's Edinburgh Magazine*, an important and conservative magazine of long standing. It was founded in 1817 by William Blackwood (1776-1834) and ran until 1980.

2 William Blackwood (1836-1912), who published in serial form a number of Conrad's important works such as "Youth" (1898), *Heart of Darkness* (1899), and *Lord Jim* (1899-1900).

3 *The Fortnightly Review*.

4 In 1898 Conrad first mentioned the idea for what appears to have become *Chance*, but he did not begin writing it until 1905 and did not complete it until 1912.

5 William Leonard Courtney (1850-1928), author and editor of *The Fortnightly Review*.

be appreciated and shall find a home easily. But perhaps You have other views for England.

Here is given the very essence of things Russian. Not the mere outward manners and customs but the Russian feeling and thought. You may safely say that. And, I think, the story is effective. It is also characteristic of the present time. Nothing of the sort had been done in English. The subject has long haunted me. Now it must come out....

Yours always<br>J Conrad.

### 3. To John Galsworthy

Someries.<br>30 Nov '08

Dearest Jack.

I am ever so glad you find Raz interesting. Your criticism as to the $II^d$ part is the very echo of my own worrying thought. And yet . . .

You see, it is all part of the general crookedness of my existence. You will not be surprised to hear that the doing of the $I^{st}$ part has been very difficult. What you see is the residue of very many pages now destroyed, but by no means wasted from an unmaterial point of view. But good work takes time; to invent an action, a march for the story which could have dispensed with part $II^d$ as it stands was a matter of meditation, of trying and re-trying for goodness knows how long. This I could not afford to do. I went on the obvious lines and on these lines I developed my narrative to give it some sort of verisimilitude. In other words I offered to sell my soul for half a crown—and now I have neither the soul nor the coin—for the novel is not finished yet. A fool's bargain—no great matter when one is young but at my age such passages embitter and discour[a]ge one beyond expression. I have no heart to think of compressing anything, for I have no illusion as to the quality of the stuff. The thing is "bad-in-itself". It should not be there at all....

Ever yours<br>J Conrad.

### 4. To Stephen Reynolds[1]

[Someries]
18 Dec 1908

My dear Stephen.

... Raz. is not finished yet. I can't turn out a novel with the polish on in eleven months—you know. But the end is just peeping above the horizon and the moral support of your superb assurance would come handy. NB[2] That does *not* mean that I want to read you fragments of the last part. Oh dear no! I would see you died [*sic*] first. I am generally ashamed rather of my work now. A lovely state of mind to be in—and helpful—and inspiring ...

Yours
J Conrad.

### 5. To Perceval Gibbon[3]

[Aldington[4]]
Saturday [11 or 18 September? 1909]

Dear Perceval.

Your remark that "surely there must be a time of the day when I don't write Razumov" has cut me to the quick. You must accustom yourself to show the most extended mercy to my sins as correspondent. There is no moment in the day when I don't hate the sight of pen and ink. And this hate at times overcomes all my other more worthy feelings such as those of love, friendship[,] politeness and even decency.

Their Serene Excellencies our Wives[5] being in active correspondence I contented myself by participating in spirit, with the alternatives of hope and fear borne with becoming stoicism. Their SS. EE's having failed in bringing about a meeting I disguised my sorrow in silence. I wish you distinc[t]ly to understand that the silence was mournful. But the swearing directed at old Raz was vivid as the lightning of hurricanes. Enough! ...

Ever yours
J. Conrad

---

1   Stephen Reynolds (1881-1919), author and social critic.
2   Short for *nota bene* or mark well (Latin).
3   Reginald Perceval Gibbon, journalist and author.
4   A village in the Ashford district of the county of Kent in southeastern England. The Conrads moved there in March 1909.
5   Maisie (Daniels) Gibbon (b. 1883) and Jessie (George) Conrad.

## 6. To Perceval Gibbon

[Aldington]
19 Dec. [1909]

Dear Gibbon,
[...] And I get yesterday a letter from P. [Pinker] telling me he hopes to have manuscript sent regularly. That I've given him nothing to sell for two years and threatening to stop short if he don't [*sic*] get end of R. in a fortnight. If he does that I shall fling the MS of Raz in the fire—and see how he likes that. He positively writes as if [I] had done nothing. You imagine how charming it is to be following the psychology of M$^r$ Razumov under these conditions. It's like working in hell. Love to you all.

Yours
J Conrad.

## 7. To John Galsworthy

[letterhead: Aldington]
22 Dec 1909

Dearest Jack
...The above, I said, were the facts on my side [figures regarding the amount of manuscript Conrad had sent to Pinker]. *Razv* wanted 15—20 thou. [words] more and was going to get that as fast as I could write them. He had the story.[1] Let him sell it. I wrote it on purpose to ease the strain.

And at last I asked him whether he really, *with the story in his possession* meant to slam the door on me (for the sake of an odd week or two), now when I was nearly through! I wanted to know, whether his letter foreshadowed *that*. Let him say yes or no.

I have been nearly out of my mind ever since. If he says yes, that was what he meant I wonder if I can restrain myself from throwing the MS in the fire. It's outrageous. Does he think I am the sort of man who wouldn't finish the story in a week if he could? Do you? Why? For what reason. Is it my habit to lie about drunk for days instead of working? I reckon he knows well enough I don't. It's a contemptuous playing with my worry. If he had said—No. I will stick to the lot—I wouldn't have been hurt. But this gratuit[o]us ignoring of my sincer-

---

1 Almost certainly a reference to Conrad's short story "The Secret Sharer," which he wrote during the latter stages of his work on *Under Western Eyes*.

ity in spirit and also in fact is almost more than I can bear. I who can hardly bear to look at the kids, who without You could not have the boy[1] at school[2] even—I wouldn't finish the book in a week if I could—unless a bribe of six pounds is dangled before me!—I sit 12 hours at the table, sleep six, and worry the rest of [the] time, feeling the age creeping on and looking at those I love. For two years I havent [*sic*] seen a picture heard a note of music, hadn't a moment of ease in human intercourse—not really.—And he talks of regular supplies of manuscript to a man who in these conditions (taking all the time together ill or well) sends him MS at the rate of 7.600 words a month; and he actually writes as if I were a swindler from whom nothing can be got unless he's pinched. Is it a swindle to write a long novel? He had better get some of his clerks to write stuff which he can sell. But 16 months for a long novel nearly done and some 57000 words of other work is not so bad—even for a man with his mind at ease, with his spirits kept up by prosperity, with his inspiration buoyed by hope. There's nothing of that for me! I don't complain dear Jack. I only state it as an argument—for when people appraise me later on with severity I wish you to be able to say:—I knew him—he was not so bad. By Jove all the moral tortures are not in prison-life. I assure you I feel sometimes as if I could drop everything and beat at the door—you understand. The thing is that, so far, I don't. But I feel now that if he stops the miserable pound a day I must throw the MS in the fire.—And indeed why not. It's nothing—it's a mere swindle—it's no good to me. The man would be a fool because that book finished would pay full half I think of my indebt[ed]ness to him. Next year even if the health is only so-so a fourth more would be paid off, after providing that pound a day and something besides, for me. But all this is vain talk. I am at the present moment unable to write a line. One must secure a certain detachment which is beyond me. I can hardly sit still. If it wasn't for dear Jess—well I don't know.

Ever yours
J Conrad.

## 8. To J.B. Pinker

[Aldington]
[12 January 1910]

My dear Pinker.

...What do you think of the tittle [*sic*] to give the book. Would *Under Western Eyes* do at all—or something of the kind? A title pertains to the

1  Conrad's son Borys (1898-1978).
2  Galsworthy often lent Conrad money to ease his financial strains.

publishing part of the business. I would not venture to ask your advice if I did not feel that strongly.

Yours sincerely<br>J. Conrad.

## 9. To John Galsworthy

[Aldington]<br>17 May. '10

Dearest Jack

I finished the revise of Raz. on the night of Wednesday last—say a week ago. For the next 24 hours I lay supine but not so broken up as I feared. Then I had to write a letter to good Robert[1]—as a matter of fact I had to write two letters. The second went off yesterday. Between whiles I went to bed and gasped. I did not even attempt to write to you. I thought that Garnett would let you know that the book was out of my hands at last, and that the stage of negociation [*sic*] has been reached. He has been most friendly and wonderfully kind, volunteering to read over and correct the clean final copy. With three superimposed revisions there were a good many phrases without grammar and even without sense to be found in the rough typed copy. And I dreaded the task of wading through all that shallow, sticky stuff again.

I am but a wretched convalescent as yet, after all. Two painful ankles and one painful wrist (the left luckily) keep me in a state of uneasy irritation. I just can hobble along for a few yards. My voice too has not come back properly. At times I am hardly audible. But that don't matter much except that Jackolo[2] imitates my extinct tones, while scolding his favourite Teddy-bear, to perfection.... While here he [Borys] gave me much of his time, very tactful with his fractious father and really of great assistance in the arranging of MS. He put in order for me 600 pp all unnumbered and considerably shuffled working very methodically and with a quiet perseverance for an hour or so every morning. With one hand only one cannot do that sort of thing easily (and in bed at that) so I was really glad to have him to help. Going off at the railway station he said to Jessie "I really think I've done some

---

1 Robert Singleton Garnett (1866-1932), a lawyer and friend of Conrad who handled some of his literary affairs during an estrangement between Conrad and Pinker.

2 Conrad's second son, John (1906-82), named after John Galsworthy.

good to Dada." He certainly comforted me not a little. He seemed well and looked strong enough....

Yours ever

J. Conrad.

## 10. To John Galsworthy

[letterhead: Capel House[1]]

15 Oct. 1911

My dearest Jack.

Yes. There is no arguing against what you say. One could attempt to explain certain things but it would be an unprofitable occupation.

You know there are about 30000 words more than the printed text. Revising while ill in bed I am afraid I have struck out whole pages recklessly. The other day I looked at the MS: 1357 pp averaging about 120 words per page. There are passages which should have remained. I wasn't in a fit state to judge them. Well—it's done now and let the critics make what they can of it. I have ordered no press-cuttings, not because I am afraid of them but that I am really indifferent to what may be said—or left unsaid....

Yours ever

J. Conrad.

## 11. To Edward Garnett[2]

[letterhead: Capel House]

20 Oct 1911.

My dear Edward.

I don't understand your picturesque allusions to packing spinach into the saucepan and the bell broth that's supposed to be the result of that culinary operation. There's just about as much or as little *hatred* in this book as in the Outcast of the Islands[3] for instance. Subjects lay

---

1 The Conrads' house in Orlestone, a small hamlet in the Ashford district of Kent. They lived there from June 1910 to March 1919.

2 Edward Garnett (1868-1937), author, critic, and brother of Robert Singleton Garnett. He was one of the reviewers for Conrad's first manuscript, *Almayer's Folly* (1895), and the two became friends thereafter. Garnett was a particularly good critic of Conrad's work and provided much sound literary advice.

3 Conrad's second novel, published in 1896. Garnett served as an important sounding board while it was being written and, according to Conrad, made the initial suggestion that he write the novel.

[*sic*] about for anybody to pick-up. I have picked up this one. And that's all there is to it. I don't expect you will believe me. You are so russianised my dear that you don't know the truth when you see it— unless it smells of cabbage-soup when it at once secures your profoundest respect. I suppose one must make allowances for your position of Russian Embassador [*sic*] to the Republic of Letters. Official pronouncements ought to be taken with a grain of salt and that is how I shall take your article in the Nation[1] which I hope to see to morrow evening when the carrier comes back from Ashford.[2] But it is hard after lavishing a "wealth of tenderness" on Tekla and Sophia, to be charged with the rather low trick of putting one's hate into a novel. If You seriously think that I have done that then my dear fellow let me tell you that you don't know what the accent of hate is. Is it possible that You haven't seen that in this book I am concerned with nothing but ideas, to the exclusion of everything else, with no arrière pensée[3] of any kind. Or are you like the Italians (and most women) incapable of conceiving that anybody ever should speak with perfect detachment, without some subtle hidden purpose, for the sake of what is said, with no desire of gratifying some small personal spite—or vanity.

As to discussing Russia it's the most chimeric of enterprises since it is there for anyone to look at. "La Russie c'est le néant"[4] Prince Bismarck[5] said in 1864—and forthwith proceeded to prove it by 20 years of the most contemptuous policy towards that "Great Power." C'est le néant. Anybody with eyes can see it.

And anyhow if hatred there were it would be too big a thing to be put into a 6/-[6] novel. This too might have occurred to you, if you had condescended to look beyond the literary horizon where all things sacred and profane are turned into copy.

Yours ever

J. Conrad.

---

1  A reference to Garnett's unsigned review of *Under Western Eyes* that appeared in *The Nation* on 21 October 1911. See Appendix B2.

2  A town in Kent not far from Capel House.

3  Literally, backward thought (French), but actually meaning ulterior motive.

4  Russia is a nothingness (French). This phrase becomes a touchstone in Conrad's essay "Autocracy and War" (1905); see Appendix F, 380, 381, 384, 385. The anecdote seems to be apocryphal.

5  Otto von Bismarck (Otto Eduard Leopold von Bismarck-Schönhausen, 1815-98), later Chancellor of Germany. In 1864, he was Minister-President and Foreign Minister of the German Kingdom of Prussia. Throughout his political career, he attempted to manipulate Russia.

6  Six shillings.

## 12. To Olivia Rayne Garnett[1]

[letterhead: Capel House]
20 Oct 1911

Dear Miss Garnett

You are a good critic. That girl [Natalia Haldin] does not move. No excuse can be offered for such a defect but there is an explanation. I wanted a pivot for the action to turn on. She had to be the pivot. And I had to be very careful because if I had allowed myself to make more of her she would have killed the artistic purpose of the book: the development of a single mood. It isn't that I was afraid or ignorant of her possibilities. Indeed they were very tempting. But it had to be a performance on one string. It had to be. You may think such self-imposed limitation a very stupid thing. But something of the kind must be done or else novel-writing becomes a mere debauch of the imagination. No doubt if I had taken another line the book would have been richer. But what I aimed at this time was an effect of virtuosity before anything else—and even to the exclusion of everything else. Still I need not have made Miss Haldin a mere peg as I am sorry to admit she is. Result of over caution.

Your kind appreciation of the book gives me great pleasure and I am glad you think it is true—as [far as it?] goes. I am quite aware it does not go very far. But the fact is that I know extremely little of Russians. Practically nothing. In Poland we have nothing to do with them. One knows they are there. And that's disagreeable enough. In exile[2] the contact is even slighter if possible if more unavoidable. I crossed the Russian frontier at the age of ten.[3] Not having been to school then I never knew Russian. I could not tell a Little Russian from a Great Russian[4] to save my life. In the book as you must have seen I am exclusively concerned with ideas....

Yours faithfully
J. Conrad.

---

1 Olivia Rayne Garnett (1871-1957), sister of Edward Garnett and Robert Singleton Garnett. Like Edward and his wife Constance (Black) Garnett (1868-1937), she was very much interested in Russia and things Russian.

2 A reference to his time in Russia (1862-68) when he accompanied his father in exile.

3 Conrad and his father were allowed to return to Poland in 1868; they settled in Kraków (Cracow) in the Austrian-controlled part of Poland.

4 Little Russia was another term for Ukraine; Great Russia was used for Russia proper.

## 13. To Macdonald Hastings[1]

[Capel House]
24 Dec 1916.

My dear Hastings

I send you this volume with my best wishes of all attainable prosperity for you and all yours.

To convey these wishes within these covers is the primary purpose. Also to show my regard for the man and his mind, by sending him what, without doubt, is the most deeply meditated novel that came from under my pen. And lastly because I really want You to read it—some day—at leisure—with detachment and with no idea at the back of your head that you must write a complimentary letter to the author. For I feel somehow that between you and me there's no need for literary civilities. We have rubbed shoulders in actual work[2]—and that does away with many conventions.

These pages represent 2 years of constant artistic preoccupation, much mental effort and about 18 months of actual writing work. When the book appeared it was all but a black frost.[3] But of late I have been seeing[?] warm[?] allusions to it as "wonderful."

Which shows that wonders will never cease. My artistic aim was to put as much dramatic spirit into the form of a novel as was possible without apparently departing from the form. It is the dramatisation of the inner feelings—and also of ideas, brought out in scene and dialogue as near as possible without the novel ceasing to be a novel and becoming a hybrid and unsatisfactory freak of presentation. I tried to keep close to scenic effects all the time. And it is in order to keep always before myself the effect of a "performance" that I invented the old teacher of languages. If you abstract the pages "off his own bat" (not perhaps 10 altogether) and the pp following the Razumov-Miss Haldin scene which ends the scenic drama I think You will find that I have come near my purpose; and the feat may interest You—in the watching of it.

Yours,
J Conrad.

---

1 Basil Macdonald Hastings (1881-1928), journalist, drama critic, and playwright.

2 Hastings adapted Conrad's novel *Victory* (1915) for the stage; it was first performed in March 1919.

3 An idiomatic translation of *un four noir* (French), literally "a cold oven," in other words, a frosty reception. Conrad probably refers to the novel's modest sales rather than its critical reception, which was generally quite warm.

# Appendix B: Contemporary Reviews

[As was typical for Conrad's novels, *Under Western Eyes* received generally favorable reviews, although the contemporary reviewers sometimes misunderstood Conrad's works. A notable exception was Edward Garnett, whose review (see Appendix B2) in *The Nation* was one of the most insightful early commentaries on the novel. While the reviews included here represent only a fraction of the many that appeared, they give a general idea of how the novel was perceived at the time.]

## 1. Anonymous, "Betrayal," *The Pall Mall Gazette* (11 October 1911): 5

Keen and merciless in exposure and meticulously searching in analysis, "Under Western Eyes" is a psychologic study of remarkable penetration, and, as a novel, is entitled to rank with the best work that Mr. Joseph Conrad has given us. We are revolted by Razumoff's betrayal of his fellow-student (though Haldin's crime merited the swift and degrading execution that was its punishment), for Haldin had sought refuge in Razumoff's rooms and had confessed to his crime under the conviction that his host was, like himself, a Nihilist. But by subtle strokes of art our sympathy—that is, at least, "a sympathy of comprehension," to use De Quincey's striking phrase as applied to "Macbeth"[1]—and perhaps something more, is enlisted with the betrayer. Except that by a quite arbitrary, and, it must be added, inartistic skipping of certain stages of his spiritual development and an equally arbitrary return to them, the narrative does not follow the sequence of events, we trace the various phases of his soul's disturbance from mere rage at being suspected by the police, through a tardy ever-growing remorse, till, purified by love, he repents, and with high courage makes full confession to an inner circle of conspirators to suffer at their cruel hands a punishment, horrible, brutal, and infinitely worse than death.

The book startles one by its amazing truth and by the intimate knowledge of the human heart that it reveals in its varied and masterly characterisation. Although, too, he still confuses the preterite[2] with the

---

1 Thomas de Quincey (1785-1859), English author. The reviewer is quoting from de Quincey's famous essay about Shakespeare's *Macbeth*, "On the Knocking at the Gate in *Macbeth*" (355), which appeared in the *London Magazine*, 8 (October 1823): 353-56.

2 Preterite tense, a tense indicating a past action or past state of being.

perfect and often uses the wrong sign of the future, Mr. Conrad's remarkable gifts as a writer of nervous and polished prose are as noteworthy here as always. Quite a masterpiece of writing, for instance, amid much that is excellent is the account of a convict's escape in Siberia. The muffled clanking of his chains, a sound he deadened with strips torn from his clothing lest it should betray his presence, is almost as unforgettable as the tapping of blind Pew's stick.[1]

## 2. [Edward Garnett], "Mr. Conrad's New Novel," *The Nation* (21 October 1911): 140-42[2]

The title of Mr. Conrad's novel is an artful one, presenting an apologia within a definition. "I cannot pretend to any complete understanding of these people and their baffling actions," the anonymous English chronicler, "a teacher of languages," seems to say to us. "I can only narrate what happened, following Mr. Razumov's diary, and my experiences with the Russian exiles in Geneva." Of course, this anonymous chronicler is merely a blank screen on which Mr. Conrad projects a series of psychological analyses of his people's deeds, moods, and temperaments. But the effect of his evasive, artistic method is artful in the extreme, reminding us of those ingenious puzzles which fall suddenly into place with a click. It is only when we look back that we recognise what a perfect whole has been framed of these imperfect parts. If to Western eyes his material seems to be eked out here and there with guess-work, to be fragmentary and puzzling, the artist has wrought it into meaning[ful] curves and a highly original pattern....

It is in these scenes of Razumov's life and moral struggles in Geneva that the irony of Mr. Conrad's method gathers weight and velocity like a wheel set rolling down-hill. In Parts I. and II. we see him skilfully arranging his chess board, in Part III. the drama of Razumov's "moral revolt" coalesces with a corrosively bitter etching of types of the revolutionary party, such as the famous Feminist, Peter Ivanovitch, his companion, Madame de S——, Laspara, the philosophic anarchist, the sinister Nikita, slayer of gendarmes and spies, but himself another [Evno] Azev, and so on. This merciless picture, which is as formidable in its indictment of the revolutionists's claims as the figures of Prince K——, General T——, and Councillor Mikulin are destructive of the Autocracy's pretensions, would seem vindictive art had not the author introduced into the group the admirable figure of

---

1  A reference to a character in the novel *Treasure Island* (1883) by Robert Louis Stevenson (1850-94), Scottish novelist, poet, and travel writer.

2  For a response to a letter that Garnett wrote to Conrad regarding the novel, see Appendix A11.

Sophia Antonovna, a woman Nihilist of the old school, who recalls the heroines of the early 'eighties. Razumov, in his unwilling intercourse with these chiefs of the circle, is ravaged by a whirling anxiety of fear, contempt, hatred, malice, and self-loathing. It is a psychological study of cynical pride sustaining the hollowness of self-disillusionment, and throwing up volcanic, fresh defensive waves of lava, that is offered us in Razumov's portrait. The study is very special, and to the English reader, who knows nought of Dostoievsky, and is touchingly ignorant of his own soul's dark places, may seem a nightmare of hallucinations, but in fact, within its narrow lines, it is illuminating in its pathological truth. The artistic intensity of the novel lies, however, less in the remarkable drawing of characteristic Russian types than in the atmospheric effect of the dark national background. With almost uncanny adroitness, Mr. Conrad has both relieved and increased the blackness of his picture by the rare, precious figure of Natalia Haldin. How he has managed to concentrate in a few "impressions," conversations, and confidences the essence, profoundly spiritual, of this exquisite type of Russian womanhood, is worth the closest examination; but he has attained a degree of fineness that is extraordinary. The poignancy of the position of the bereaved mother watching for the arrival of her dead son is much heightened by the ironical fact that Haldin, in his last letter to his sister, has commended Razumov as "a man of unstained, lofty, and solitary existence" [146]. In a few passages, such as on page 133 [146], this irony is thrust home too obviously, but the author soon retrieves this false step. In other passages the bitterness and irony of the artistic treatment seem to ignite in a flame to light up the obscurities of this drama of ignoble egotism and impure motives. It is, however, in the suggestiveness of the national background of the illusions of frustrated and blighted generations, stretching ominously like a gloomy curtain behind the figures in the drama, that the author's special triumph lies. Readers of "The Heart of Darkness" [sic] will recall Mr. Conrad's special power of concentrating and blending the tragic essence of human stupidity and human futility with a poetic description of a place and an atmosphere. In "Under Western Eyes" he has concerned himself exclusively with flying aspects of Russia's mournful internal history, which many of her chief writers associate with deep-rooted vices in the national blood. And he has artfully underscored the stigma by skilfully placing his fanatical and impotent circle of "reformers" against the bourgeois placidity and indifference of modern Switzerland. There is something almost vitriolic in Mr. Conrad's scathing rejection of the shibboleths of humanitarian lovers of their kind, and we confess to an enjoyment, positively indefensible, in such perfect little scenes as the one where we see the tortured Mr. Razumov seeking solitude on the little islet, "a perfection of puerile neatness" [258], where stands the exiled effigy of Jean Jacques Rousseau.

There are pages, indeed not a few, where the talk between the characters seems a little strained, or obviously arranged for the particular purpose of the drama. But such flaws escape clean from the memory when we reach the last chapter of Razumov's confession of his crime to Miss Haldin, and, later, to the circle of exiles. The sinister force of the last twenty pages has the effect of a thunderbolt cleaving the brooding, sultry air. Here Mr. Conrad is at his best, and many of his pages may be placed by the side of notable passages in Turgenev and Dostoievsky, to both of which great masters Mr. Conrad bears affinities and owes a debt.

### 3. Anonymous, "New Novels," *The Athenæum* (21 October 1911): 483-84

Mr. Conrad reveals once again in his latest book the remarkable psychological subtlety which has always characterized his work. His synthesis of a mood, of a frame of mind, of emotional conditions, usually on the side of tragedy, is something quite by itself in English fiction. His novels virtually consist of these various syntheses. Take, for example, "Lord Jim," "The Nigger of the Narcissus," "The Heart of Darkness," [*sic*] even his earliest work "Almayer's Folly," and this his latest. Here he is building up about a case of almost venial treachery all through the three hundred odd pages. Razumov betrayed to the Russian authorities, on an impulse which was not altogether fear, a man who had trusted him under a misapprehension as to his political views. The man was hanged, and thenceforward Razumov becomes the theatre of a tragedy in remorse. It is a mordant[1] piece of work, full of that atmosphere which the author alone controls. It is very un-English work—indeed, the book reads like a translation from some other tongue, presumably Russian. It shows definite affinities with the great Russian novels. As always, Mr. Conrad is reckless in the form of his narrative, which in this instance is at times tiresome. He has some astonishing and vivid pictures of revolutionaries in exile; and one gets a general impression of the ineffectiveness, stupidity, and hopelessness of the agents of the Cause.

---

1  Sharply critical, biting, or caustic.

## 4. Anonymous, "*Under Western Eyes* by Joseph Conrad," *The Academy* (2 December 1911): 699-700

Mr. Conrad is a great stylist. His latest book is written in fresh and vivid language, with powerful vision, and an extraordinary subtlety in the portrayal of emotions. His characters express as clearly as may be the complex problems which rend them, the hopeless cynicism, almost fatalism, with which they wait in tragic and hopeless courage for the end. Even Mr. Conrad cannot fathom the unfathomable, and he does not solve for us the mystery of the Russian character, dogged in conviction, illogical in action, entirely incapable of interregna[1] of curious detachment, and flights in quests of the trivial. With these people of ice and fire an apparently simple proposition is caught up in a cloud of mysticism, expressed in strange vocabularies, and made terrible by imaginings. The national temperament, strange fusing of extreme simplicity and diabolical cunning, sets class against class, sister against brother. Capable of passionate sincerity and intense suffering in the chill isolation in which each one must live a secret life apart, small wonder that existence for them is an undesirable thing, a tragedy of errors....

Motive and action are finely pointed in character-studies of masterly drawing and finish. The psychology is marvellous. One is absorbed in its depths, amazed at its artistry and balance and hurled with dynamic force along the pathways of its reasoning.

## 5. Frederic Taber Cooper, "The Clothing of Thoughts and Some Recent Novels," *The Bookman* (December 1911): 439-45

The foreign strain has always been apparent in Mr. Conrad's writings, but never more so than in his latest volume, *Under Western Eyes*. And this is only natural, because the chief purpose of the book is to interpret one nationality to another, to reveal and explain the spirit of Russia to Western Europe. The theme of the story, nihilism, anarchy, torture, exile, and all the nameless things that Siberia stands for, stamp the volume as distinctly a new departure on the part of Mr. Conrad. But although the theme is new, the method is unmistakably identical with that of *Heart of Darkness*, of *Lord Jim*, of *Children of the Sea*.[2] It does not make the slightest difference whether he is picturing the toss and tumble of ocean waves, the depths and darkness of an African forest, or the unfathomed impulses and treacheries of human

---

1 Periods of freedom from the usual ruling authority.
2 *The Nigger of the "Narcissus"* was first published in America in 1897 under the title *Children of the Sea*.

hearts, there is always in Mr. Conrad's writing that same wonderful ability to make us see, that inimitable suggestiveness that shows us a hundred things behind the specific details that he has chosen to mention. *Under Western Eyes* suggests a comparison with *Falk*,[1] in so far as its central theme is the study of a man haunted by remorse; but here the resemblance stops, because *Falk* dealt with an isolated case, a man whose self-loathing springs from his having been a victim of the blind savagery of nature, while in *Under Western Eyes*, the central figure merely represents an extreme case of the sort of individual injustice constantly begotten by existing conditions in a country seething with revolt.... *Under Western Eyes* will never rank with *Lord Jim* and just one or two other volumes that stand conspicuously as Mr. Conrad's finest achievements. None the less, it is a rather big book and one which no critical estimate of Mr. Conrad's life work could afford to ignore.

### 6. Anonymous, "*Under Western Eyes* by Joseph Conrad," *Catholic World* (January 1912): 535-36

We have here a minute study of Russian character, particularly in relation to political and national aspirations. Mr. Conrad was born in Russian dominions and passed his early childhood in Siberia, and he seems to have imbibed an intimate knowledge of not only the manners and customs but of that indefinable atmosphere which characterizes and differentiates the various races of the world. This, with his great ability for synthetic writing, helps to bring him through a work which would prove an impossibility for most contemporary writers. He bases a well-proportioned book on the frail incident of one student's visit to another.... As in all his other books, Mr. Conrad rejects the conventional construction adopted by novelists. He plans and erects after his own genius which leaves a stamp of originality on every page. His character-sketching is done with a masterly hand. Razumov is one of those creations of imagination which live with a living, palpitating heart. Mr. Conrad is to be congratulated on this fine study of human nature, a study that will rank near that of *Lord Jim*. The peculiar thing about *Under Western Eyes* is the vein of anticipation which runs through it, and which draws on the reader page by page, holding his attention through many a long paragraph of psychological speculation. This sense of anticipation is not obtained by any mere trickery of a literary craftsman, but by the slow, logical development of the story. From

---

1   "Falk," a lengthy story written in 1901 but not published until 1903 (when it was included in the volume *Typhoon and Other Stories*), presumably because it broached the subject of cannibalism. In the story, Falk is haunted by his once having participated in cannibalism in order to survive.

whatever standpoint the book may be viewed it must be described as a remarkable piece of work.

## 7. Anonymous, "Recent Fiction and the Critics," *Current Literature* 52 (February 1912): 236-37

What Henry James[1] accomplishes for the sophisticated people of England, Joseph Conrad accomplishes for the sophisticated folk of Russia: he renders them comprehensible to the great world lying to the West of them. Russia, immense and seething, is still a riddle to most of us. The Russian spirit has to be revealed to Western eyes. This ... is a tremendous undertaking, for we think that we know what Russia needs and why she needs it, and the author has to puncture our self-conceit before he can put true notions in the place of false ones. His latest book [*Under Western Eyes*] is written by Mr. Conrad in the guise of an English professor in Geneva who has had access to the self-revealing diary of the hero, Razumov. It is a study in remorse, and, as such, is appropriately keyed in the poignant pitch of personal anguish which made some of Mr. Conrad's earlier volumes so compelling in their appeal to the emotions.... The characters and their ways of thinking seem compellingly true. Mr. Conrad's father was a Russian [sic] and the son's long residence in England. As well as his artistic self-detachment, renders his Russian characters better understood than are those of writers who are more exclusively Russian. He is often, of course, compared with Tolstoy, Dostoievsky, and Turgeniev. His individuality refracts now and again in a way to warrant the comparison: but Mr. Conrad possesses angles of refraction that are all his own....

---

1 Henry James (1843-1916), American novelist and short story writer.

# Appendix C: Contemporary Accounts of the Assassination of de Pleve

[This appendix contains several accounts of de Pleve's assassination as they appeared in *The Times* in London. As can be seen, a great deal of confusion and fear surrounded the event and its aftermath. Also included is an account from the *Illustrated London News*. In addition to these newspaper accounts are two first-hand accounts, one by an English journalist who happened to be present and the other by one of the organizers of the assassination. Details of the attack differ on many points from those in *Under Western Eyes* because Conrad combined elements from the assassinations of both de Pleve and Aleksandr II, as well as inventing details from his own imagination.]

## 1. Anonymous, "Assassination of M. De Plehve: A Bomb Hurled in St. Petersburg," *The Times* (29 July 1904): 3

St. Petersburg, July 28.

As M. de Plehve, the Minister of the Interior, was driving to the Warsaw railway station[1] here this morning, a bomb was thrown under his carriage, and the Minister was killed.

Noon.

M. de Plehve was on his way to Peterhof[2] about 10 o'clock this morning in order to make his report to the Tsar,[3] when just as his carriage was passing in front of the Hôtel de Varsovie, which is close to the St. Petersburg terminus of the Warsaw Railway, a man suddenly rushed out of the restaurant attached to the hotel and hurled a bomb at the Minister's carriage.

The explosion was terrific. The Minister was killed on the spot, so also was the coachman. The carriage and the horses were shattered to atoms. The body of the Minister was terribly mutilated, the left arm and both legs being torn from it.

The man who threw the bomb was at once, in spite of the confusion that prevailed, surrounded and arrested.

---

1  A main railway station in St. Petersburg, built in 1850.
2  A collection of gardens and palaces built under the direction of Peter the Great; it lies a short distance south and west of St. Petersburg.
3  Nikolai II (Nikolai Aleksandrovich) (1868-1918).

1:40 P.M.

It seems that M. de Plehve's actual destination was the Baltic Railway Station.[1] The Warsaw Station, close to which the crime was perpetrated, lay on his line of route. Some persons who were driving in hired carriages which happened to be passing at the time were injured by the explosion of the bomb.

It now appears to be not altogether certain that the man arrested was the actual criminal.

2:20 P.M.

The man arrested as being the assassin of M. de Plehve is a Jew. He has so far declined to give his name.

2:35 P.M.

The thoroughfare in which the assassination of M. de Plehve took place was the Ismailovsky Prospect, situated about 100 yards from the Warsaw Railway Station. The Tsar is accustomed to receive the various Ministers on certain fixed days—Thursday is the day for the reception of the Minister of the Interior—and, as M. de Plehve always went at the same hour, the assassin was able to time the Minister's arrival almost to the second.

The force of the explosion must have been terrific. All the windows in the vicinity of the scene of the murder are shattered. The roadway is still littered with the *débris* of the carriage. It is reported that several other lives have been lost, and that a woman and a child are among the victims.

The street is thronged with police, mounted and on foot, and all traffic is forbidden in that thoroughfare.

It is no exaggeration to say that the outrage has thrown St. Petersburg into a state of consternation.

2:59 P.M.

Every hour fresh details of the crime which has filled the city with horror come to hand. The act was committed just as the carriage reached the bridge at the Warsaw Station. On this side of the bridge, on the right-hand side, stands the Warsaw Restaurant. Just before M. de Plehve's carriage arrived some bystanders noticed a young man looking out of one of the windows watching the street and all that was passing very attentively. When the Minister's carriage came into sight this man was seen to become more intensely on the alert, and as the equipage came opposite the house he was observed to throw something through the window.

---

1   A main railway station in St. Petersburg, built in 1857.

According to one version the bomb fell under the carriage, according to another it fell into it. In either case the destruction wrought was frightful. The unhappy Minister was blown in pieces. Head, arms and legs were torn from the trunk. As soon as possible the police threw a cloth over the remains. Of the carriage only the hind wheels remain. The rest is reduced to fragments. The concussion produced by the explosion was such that all the windows of the station, which faces the bridge, were smashed.

The assassin was seized as he was attempting to leave the restaurant. On his face were marks of blood. A crowd collected very quickly round the restaurant, but dispersed in haste when the report was spread that the murderer had another bomb upon him. It is said that this was quite true, and that the murderous engine was speedily taken away from him.

7:50 P.M.

The assassin had put on the uniform of an official of the Warsaw Railway in order to avoid suspicion while awaiting the arrival of M. de Plehve's carriage.

The police are maintaining a strict watch over the Hôtel de Varsovie, and none of the staff or of the guests are allowed to leave the premises.

10 P.M.

A requiem service in memory of the late M. de Plehve was held at the Ministry of the Interior this evening. There was a large attendance, which included the members of the Diplomatic Body, numerous high Court dignitaries, State officials, and many leading members of St. Petersburg society.

It now appears that the assassin was himself so severely injured by the explosion of the bomb that his recovery is doubtful. He was rendered insensible, but regained consciousness this evening, and was interrogated.

M. Durnovo,[1] Senator and Assistant to the late M. de Plehve, has been appointed Minister of the Interior *ad interim*.[2]

July 29.

It is believed that M. de Plehve's assassin had several accomplices. He obstinately refuses to divulge his name. The bomb consisted of a small tin box filled with explosives and scraps of metal.

---

1  Pëtr Nikolaevich Durnovo (1845-1915), statesman and security chief; he served as acting Minister of the Interior from 1904 until his dismissal in 1906.

2  Literally, "for the intervening time" (Latin), but here meaning "temporarily."

The number of persons injured is now stated to be 18. Six cases have been substantiated, among the wounded being two officers, a reservist, a woman, and a child. The violence of the explosion was so great that splinters of the carriage were driven into M. de Plehve's body and his head was nearly severed.

The assassin has been removed to the Alexander Hospital.[1] His condition is critical.

As the Minister of Justice was driving to Peterhof at 2 o'clock in the afternoon to report to the Tsar, stones were thrown at him, and the windows of his carriage were broken. The assailants were not discovered.

The crime had been expected for a long time, as it was known that M. de Plehve was a marked man among the revolutionaries. Only a short time ago the police heard of a plot against him and arrested five persons who were found with bombs in their possession on the road to the Winter Palace,[2] where M. de Plehve was driving on the day in question. In the present case it was known that a conspiracy existed, but the Minister of Justice, M. Muravieff,[3] was believed to be the sole object of it.

## 2. Anonymous, "The Murder of M. De Plehve," *The Times* (1 August 1904): 3

St. Petersburg, July 31.

The Tsar and Tsaritsa[4] have sent a telegram to de Plehve's widow[5] expressing their heartfelt sympathy with her in her heavy and unexpected trouble.

The funeral of M. de Plehve took place to-day. The removal of the body was preceded by a religious service at the chapel attached to the apartments of the late Minister at the Ministry of the Interior, at which the Metropolitan Antonius[6] officiated. Among those present

---

1 St. Petersburg's first public hospital, which opened in 1841.

2 Winter residence of the Russian tsars, built in St. Petersburg between 1754 and 1762.

3 Nikolai Valerianovich Murav'ev (1850-1908), who served in that capacity from 1894 until 1905. He escaped an assassination attempt in 1905.

4 Nikolai II's wife, Aleksandra Fëdorovna of Hesse (1872-1918).

5 Zinaida Nikolaevna Uzhumetskaia-Gritsevich de Pleve (d. 1921).

6 Antonius (Aleksandr Vasil'evich Vadkovskii) (1846-1912), Metropolitan of Saint Petersburg and Ladoga (1898-1912); in the Russian Orthodox Church, a metropolitan is an ecclesiastical position ranking between an archbishop and a bishop.

were the Emperor,[1] the Empress Dowager,[2] the Hereditary Grand Duke Michael,[3] all the other Grand Dukes, the Grand Duchesses, the members of the Diplomatic Body, all the Ministers, and the members of the Council of State. An immense number of wreaths and other floral offerings, both natural and artificial, had been sent, including three wreaths from the provincial Governors of Finland.[4] At the conclusion of the service, the remains were removed with great ceremony to the cemetery of the Novodievitchi Monastery[5] for interment by the side of the late Minister's relations.

Paris, July 31.

A telegram from St. Petersburg states that as a consequence of the assassination of M. de Plehve, about 1,000 persons were arrested yesterday.

### 3. Anonymous, "The Murder of M. De Plehve (From Our Russian Correspondents)," *The Times* (2 August 1904): 3

The following extract from a private letter of July 27 from St. Petersburg may be of some interest:—

"On hearing the news of the murder of M. De Plehve, I went to the Warsaw Station, near which the deed had been committed. At the last block of houses in the Ismailovsky Prospekt, before the bridge over the Obvodny Canal,[6] traffic was partially stopped, and a considerable crowd had gathered. A large force of city police was in possession. To all questions as to what had occurred they merely replied:—'We do not know anything; we have orders.' On inquiring if I could go to the Warsaw Station, I was directed to go round the block to the right. This I did, crossing the canal by a bridge higher up and returning by that opposite the station. Here I saw some traces of the deed. The carriage in which the unfortunate Minister had been driving had been blown into fragments, and parts of it were scattered about all over the street; the footboard was on the side-walk. In the middle of the road were some other

---

1 Nikolai II.
2 Mariia Fëdorovna, Marie Sophie Frederikke Dagmar (1847-1928), mother of Nikolai II and widow of Aleksandr III (Aleksandr Aleksandrovich) (1845-94).
3 Grand Duke Michael (Mikhail Aleksandrovich) of Russia (1878-1918), son of Aleksandr III and younger brother of Nikolai II.
4 Finland was a Russian province from the time of its defeat at the hands of Aleksandr I (Aleksandr Pavlovich) (1777-1825) in 1809 until it declared independence in 1917, following the Russian Revolution.
5 Built in 1524 and located on the River Moskva in Moscow.
6 A canal connecting the Neva River and the Ekateringofka River.

parts of the vehicle, with ominous red stains. On the opposite side of the road (the Minister was driving on the right side, as is the rule of the road in St. Petersburg) is a huge drapery establishment several stories high. Almost every window in it for a distance of about 100 yards up the street was smashed; on the near side, occupied by the lower buildings, chiefly of one story, the glass was shivered into dust. A large stand camera, belonging to the police photographer, was placed on the bridge to photograph the scene of the murder. The crowd, which was allowed to pass relatively near on this side, was, however, moved on rapidly, so that it was impossible to take more than a cursory glance. With their customary indifference, the people showed hardly any trace of excitement, and seemed to regard the affair with little more concern or even curiosity than if it had been an ordinary street accident. They were discussing it in the neighbouring streets, but apparently with the utmost apathy.

"M. de Plehve, besides being Minister of the Interior, was practically the Prime Minister, for, as there is no collective Cabinet responsibility in Russia, it is always one man, of greater ability or self-assertion than his colleagues, who is the leading spirit in the Government. Moreover, as Minister of the Interior, he exercised the chief control over all the seven different police organizations of Russia and directly inspired those methods of repression which have been so exceptionally conspicuous of late.

"I have been informed on good authority that the revolutionists intimated to the Emperor a short time ago that, as they did not regard him as primarily responsible for the policy of repression, they would not make any attempts against him personally; but that they would be inexorable towards those of his Ministers with whom lay the real responsibility."

### 4. Anonymous, "The Assassination of M. de Plehve," *The Illustrated London News* (6 August 1904): 184

There is no diminution in the signs of internal unrest in Russia. Conspiracies against the hard dealing of Ministers are rife, and the latest of these has been successful. Sipiaguine[1] and Bobrikoff[2] have been fol-

---

1 Dmitrii Sergeevich Sipiagin (1853-1902) was Minister of the Interior of Russia from 1900 until 1902 when he was assassinated; see below, 359, note 2.

2 Nikolai Ivanovich Bobrikov (1839-1904), a Russian army officer and later Governor-General of Finland (1898-1904). In 1903, Nikolai II gave him dictatorial powers. He was assassinated by Evgenii Shauman (1875-1904), who subsequently committed suicide.

lowed by de Plehve, the Minister of the Interior, who on July 28 fell by the assassin's hand; The Minister was driving to the Warsaw Railway-Station at St. Petersburg on his way to pay an official visit to the Czar at Peterhof, and as he was passing a small hotel near the station a man approached the carriage and flung beneath it an infernal machine of tremendous power. There was a deafening explosion, the carriage was shattered, the Minister and his coachman were instantly killed, fifteen of the bystanders were wounded, and the murderer himself was removed suffering from terrible injuries. The assailant's identity has not been officially disclosed; but according to some reports he is a student, either a Jew or a Finn.[1] The assassin made no attempt to deny the crime. In spite of his desperate condition he attempted before his arrest to blow out his brains with a revolver, which was, however, taken from him in time. He is since reported to have died of his wounds. The late Minister had raised himself from obscure beginnings. His ideal was the preservation of autocracy, which principle he desired to develop to its utmost limit. On taking office he reorganised the police system on French lines, and the grievous methods of Russian espionage became tenfold more burdensome. Little attempt was made to disguise the popular satisfaction at de Plehve's murder. One of his last acts of severity was to replace the murdered Governor of Finland by Prince Obolenski,[2] a greater martinet[3] than Bobrikoff.

## 5. From E.J. Dillon, *The Eclipse of Russia* (New York: George H. Doran, 1918), 133

On the historic day I was driving over the badly paved streets of Petersburg to the landing-place for steamers to meet a friend who was coming from Ireland to stay with me. My droshky[4] was in the street leading to the Warsaw railway station when two men on bicycles glided past, followed by a closed carriage, which I recognised as that of the all-powerful minister. Suddenly the ground before me quivered, a tremendous sound as of thunder deafened me, the windows of the

---

1  Jews and Finns numbered highly in the various revolutionary groups in Russia, the Finns seeking independence from Russia and the Jews seeking better treatment and an end to discrimination and pogroms.
2  Ivan Mikhailovich Obolenskii (1853-1910), Governor-General of Finland from 1904 to 1905.
3  A strict disciplinarian.
4  A low, four-wheeled Russian carriage without a top.

houses on both sides of the broad street rattled, and the glass of the panes was hurled on to the stone pavement. A dead horse, a pool of blood, fragments of a carriage, and a hole in the ground were parts of my rapid impressions. My driver was on his knees devoutly praying and saying that the end of the world had come. I got down from my seat and moved towards the hole, but a police officer ordered me back, and to my questions replied that the minister Plehve had been blown to fragments. The man who materially contributed to condemn him to death, and who had the sentence thus effectively carried out, was the favourite spy of the government and member of the Social Revolutionary Council, [Evno] Azeff.[1] In truth it was a mad world.

Plehve's end was received with semi-public rejoicings. I met nobody who regretted his assassination or condemned the authors. This attitude towards crime, although by no means new, struck me as one of the most sinister features of the situation, and I gave expression to my apprehension of its consequences. Far more surprising was the attitude of the government towards its own agent, Azeff, who conceived and concerted the misdeed and saw it carried out. This monster was allowed to remain in the government service, and even after he had the Tsar's uncle, the Grand Duke Sergius,[2] assassinated he was kept on, and his services were deemed to be invaluable and indispensable!

## 6. From Boris Savinkov,[3] *Memoirs of a Terrorist*. Trans. Joseph Shaplen (New York: Albert & Charles Boni, 1931), 58–70

On July 15,[4] between eight and nine o'clock in the morning, I met [Egor Sergeevitch] Sazonov at the Nikolayevsky,[5] and [Ivan Platonovitch] Kaliayev at the Warsaw railway station. They were dressed as they were the week before: Sazonov as a railway employee and Kaliayev as a porter. Borishansky and Sikorsky[6] arrived at the

---

1 See 45, 241, 324, 339.

2 Grand Duke Sergei Aleksandrovich of Russia (1857-1905), uncle to Nikolai II and fifth son of Aleksandr II, was assassinated at the Kremlin by the Socialist-Revolutionary Ivan Platonovitch Kalyiaev (1877-1905), who was hanged shortly thereafter.

3 Boris Viktorovich Savinkov (1879-1925), a leader of the Socialist-Revolutionaries, who opposed both tsarist Russia and soviet Russia. Shortly after being captured by the Soviets in 1924, Savinkov died in prison. Accounts conflict as to whether he committed suicide or was murdered by prison authorities.

4 28 July, according to the Western calender.

5 Nikolaevskii Palace, completed in 1861.

6 David Borishanskii and Shimel'-Leiba Vulfovitch Sikorskii (1884-1927), members of the Socialist-Revolutionaries.

Warsaw station from Dvinsk[1] on the next train. They had spent the last few days in Dvinsk. While I was waiting for the comrades, Dulebov[2] harnessed his horse at his livery stable and came to the Northern Hotel, where Schweizer[3] lived. Schweizer got into the cab and distributed the bombs at the appointed place, at the corner of the Ofllzerskaya and Torgovoya streets, near the Marinsky Theatre.[4] The twelve-pound bomb was given to Sazonov. It was cylindrical in form, wrapped in a newspaper and tied with a string. Kaliayev's bomb was in a handkerchief. Kaliayev and Sazonov did not conceal their bombs. They carried them openly in their hands. Borishansky and Sikorsky concealed theirs under their mantles.[5]

The transfer of the bombs was without a hitch this time. Schweizer went home. Dulebov took up a station at the Technological Institute[6] along the Zagorodny Prospect. Here he was to wait for me to learn of the result. Matzeyevsky[7] stood with his cab along the Obvodny Canal. The rest, i.e., Sazonov, Kaliayev, Borishansky, Sikorsky and I assembled at the Pokrov Church on the Sadovaya street. From here they were to go in prearranged order, one after another—Borishansky first, Sazonov second, Kaliayev third and Sikorsky fourth—along the Anglisky Prospect and Droviannaya street to the Obvodny Canal and, turning along the canal past the Baltic and Warsaw stations, they were to meet Von Plehve on the Izmailovsky Prospect. The time was so calculated that by walking at a normal pace they were to meet Von Plehve along the Izmailovsky Prospect, somewhere between the Obvodny Canal and the First Regiment Armory. They walked at a distance of forty paces from each other. This was done to lessen the danger from detonation of the explosion. Borishansky was to permit Von Plehve to pass and, later, to bar his way back to his villa. Sazonov was to hurl the first bomb.

It was a bright, sunny day. As I approached the Pokrov Church square I saw this picture. Sazonov, sitting on a bench, was telling Siko-

---

1  Daugavpils, a city in southern Latvia, along the Daugava River.

2  Egor Olimpievich Dulebov (1883/4-1908), one of the assassins of Nikolai Modestovich Bogdanovich, governor of Ufa province, in 1903.

3  Maksimilian Il'ich Shveitser (1881-1905) blew himself up the following year while making a bomb.

4  The Imperial Mariinskii Theatre is a famous opera and ballet theater, hosting the premieres of many of the world's most famous ballets.

5  Cloaks or loose-fitting robes.

6  Saint Petersburg State Institute of Technology, established in 1828.

7  Iosif Matseevskii, a member of the Socialist-Revolutionaries, who later joined the Polish Socialist party.

rsky in great detail how and where to sink[1] his bomb. Sazonov was calm and did not appear to think of himself at all. Sikorsky listened to him attentively. At a distance, on a bench, sat the usually imperturbable Borishansky, and beyond him, at the church gate, stood Kaliayev, with his hat off, crossing himself before an ikon.

I went over to him.

"Yanek!"

He turned, as he crossed himself.

"Is it time to go?"

I looked at my watch. It was twenty minutes to ten.

"Of course, it's time. Go."

From the bench farthest removed rose Borishansky. Without hurrying, he walked toward the Peterhoff Prospect. Sazonov and Sikorsky followed him. Sazonov smiled, shook Sikorsky's hand and quickly, head high, followed Borishansky. Kaliayev still did not move.

"Yanek."

"Well, what?"

"Go."

He kissed me and hurriedly, with easy, beautiful gait, moved to overtake Sazonov. Sikorsky slowly followed. I followed them with my eyes. The sun's rays played on Sazonov's brass buttons. He carried his bomb in his right hand, between the elbow and the shoulder. It was evident the thing was too heavy for him.

I turned back along the Sadovaya and through the Voznesensky [Prospekt] to the Izmailovsky Prospect, with the intention of reaching the area where the assassination was to take place. By the very appearance of the street I perceived that Von Plehve was about to pass. The assembled police officials were intensely on the alert. There was a general atmosphere of nervousness and tension. Here and there on the street corners were plain-clothes men.

When I approached the Seventh Regiment Armory I saw a policeman standing rigidly at attention. At the same moment, on the Obvodny Canal bridge, I saw Sazonov. He walked as before—head high and carrying his bomb so that it touched his shoulder. And immediately, behind me, dashed by the carriage with two black horses. There was no liveried lackey[2] on the coach box, but at the left wheel, on a bicycle, rode a detective. Later it developed he was Friedrich Hartman,[3] an agent of

---

1 Abandon.
2 Uniformed footman.
3 Fridrikh Gartman, a member of the Secret Police and Pleve's main bodyguard.

the Secret Political Police. Behind him were two more detectives in a cab. I recognized Von Plehve.

Several seconds passed. Sazonov disappeared in the crowd, but I knew that he was walking now along the Izmailovsky Prospect, parallel with the Warsaw Hotel. These few seconds seemed to me interminably long. Suddenly the monotonous noise of the street was broken by a strange, heavy, ponderous thud. It was as if someone had struck an iron plate with a heavy hammer. At the same moment there was a wail of broken windows round about. From the ground rose a thin column of grayish-yellow smoke, almost black at the edges. It grew thicker and thicker until it covered the whole street and then disappeared as quickly as it had come. I thought that through the smoke I saw some black fragments.

For a moment I almost lost consciousness. But I expected the explosion and quickly regained my self-control. I ran across the street to the Warsaw Hotel and heard someone shouting: "Don't run: there will be another blast. . . ."

When I came to the place of the explosion the smoke had already dispersed. There was a smell of burning. Before me, in the dusty street, about four feet from the pavement, I saw Sazonov. He was on the ground, reclining with his left arm on the stones and his head cocked to the right. His cap had been blown off and his dark-chestnut locks fell in disorder upon his brow. His face was pale. Here and there on his brow and cheeks were little streams of blood. The eyes were dim and half-closed. A black spot of blood, beginning at the abdomen, grew wider and wider, ending in a large crimson pool at his feet.

I bent over him and gazed into his face. Suddenly the thought struck me that he was dead, and at the same moment I heard a voice behind me:

"And the minister? They say the minister escaped."

I then concluded that Von Plehve was alive.

I was still bending over Sazonov. A police captain, pale, with trembling jaw (I recognized in him Captain Perepelitzin, who was well known to me), approached. Waving his white-gloved hands nervously he said:

"Go away, Sir, go away. . . ." I turned and walked along the middle of the street in the direction of the Warsaw station. On leaving, I did not notice that a few paces from Sazonov lay Von Plehve's mutilated corpse, surrounded by fragments of his carriage. A crowd of stone masons and dust-covered bricklayers was running in my direction. They were shouting. Crowds of people were also running on the pavements. All I could think, however, was:

"Von Plehve is alive. Sazonov is killed."

I wandered long about the city, until quite mechanically I found myself before the Technological Institute. Dulebov was still waiting for me there. I got into his cab.

"Well, what's happened?" he turned to me.

"Von Plehve is alive."

"And Yegor?"

"Dead."

Dulebov's eyes filled with tears. His jaws trembled. But he said nothing. In about five minutes he again turned to me:

"And what now?"

"On the way back, at four o'clock."

He shook his head in approval. Then I said:

"At three o'clock I will give you a bomb. Wait for me again at the Technological Institute."

After bidding him good-bye, I went to the Yusupov Garden[1] where all those participating in the assassination were to meet in the event of failure. I hoped that not all had been arrested and that they had preserved their bombs. It was my intention to try again to kill Von Plehve on his way back from Peterhoff. We knew that he usually returned from the Czar between three and four o'clock. Dulebov, myself and those who might be still alive were to hurl the bombs.

I found no one in the Yusupov Gardens.

Kaliayev had walked all the time behind Sazonov, at an even distance of forty feet. When Sazonov reached the bridge across the Obvodny Canal, Kaliayev noticed that he suddenly increased his pace. He realized that Sazonov had spotted the carriage. As Von Plehve and Sazonov approached each other, Kaliayev was already on the bridge and from the elevation observed the explosion and the destruction of the carriage. For a moment he was confused. He could not determine the effect of the blast and whether it was now up to him to hurl the second bomb. While contemplating the situation, he suddenly saw the blood-stained horses, dragging fragments of the carriage wheels behind them, dashing forward across the bridge. He observed also the excited crowds running in all directions. Perceiving the wheel fragments he understood that Von Plehve was killed. He turned toward the Warsaw station and walked slowly in the direction of Sikorsky. On the way he was stopped by some janitor.

"What's happened?"

"I don't know."

"Are you coming from there?"

"Yes, from there."

---

1  The gardens of the Yusupov Palace, located on the Fontanka River, were opened to the general public in 1863 and became a popular place to visit.

"Then why don't you know?"

"How am I to know? They say a cannon blew off."

Kaliayev sank his bomb in the pond and, in accordance with our understanding, left at noon for Kiev.[1]

Borishansky heard the explosion behind him. Realizing that Von Plehve would not return he, too, got rid of his bomb and departed from St. Petersburg.

As we had expected, Sikorsky failed to do as he was told. Instead of going to Petrovsky Park,[2] hire a boat and row out to sea, he hired a skiff at the Engineering Institute[3] to go across the Neva[4] and, in the presence of the boatman, close to the battleship "Slava," then in process of construction,[5] threw his bomb into the water. The boatman demanded to know what he was doing. Thereupon, without replying, Sikorsky offered him ten roubles. The boatman took him to the police station.

Sikorsky's bomb could not be found immediately and his participation in the assassination of Von Plehve could not, therefore, be proven, until, finally in the fall, some workmen of the Kolotilin fisheries dragged the bomb out in their net and delivered it to their plant.

Failing to find any of our group in the Yusupov Garden I went to a bath house in Cossack lane, rented a room and lay down on a couch. I remained there two hours, until, according to my calculations, it was time to go to find Schweizer and prepare for the second attempt to kill Von Plehve. Emerging on the Nevsky[6] I mechanically bought a newspaper from a vendor. Displayed prominently on the front page was a portrait of Von Plehve, draped in black. Below was his obituary. Shortly after ten o'clock the wounded Sazonov was taken to the Alexandrovsky Hospital for Laborers, where in the presence of Minister of Justice [Nikolai Valerianovich] Muraviev, an operation was performed upon him. In accordance with the rules of the Terrorist Brigade he flatly declined to reveal his name or to divulge any information.

From prison he sent us the following letter:

---

1  Capital of Ukraine, located on the Dnepr River in north-central Ukraine; also known as Kyiv.

2  Savinkov apparently means Petrovskii Island, which lies between the Malaia Neva River and the Zhdanovka River, from which one could row out to the Gulf of Finland.

3  Gorny Institute (now Saint Petersburg Mining Institute), established in 1773.

4  A river in the Leningrad province in northwestern Russia, whose mouth is at St. Petersburg.

5  The battleship *Slava*, which was begun in 1902 at the Baltic Works in St. Petersburg and completed in June of 1905.

6  Nevskii Prospekt, the main road in St. Petersburg.

"When I was arrested my whole face was bathed in blood; the eyes were out of their sockets; in my right side there was a gaping hole; two toes were torn from my left foot; the sole was crushed. I was well-nigh mortally wounded. The police agents, masquerading as doctors, kept waking me, and would not let me rest. They repeated again and again the horrors of the explosion, and told me lies about 'the little Jew' Sikorsky. It was torture!

"The enemy is contemptible without limit. It is dangerous to surrender oneself to them alive. Please let this be known. Farewell, dear comrades! I salute the rising sun of liberty!

"Dear brothers, comrades! My play is finished. I do not know whether I played my part well, but I am eternally grateful for the confidence you have shown me. You made it possible for me to experience an incomparable, a moral satisfaction. This satisfaction silenced the pain I suffered after the explosion. I had hardly awakened from my operation when I breathed with relief. At last, it was all over. I was ready to sing and shout for joy. After the explosion I lost consciousness. On coming to, and not knowing how seriously I was wounded, I wanted to escape arrest by suicide, but my hand was too weak to grasp my revolver. I was captured. For several days I was in delirium. For three weeks my eyes were covered with bandages. For two months I could not move from my bed, and I was fed, like a child, by strange hands. The police, naturally, took advantage of my helplessness. The police agents listened in on my delirium. Under the guise of doctors and hospital assistants they wakened me as soon as I would fall asleep. They kept on repeating to me the horrors of the Izmailovsky Prospect.[1] They kept me in a state of feverish excitement. They tried in every way to make me believe that S. [Sikorsky] had betrayed us. They said he told them that a few days before July 15 he had met someone (some old woman) in Vilna,[2] that another Jew, in an English coat, was also under arrest, and that S. had identified him as a comrade from Byelostok.[3] Fortunately, the police agents could not gain much from my illness. I think I remember everything I said in my delirium, but that is not important if you take proper precautions. There is one stupidity, one crime I cannot forgive myself. I cannot understand how I could reveal my name after keeping silent for three weeks. Comrades! Be lenient with me. I already feel myself crushed. If you would only realize how I suffered, how I still suffer, knowing that I talked in my delirium. And I was helpless to do anything. How could I help myself? To bite off

---

1   I.e., the carnage resulting from the explosion that killed de Pleve.
2   Vil'nius, the capital and largest city in Lithuania, located in the southeastern part of the country.
3   Białystok, a city in northeastern Poland.

my tongue? But I had no strength for this. I was so weak. I wanted only to die—or to get well quickly. I am also very much concerned, dear brothers-comrades, lest I may have done wrong in my explanations of the party's tasks. As you know, in my views on terror I am a disciple of the 'Narodnaya Volia'[1] and disagree therein with the party program. So that when the time came for me to appear before the court I felt that I was in a false position. I should have ignored my personal views and spoken only of the party program. Did I commit a wrong against the party? If so, I beg you to forgive me. Let the party declare publicly that I was mistaken, and that it is not responsible for the words of its individual members, particularly one who is ill, like myself. I am not yet entirely well. The blow in the head was too strong. This is all that weighs upon my conscience, and I wanted all the time to confess before you, dear comrades. If I be only an individual who has wronged the common cause, let the fact remain and let it speak for itself: I have tried consciously to diminish its importance.

"I welcome the new ideas that are making themselves felt on the question of terror. Let us remain to the end disciples of the 'Narodnaya Volia.' I did not at all expect that I would not be killed and I do not rejoice at the verdict: what joy is there to be the captive of the Russian government? Let us hope it will not be for long. I look upon this verdict as a condemnation of the judges who sentenced to death Stepan, Gregory Andreyevitch[2] and others. Dear brothers-comrades! I embrace you and kiss you warmly. This missive is only for you, my close comrades. I ask you, therefore, not to make it public. Let my farewell greeting to you be the words I uttered when I gazed upon our stricken foe and when it seemed that I myself was dying: 'Long live the Terrorist Brigade!' 'Down with Absolutism!' Good-bye. Live on. Work.

"Affectionately, brothers-comrades,

"Your

"YEGOR."

---

1 People's will (Russian): a reference to the People's Will wing of the Land and Freedom Party. See 12-13, 144, 276, and Appendix E.

2 A reference to Stepan Valerianovich Balmashov (1881-1902) and Grigorii Andreevich Gershuni (1870-1908). Balmashov was a student Revolutionary-Socialist who gained entrance into Mariinskii Palace by posing as an aide-de-camp of the Tsar and who proceeded to assassinate Dmitrii Sergeevich Sipiagin, Minister of the Interior, in 1902. Balmashov was hanged shortly after the assassination. Gershuni, one of the founders of the Socialist-Revolutionary Party and one of the organizers of Sipiagin's assassination, was sentenced to death in 1904, although the sentence was commuted to life in prison. Gershuni escaped from prison and fled to the West, where he died of tuberculosis in 1908. The "others" to whom Sazonov refers probably include those tried along with Gershuni in their February 1904 trial.

Subsequently Sazonov wrote us as follows:

"To My Comrades in the Cause.

"Dear brothers-comrades! A year and a half has passed since I was taken from your ranks. But torn from you in body, I have not for a moment ceased to live with you in all my thought. Amid the thunder of the revolutionary tempest that has swept over the country, I have listened with particular interest for the voice of the T.B. (Terrorist Brigade of the Socialists-Revolutionists) and its voice has not been lost in the mighty chorus of the revolution. The T.B. has always known how to give the proper answer to the problems of life. With exaltation I greeted its victories; with anguish—its failures; these are, however, quite natural in any great and live work. With a feeling of deep pain, with love and adoration I bow before the graves of the fallen. And the end is not yet. Judging by all the circumstances it will still be necessary for the T.B. to appear upon the historical arena. Keeping in mind the tasks yet to be done and the sacrifices they will demand, I feel compelled to recall the past. I cannot refrain from telling you, brothers-comrades, how happy I have been to recall you to my mind, your loving, purely fraternal attitude toward me, the confidence you placed in me when you entrusted me with such a responsible task as that of July 15. For me, it would have been a thousand times worse than death to defile your love, to prove myself beneath your confidence, to becloud in any way the work of the T.B., the whole greatness of which I am the first to recognize and before which I stand in awe. Fate had almost played evil pranks upon me. I was wounded, but not killed. Having lost all power of control over myself, I almost became, in my delirium, an involuntary traitor. I was compelled to experience that which is most repulsive to a revolutionist: the Judas kisses and embraces of police agents who, taking advantage of my helplessness and of the fact that my bandage deprived me of sight, appeared before me under the neutral flag of physicians and hovered around me like hungry wolves. During the four months before the trial I was in a terrible state of ignorance as to the consequences of my delirium, in fear for my comrades, for the cause, in doubt as to whether I had not betrayed them. Only the success of the cause and the intoxication of victory gave me strength to survive my illness and to withstand the superhuman tortures of the soul. Fortunately, the delirium passed safely. But after my illness and spiritual sufferings, I appeared at the trial very weak, with my mind crushed by the explosion and the knocks and blows of police spies, hardly able to master my thoughts and tongue. In such a state it was my duty not to speak before the court, in order that I might not misrepresent the party program. I would have acted thus had not something occurred before which compelled me to explain. I mean the statement I made to the district attorney on July 15, immediately after I awoke from my operation. I do not know whether I can survive it, but it appeared incumbent upon me to declare immediately that I was a member of the Terrorist Brigade of the Party of Socialists-Revolutionists and that the man who perished in the explosion at the Northern Hotel was my comrade in the cause. It had been understood that I was merely to confirm Pokotilov's[1] membership in the T.B.—nothing more. But the district attorney asked me about the aims of the T.B. and I, without realizing that I was violating the party principle 'to give no information' did give an explanation and in rather militant form (the very same explanation which is embodied in the indictment). Why did I do that? Why did I violate the principle and introduce a dissonance in the interpretation of the party program? Because during the inquiry I had several times almost lost consciousness, pleaded that it be discontinued and begged to be given water lest I faint. Up until the moment of the trial I worried little about the information I divulged. But later, when it came time to think what to say before the court if I were called upon to speak, I quickly perceived the disharmony between my words and the party program. The realization of this, more than anything else, compelled me to try and express only the official party point of view. Several days before the trial I wrote down what I intended to say. I tried not to go to the extreme, and, as it developed, leaned too much in the other direction. Moreover, it was so difficult to express oneself in court that I paid a high price for the opportunity to speak. At first they would not let me speak at all pending conclusion of the evidence and I was enabled to speak only upon the insistence of (prosecutor) Karabchevsky.[2] I was interrupted and interfered with at every word, I lost the thread of my speech. Tortured, I swallowed much; now and then words came from my lips accidentally which I would have gladly taken back immediately. After the trial I felt all broken up and bitten with remorse at having supported by my participation the whole comedy of the trial. So that when later I had been informed that you were quite satisfied with what I had said, the information rang in my ears like irony. I wrote you about this immediately after the trial, dear comrades, in explanation of the mistakes into which I fell involuntarily. I feel the

---

1  Aleksei Dmitrievich Pokotilov (1879-1904) blew himself up while making a bomb a few months before de Pleve's assassination.

2  The famous Russian lawyer Nikolai Platonovich Karabchevskii (1851-1925), who was actually Sazonov's defense lawyer. The translator mistakenly refers to him here as the prosecutor of the case.

need of repeating it again now, in order that there may be no misunderstanding between me and those of you who may be called upon to sacrifice themselves. It is absolutely essential to my happiness to preserve the consciousness of complete solidarity with you on all questions of life and our program. To all those doomed to die I send my special greeting and hope that in good health, physical and moral, they may carry forward to the end and with honor the banner of the organization. I greet you, dear comrades! Courage and success! Let us hope that soon it will no longer be necessary to wage our fight by terroristic means and that we will win the opportunity to work for our socialist ideals under conditions more commensurate with human strength.

"Your<br>"Yegor.

"P.S. I ask that this note be delivered to those for whom it is intended, i.e., the T.B.; and not to other, even though carefully chosen persons, which seems to have been the case with my first note."

Tried together with Sazonov was Schimel-Leiba Vulfovitch Sikorsky, a citizen of the town of Knishin[1] and a leather worker by trade, who from his fourteenth year had worked in a factory, first in Knishin, later in the town of Kriniki,[2] and subsequently in Byelostok. In Kriniki he first became acquainted with the revolutionary parties, but joined the Party of Socialists-Revolutionists only in Byelostok. There he also made the acquaintance of Borishansky, who, as I have mentioned before, brought him into the Terrorist Brigade, in June, 1904.

Sazonov and Sikorsky were tried November 30, 1904, before a jury in the St. Petersburg High Court. Sazonov was defended by Kazorinov.[3] Both defendants were deprived of all rights and property. Sazonov was sentenced to hard labor for life and Sikorsky to 20 years. This comparatively mild verdict (it had been expected by all, including Sazonov himself, that they would be tried before a military tribunal and hanged) is to be explained by the fact that with the appointment of Prince Sviatopolk-Mirsky[4] to succeed Von Plehve as minister of the interior, the government had decided to pursue a somewhat milder policy and not to arouse public opinion by imposing death sentences.

Like Sikorsky, Sazonov was after the trial incarcerated in Schlues-

---

1 Knyszyn, a town in northeastern Poland.

2 A town in northeastern Poland.

3 Kazarinov was Sikorskii's lawyer, not Sazonov's.

4 Pëtr Danilovich Sviatopolk-Mirskii (1857-1914). He was dismissed from his position as Minister of the Interior on 15 January 1905, after the events of Bloody Sunday.

selburg fortress. By the Manifesto of October, 1905, their sentences were reduced. In 1906 they were transferred from Schluesselburg to the Akatui prison[1] in Siberia. (While in Siberia Sazonov committed suicide by soaking himself in kerosene and setting himself on fire.[2] He did this in protest against mistreatment of political prisoners by the authorities.)

---

1  Akatui Katorga Prison in eastern Siberia, constructed in 1888.
2  Savinkov appears to be mistaken here. Sazonov is instead reputed to have committed suicide by taking an overdose of morphine on 28 November 1909.

# Appendix D: Illustrations of the Assassination of de Pleve

[This appendix contains four photographs related to the assassination of de Pleve. The first two are of the Minister and his assassin. The others are two views of de Pleve's exploded carriage. The photograph of de Pleve is reprinted from the Gosudarstvennaia Kantseliariia's book *Gosudarstvennaia Kantseliariia 1810-1910*. St. Petersburg: Gosudarstvennaia Tipografiia, 1910. The others are reprinted from Viktor Petrovich Obninskii's *Poslednii samoderzhets, Ocherki zhizni i tsarstvovaniia imperatora Rossii Nikolaia II-go*. Berlin: Eberhard Frowein, 1912.]

## 1. Viacheslav Konstantinovich de Pleve, Russian Minister of the Interior

## 2. Egor Sazanov, Assassin of de Pleve

### 3. de Pleve's Exploded Carriage (view one)

### 4. de Pleve's Exploded Carriage (view two)

# Appendix E: The Central Committee of the Party of Socialist-Revolutionaries, "To the Whole Russian Peasantry" (July 1904)

[This manifesto, released by the Socialist-Revolutionary Party just after the assassination of de Pleve, explains and justifies the attack on the Minister of the Interior. It also provides insight into the thinking of the Socialist-Revolutionaries and their rhetorical approach to the Russian masses.]

## To the Whole Russian Peasantry[1]

*In struggle you will find your rights![2]*

On 15 July 1904, in accordance with the decision of the Fighting Organisation of the Socialist-Revolutionary Party, the Minister of Internal Affairs Vyacheslav Konstantinovich von Plehve was killed.

Von Plehve had been a Minister for two years and 105 days. Before him the Minister had been Dmitriy [Sergeyevich] Sipyagin. Sipyagin had been killed for his crimes against the people on 2 April 1902 by Stepan Valerianovich Balmashov, in accordance with the decision of the Socialist-Revolutionaries' Fighting Organisation.

In appointing von Plehve, the Tsar intended to put a halt to the people's revolution—the people's uprising against the tsar's, landowners' and bosses' oppression.

The Minister of Internal Affairs is invested with enormous power. All Russia is in his hands. All the governors, all the land captains, and the entire police are answerable to him, right down to the lowest village policeman. Above the Minister stands only the Tsar. The Minister is answerable to the Tsar alone.

This power was invested in von Plehve in order to keep the people in slavery. Von Plehve was the pillar which was supposed to prop up the crumbling wall of autocracy. And von Plehve earned the Tsar's trust. He did everything to suppress the people's dissatisfaction. He

---

1 This text is a translation by Dr. Francis King of a leaflet issued by the Party of Socialist-Revolutionaries Central Committee in July 1904.

2 This appears to have been the main slogan of the Social-Revolutionary Party, since it also appears as the epigraph for other manifestoes from the party.

lavished the people's money on the police, on prisons, and on kangaroo courts. Nor did he spare the people's blood.

On von Plehve's orders, troops, Cossacks and the police were used to defend the factory owners and protect the autocracy against the robbed and oppressed people. Workers and peasants were beaten, cut down, shot, imprisoned, sent to Siberia and exiled. All this was because the people had ceased to bear the bosses' yoke patiently. All this was to reinforce the crumbling bastion of autocracy.

As soon as he had been appointed Minister, in April 1902, von Plehve set off for Khar'kov[1] and Poltava,[2] in order personally to oversee the retribution against the peasants for having tried to get their land and freedom.[3]

At his insistence the peasants, pacified, humiliated, ruined and condemned, in addition to all the punishments already inflicted upon them, had to pay a tax to the landowners as a form of bail. Seeing the growing discontent in the countryside, von Plehve introduced a new village police force, the *strazhniki*. They have swarmed all over the countryside like locusts. Everywhere these bloodhounds sniff out the spirit of discontent, seize the true servants of the people, drive them into jail and thence into exile in northern hovels. Under von Plehve's rule the black cloud of oppression and arbitrariness has hung more heavily over the people than ever before. The all-powerful Minister's police have suppressed everyone and everything. It seemed as if justice had been driven off the face of the earth, and that the dark reign of injustice would last for ever in Russia. Von Plehve did what he liked, and it seemed that there was no force that could call him to account.

But the power of the people is great. Tsarist ministers cannot suppress the will of the people.[4] The Minister did not want to reckon with the people, he did not want to give an account of himself or his actions. Surrounded by a thick wall of police, the Minister thought he was beyond the reach of the people's judgement.

But that judgement came. The thunder of the people's anger has struck this contemptible enemy of the people. Von Plehve has paid with his life for the hunger, the want, the robbery, the torture, the groans and the deaths of millions of working people.

The Party of Socialist-Revolutionaries, which fights in the front

---

1 City at the convergence of the Lopan', Uda, and Khar'kov rivers in the Khar'kov province of northeastern Ukraine; also known as Kharkiv.
2 City on the Vorskla River in the Poltava province of eastern Ukraine.
3 Likely an allusion to the Land and Freedom party that arose in 1876 and advocated land reform and political liberties. Some party members advocated political assassination as a means to achieve their ends.
4 Probably an allusion to the People's Will wing of the Land and Freedom party.

ranks of the awakening people, sentenced this villain to death in the name of and on behalf of the people. The sentence has been carried out by its Fighting Organisation.

Von Plehve was one of the pillars which held up the wall of autocracy, a wall which blocked the people's path to freedom and happiness.

If you chop down the pillars, the wall will fall.

But the death of von Plehve does not put an end to the struggle against oppression. Von Plehve was not the only one. He was just one of the most malicious enemies of the people. Only the people themselves can tear down the whole wall and destroy utterly all the evil which presses down on the people.

We, the Socialist-Revolutionaries, ceaselessly call on the people to struggle for the people's cause. We do so by word and by example. We invite into our ranks everybody who no longer wishes to wait, but who wants to win *land* and *freedom*[1] for the people.

Let the explosion of 15 July thunder across all Russia and awaken all those who have not yet stirred for the great cause of the liberation of the people.

*Down with the autocracy!* We demand that elected representatives of the whole country should consider and decide upon the reconstruction of all our institutions in the interests of the working people. We demand the convocation of a Constituent Assembly!

*Down with arbitrariness and violence!* We demand full freedom of conscience, speech, the press, assembly, trade unions and strikes! We demand the repeal of all laws which restrict the rights of those nationalities forcibly imprisoned in the Russian Tsardom.

*Down with the unaccountable bureaucracy!* We demand that all in responsible positions be elected, removable and answerable before the courts!

*Down with the landowners!* We demand an end to the trade in our mother earth, and demand that all land pass into the control and use of the whole working agricultural population!

*Down with the capitalists!* We demand that everything created by the labour of the working people should pass to them, should be for the common benefit, and should not go into the pockets of a bunch of useless layabouts!

*Down with the war!* We demand peace and fraternity between the peoples, we demand that every people have the right freely to decide its own fate, we demand general disarmament and the replacement of standing armies by a people's militia. We demand an immediate end

---

1 Probably another allusion to the Land and Freedom party.

to this terrible, destructive and bloody war with Japan,[1] of no use to the working people!

Comrades! The struggle continues! In struggle we will find our rights!

The Central Committee of the Party of Socialist-Revolutionaries!

---

1  A reference to the Russo-Japanese War of 1904-05.

# Appendix F: Joseph Conrad, "Autocracy and War" (1905)

[This essay, published just a few years before *Under Western Eyes*, is Conrad's most complete statement of his political views regarding Russia. It outlines his criticism of Russian autocracy and provides a strong background for the political views that appear in the novel. The essay, occasioned by the events of the Russo-Japanese War of 1904-05, is an ominous prophecy of historical events that were soon to take place.]

## Autocracy and War[1]

From the firing of the first shot on the banks of the Sha-ho the fate of *the* great battle of this war hung in the balance for more than a fortnight.[2] The famous three-day battles, for which history has reserved the recognition of special pages, sink into insignificance before the struggles in Manchuria engaging half a million men on fronts of sixty miles, struggles lasting for weeks, flaming up fiercely and dying away from sheer exhaustion, to flame up again in a desperate persistence, and end—as we have seen them more than once—not from the victor obtaining a crushing advantage, but through the mortal weariness of the combatants.

We have seen these things, though we have seen them only in the cold, silent, colourless print of books and newspapers. In stigmatising the printed world as cold, silent, and colourless, I have no intention of putting a slight upon the fidelity and the talents of men who have provided us with words to read about the battles in Manchuria. I only wished to suggest that from the nature of things the war in the Far East has been made known to us, so far, in a pale and grey reflection of its terrible and monotonous phases of pain, death, sickness; a reflection seen in the perspective of thousands of miles, in the dim atmosphere of official reticence, through the veil of inadequate words. Inadequate, I say, because what had to be reproduced is beyond the common expe-

---

1 First published in *The Fortnightly Review* (1 July 1905): 1-21, and later collected in Conrad's *Notes on Life and Letters* (1921).
2 A battle fought on the Sha-Ho River in central Manchuria (northeastern China) that lasted from 5 October to 17 October 1904. The battle was not decisive for either side and occurred during the Russo-Japanese War, which began on 8 February 1904 and lasted until 5 September 1905, with Japan the eventual victor.

rience of war, and our imagination, luckily for our peace of mind, has remained a slumbering faculty, notwithstanding the din of humanitarian talk and the real progress of humanitarian ideas. Direct vision of the fact, or the stimulus of a great art, can alone make it turn and open its eyes heavy with blessed sleep; and even there, as against the testimony of the senses and the stirring up of emotion, that saving callousness which reconciles us to the conditions of our existence, will assert itself under the guise of assent to fatal necessity or in the enthusiasm of a purely esthetic admiration of the rendering. In this age of knowledge our sympathetic imagination, to which alone we can look for the ultimate triumph of concord and justice,[1] remains strangely impervious to information, however correctly and even picturesquely conveyed. As to the vaunted eloquence of a serried[2] array of figures, it has all the futility of precision without force. It is the exploded superstition of enthusiastic statisticians. An overworked horse falling in front of our windows, a man writhing under a cart-wheel in the street, awaken more genuine emotion, more horror, pity, and indignation, than the stream of reports, appalling in their monotony, of tens of thousands of decaying bodies tainting the air of the Manchurian plains, of other tens of thousands of maimed bodies groaning in ditches, crawling on the frozen ground, filling the field hospitals; of the hundreds of thousands of survivors no less pathetic and even more tragic in being left alive by fate to the pitiable exhaustion of their pitiful toil.

An early Victorian, or perhaps a pre-Victorian, sentimentalist, looking out of an upstairs window, I believe, at a street—perhaps Fleet-street[3] itself—full of people, is reported, by an admiring friend,

---

1  A phrase that Conrad uses with some frequency: as well as three other occurrences in this essay (382, 384, 397), it also appears in *The Mirror of the Sea* (Doubleday, 1928, 193), in "A Note on the Polish Problem" (*Notes on Life and Letters*, 112), and in *Under Western Eyes* (289). The phrase appears to have its origins in Roman thought concerning two elements necessary for a stable society, virtues embodied in the Roman gods Concordia and Justitia.

2  Close or pressed together, usually referring to soldiers, but in this case a closely reasoned and compact argument.

3  Conrad is referring to a passage from "The Londoner," an unsigned column by Charles Lamb (1775-1834): "This passion for crowds is no where feasted so full as in London. The man must have a rare *recipe* for melancholy, who can be dull in Fleet-street. I am naturally inclined to *hypochondria*, but in London it vanishes, like all other ills. Often, when I have felt a weariness or distaste at home, have I rushed out into her crowded Strand, and fed my humour, till tears have wetted my cheek for inutterable sympathies with the multitudinous moving picture, which she never fails to present at all hours, like shifting scenes of a skilful Pantomime" (*Morning Post and Gazetteer*, 1 February 1802, 3). Fleet Street is a famous street in London, traditionally the home of the British press, named for the River Fleet which flows near it.

to have wept for joy at seeing so much life. These arcadian tears, this facile emotion worthy of the golden age, comes to us from the past, with solemn approval, after the close of the Napoleonic wars,[1] and before the series of sanguinary surprises held in reserve by the nineteenth century for our hopeful grandfathers. We may well envy them their optimism of which this anecdote of an amiable wit and sentimentalist presents an extreme instance, but still, a true instance, and worthy of regard in the spontaneous testimony to that trust in the life of the Earth, triumphant at last in the felicity of her children. Moreover, the psychology of individuals, even in the most extreme instances, reflects the general effect of the fears and hopes of its time. Wept for joy! I should think that now after eighty years the emotion would be of a sterner sort. One could not imagine anybody shedding tears of joy at the sight of much life in a street, unless, perhaps, he were an enthusiastic officer of a general staff or a popular politician, with its career yet to make. And hardly even that. In the case of the first tears would be unprofessional, and a stern repression of all signs of joy at the provision of so much food for powder more in accord with the rules of prudence: the joy of the second would be checked before it found issue in weeping by anxious doubts as to the soundness of these electors' views upon the question of the hour, and the fear of missing the consensus of their votes.

No! It seems that such a tender joy would be misplaced now as much as ever during the last hundred years, to go no further back. The end of the eighteenth century was, too, a time of optimism and of desperate mediocrity in which the French Revolution[2] exploded like a bomb-shell. In its lurid blaze the insufficiency of Europe, the inferiority of minds, of military and administrative systems, stood exposed with pitiless vividness. And there is but little courage in saying at this time of the day that the glorified French Revolution itself, except for its destructive force, was in essentials a mediocre phenomenon. The parentage of that great social and political upheaval was intellectual, the idea was elevated: but it is the bitter fate of the idea to lose its royal form and power, to lose its "virtue" the moment it descends from its solitary throne to work its will amongst the people. It is a king whose destiny is never to know the obedience of his subjects except at the cost of degradation. The degradation of the ideas of freedom and

---

1 After becoming ruler of France in 1799, Napoleon Bonaparte pursued a series of military campaigns across Europe until his eventual defeat at the Battle of Waterloo on 18 June 1815.

2 The French Revolution occurred from 1789 until Napoleon's rise to power in 1799. The revolution is particularly noted for its bloody campaign against the French monarchy and aristocracy (the Reign of Terror) and as the first example of the overthrow of a monarchical power in Europe by the populace.

justice at the root of the French Revolution is made manifest in the person of its heir; a personality without law or faith, whom it has been the fashion to represent as an eagle,[1] but who was, in truth, much more like a sort of vulture preying upon the body of a Europe which did, indeed, for some dozen of years resemble very much a corpse. The subtle and manifold influence for evil of the Napoleonic episode as a school of violence, as a sower of national hatreds, as the direct provocator of obscurantism and reaction, of political tyranny and injustice, can not well be exaggerated.

The nineteenth century began with wars which were the issue of a corrupted revolution.[2] It may be said that the twentieth begins with a war which is like the explosive ferment of a moral grave, whence may yet emerge a new political organism to take the place of a gigantic and dreaded phantom. For a hundred years the ghost of Russian might overshadowing with its fantastic bulk the councils of central and western Europe sat upon the gravestone of autocracy, cutting off from air, from light, from all knowledge of themselves and of the world, the buried millions of Russian people. Not the most determined cockney sentimentalist could have had the heart to weep for joy at the thought of its teeming numbers! And yet they were living, they are alive yet, since through the mist of print we have seen their blood freezing crimson upon the snow of the squares and streets of St. Petersburg,[3] since their generations born in the grave are yet alive enough to fill the ditches and cover the fields of Manchuria with their torn limbs, their maimed trunks, to send up from the frozen ground of battle-fields a chorus of groans calling for vengeance from Heaven, to kill and retreat, or kill and advance, without intermission or rest, for twenty hours, for fifty hours, for whole days, for whole weeks of fatigue, hunger, cold, and murder—till their ghastly labour worthy of a place amongst the punishments of Dante's Inferno,[4] passing through the stages of courage, of fury, of hopelessness, sinks into the night of crazy despair.

It seems that in both armies many men are driven beyond the bounds of sanity by the stress of moral and physical misery. Great

---

1 Napoleon replaced the fleur-de-lys (the symbol of the French monarchy) with an eagle.

2 A reference to the Napoleonic wars.

3 A reference to the revolution that began on 22 January 1905 in St. Petersburg with "Bloody Sunday," the massacre of peaceful demonstrators who were led by Father Georgii Apollonovich Gapon.

4 A reference to *The Inferno* by Italian poet Dante Alighieri (1265-1321), the first part of his famous poem *The Divine Comedy* (1307-21); it depicts the sins and suffering of those in Hell.

numbers of soldiers and regimental officers go mad as if by way of protest against the peculiar sanity of a state of war: mostly amongst the Russians, of course. The Japanese have in their favour the tonic effect of success; and the innate gentleness of their character stands them in good stead. But the Japanese Grand Army has yet another advantage in this nerve-destroying contest, which for endless, arduous, toil of killing surpasses all the wars of history. It has a base for its operations; a base of a nature beyond the concern of the many books written upon the so-called art of war, which, considered by itself, purely as an exercise of human ingenuity, is at best only a thing of well-worn, simple artifices. The Japanese Army has for its base a reasoned conviction; it has behind it the profound belief in the right of a logical necessity to be appeased at the cost of so much blood and treasure. And in that belief, whether well or ill founded, that army stands on the high ground of conscious assent, shouldering deliberately the burden of a long-tried faithfulness. The other people (since each people is an army nowadays), torn out from a miserable quietude resembling death itself, hurled across space, amazed, without starting point of its own or knowledge of the aim, can feel nothing but the horror-stricken consciousness of having mysteriously become the plaything of a black and merciless fate.

The profound, the instructive nature of this war is resumed by the memorable difference in the spiritual state of the two armies: the one forlorn and dazed on being driven out from an abyss of mental darkness into the red light of a conflagration, the other with the full knowledge of its past and its future, "finding itself" as it were at every step of the trying war before the eyes of an astonished world. The greatness of the lesson has been dwarfed for most of us by an often half-unconscious prejudice of race-difference. The West having managed to lodge its hasty foot on the neck of the East is prone to forget that it is from the East that the wonders of patience and wisdom have come to a world of men who set the value of life in the power to act rather than in the faculty of meditation. It has been dwarfed by this, and it has been obscured by a cloud of considerations with whose shaping wisdom and meditation had little or nothing to do; by the weary platitudes on the military situation which (apart from geographical conditions) is the same everlasting situation that has prevailed since the times of Hannibal and Scipio,[1] and further back yet, since the beginning of historical record—since prehistoric times, for that matter; by the conventional expressions of horror at the tale of maiming and

1 Hannibal (247-c. 181 BC) led Carthage against Rome during the Second Punic War (218-201 BC). He was defeated by the Roman general Publius Cornelius Scipio Africanus (236-c. 183 BC) at the Battle of Zama (202 BC).

killing; by the rumours of peace with guesses more or less plausible as to its conditions. All this is made legitimate by the consecrated custom of writers in such time as this—the time of a great war. More legitimate in view of the situation created in Europe are the speculations as to the course of events after the war. More legitimate, but hardly more wise than the irresponsible talk of strategy that never changes, and of terms of peace that do not matter.

And above it all, unaccountably persistent—unaccountably, unless on the theory that there is no evidence-subduing awe like the fear inspired by the appearances of brute force—the decrepit old, hundred years old, spectre of Russia's might[1] still faces Europe from above the teeming grave of Russian people. This dreaded and strange apparition, bristling with bayonets, armed with chains, hung over with holy images, that something not of this world, partaking of a ravenous Ghoul, of a blind Djinn[2] grown up from a cloud, and of the Old Man of the Sea,[3] still faces us with its old stupidity, with its strange mystical arrogance, stamping its shadowy feet upon the gravestone of autocracy, already cracked beyond repair by the torpedoes of Togo's fleet[4] and the guns of Oyama,[5] already heaving in the blood-soaked ground with the first stirrings of a resurrection.

Never before had the Western world the opportunity to look so deep into the black abyss which separates a soulless autocracy posing as, and even believing itself to be, the arbiter of Europe, from the benighted, starved souls of its people. This is the real object-lesson of this war, its unforgettable information. And this war's true mission, disengaged from the economic origins of that contest, from doors open or shut, from the fields of Korea for Russian wheat or Japanese rice, from the ownership of ice-free ports and the command of the waters of the East—its true mission was to lay a ghost.[6] It has accomplished it. Whether Kuropatkin[7] was incapable or unlucky, whether or

---

1   A reference to Russia's reputation as the supreme military power on land during most of the nineteenth century after Napoleon's defeat in 1815.

2   A Jinn or Jinni, a class of spirits lower than angels in Muslim mythology and capable of exercising supernatural powers.

3   In Greek mythology, a sea god noted for wisdom and prophecy. The name is used for various sea gods including Nereus and Proteus.

4   Heihachirō Tōgō (1848-1934), commander of the Japanese fleet.

5   Iwao Ōyama (1842-1916), commander of the Japanese army in Manchuria.

6   I.e., to lay it to rest. The war was fought over control of Korea and Port Arthur in southern Manchuria in order that Japan could have greater access to naval bases and thus more easily secure colonies.

7   General Aleksei Nikolaevich Kuropatikin (1848-1925), commander-in-chief of the Russian forces.

not Russia issuing next year, or the year after next, from behind a rampart of piled-up corpses will win or lose a fresh campaign—are minor considerations. The task of Japan is done; the mission accomplished; the ghost of Russian might is laid. Only Europe, accustomed so long to the presence of that portent, seems unable to comprehend that, as in the fables of our childhood, the twelve strokes of the hour have rung, the cock has crowed, the apparition has vanished—never to haunt again this world which has been used to gaze at it with vague dread and many misgivings.

It was a fascination. And the hallucination still lasts as inexplicable in its persistence as in its duration. It seems so unaccountable, that the doubt arises as to the sincerity of all that talk as to what Russia will or will not do, whether it will raise or not another army, whether it will bury the Japanese in Manchuria under seventy millions of sacrificed peasants' caps (as her Press boasted a little more than a year ago) or give up to them that jewel of her crown, Saghalien,[1] together with some other things; whether, perchance, as an interesting alternative, it will make peace on the Amur[2] in order to make war beyond the Oxus.[3]

All these speculations (with many others) have appeared gravely in print; and if they have been gravely considered by only one reader out of each hundred, there must be something subtly noxious to the human brain in the composition of newspaper ink; or else it is that the large page, the columns of words, the leaded headings, exalt the mind into a state of feverish credulity. The printed voice of the Press makes a sort of still uproar, taking from men both the power to reflect and the faculty of genuine feeling; leaving them only the artificially created need of having something exciting to talk about.

The truth is that the Russia of our fathers, of our childhood, of our middle-age; the testamentary Russia of Peter the Great[4]—who imagined that all the nations were delivered into the hand of Tsardom—can do nothing. It can do nothing because it does not exist. It has vanished for ever at last, and as yet there is no new Russia to take the place of that ill-omened creation, which, being a fantasy of a madman's brain,

---

1  Sakhalin Island, located north of Japan's Hokkaidō island between the Tatar Strait and the Sea of Okhotsk. At the end of the Russo-Japanese War, Russia ceded the southern half of the island to Japan.

2  A river in eastern Asia that runs through Siberia, Mongolia, and China and empties into the Tatar Strait.

3  Older name for Amu-Dar'ia or the Amu River. It forms part of the border between Afghanistan and several former Russian provinces, such as Turkmenistan, and eventually empties into the Aral Sea.

4  Tsar from 1682 to 1725, particularly known for his attempts to westernize Russia and transform it into what would become the Russian Empire.

could in reality be nothing else than a figure out of a nightmare seated upon a monument of fear and oppression.[1]

The true greatness of a State does not spring from such a contemptible source. It is a matter of logical growth, of faith and courage. Its inspiration springs from the constructive instinct of the people, governed by the strong hand of a collective conscience and voiced in the wisdom and counsel of men who seldom reap the reward of gratitude. Many States have been powerful, but, perhaps, none have been really great—as yet. That the position of a State in reference to the moral methods of its development can be seen only historically, is true. Perhaps mankind has not lived long enough for a comprehensive view of any particular case. Perhaps no one will ever live long enough; and perhaps this earth shared out amongst our clashing ambitions by the anxious arrangements of statesmen shall come to an end before we attain the felicity of greeting with unanimous applause the perfect fruition of a great State. It is even possible that we are destined for another sort of bliss altogether: that sort which consists in being perpetually duped by false appearances. But whatever political illusion the future may hold out to our fear or our admiration, there will be none, it is safe to say, which in the magnitude of anti-humanitarian effect will equal that phantom now driven off the world by the thunder of thousands of guns, none that in its retreat will cling with an equally shameless sincerity to more unworthy supports, to the moral corruption and mental darkness of slavery, to the mere brute force of numbers.

This very ignominy of infatuation should make clear to men's feelings and reason that the downfall of Russia's might is unavoidable. Spectral it lived and spectral it disappears without leaving the memory of a single generous deed, of a single service rendered—even involuntarily—to the polity of nations. Other despotisms there have been, but none whose origin was so grimly fantastic in its baseness, and the beginning of whose end was so gruesomely ignoble. What is amazing is the myth of its irresistible strength which is dying so hard.

Considered historically, Russia's influence in Europe seems the most baseless thing in the world; a sort of convention invented by diplomatists for some dark purpose of their own, one would suspect, if the lack of grasp upon the realities of any given situation were not a characteristic in the management of international relations. A glance back at the last hundred years shows the invariable, one may say the logical, powerlessness of Russia. As a military power it has never

---

1   In his edition of *Notes on Life and Letters* (415), J.H. Stape suggests that this is a reference to the bronze equestrian statue of Peter the Great in St. Petersburg. It was commissioned by Catherine the Great and sculpted by Étienne-Maurice Falconet (1716-91) in 1782.

achieved by itself a single great thing. It has been indeed able to repel an ill-considered invasion,[1] but only by having recourse to the extreme methods of desperation. In its attacks upon its specially-selected victim this giant always struck as if with a withered right hand. All the Turkish campaigns[2] prove that, from Potemkin's[3] time to the last Eastern war in 1878,[4] entered upon with every advantage that a well-nursed prestige and a carefully fostered fanaticism can give. Even the half-armed were always too much for the might of Russia, or, rather, of the Tsardom. It was victorious only against the practically disarmed, as, in regard to its ideal of territorial expansion, a glance at a map will prove sufficiently. As an ally Russia has been always unprofitable, taking her share in the defeats rather than in the victories of her friends, but always pushing her own claims with the arrogance of an arbiter of military success. She has been unable to help to any purpose a single principle to hold its own, not even the principle of authority and legitimism which Nicholas the First[5] had declared so haughtily to rest under his especial protection; just as Nicholas the Second[6] has tried to make the maintenance of peace on earth his own exclusive affair. And the first Nicholas was a good Russian; he held the belief in the sacredness of his realm with such an intensity of faith that he could not survive the first shock of doubt. Rightly envisaged, the Crimean war[7] was the end of what remained of absolutism and legitimism[8] in Europe. It threw the

---

1  A reference to Napoleon's invasion of Russia in 1812. Although the French forces reached as far as Moscow, they were forced to make a disastrous retreat (during which most of their troops were lost) as a result of the Russian army's scorched-earth policy during its own retreat that had left no supplies behind.

2  An extensive series of war fought between Russia and the Turkish Ottoman Empire during the following years:1676–81, 1687, 1689, 1695-96, 1710-12, 1735-39, 1768-74, 1787-91, 1806-12, 1828-29, 1853-56, and 1877-78. Russia fought these campaigns in an attempt to expand its southern borders, particularly to obtain a port on the Black Sea.

3  Grigorii Aleksandrovich Potëmkin (1739-91), Russian army officer, statesman, and lover of Catherine the Great. He is particularly known for his efforts to expand Russia's southern borders into Crimea.

4  A reference to the Russo-Turkey War of 1877-78 in which a Russian victory resulted in significantly increased influence in the Balkans.

5  Nikolai I, tsar of Russian from 1825 to 1855, was especially known for his role in solidifying autocratic rule.

6  Nikolai II, tsar of Russia from 1895 to 1917, another strong defender of autocracy and the last Russian emperor; he was executed after the Russian Revolution of 1917.

7  The Crimean War of 1853-56 between Russia and the forces of the Ottoman Turks, England, France, and Sardinia-Piedmont.

8  A person ruling based upon legitimacy.

way open for the liberation of Italy.[1] The war in Manchuria makes an end of absolutism in Russia, whoever has got to perish from the shock behind a rampart of dead ukases,[2] manifestoes, and rescripts.[3] In the space of a short fifty years the self-appointed Apostle of Absolutism and the self-appointed Apostle of Peace, the Augustus[4] and the Augustulus[5] of the *régime* that was wont to speak contemptuously to European Foreign Offices in the beautiful French phrases of Prince Gorchakov,[6] have fallen victims, each after his kind, to their shadowy and dreadful familiar, to the phantom, part Ghoul, part Djinn, part Old Man of the Sea, with beak and claws and a double head, looking greedily both East and West on the confines of two continents.

That nobody through all that time penetrated the true nature of the monster it is impossible to believe. But of the many who must have seen, all were either too modest, too cautious, perhaps too discreet, to speak; or else were too insignificant to be heard or believed. Yet not all.

In the very early 'sixties Prince Bismarck, then about to leave his post of Prussian Minister in St. Petersburg,[7] called—so the story goes—upon another distinguished diplomatist. After some talk upon the general situation, the future Chancellor of the German Empire remarked that it was his practice to resume[8] the impressions he carried out of every country where he had made a long stay, in a short sentence, which he caused to be engraved upon some trinket. "I am leaving this country now and this is what I bring away from it," he continued, taking off his finger a new ring to show his colleague the inscription inside: "*La Russie c'est le néant.*"[9]

Prince Bismarck had the truth of the matter, and was neither too modest nor too discreet not to speak out. Certainly he was not afraid of not being believed. Yet he did not shout his knowledge from the house-tops. He meant to have the phantom for his accom-

---

1   A reference to the war of 1859 in which Piedmont (in northwestern Italy) and its ally France sought to oust Austrian troops from Piedmont.

2   Legally-binding orders or proclamations by a Russian emperor.

3   Official decrees or pronouncements.

4   Gaius Octavius, later Cæsar Augustus (63 BC-AD 43), the first Roman emperor, whose reign was marked by the peace he restored to the empire following the Civil War (49-46 BC).

5   A derogatory diminutive for Augustus.

6   Aleksandr Mikhailovich Gorchakov (1798-1883), Russia's foreign minister from 1856 to 1882.

7   Bismarck was the Prussian ambassador to Russia from 1859 to 1862; he became chancellor in 1871.

8   To summarize briefly.

9   See Appendix A11, 335, note 4.

plice in an enterprise which has set the clock of peace back for many a year.

He had his way. The German Empire has been an accomplished fact for more than the third part of a century—a great and solid legacy left to the world by the ill-omened phantom of Russia's might.

It is that last that is disappearing now—unexpectedly, astonishingly, as if by a touch of that wonderful magic for which the East has always been famous. The pretence of belief in its existence will no longer answer anybody's purposes (now Prince Bismarck is dead) unless the purposes of the writers of sensational paragraphs as to this *Néant* making an armed descent upon the plains of India.[1] That sort of folly would be beneath notice if it did not distract attention from the real problem created for Europe by the war in the Far East.

For good or evil in the working-out of her destiny, Russia is bound to remain a *Néant* for many long years, in a more even than the Bismarckian sense. The very fear of this spectre being gone it behoves us to consider its legacy—the fact (no phantom that) accomplished in Central Europe by its help and connivance.

The German Empire may feel at bottom the loss of an old accomplice always amenable to confidential whispers of a bargain; but in the first instance it cannot but rejoice at the fundamental weakening of a possible obstacle to its instincts of territorial expansion. There is a removal of that latent feeling of restraint which the presence of a powerful neighbour, however implicated with you in a sense of common guilt, is bound to inspire. The common guilt of the two Empires is defined precisely by their frontier line running through the Polish provinces. Without indulging in excessive feelings of indignation at that country's partition,[2] or going so far as to believe—with a late French politician—in the "immanent justice of things,"[3] it is clear that a material situation, based upon an essentially immoral transaction, contains the germ of fatal differences in the temperament of the two partners in iniquity—whatever it is. Germany has been the evil counsellor of Russia on all the questions of her Polish problem. Always urging the adoption of the most repressive measures with a perfectly logical duplicity, Prince Bismarck's Empire has taken care to couple the neighbourly offers of military assistance with its merciless advice. The thought of the Polish provinces accepting a frank reconciliation

---

1 A fear in England throughout much of the nineteenth century.
2 A reference to the first (1772), second (1793), and third (1795) partitions of Poland among Prussia, Russia, and Austria-Hungary, the last of which resulted in the complete disappearance of an autonomous Poland.
3 A comment attributed to Léon Gambetta (1838-82), French statesman and republican.

with a humanised Russia and bringing the weight of homogeneous loyalty to within a few score of miles of Berlin[1] has been always intensely distasteful to the arrogant Germanising tendencies of the other partner in iniquity. And, besides, the way to the Baltic provinces leads over the Niemen[2] and over the Vistula.[3]

And now, when there is a possibility of serious internal disturbances destroying the sort of order autocracy had kept in Russia, the road over these rivers is seen wearing a more inviting aspect. At any moment the pretext of armed intervention may be found in a revolutionary outbreak provoked by socialists, perhaps—but at any rate by the political immaturity of the enlightened classes and by the political barbarism of the Russian people. The throes of Russian resurrection will be long and painful. This is not the place to speculate upon the nature of these convulsions; but there must be some violent break-up of the lamentable tradition, a shattering of the social, of the administrative—perhaps of the territorial—unity.

Voices have been heard saying that the time for reforms in Russia is already past. This is the superficial view of a more profound truth that for Russia there has never been such a time within the memory of mankind. It is impossible to initiate any sort of reform upon a phase of blind absolutism, and in Russia there has never been anything else to which the faintest tradition could, after ages of error, go back as to a parting of the ways.

In Europe the monarchical principle stands justified in its struggle with the growth of political liberty by the evolution of the idea of nationality as we see it concreted at the present time, by the inception of that wider solidarity grouping together around the standard of absolute power these larger agglomerations of mankind. This service of unification, creating close-knit communities possessing the ability, the will, and the power to pursue a common ideal, has prepared the ground for the advent of a still larger understanding: for the solidarity of Europeanism, which must be the next step towards the advent of Concord and Justice; an advent that, however delayed by the cowardly worship of force and the evil passions of national selfishness, has been, and remains, the only possible goal of our progress.

The conceptions of legality, of larger patriotism, of national duties and aspirations have grown under the shadow of the unlimited monar-

---

1   The capital city of Germany, located in the northeastern part of the country.

2   A major river in eastern Europe (also known as the Neman River) beginning in Belarus, flowing through Lithuania, and emptying into the Baltic Sea.

3   The longest river in Poland (also known as the Wisła), beginning near the borders of Slovakia and the Czech Republic and emptying into the Gulf of Gdańsk.

chies of Europe, which were the creations of historical necessity. There were seeds of wisdom in their very violences and abuses. They had a past and a future; they were human. But under the shadow of Russian autocracy nothing could grow. Russian autocracy succeeded to nothing; it had no historical past, and it cannot hope for a historical future. It can only end. By no industry of investigation, by no fantastic stretch of benevolence, can it be presented as a phase of development through which a society, a State, must pass on the way to the full consciousness of its destiny. It lies outside the stream of progress. This despotism has been utterly un-European. And neither has it been Asiatic in its nature. Oriental despotisms belong to the history of mankind; they have left their trace on our minds and our imagination by their splendour, by their culture, by their art, by the exploits of great conquerors. The record of their rise and decay has an intellectual value; they are in their origins and their course the manifestations of human needs, the instruments of racial temperament, of conquering force, of faith and fanaticism. The Russian autocracy as we see it now is a thing apart. It is impossible to assign to it any rational origin in the vices, the misfortunes, the necessities, or the passions of mankind. This despotism has neither an European nor an Oriental parentage; more, it seems to have no root either in the institutions or the follies of this earth. What strikes one with a sort of awe is just this something inhuman in its character. It is like a visitation, like a curse from Heaven falling in the darkness of ages upon the immense plains of forest and steppe[1] lying dumbly on the confines of two continents: a true desert harbouring no spirit either of the East or of the West.

This pitiful fate of a country held by an evil spell, suffering from an awful visitation for which the responsibility cannot be traced either to her sins or her follies, has made Russia as a nation so difficult to understand by Europe. From the very first ghastly dawn of her existence as a State she had to breathe the atmosphere of despotism; she found nothing but the arbitrary will of an obscure autocrat at the beginning and end of her organisation. Hence arises her impenetrability to whatever is true in Western thought. Western thought, when it crosses her frontier, falls under the spell of her autocracy and becomes a noxious parody of itself. Hence the contradictions, the riddles of her national life, which are looked upon with such curiosity by the rest of the world. The curse had entered her very soul; autocracy, and nothing else in the world, has moulded her institutions, and with the poison of slavery drugged the national temperament into the apathy of a hope-

---

1   A plain without trees, also associated with the Steppe running from Hungary eastward to Manchuria.

less fatalism. It seems to have gone into the blood, tainting every mental activity in its source by a half-mystical, insensate, fascinating assertion of purity and holiness. The Government of Holy Russia,[1] arrogating to itself the supreme power to torment and slaughter the bodies of its subjects like a God-sent scourge,[2] has been most cruel to those whom it allowed to live under the shadow of its dispensation. The worst crime against humanity of that system we behold now crouching at bay behind vast heaps of mangled corpses is the ruthless destruction of innumerable minds. The greatest horror of the world—madness—walked faithfully in its train. Some of the best intellects of Russia, after struggling in vain against the spell, ended by throwing themselves at the feet of that hopeless despotism as a giddy man leaps into an abyss.[3] An attentive survey of Russia's literature, of her church, of her administration, and the cross-currents of her thought, must end in the verdict that the Russia of to-day has not the right to give her voice on a single question touching the future of humanity, because from the very inception of her being the brutal destruction of dignity, of truth, of rectitude, of all that is fruitful in human nature has been made the imperative condition of her existence. The great governmental secret of that imperium[4] which Prince Bismarck had the insight and the courage to call *Le Néant*, has been the extirpation of every intellectual hope. To pronounce in the face of such a past the word Evolution, which is precisely the expression of the highest intellectual hope, is a gruesome pleasantry. There can be no evolution out of a grave. Another word of less scientific sound has been very much pronounced of late in connection with Russia's future, a word of more vague import, a word of dread as much as of hope—Revolution.

In the face of the events of the last four months, this word has sprung instinctively, as it were, on grave lips, and has been heard with solemn forebodings. More or less consciously Europe is preparing

---

1  A common expression, probably with its origins in mediæval times, equivalent to the "Holy Roman Empire" in the sense of suggesting a divinely-appointed political entity. Conrad's use of the term here is clearly ironic.

2  Perhaps a reference to Attila (c. 406-53), also known as the Scourge or God or *Flagellum Dei* (Latin), who rampaged across Europe during his reign as king of the Huns (c. 433-53) and has become an image of ruthlessness and cruelty; more generally, a scourge can refer to a kind of whip used for chastisement or penance.

3  Councillor Mikulin makes a similar comment to Razumov: "You shall be coming back to us. Some of our greatest minds had to do that in the end" (263).

4  A Latin word meaning "command" or "empire," referring to the supreme executive power of the Roman rulers and encompassing both military and civil affairs.

herself for a spectacle of much violence and perhaps of an inspiring nobility of greatness. And there will be nothing of what she expects. She will see neither the anticipated character of the violence nor yet any signs of generous greatness. Her expectations, more or less vaguely expressed, give the measure of her ignorance of that *Néant* which for so many years had remained hidden behind the phantom of invincible armies.

*Néant!* In a way, yes! And yet perhaps Prince Bismarck has let himself be led away by the seduction of a good phrase into the use of an inexact term. The form of his judgment had to be pithy, striking, engraved within a ring. If he erred, then, no doubt, he erred deliberately. The saying was near enough the truth to serve, and perhaps he did not want to destroy utterly by a more severe definition the prestige of the sham that could not deceive his genius. Prince Bismarck has been really complimentary to the useful phantom of the autocratic might. There is an awe-inspiring idea of infinity conveyed in the word *Néant*—and in Russia there is no idea. She is not a *Néant*; she is and has been simply the negation of everything worth living for. She is not an empty void, she is a yawning chasm open between East and West; a bottomless abyss that has swallowed up every hope of mercy, every aspiration towards personal dignity, towards freedom, towards knowledge; every ennobling desire of the heart, every redeeming whisper of conscience. Those that have peered into that abyss, where the dreams of Panslavism,[1] of universal conquest, mingled with the hate and contempt for Western ideas, drifted impotently like shapes of mist, know well that it is bottomless; that there is in it no ground for anything that could in the remotest degree serve even the lowest interests of mankind—and certainly no ground ready for a revolution.

The sin of the old European Monarchies was not the absolutism inherent in every form of government; it was the inability to alter the forms of their legality, grown narrow and oppressive with the march of time. Every form of legality is bound to degenerate into oppression, and the legality in the forms of monarchical institutions sooner, perhaps, than any other. It has not been the business of monarchies to be adaptive from within. With the mission of uniting and consolidating the particular ambitions and interests of feudalism[2] in favour of a

---

1   A movement originally aimed at the unity of all Slavic peoples. Later, Russia used the idea as a political tool to justify and push for Russian rule of all Slavic peoples and nations.

2   A system of rule prevalent in Europe, particularly during the Middle Ages, in which a lord provided land to vassals in exchange for services. A similar system existed in Russia until the latter part of the nineteenth century.

larger conception of a State, of giving self-consciousness, force, and nationality to the scattered energies of thought and action, they were fated to lag behind the march of ideas they had themselves set in motion in a direction they could neither understand nor approve. Yet, for all that, the thrones still remain, and what is more significant, perhaps, many of the dynasties, too, have survived. The revolutions of European States have never been in the nature of absolute protests *en masse*[1] against the monarchical principle: they were the uprising of the people against the oppressive degeneration of legality. But there never has been any legality in Russia; she is a negation of that as of everything else having its root in reason or conscience. The ground of every revolution had to be intellectually prepared. A revolution is a short cut in the rational development of national needs in response to the growth of world-wide ideals. It is conceivably possible for a monarch of genius to put himself at the head of a revolution without ceasing to be the king of his people. For the autocracy of Holy Russia the only conceivable self-reform is—suicide.

The same relentless fate holds in its grip the all-powerful ruler and his helpless people. Wielders of a power purchased by an unspeakable baseness of subjection to the Khans of the Tartar horde,[2] the Princes of Russia who, in their heart of hearts, had come in time to regard themselves as superior to every monarch of Europe, have never risen to be the chiefs of a nation. Their authority has never been sanctioned by popular tradition, by ideas of intelligent loyalty, of devotion, of political necessity, of simple expediency, or even by the power of the sword. Its only sanction has been the fear of the lash. Thus debarred from attaining to the dignity of chiefs, they have remained mere owners of slaves, asserting with half-mystical vanity the divine origin of the evil thing which had made them and their people its own. In whatever form of upheaval Autocratic Russia is to find her end, it can never be a revolution fruitful of moral consequences to mankind. It can not be anything else but a rising of slaves. It is a tragic circumstance that the only thing one can wish to that people who had never seen face to face either law, order, justice, right, truth about itself or the rest of the world, who had known nothing outside the capricious will of its irresponsible masters, is that it should find in the approaching hour of need, not an organiser

---

1   As a group or whole (French).

2   A reference to the Tatar rule of most of Russia from the thirteenth century to the fifteenth century. The original conquerors became known as the Golden Horde. During the Tatar rule, Russian leaders were expected to pay homage to the Tatar rulers or Khans; see 151.

or a law-giver with the wisdom of a Lycurgus[1] or a Solon[2] for their service, but at least the force of energy and desperation in some as yet unknown Spartacus.[3]

A brand of hopeless moral and mental inferiority is set upon Russian achievements; and the coming events of her internal changes, however appalling they may be in their magnitude, will be nothing more impressive than the convulsions of a colossal body. As her boasted military force that, corrupt in its origin, has ever struck no other but faltering blows, so her soul, kept benumbed by her temporal and spiritual master with the poison of tyranny and superstition, will find itself on awakening possessed of no language, a monstrous full-grown child having first to learn the ways of living thought and articulate speech. It is safe to say that tyranny assuming a thousand protean[4] shapes will remain clinging to her struggles for a long time before her blind multitudes succeed at last in trampling her out of existence under their million bare feet.

That would be the beginning. What is to come after? The conquest of freedom to call your soul your own is only the first step on the road to excellence. We, in Europe, having gone a step or two further, have had the time to forget how little that freedom means. To Russia it must seem everything. A prisoner shut up in a noisome dungeon concentrates all his hope and desire on the moment of stepping out beyond the gates. It appears to him pregnant with an immense and final importance; whereas what is important is the spirit in which he will draw the first breath of freedom, the counsels he will hear, the hands he may find extended, the endless days of toil that must follow, wherein he will have to build his future with no other material but what he can find within himself.

It would be vain for Russia to hope for the support and counsel of collective wisdom. Since 1870 (as a distinguished statesman of the old tradition disconsolately exclaimed): "*Il n'y a plus d'Europe!*"[5] There is, indeed, no Europe. The idea of a Europe united in the solidarity of her dynasties, which for a moment seemed to dawn on the horizon of the

---

1   Legendary lawgiver of the seventh or eighth century BC who, according to tradition, founded most of Sparta's laws and government institutions.

2   Athenian statesman and poet (c. 630–c. 559 BC) who is often credited with laying the foundations for Athenian democracy.

3   Gladiator and slave (d. 71 BC) who led a two-year slave revolt against Rome, which was eventually suppressed.

4   Variable; versatile.

5   Europe is no more (French). Louis-Adolphe Thiers (1797-1877) is reputed to have made this statement when unable to rally European support against Prussia in 1870.

Vienna Congress[1] through the subsiding dust of Napoleonic alarums and excursions,[2] has been extinguished by the larger glamour of less restraining ideals. Instead of the doctrine of solidarity it was the doctrine of nationalities much more favourable to spoliations[3] that came to the front, and since its greatest triumphs at Sadowa[4] and Sedan[5] there is no Europe. Meanwhile, till the time comes when there will be no frontiers, there are alliances so shamelessly based upon the exigencies of suspicion and mistrust that their cohesive force waxes and wanes with every year, almost with the event of every passing month. This is the atmosphere Russia will find when the last rampart of tyranny has been beaten down. But what hands, what voices will she find on coming out into the light of day? An ally she has yet who more than any other of Russia's allies has found that she had parted with lots of solid substance in exchange for a shadow. It is true that the shadow was indeed the mightiest, the darkest that the modern world had ever known—and the most overbearing. But it is fading now, and the tone of truest anxiety as to what is to take its place will come, no doubt, from that and no other direction; and no doubt, also, it will have that note of generosity which even in the moments of greatest aberration is seldom wanting in the voice of the French people.

Two neighbours Russia will find at her door. Austria, traditionally unaggressive whenever her hand is not forced, ruled by a dynasty of uncertain future, weakened by her duality, can only speak to her in an uncertain, bi-lingual phrase. Prussia, grown in something like sixty years from an almost pitiful dependant into a bullying friend and evil-counsellor of Russia's masters, may, indeed, hasten to extend a strong hand to the weakness of her exhausted body, but, if so, it will be only with the intention of tearing away the long-coveted part of her substance.[6]

---

1  The Congress of Vienna was held from 1 September 1814 to 9 June 1815 among the major European powers in an attempt to redraw the borders in Europe after the fall of Napoleonic France.

2  Confused noise and bustle.

3  Plunderings or pillagings; destruction.

4  Battle of Sadowa or Battle of Königgrätz (3 July 1866), a decisive Prussian victory over Austria during the Seven Weeks' War (1866), also known as the Austro-Prussian War.

5  Battle of Sedan (1 September 1870), a decisive Prussian victory over France in the Franco-German War (1870-71), also known as the Franco-Prussian War.

6  A somewhat prophetic statement since Germany would declare war on Russia shortly after the onset of the First World War, the "long-coveted part" being German-speaking territories under Russian rule.

Pangermanism[1] is by no means a shape of mists, and Germany is anything but a *Néant* where thought and effort are likely to lose themselves without sound or trace. It is a powerful and voracious organism, full of unscrupulous self-confidence, whose appetite for aggrandisement will only be limited by the power of helping itself to the severed members of its friends and neighbours. The era of wars so eloquently denounced by the old Republicans[2] as the peculiar blood-guilt of dynastic ambitions is by no means over yet. They will be fought out differently, with lesser frequency, with an increased bitterness and the savage tooth-and-claw obstinacy of a struggle for existence. They will make us regret the time of dynastic ambitions, with their human absurdity moderated by prudence and even by shame, by the fear of personal responsibility and the regard paid to certain forms of conventional decency. For, if the monarchs of Europe have been derided for addressing each other as "brother" in autograph communications, that relationship was at least as effective as any form of brotherhood likely to be established between the rival nations of this continent, which, we are assured on all hands, is the heritage of democracy. In the ceremonial brotherhood of monarchs the reality of blood ties entered often for what little it is worth as a drag on unscrupulous desires of glory or greed. Besides, there was always the common danger of exasperated peoples, and some respect for each other's divine right.[3] No leader of a democracy without other ancestry but the sudden shout of a multitude, and debarred by the very condition of his power from even thinking of a direct heir, will have any interest in calling brother the leader of another democracy—a chief as fatherless and heirless as himself.

The war of 1870,[4] brought about by the Third Napoleon's half-generous, half-selfish adoption of the principle of nationalities,[5] was the first war characterised by a special intensity of hate, by a new note

---

1  A movement that was particularly prominent in the late nineteenth and early twentieth centuries, intended to unify all German-speaking peoples and countries; it was also used as a justification for German expansionist actions in Europe, particularly later during the Nazi era.

2  A reference to figures such as Giuseppe Mazzini, Giuseppe Garibaldi (1807-82), and Léon Gambetta, who fought for republican principles of government in Europe and sought to throw off the old monarchical system.

3  A reference to the concept of divine right of kings: i.e., that kings were appointed by God to rule over their people.

4  The Franco-German War, in which Prussia defeated France.

5  Napoleon III, Charles-Louis-Napoleon Bonaparte (1808-73), opposed Prussia's attempt to place an ally on the vacant Spanish throne. He argued for the principle of nationality, though he was actually more interested in impeding the spread of Prussian influence in Europe.

in the tune of an old song for which we may thank the Teutonic[1] thoroughness. Was it not that excellent *bourgeoise*,[2] Princess Bismarck[3] (to keep only to great examples), who was so righteously anxious to see men, women, and children—emphatically the children, too—of the abominable French nation massacred off the face of the earth? This illustration of the new war-temper is artlessly revealed in the prattle of the amiable Busch,[4] the Chancellor's pet "reptile"[5] of the Press. And this was supposed to be a war for an idea! Too much, however, should not be made of that good wife's and mother's sentiments any more than of the good First Emperor William's[6] tears, shed so abundantly after every battle, by letter, telegram, and otherwise, during the course of the same war, before a dumb and shame-faced continent. These were merely the expressions of the simplicity of a nation which more than any other has a tendency to run into the grotesque. There is worse to come.

To-day, in the fierce grapple of two nations of different race,[7] the short era of national wars seems about to close. No war will be waged for an idea. The "noxious idle aristocracies"[8] of yesterday fought without malice for an occupation, for the honour, for the fun of the thing. The virtuous, industrious democratic States of to-morrow may yet be reduced to fighting for a crust of dry bread, with all the hate, ferocity and fury that must attach to the vital importance of such an issue. The dreams of sanguine humanitarians raised almost to ecstasy about the year 'fifty of the last century by the moving sight of the

---

1 Germanic.

2 A middle-class woman, particularly of the mercantile class (French).

3 Jeanne Frederika Charlotte Dorothea Eleanore von Bismarck (1824-94), wife of Otto von Bismarck.

4 Julius Hermann Moritz Busch (1821-99), German publicist. He became one of Bismarck's press agents and was closely associated with him, publishing several books and pamphlets favorable toward Bismarck.

5 In the sense of "crawling" or "groveling," rather than "venomous." In other words, Conrad refers to the press being in the service of Bismarck.

6 Wilhelm I, Wilhelm Friedrich Ludwig (1797-1888), became king of Prussia in 1861 and emperor of Germany in 1871.

7 I.e., Russia and Japan.

8 It is uncertain whom, if anyone, Conrad is quoting here, although the quotation bears some similarity to a comment by the French novelist Anatole France (1844-1924) regarding French Naturalist novelist Émile Zola (1840-1902): that Zola "attacks with vigorous hatred an idle, frivolous society, a base and noxious aristocracy" (as quoted by J.G. Patterson in his *A Zola Dictionary* [Routledge, 1912], xxii).

Crystal Palace[1]—crammed full with that variegated rubbish which it seems to be the bizarre fate of humanity to produce for the benefit of a few employers of labour—have vanished as quickly as they had arisen. The golden hopes of peace have in a single night turned to dead leaves in every drawer of every benevolent theorist's writing-table. A swift disenchantment overtook the incredible infatuation which could put its trust in the peaceful nature of industrial and commercial competition.

Industrialism and commercialism—wearing high-sounding names in many languages (*Welt-Politik*[2] may serve for one instance), picking up coins behind the severe and disdainful figure of science whose giant strides have widened for us the horizon of the universe by some few inches—stand ready, almost eager, to appeal to the sword as soon as the globe of the earth has shrunk beneath our growing numbers by another ell[3] or so. And democracy, which has elected to pin its faith to the supremacy of material interests,[4] will have to fight their battles to the bitter end, on a mere pittance—unless, indeed, some statesman of exceptional ability and overwhelming prestige succeeds in carrying through an international understanding for the delimitation of spheres of trade all over the earth, on the model of the territorial spheres of influence marked in Africa to keep the competitors for the privilege of improving the nigger (as a buying machine) from flying prematurely at each other's throats.

This seems the only expedient at hand for the temporary maintenance of European peace, with its alliances based on mutual distrust, the preparedness for war as its ideal, and the fear of wounds, luckily stronger, so far, than the pinch of hunger, for its only guarantee. The true peace of the world will be a place of refuge much less like a beleaguered fortress and more, let us hope, in the nature of an inviolable temple. It will be built on less perishable foundations than those of material interests. But it must be confessed that the architectural

---

1 A famous glass and iron structure designed by Sir Joseph Paxton (1801-65), which housed the Great Exhibition of 1851 in Hyde Park in London. It became symbolic of the triumph of science and technology during the nineteenth century.

2 Literally, "world politics" (German), but used specifically by Germany during the latter part of the nineteenth century to mean a policy in which they sought to increase their power by acquiring greater colonial holdings and increased military production.

3 A unit of measurement, varying in length; for example, in England 45 inches, while in Scotland 37.2 inches.

4 An expression that appears repeatedly, with extremely negative connotations, in Conrad's *Nostromo* (1904) and implying soulless economic priorities.

aspect of the universal city remains as yet inconceivable—that the very ground of its erection has not been cleared of the jungle.

Never before in history has the right of war been more fully admitted in the rounded periods of public speeches, in books, in public prints, in all the public works of peace, culminating in the establishment of the Hague Tribunal[1]—that solemnly official recognition of the Earth as a House of Strife. To him whose indignation is qualified by a measure of hope and affection, the efforts of mankind to work its own salvation present a sight of disarming comicality. After clinging for ages to the steps of the heavenly throne, they are now, without modifying much their attitude, trying with touching ingenuity to steal one by one the thunderbolts of their Jupiter.[2] They have removed war from the list of heaven-sent visitations that could only be prayed against; they have erased its name from the supplication against the wrath of war, pestilence and famine, as it is found in the litanies[3] of the Roman Church; they have dragged the scourge down from the skies and have made it into a calm and regulated institution. At first sight the change does not seem for the better. Jove's thunderbolt looks a most dangerous plaything in the hands of the people. But a solemnly established institution begins to grow old at once in the discussion, abuse, worship, and execration of men. It grows obsolete, odious, and intolerable; it stands fatally condemned to an unhonoured old age.

Therein lies the best hope of advanced thought, and the best way to help its prospects is to provide in the fullest, frankest way for the conditions of the present day. War is one of its conditions; it is its principal condition. It lies at the heart of every question agitating the fears and hopes of a humanity divided against itself. The succeeding ages have changed nothing except the watchwords[4] of the armies. The intellectual stage of mankind being as yet in its infancy, and States, like most individuals, having but a feeble and imperfect consciousness of the worth and force of the inner life, the need of making their existence manifest to themselves is determined in the direction of physi-

---

1  The Permanent Court of Arbitration or Hague Tribunal, located in The Hague, Netherlands, established in 1899 as a means of arbitrating international disputes.

2  The chief Roman God, worshiped as the god of thunder and lightning, and often depicted as hurling lightning bolts; also known as Jove.

3  A reference to the *Litaniæ Sanctorum* or Litany of the Saints, a prayer containing the Latin line "A peste, fame, et bello" (from pestilence, famine, and war) spoken by the officiating priest, to which the people respond, "Libera nos, Domine" (Lord, deliver us).

4  In the original sense of military password; Conrad uses it on p. 396 in the modern sense of principle or slogan.

cal activity. The idea of ceasing to grow in territory, in strength, in wealth, in influence—in anything but wisdom and self-knowledge—is odious to them as an omen of the end. Action, in which is to be found the illusion of a mastered destiny, can alone satisfy our uneasy vanity and lay to rest the haunting fear of the future—a sentiment concealed, indeed, but proving its existence by the force it has, when invoked, to stir the passions of a nation. It will be long before we have learned that in the great darkness before us there is nothing that we need fear. Let us act lest we perish—is the cry. And the only form of action open to a State can be of no other than aggressive nature.

There are many kinds of aggressions, though the sanction of them all is one and the same—the magazine rifle of the latest pattern. In preparation for or against such a form of action the States of Europe are spending now such moments of uneasy leisure as they can snatch from the labours of factory and counting-house.

Never before had war received so much homage at the lips of men, never has it reigned with less undisputed sway in their minds. It has harnessed science to its gun-carriages; it has enriched a few respectable manufacturers, scattered doles of food and raiment amongst a few thousand skilled workmen, devoured the first youth of whole generations, and reaped its harvest of countless corpses. It has perverted the intelligence of men, women, and children, and has made the speeches of Emperors, Kings, Presidents, and Ministers monotonous with ardent protestations of fidelity to peace. Indeed, it has made peace altogether its own—it has modelled it on its own image: a martial, overbearing, war-lord sort of peace, with a mailed[1] fist, and turned-up moustaches, ringing with the din of grand manœuvres, eloquent with allusions to glorious feats of arms; it has made it so magnificent as to be almost as expensive to keep up as itself. And it has taken even more upon itself. As if it were the prophet of a new faith it has sent out apostles of its own, who at one time went about (mostly in newspapers) preaching the gospel of the mystic sanctity of its sacrifices, and the regenerating power of spilt blood, to the poor in mind—whose name is legion.[2]

It has been observed that in the course of earthly greatness such a day of culminating triumph is often paid by a morrow of sudden extinction. Let us hope so. Yet the dawn of that day of retribution may be a long time breaking above a dark horizon. War is with us now; and, whether this one ends soon or late, war will be with us again. And it is the way of true wisdom for men and States to take account of things as they are.

---

1  Armor composed of chain-work, interlaced rings, overlapping plates.
2  See Luke 8:30: "And Jesus asked him, saying, What is thy name? And he said, Legion: because many devils were entered into him." (See also Mark 5:9.)

Civilisation has done its little best by our sensibilities for whose growth it is responsible. It has managed to remove the sights and sounds of battlefields away from our doorsteps. But it cannot be expected to achieve the feat always and under every variety of circumstance. Some day it must fail. Then we shall have a wealth of appallingly unpleasant sensations brought home to us with painful intimacy, while the apostles of war's sanctity will crawl away swiftly into the holes where they belong, somewhere in the yellow basements of newspaper offices. It is not absurd to suppose that whatever war comes to us next it will not be a distant war of *revanche*[1] waged by Russia either beyond the Amur or beyond the Oxus.

The Japanese armies have laid that ghost for many a year. They have laid it for ever, because the Russia of the future will not, for the reasons explained above, be the Russia of to-day. It will have not the same thoughts, resentments, or aims. It is even a question whether it will preserve its gigantic frame unaltered and unbroken. All speculation loses itself in the magnitude of the events made possible by the defeat of an Autocracy whose only shadow of a title to existence was the invincible power of military conquest. That it will have a miserable end in harmony with its base origin and inglorious life does not seem open to doubt. The problem of the immediate future is posed not by the eventual manner but by the approaching fact of its disappearance.

The Japanese armies, in laying the oppressive ghost, have not only accomplished what will be recognised historically as an important mission in the world's struggle against all forms of evil, they have also created a situation. They have created a situation in the East which they are competent to manage by themselves; and in doing this they have brought about a change in the condition of the West with which Europe is not well prepared to deal. The common ground of concord, good faith and justice is not sufficient to establish an action upon; since the conscience of but very few men amongst us, and that of no single Western nation as yet, will brook the restraint of abstract ideas as against the fascination of a material advantage. And eagle-eyed wisdom alone cannot take the lead of human action, which in its nature must for ever remain short-sighted. The trouble of the civilised world is the want of a common conservative principle abstract enough to give the impulse, practical enough to form the rallying point of international action tending towards the restraint of particular ambitions. Peace tribunals instituted for the greater glory of war will not replace it. Whether such a principle exists—who can say? If it does not then it ought to be invented. A sage with a sense of humour and a

---

1  Revenge (French).

heart of compassion should set about it without loss of time, and a solemn prophet full of words and fire ought to be given the task of preparing the minds. So far there is no trace of such a principle anywhere in sight; even its plausible imitations (never very effective) have disappeared long ago before the doctrine of national aspirations. *Il n'y a plus d'Europe*—there is only an armed and trading continent, the home of slowly maturing economical contests for life and death, and of loudly-proclaimed world-wide ambitions. There are also other ambitions not so loud, but deeply rooted in the envious acquisitive temperament of the last comer amongst the great Powers of the continent, whose feet are not exactly in the ocean—not yet—and whose head is very high up—in Pomerania,[1] the breeding-place of such precious Grenadiers[2] that Prince Bismarck (whom it is a pleasure to quote) would not have given the bones of one of them for the settlement of the old Eastern Question.[3] But times have changed, since, by way of keeping up, I suppose, some old barbaric German rite, the faithful servant of the Hohenzollerns[4] was buried alive to celebrate the accession of a new Emperor.[5]

Already the voice of surmises has been heard hinting tentatively at a possible re-grouping of European Powers. The alliance of the three Empires[6] is supposed possible. And it may be possible. The myth of Russia's power is dying very hard—hard enough for that combination to take place—such is the fascination that a discredited show of numbers will still exercise upon the imagination of a people trained to the worship of force. Germany may be willing to lend its support to a tottering autocracy for the sake of an undisputed first place in such a combination—and of a preponderating voice in the settlement of every question in that south-east of Europe which merges into Asia. No principle being involved in such an alliance of mere expediency, it

---

1  At that time, Pomerania was a province of Prussia constituting what would be parts of present-day Germany and Poland on the south coast of the Baltic Sea.

2  Originally, soldiers who threw grenades, but later meaning the best soldiers.

3  In a speech of 5 December 1876, Bismarck famously remarked that the Baltics were not worth the bones of a single Pomeranian grenadier.

4  The House of Hohenzollern or the Hohenzollern Dynasty was the ruling house of Brandenburg-Prussia and Imperial Germany from the fifteenth century to the twentieth century.

5  Wilhelm II, Friedrich Wilhelm Albert Viktor (1859-1941), who became German Emperor in 1888, and forced the "faithful servant" Bismarck to resign in 1890. The "barbaric German rite" is a reference to the ancient practice of burying the king's councillors with him.

6  Prussia, Russia, and Austria-Hungary.

would never be allowed to stand in the way of Germany's other ambitions. The fall of autocracy would bring its restraint automatically to an end. Thus it may be believed that the support Russian despotism may get from its once humble friend and client will not be stamped by that thoroughness which is supposed to be the mark of German superiority. Russia weakened down to the second place, or Russia eclipsed altogether during the throes of her regeneration, will answer equally well the plans of German policy—which are many and various and often incredible, though the aim of them all is the same: aggrandisement of territory and influence, with no regard to right and justice, either in the East or in the West; for that and no other is the true note of your *Welt-politik* which desires to live.

The German eagle[1] with a Prussian head looks all round the horizon not so much for something to do that would count for good in the records of the earth, as simply for something good to get. He gazes upon the land and upon the sea with the same covetous steadiness, for he has become of late a maritime eagle, and has learned to box the compass.[2] He gazes north and south, and east and west, and is inclined to look intemperately upon the waters of the Mediterranean when they are blue.[3] The disappearance of the Russian phantom has given a foreboding of unwonted freedom to the *Welt-politik*. According to the national tendency this assumption of Imperial impulses would run into the grotesque were it not for the spikes of the pickelhaubes[4] peeping out grimly from behind. Germany's attitude proves that no peace for the earth can be found in the expansion of material interests which she seems to have adopted exclusively as her only aim, ideal, and watchword. For the use of those who gaze half-unbelieving at the passing away of the Russian phantom, part Ghoul, part Djinn, part Old Man of the Sea, and wait half-doubting for the birth of a nation's soul in this age

---

1  The coat of arms of Germany prominently features a black eagle with red beak and talons; the Prussian coat of arms featured a similar eagle.

2  I.e., to look all around. In maritime navigation, this meant to call out the 32 points on the compass in order beginning at north and moving clockwise, but in practice it can mean beginning the process at any compass point and moving either clockwise or counterclockwise.

3  In his edition of *Notes on Life and Letters* (420), Stape sees this comment as an allusion to Wilhelm II's declaration on 31 March 1905 supporting Moroccan independence, which would benefit German trade and frustrate a clandestine plan by Spain and France to partition Morocco.

4  Spiked helmets (German); *Pickelhauben* is the correct plural in German.

which knows no miracles, the once famous saying of poor Gambetta,[1] tribune of the people (who was simple and believed in the "immanent justice of things") may be adapted in the shape of a warning that, so far as a future of liberty, concord and justice is concerned: *"Le Prussianisme—voilà l'ennemi!"*[2]

---

1 Léon Gambetta, who was instrumental in bringing about a republican government in France in 1871.

2 Prussia—There is the enemy! (French), an allusion to Gambetta's comment "Le cléricalisme? voilà l'ennemi!" ("Clericalism? There is the enemy!")

# Select Bibliography

## Biography

Baines, Jocelyn. *Joseph Conrad: A Critical Biography*. London: Weidenfeld & Nicolson, 1959.

Karl, Frederick R. *Joseph Conrad: The Three Lives, A Biography*. New York: Farrar, Straus, and Giroux, 1979.

Najder, Zdzisław. *Joseph Conrad: A Life*. Rochester, NY: Camden House, 2007.

## General Criticism

Berthoud, Jacques. *Joseph Conrad: The Major Phase*. Cambridge: Cambridge UP, 1978.

Fleishman, Avrom. *Conrad's Politics: Community and Anarchy in the Fiction of Joseph Conrad*. Baltimore: Johns Hopkins UP, 1967.

Guerard, Albert J. *Conrad the Novelist*. Cambridge, MA: Harvard UP, 1958.

Hay, Eloise Knapp. *The Political Novels of Joseph Conrad: A Critical Study*. Chicago: U of Chicago P, 1963.

Hewitt, Douglas. *Conrad: A Reassessment*. 3rd ed. Cambridge: Bowes & Bowes, 1975.

Moser, Thomas C. *Joseph Conrad: Achievement and Decline*. Cambridge, MA: Harvard UP, 1957.

Sherry, Norman. *Conrad's Eastern World*. Cambridge: Cambridge UP, 1966.

———. *Conrad's Western World*. Cambridge: Cambridge UP, 1971.

Warren, Robert Penn. "Introduction." Nostromo *by Joseph Conrad*. New York: Modern Library, 1951, vii–xxxix.

Watt, Ian. *Conrad in the Nineteenth Century*. Berkeley: U of California P, 1979.

Zabel, Morton Dauwen. "Editor's Introduction." *The Portable Conrad*. New York: Viking Press, 1947, 1-47.

## Articles, Books, and Book Chapters on *Under Western Eyes*

Adams, Barbara Block. "Sisters under Their Skins: The Women in the Lives of Raskolnikov and Razumov." *Conradiana* 6.2 (May 1974): 113-24.

Andersen, Mildred C. "Conrad's Perspectives on Dostoevsky's *Crime and Punishment*: An Examination of *Under Western Eyes.*" In *Joseph Conrad: East European, Polish, and Worldwide*. Ed. Wiesław Krajka. Boulder, CO: East European Monographs, 1999, 61-86.

Andreas, Osborn. *Joseph Conrad: A Study in Non-Conformity*. New York: Philosophical Library, 1959, 127-34.

Armstrong, Paul. "Cultural Differences in Conrad and James: *Under Western Eyes* and *The Ambassadors.*" *REAL* 12 (1996): 143-62.

Aroumi, Michel. "The Avatars of the Lord of the Apocalypse in *Under Western Eyes.*" In *Beyond the Roots: The Evolution of Conrad's Ideology and Art*. Ed. Wiesław Krajka. Boulder, CO: East European Monographs, 2005, 299-317.

Asaduddin, M. *Joseph Conrad: Between Culture and Politics*. New Delhi, India: Creative Books, 1994, 127-50.

Ash, Beth Sharon. *Writing in Between: Modernity and Psychosocial Dilemma in the Novels of Joseph Conrad*. New York: St. Martin's Press, 1999, 253-305.

Bardolphe, Jacqueline. "Ngugi wa Thiong'o's *A Grain of Wheat* and *Petals of Blood* as Readings of Conrad's *Under Western Eyes* and *Victory.*" *The Conradian* 12.1 (May 1987): 32-49.

Berman, Jeffrey. *Joseph Conrad: Writing as Rescue*. New York: Astra Books, 1977, 129-48.

———— and Donna Van Wagenen. "*Under Western Eyes*: Conrad's Diary of a Writer?" *Conradiana* 9.3 (autumn 1977): 269-74.

Bernstein, Stephen. "Conrad and Postmodernism: *Under Western Eyes.*" *The Conradian* 20.1-2 (spring & autumn 1995): 31-56.

————. "Conrad and Rousseau: A Note on *Under Western Eyes.*" *Journal of Modern Literature* 19.1 (summer 1994): 161-63.

Berthoud, Jacques. "Anxiety in *Under Western Eyes.*" *The Conradian* 18.1 (autumn 1993): 1-13.

Biskupski, M.B. "Conrad and the International Politics of the Polish Question, 1914-1918: Diplomacy, *Under Western Eyes*, or Almost *The Secret Agent.*" *Conradiana.* 31.2 (summer 1999): 84-98.

Boyle, Ted E. *Symbol and Meaning in the Fiction of Joseph Conrad*. The Hague: Mouton, 1965, 195-217.

Busza, Andrzej. "Conrad's Tale of Two Cities." *L'Époque Conradienne* 19 (1993): 107-18.

————. "Rhetoric and Ideology in Conrad's *Under Western Eyes.*" In *Joseph Conrad: A Commemoration*. Ed. Norman Sherry. London: Macmillan, 1976, 105-18.

————. "'Usque ad Finem': *Under Western Eyes, Lord Jim*, and Conrad's Red Uncle." *The Conradian* 25.2 (spring 2000): 64-71.

Cady, Louise Lamar. "On Conrad's Compositional Effects in

Razumov's Decision to Betray Haldin." *West Virginia University Philological Papers* 22 (1975): 59-62.

Caminero-Santangelo, Byron. *African Fiction and Joseph Conrad.* Albany: SUNY Press, 2005, 49-67.

Carabine, Keith. "Conrad, Pinker, and *Under Western Eyes*: A Novel." *The Conradian* 10.2 (November 1985): 144-53.

―――. "Construing 'Secrete' and 'Diabolism' in *Under Western Eyes*: A Response to Frank Kermode." In *Conrad's Literary Career.* Ed Keith Carabine, Owen Knowles, and Wiesław Krajka. Boulder, CO: East European Monographs, 1992, 187-210.

―――. "Eating Dog in Conrad's *A Personal Record* and *Razumov.*" *Notes and Queries* 38.3 (September 1991): 336-37.

―――. "From *Razumov* to *Under Western Eyes*: The Case of Peter Ivanovitch." *Conradiana* 25.1 (spring 1993): 3-29.

―――. *The Life and the Art: A Study of Conrad's "Under Western Eyes."* Amsterdam: Rodopi, 1996, 209-51.

―――. "Man's 'Ingenuity in Error': Construing and Self-Deception in *Julius Cæsar* and *Under Western Eyes.*" *The Conradian* 10.2 (November 1985): 94-115.

―――. "'No Action is Simple': Betrayal and Confession in Conrad's *Under Western Eyes* and Ngugi's *A Grain of Wheat.*" In *Conrad at the Millennium: Modernism, Postmodernism, Postcolonialism.* Ed. Gail Fincham and Attie M. de Lange with Wiesław Krajka. Boulder, CO: Social Science Monographs, 2001, 233-71.

―――. *"Under Western Eyes."* In *The Cambridge Companion to Joseph Conrad.* Ed J.H. Stape. Cambridge: Cambridge UP, 1996, 122-39.

―――. "'Where to?': A Comparison of Dostoevsky's *Crime and Punishment* and Conrad's *Under Western Eyes.*" In *Inter-Relations: Conrad, James, Ford and Others.* Ed. Keith Carabine and Max Saunders. Boulder, CO: Social Science Monographs, 2003, 211-60.

Cobley, Evelyn. "Political Ambiguities in *Under Western Eyes* and *Doktor Faustus.*" *Canadian Review of Comparative Literature/Revue canadienne de littérature comparée* 10.3 (September 1983): 377-88.

Cooper, Christopher. *Conrad and the Human Dilemma.* New York: Barnes & Noble, 1970, 62-104.

Cousineau, Thomas J. "The Ambiguity of Razumov's Confession in *Under Western Eyes.*" *Conradiana* 18.1 (spring 1986): 27-40.

Cox, C.B., Ed. *Conrad*: Heart of Darkness, Nostromo, Under Western Eyes, *A Casebook.* London: Macmillan, 1981.

―――. *Joseph Conrad: The Modern Imagination.* London: J.M. Dent & Sons, 1974, 102-17.

Crankshaw, Edward. "Conrad and Russia." In *Joseph Conrad: A Commemoration.* Ed. Norman Sherry. London: Macmillan, 1976, 91-104.

Curle, Richard. *Joseph Conrad and His Characters: A Study of Six Novels*. London: William Heinemann, 1957, 145-83.

Daleski, H.M. *Joseph Conrad: The Way of Dispossession*. London: Faber and Faber, 1977, 184-209.

Dalipagic-Csizmazia, Catherine. "Razumov and Raskolnikov: The Path of Torments." *L'Époque Conradienne* 19 (1993): 71-84.

Davidson, Arnold E. *Conrad's Endings: A Study of the Five Major Novels*. Ann Arbor, MI: UMI Research Press, 1984, 71-86.

Davis, Roderick. "Under Eastern Eyes: Conrad and Russian Reviewers." *Conradiana* 6.2 (May 1974): 126-30.

———. "*Under Western Eyes*: 'The Most Deeply Meditated Novel.'" *Conradiana* 9.1 (spring 1977): 59-75.

De Marco, Nick. *"Liberty" and "Bread": The Problem of Perception in Conrad, a Critical Study of* Under Western Eyes. Chieti, Italy: Marino Solfanelli Editore, 1991.

DiSanto, Michael John. *Under Conrad's Eyes: The Novel as Criticism*. Montreal: McGill-Queen's UP, 2009, 132-62.

Dobrinsky, Joseph. *The Artist in Conrad's Fiction: A Psychocritical Study*. Ann Arbor, MI: UMI Research Press, 1989, 77-99.

Eagleton, Terry. *Exiles and Émigrés: Studies in Modern Literature*. New York: Schocken Books, 1970, 23-32.

Eggert, Paul. "Variant Versions and International Copyright: The Case of Joseph Conrad's *Under Western Eyes*." In *Varianten—Variants—Variantes*. Ed. Bodo Plachta. Tübingen, Germany: Max Niemeyer, 2005, 201-12.

Fincham, Gail. "'To make you see': Narration and Focalization in *Under Western Eyes*." In *Joseph Conrad: Voice, Sequence, History, Genre*. Ed. Jakob Lothe, Jeremy Hawthorn, and James Phelan. Columbus: Ohio State UP, 2008, 60-80.

Fleishman, Avrom. "Speech and Writing in *Under Western Eyes*." In *Joseph Conrad: A Commemoration*. Ed. Norman Sherry. London: Macmillan, 1976, 119-28.

Fogel, Aaron. *Coercion to Speak: Conrad's Poetics of Dialogue*. Cambridge, MA: Harvard UP, 1985, 180-218.

Fothergill, Anthony. "Conrad's 'Nightmarish Meanings': Betraying the Tradition in *Nostromo* and *Under Western Eyes*." *L'Époque Conradienne* 18 (1992): 11-24.

———. "Signs, Interpolations, Meanings: Conrad and the Politics of Utterance." *The Conradian* 22.1-2 (spring-winter 1997): 39-57.

Fraser, Gail. *Interweaving Patterns in the Works of Joseph Conrad*. Ann Arbor, MI: UMI Research Press, 1988, 111-33.

Fraser, Jennifer Margaret. "'A matter of tears': Grieving in *Under Western Eyes*." In *Conrad in the Twenty-First Century: Contemporary*

*Approaches and Perspectives*. Ed. Carola M. Kaplan, Peter Mallios, and Andrea White. New York: Routledge, 2005, 251-65.

Fries, Maureen. "Feminism-Antifeminism in *Under Western Eyes*." *Conradiana* 5.2 (May 1973): 56-65.

Gekoski, R.A. *Conrad: The Moral World of the Novelist*. New York: Barnes & Noble, 1978, 152-71.

Gilliam, Harriet. "The Daemonic in Conrad's *Under Western Eyes*." *Conradiana* 9.3 (autumn 1977): 219-36.

———. "Russia and the West in Conrad's *Under Western Eyes*." *Studies in the Novel* 10.2 (summer 1978): 218-33.

———. "Time in Conrad's *Under Western Eyes*." *Nineteenth-Century Fiction* 31.4 (March 1977): 421-39.

———. "Two Russians in the West: Conrad's Razumov and Count Razumovsky." *Journal of Modern Literature* 6 (1977): 311-15.

———. "Vision in Conrad's *Under Western Eyes*." *Texas Studies in Literature and Language* 19.1 (spring 1977): 24-41.

Gillies, M.A. "Conrad's *The Secret Agent* and *Under Western Eyes* as Bergsonian Comedies." *Conradiana* 20.3 (autumn 1988): 195-213.

Gillon, Adam. "Conrad's Satirical Stance in *Under Western Eyes*: Two Strange Bedfellows—Prince Roman and Peter Ivanovitch." *Conradiana* 18.2 (summer 1986): 119-28.

GoGwilt, Christopher. *The Invention of the West: Joseph Conrad and the Double-Mapping of Europe and Empire*. Stanford, CA: Stanford UP, 1995, 142-79.

Goldman, Michael. "*Under Western Eyes* and the Satanic Script." *Hebrew University Studies in Literature and the Arts* 13.1 (spring 1985): 63-97.

Goodin, George. "The Personal and the Political in *Under Western Eyes*." *Nineteenth-Century Fiction* 25.3 (December 1970): 327-42.

Goonetilleke, D.C.R.A. *Joseph Conrad: Beyond Culture and Background*. New York: St. Martin's Press, 1990, 60-71.

Graham, Kenneth. "'Like a Traveller in a Strange Country': Narrative Dynamics in *Under Western Eyes*." In *Studies in English and American Literature: In Honour of Witold Ostrowski*. Ed. Irena Janicka-Świderska. Warsaw: Państwowe Wydawnictwo Naukowe, 1984, 63-70.

Greaney, Michael. *Conrad, Language, and Narrative*. Cambridge: Cambridge UP, 2002, 152-69.

Gurko, Leo. "*Under Western Eyes*: Conrad and the Question of 'Where to?'" *College English* 21.8 (May 1960): 445-52.

Hagan, John. "Conrad's *Under Western Eyes*: The Question of Razumov's 'Guilt' and 'Remorse.'" *Studies in the Novel* 1.3 (fall 1969): 310-22.

Hamilton, Alissa. "The Construction and Deconstruction of

National Identities through Language in the Narratives of Ngũgĩ wa Thiong'o's *A Grain of Wheat* and Joseph Conrad's *Under Western Eyes.*" *African Languages and Cultures* 8.2 (1995): 137-51.

Hampson, Robert. *Joseph Conrad: Betrayal and Identity.* London: Macmillan, 1992, 167-95.

Haugh, Robert F. *Joseph Conrad: Discovery in Design.* Norman: U of Oklahoma P, 1957, 119-35.

Hawthorn, Jeremy. *Joseph Conrad: Language and Fictional Self-Consciousness.* London: Edward Arnold, 1979, 102-28.

———. *Joseph Conrad: Narrative Technique and Ideological Commitment.* London: Edward Arnold, 1990, 236-59.

———. *Sexuality and the Erotic in the Fiction of Joseph Conrad.* London: Continuum, 2007, 131-52.

Heimer, Jackson W. "The Betrayer as Intellectual: Conrad's *Under Western Eyes.*" *Polish Review* 12.4 (autumn 1967): 57-68.

Henricksen, Bruce. *Nomadic Voices: Conrad and the Subject of Narrative.* Urbana: U of Illinois P, 1992, 137-60.

Hepburn, Allan. "Above Suspicion: Audience and Deception in *Under Western Eyes.*" *Studies in the Novel* 24.3 (fall 1992): 282-97.

Hervouet, Yves. "Conrad's Debt to French Authors in *Under Western Eyes.*" *Conradiana* 14.2 (summer 1982): 113-25.

Higdon, David Leon. "Chateau Borel, Pétrus Borel, and Conrad's *Under Western Eyes.*" *Studies in the Novel* 3.1 (spring 1971): 99-102.

———. "Conrad among the Bibliographers: Monsters or Handmaidens?" *The Conradian* 6.1 (April 1980): 5-18.

———. "Conrad, *Under Western Eyes*, and the Mysteries of Revision." *Review of English Studies* n.s. 39.154 (May 1988): 231-44.

———. "Conrad's Clocks." *The Conradian* 16.1 (September 1991): 1-18.

———. "Edward Garnett's Copy of *Under Western Eyes.*" *The Conradian* 10.2 (November 1985): 139-43.

———. "'The End Is the Devil': The Conclusions to Conrad's *Under Western Eyes.*" *Studies in the Novel* 19.2 (summer 1987): 187-96.

———. "'His Helpless Prey': Conrad and the Aggressive Text." *The Conradian* 12.2 (November 1987): 108-21.

———. "Joseph Conrad and Michael Straight." *The Conradian* 8.2 (summer 1983): 44-47.

———. "Pascal's Pensée 347 in *Under Western Eyes.*" *Conradiana* 5.2 (May 1973): 81-83.

———. "The Unrecognized Second Edition of Conrad's *Under Western Eyes.*" *Studies in Bibliography* 40 (1987): 220-25.

———. "'Word for Word': The Collected Editions of Conrad's *Under Western Eyes.*" *Conradiana* 18.2 (summer 1986): 129-36.

———— and Robert F. Sheard. "Conrad's 'Unkindest Cut': The Canceled Scenes in *Under Western Eyes.*" *Conradiana* 19.3 (autumn 1987): 167-81.

Holywood, Paul. "*Under Western Eyes.*" In *A Joseph Conrad Companion.* Ed. Leonard Orr and Ted Billy. Westport, CT: Greenwood Press, 1999, 195-230.

Humphries, Reynold. "The Representation of Politics and History in *Under Western Eyes.*" *Conradiana* 20.1 (spring 1988): 13-32.

————. "'The Secret of Composition': Reading, Writing and Narrative in *Under Western Eyes.*" *L'Époque Conradienne* 12 (1986): 95-114.

Hunter, Allan. *Joseph Conrad and the Ethics of Darwinism: The Challenges of Science.* London: Croom Helm, 1983, 220-40.

Izsak, Emily K. "*Under Western Eyes* and the Problems of Serial Publication." *Review of English Studies* 23 (November 1972): 429-44.

Johnson, Bruce. *Conrad's Models of Mind.* Minneapolis: U of Minnesota P, 1971, 140-58.

Johnston, John H. "*The Secret Agent* and *Under Western Eyes*: Conrad's Two Political Novels." *West Virginia University Philological Papers* 17 (1970): 57-71.

Kaplan, Carola M. "Conrad's Narrative Occupation of/by Russia in *Under Western Eyes.*" *Conradiana* 27.2 (summer 1995): 97-114.

————. "The Spectre of Nationality in Henry James' *The Bostonians* and in Joseph Conrad's *Under Western Eyes.*" In *Literature and Exile.* Ed. David Bevin. Amsterdam: Rodopi, 1990, 37-54.

Karl, Frederick R. "The Rise and Fall of *Under Western Eyes.*" *Nineteenth-Century Fiction* 13.4 (March 1959): 313-27.

Kaye, Julian B. "Conrad's *Under Western Eyes* and Mann's *Doctor Faustus.*" *Comparative Literature* 9.1 (winter 1957): 60-65.

Kelley, Robert E. "'This Chance Glimpse': The Narrator in *Under Western Eyes.*" *University Review* 37.4 (June 1971): 285-90.

Kermode, Frank. "Secrets and Narrative Sequence." *Critical Inquiry* 7.1 (autumn 1979): 83-101.

————. "*Under Western Eyes* Revisited." In *Rereading Texts/Rethinking Critical Presuppositions: Essays in Honour of H.M. Daleski.* Frankfurt, Germany: Peter Lang, 1997, 263-73.

Kim, Jong-Seok. "Vision, Illusion, and Misinterpretation in Conrad's *Under Western Eyes.*" *English Language and Literature* 49.4 (2003): 955-79.

Kirschner, Paul. "The French Face of Dostoevsky in Conrad's *Under Western Eyes*: Some Consequences for Criticism." *Conradiana* 30.3 (fall 1998): 163-82.

————. "'Making You *See* Geneva': The Sense of Place in *Under Western Eyes.*" *L'Époque Conradienne* 14 (1988): 101-27.

————. "Revolution, Feminism and Conrad's Western 'I.'" *The Conradian*. 10.1 (May 1985): 4-25.

————. "Topodialogic Narrative in *Under Western Eyes* and the Rasoumoffs of 'La Petite Russie.'" In *Conrad's Cities: Essays for Hans van Marle*. Ed. Gene M. Moore. Amsterdam: Rodopi, 1992, 223-54.

Knowles, Owen. "*Under Western Eyes*: A Note on Two Sources." *The Conradian* 10.2 (November 1985): 154-61.

La Bossiere, Camille R. "'A Matter of Feeling': A Note on Conrad's Comedy of Errors in *Under Western Eyes*." *Thalia* 2.1-2 (1979): 35-38.

Larson, Jil. "Promises, Lies, and Ethical Agency in *Under Western Eyes*." *Conradiana* 29.1 (spring 1997): 41-58.

Laskowsky, Henry J. "Conrad's *Under Western Eyes*: A Marxian View." *Minnesota Review* 11 (1978): 90-104.

Leavis, L.R. "Guilt, Love and Extinction: *Born in Exile* and *Under Western Eyes*." *Neophilologus* 85.1 (January 2001): 153-62.

Lee, Man-Sik. "Razumov's Moral Growth in Joseph Conrad's *Under Western Eyes*." *Nineteenth Century Literature in English* 9 (2005): 261-80.

Levin, Yael. "The Moral Ambiguity of Conrad's Poetics: Transgressive Secret Sharing in *Lord Jim* and *Under Western Eyes*." *Conradiana* 39.3 (fall 2007): 211-28.

————. *Tracing the Aesthetic Principle in Conrad's Novels*. New York: Palgrave Macmillan, 2008, 73-103.

Lewitter, L.R. "Conrad, Dostoevsky, and the Russo-Polish Antagonism." *Modern Language Review* 7.3 (July 1984): 653-63.

Long, Andrew. "The Secret Policeman's Couch: Informing, Confession, and Interpellation in Conrad's *Under Western Eyes*." *Studies in the Novel* 35.4 (winter 2003): 490-509.

Lothe, Jakob. *Conrad's Narrative Method*. Oxford: Clarendon Press, 1989, 263-93.

Lovely, Deborah. "'But I digress': The Teacher in *Under Western Eyes* as a Model for Political Engagement." *West Virginia University Philological Papers* 36 (1990): 30-37.

Lucking, David. *Conrad's Mysteries: Variations on an Archetypal Theme*. Lecce, Italy: Edizioni Milella, 1986, 196-219.

Luyat, Anne. "Betrayal and Revelation: The Double Source of Tragedy in *Under Western Eyes*." *L'Époque Conradienne* 18 (1992): 153-62.

Maissonat, Claude. "The Agency of the Letter and the Function of the Textual Voice in *Under Western Eyes*." *The Conradian* 34.2 (autumn 2009): 90-109.

Martin, W.R. "Compassionate Realism in Conrad and *Under Western Eyes*." *English Studies in Africa* 17.2 (September 1974): 89-100.

Mathew, Anita. "An Eastern Appreciation of Joseph Conrad: His Treatment of Evil in 'Heart of Darkness' and *Under Western Eyes*." In *Joseph Conrad: East European, Polish, and Worldwide*. Ed. Wiesław Krajka. Boulder, CO: East European Monographs, 1999, 311-27.

Matlaw, Ralph E. "Dostoevskii and Conrad's Political Novels." In *Dostoevskii and Britain*. Ed. W.J. Leatherbarrow. Oxford: Berg, 1995, 229-48.

Melnick, Daniel C. "*Under Western Eyes* and Silence." *Slavic and East European Journal* 45.2 (summer 2001): 231-42.

Meyer, Bernard C. "Conrad and the Russians." *Conradiana* 12.1 (1980): 13-21.

Michel, Lois A. "The Absurd Predicament in Conrad's Political Novels." *College English* 23.2 (November 1961): 131-36.

Moore, Gene M. "Chronotopes and Voices in *Under Western Eyes*." *Conradiana* 18.1 (spring 1986): 9-25.

———. "Conrad's *Under Western Eyes*." *Explicator* 49.2 (winter 1991): 103-04.

Moser, Thomas C. "An English Context for Conrad's Russian Characters: Sergey Stepniak and the Diary of Olive Garnett." *Journal of Modern Literature* 11.1 (March 1984): 3-44.

———. "Ford Madox Hueffer and *Under Western Eyes*." *Conradiana* 15.3 (autumn 1983): 163-80.

Mozina, Andrew. *Joseph Conrad and the Art of Sacrifice: The Evolution of the Scapegoat Theme in Joseph Conrad's Fiction*. New York: Routledge, 2001, 75-105.

Mukerji, N. "The Problem of Point of View in *Under Western Eyes*." *Bulletin of The Department of English (Calcutta University)* n.s. 8.2 (1972-73): 73-80.

Najder, Zdzisław. "Conrad and Rousseau: Concepts of Man and Society." In *Joseph Conrad: A Commemoration*. Ed. Norman Sherry. London: Macmillan, 1976, 77-90.

Okuda, Yoko. "*Under Western Eyes* and Soseki's *Kokoro*." *The Conradian* 30.1 (spring 2005): 59-70.

———. "*Under Western Eyes*: Words and the Living Body." *The Conradian* 16.1 (September 1991): 19-36.

Osborne, Roger. "Joseph Conrad's *Under Western Eyes*: The Serials and First Editions." *Studies in Bibliography* 54 (2001): 301-16.

———. "The Typescript Versions of Conrad's *Under Western Eyes*: Motivations, Intentions and Editorial Possibilities." *Bibliographical Society of Australia and New Zealand Bulletin* 26.2 (2002): 105-18.

Paccaud, Josiane. "Conrad's Technique of Free Indirect Discourse in *Under Western Eyes*." *Conradiana* 22.1 (spring 1990): 54-65.

———. "Hypertextuality in Joseph Conrad's *Under Western Eyes*." *Cahiers victoriens et édouardiens* 29 (April 1989): 73-82.

———. "The Meaning of Mr Razumov's Betrayal in Conrad's *Under Western Eyes*." *L'Époque Conradienne* 12 (1986): 65-73.

———. "Mr. Razumov's 'Disease of Perversity': Of Artistic Lies in Conrad's *Under Western Eyes*." *Forum for Modern Language Studies* 24.2 (April 1988): 111-25.

———. "The Name-of-the-Father in Conrad's *Under Western Eyes*." *Conradiana* 18.3 (autumn 1986): 204-18.

———. "*Under Western Eyes* and *Hamlet*: Where Angels Fear to Tread." *Conradiana* 28.2 (summer 1996): 83-85.

Panagopoulos, Nic. *The Fiction of Joseph Conrad: The Influence of Schopenhauer and Nietzsche*. Frankfurt, Germany: Peter Lang, 1998, 129-63.

Panichas, George A. *Joseph Conrad: His Moral Vision*. Mercer, GA: Mercer UP, 2005, 79-98.

Patterson, John. "A Note on 'Namelessness' in *Under Western Eyes* and *Resurrection*." *Conradiana* 10.2 (summer 1978): 169-70.

Peacock, Noel. "The Russian Eye: Surveillance and the Scopic Regime in *Under Western Eyes*." In *Conrad and Poland*. Ed. Alex S. Kurczaba. Boulder, CO: East European Monographs, 1996, 113-33.

Perera, S.W. "Confession and Assertion in Conrad's *Under Western Eyes*." *Sri Lanka Journal of the Humanities* 21.1-2 (1995): 42-56.

Pudełko, Byrgida. "Female Portrayals in Conrad's *Under Western Eyes* and Turgenev's *On the Eve* and *Virgin Soil*." *L'Époque Conradienne* 34 (2008): 29-37.

Purdy, Dwight H. "Creature and Creator in *Under Western Eyes*." *Conradiana* 8.3 (autumn 1976): 241-46.

———. "'Peace that Passeth Understanding': The Professor's English Bible in *Under Western Eyes*." *Conradiana* 13.2 (summer 1981): 83-93.

Rachman, Shalom. "Personal Moral Sensibility in Conrad's *Under Western Eyes*." *Studies in the Twentieth Century* 9 (spring 1972): 59-75.

Rado, Lisa. "Walking through Phantoms: Irony, Skepticism, and Razumov's Self-Delusion in *Under Western Eyes*." *Conradiana* 24.2 (summer 1992): 83-99.

Raval, Suresh. *The Art of Failure: Conrad's Fiction*. Boston: Allen & Unwin, 1986, 126-47.

Ressler, Steve. *Joseph Conrad: Consciousness and Integrity*. New York: New York UP, 1988, 98-141.

Rice, Tom. "Condomization in *The Secret Agent* and *Under Western Eyes*." *Conradiana* 40.2 (summer 2008): 129-45.

Rieselbach, Helen Funk. *Conrad's Rebels: The Psychology of Revolution in the Novels from* Nostromo *to* Victory. Ann Arbor, MI: UMI Research Press, 1985, 59-85.

Rising, Catharine. "Raskolnikov and Razumov: From Passive to Active Subjectivity in *Under Western Eyes*." *Conradiana* 33.1 (spring 2001): 24-39.

Rødstøl, Knut. "The Subversions of the 'debauch of the imagination': Ethics and Aesthetics in *Under Western Eyes*." In *Conrad in Scandinavia*. Ed. Jakob Lothe. Boulder, CO: Social Science Monographs, 1995, 225-49.

Romanick, Debra. "Politics, Martyrdom and the Legend of Saint Thekla in *Under Western Eyes*." *Conradiana* 32.2 (summer 2000): 144-57.

———. "Victorious Wretch?: The Puzzle of Haldin's Name in *Under Western Eyes*." *Conradiana* 30.1 (spring 1998): 44-52.

Rosenfield, Claire. *Paradise of Snakes: An Archetypal Analysis of Conrad's Political Novels*. Chicago: U of Chicago P, 1967, 123-72.

Ryol, Kim Sung. "The Wanderings of Cain: *Under Western Eyes* as Ethical Drama," *Nineteenth Century Literature in English* 6.2 (autumn 2002): 103-28.

Saveson, John E. *Conrad, the Later Moralist*. Amsterdam: Rodopi, 1974, 71-91.

Schleifer, Ronald. "Public and Private Narrative in *Under Western Eyes*." *Conradiana* 9.3 (autumn 1977): 237-54.

Schwarz, Daniel R. *Conrad:* Almayer's Folly *to* Under Western Eyes. Ithaca, NY: Cornell UP, 1980, 195-211.

Secor, Robert. "The Function of the Narrator in *Under Western Eyes*." *Conradiana* 3.1 (autumn 1970-1971): 27-38.

Sewlall, Harry. "Crime and Punishment: An Intertextual Dialogue between Conrad's *Under Western Eyes* and Dostoevsky's *Crime and Punishment*." In *A Return to the Roots: Conrad, Poland and East-Central Europe*. Ed. Wiesław Krajka. Boulder, CO: East European Monographs, 2005, 211-31.

———. "Writing from the Periphery: The Case of Ngugi and Conrad." *English in Africa* 30.1 (May 2003): 55-69.

Simmons, Allan H. "*Under Western Eyes*: The Ludic Text." *The Conradian* 16.2 (May 1992): 18-37.

Smith, David R. "Dostoevsky and Conrad." *The Conradian* 15.2 (January 1991): 1-11.

———. Ed. *Joseph Conrad's* Under Western Eyes: *Beginnings, Revisions, Final Forms*. Hamden, CT: Archon Books, 1991.

Spence, Gordon. "The Feminism of Peter Ivanovitch." *Conradiana* 29.2 (summer 1997): 113-22.

Stewart, J.I.M. *Joseph Conrad*. New York: Dodd, Mead & Co., 1968, 185-208.

Stine, Peter. "Joseph Conrad's Confession in *Under Western Eyes*." *Cambridge Quarterly* 9.2 (1980): 95-113.

Sturgess, Philip J.M. "Duplicity and Design in *Under Western Eyes*." In *Studies in English and American Literature: In Honour of Witold Ostrowski*. Ed. Irena Janicka-Świderska. Warsaw: Państwowe Wydawnictwo Naukowe, 1984, 159-64.

Sung, Kilho. "Intertextuality within Conrad: An Intratextual Reading of *Under Western Eyes* and 'The Secret Sharer.'" *Studies in Modern Fiction* 11.2 (winter 2004): 311-42.

Swanson, Donald R. "The Observer Observed: Notes on the Narrator of *Under Western Eyes*." In *Renaissance and Modern: Essays in Honor of Edwin M. Moseley*. Ed. Murray J. Levith. Saratoga Springs, NY: Skidmore College, 1976, 109-18.

Szittya, Penn R. "Metafiction: The Double Narration in *Under Western Eyes*." *ELH* 48.4 (winter 1981): 817-40.

Tanner, Tony. "Nightmare and Complacency: Razumov and the Western Eye." *Critical Quarterly* 4.3 (autumn 1962): 197-214.

Thomas, Brian. "The Symbolism of Textuality in Joseph Conrad's *Under Western Eyes*: Razumov as Literalist of the Imagination." *Conradiana* 28.3 (autumn 1996): 215-27.

Thomas, Claude. "Structure and Narrative Technique of *Under Western Eyes*." *Cahiers victoriens et édouardiens* 2 (1975): 205-22.

Towheed, Shafquat. "Geneva v. Saint Petersburg: Two Concepts of Literary Property and the Material Lives of Books in *Under Western Eyes*." *Book History* 10 (2007): 169-91.

Toy, Phyllis. "Joseph Conrad's *Under Western Eyes*: The Language of Politics and the Politics of Language." In *Joseph Conrad: East European, Polish and Worldwide*. Ed. Wiesław Krajka. Boulder, CO: East European Monographs, 1999, 41-59.

Vineberg, Steve. "Two Routes into Conrad: On Filming *Under Western Eyes* and *An Outcast of the Islands*." *Literature/Film Quarterly* 15.1 (1987): 22-27.

Viswanathan, Jacqueline. "Point of View and Unreality in Brontë's *Wuthering Heights*, Conrad's *Under Western Eyes* and Mann's *Doktor Faustus*." *Orbis Litterarum* 29 (1974): 42-60.

Wasiolek, Edward. "Conrad and Dostoevsky, and Natalia and Sonia." *International Fiction Review* 17.2 (summer 1990): 96-103.

Watts, Cedric. "Stepniak and *Under Western Eyes*." *Notes and Queries* 13.11 (November 1966): 410-11.

————. "*Under Western Eyes*: The Haunted Haunts." *The Conradian* 34.2 (Autumn 2009): 35-50.

West, Russell. *Conrad and Gide: Translation, Transference and Intertexuality*. Amsterdam: Rodopi, 1996, 103-34.

Wheatley, Alison E. "An Experiment in Understanding: Narrative Strategies of Association and Accumulation in Conrad's *Under Western Eyes*." *Journal of Narrative Theory*. 30.2 (summer 2000): 206-36.

Wheeler, Marcus. "Russia and Russians in the Works of Conrad." *Conradiana* 12.1 (spring 1980): 23-36.

White, Margaret Ann Rusk. "Peter Ivanovitch's Escape: A Possible Source Overlooked." *Conradiana* 21.1 (spring 1980): 72-80.

Winner, Anthony. *Culture and Irony: Studies in Joseph Conrad's Major Novels*. Charlottesville: UP of Virginia, 1988, 92-124.

Wollaeger, Mark A. *Joseph Conrad and the Fictions of Skepticism*. Stanford, CA: Stanford UP, 1990, 170-92.

Wutawunashe, Jonathan. "The Manipulation of the Reader's Sympathy in Conrad's *Under Western Eyes*." *Opus* 4 (1979): 28-30.

Zabel, Morton Dauwen. "Introduction." *Under Western Eyes* by Joseph Conrad. Garden City, NY: Anchor Books, 1963, ix-lviii.

Zellar, Leonard. "Conrad and Dostoevsky." In *The English Novel in the Nineteenth Century: Essays on the Literary Mediation of Human Values*. Ed. George Goodin. Urbana: U of Illinois, P, 1972, 214-23.